Cross Purposes

A Martin Quint Novel

To Clark –

Enjoy !

Stephen D. Senturia

Steve Sint

FriesenPress

Suite 300 - 990 Fort St
Victoria, BC, V8V 3K2
Canada

www.friesenpress.com

ISBN
978-1-5255-3650-2 (Hardcover)
978-1-5255-3651-9 (Paperback)
978-1-5255-3652-6 (eBook)

1. FICTION, LITERARY

Distributed to the trade by The Ingram Book Company

Author's Preface

When I wrote my first novel, *One Man's Purpose,* my goal was to tell the story of a first-rate academic institution, run by smart, competent people, where in spite of everyone's best intentions, things could still go badly wrong. I placed the story at the fictional Cambridge Technology Institute, a look-alike for the Massachusetts Institute of Technology, where I spent thirty-six happy years on the faculty. That book ended with the protagonists, Martin Quint and his wife, Jenny, having moved to Bottlesworth College, an equally fictional institution located in the town of Brimfield Junction, Maine. *Cross Purposes* takes up their story almost a year after their move.

Those familiar with the geography will recognize that I have modeled this new locale, very loosely, on Brunswick, Maine, and its famous and quite excellent Bowdoin College. But remember, this is a work of fiction. I am making no statements about Bowdoin or how it is run. Indeed, the Bowdoin leadership would not recognize the way I have structured the Bottlesworth administration. But books like this need to be placed somewhere, and I like the crisp visualization that comes from imagining a real town and a real college.

This is truly a work of fiction. All the characters are fictional. The situations and events are fictional. But the emotions, I hope, are real.

Stephen D. Senturia
Brookline, MA

Cross Purposes

Prologue: May 26, 2015

Sylvia Palmer was seated at her desk in the Grant Street law offices of Wilkins and Palmer, LLC. She was gazing blankly at the Pittsburgh skyline when her assistant bustled in wearing a big smile.

"Found him. He's not in Cambridge. He's on leave as a Visiting Professor of Physics at Bottlesworth College. It's in Maine. You want me to call him?"

"Well done," said Sylvia. "At least we know where to find him. But our first contact needs to be written. Change the address on my letter and set up delivery with Wilshire."

"Why not FedEx? He'll have it tomorrow."

"FedEx accepts just signatures. I need more. Instruct Wilshire to require photo ID and to photograph it as confirmation. I'm hoping for Andrew's sake that we won't need it, but if he balks, I'll want evidence that will stand up in court."

"Shouldn't I call ahead to verify that he's there? Academic types tend to scatter after Memorial Day."

"No. Wilshire will track him down. I'm pretty sure his native curiosity will get him to sign. I don't want him refusing the letter and then having to file a suit in Maine or Massachusetts just to get his attention."

* **1** *

Martin scanned the entries on the pale yellow grade sheet one last time and muttered, "Okay. That's it. I'm done." He reached for the pen perched in his personally inscribed desk set, a departure gift from the editorial board of the *Journal of Semiconductor Materials Technology*. After scrawling his signature, he added the date, chuckling over this being the seventh day of May. On the seventh day, says the Bible, God rested, but Martin didn't plan to rest. No, no, no. Not today. He reperched the pen and, giving the paper two crisp folds, slid it into the bright orange Registrar's envelope marked "Grades: Confidential."

The early morning mist had stopped, and the gardeners were once again out with their riding mowers and weed whackers, snarling and sputtering their way around the Central Quad, grooming for the graduation a week hence. Leaving his office, he descended the two flights of granite stairs, whose gentle undulations bore silent witness to the countless footsteps of generations of students, and emerged into the renovated lobby with its photo arcade of the School of Science Faculty.

The lobby renovation, completed last fall, had been done at the urging of the Department of Environmental Science supported by a gaggle of undergraduate activists who wanted to make the campus greener. The ornate carved wood panels surrounding the entry, part of the original 1875 construction, had been ripped out and consigned to the campus warehouse on the Clements Corner Road, creating enough lateral space for the installation of a revolving door next to the existing wheelchair-friendly door. Tasteful signs were posted as a reminder to please use the revolving door, as it would save eighty-five percent of the energy lost when opening the regular door. Reminders notwithstanding, most of the students and many of the faculty continued to use the

older door, causing Martin to shake his head in recurrent disappr
He chose the revolving door and started directly across the Ceɪ.ɪ.ɑɪ
Quad toward College Hall, scattering a trio of robins who were reaping
bounty from the damp, stirred-up lawn.

The Quad was empty of students, with exams over and the celebration of commencement still days ahead. He looked to his right as he
always did, picking out the second-story window in Corey Hall where
his father's office had been, reminding him once again of their bitter
fights when he was a teenager and their bit-by-bit transition to genuine
fondness in adulthood. He missed that fondness, their friendship. Still,
here he was, back in Brimfield Junction, a faculty member instead of a
faculty brat. These oak trees were part of his life. This very quadrangle,
now perfumed with the smell of fresh-cut grass, had been one of his
childhood playgrounds, but not always happily. A furtive glance toward
the white picket fence surrounding the founder's gravesite evinced a
gibbous image of his mother, shimmering like Banquo's ghost, a vague
memory from childhood, a mysterious void, a persistent bad dream.
Why did she leave?

As Martin dropped off his grades in College Hall, a puff of pride
swelled in his chest. His new version of Electricity and Magnetism
had just received the highest student evaluation scores the Physics
Department had ever seen. Bottlesworth College might be a small
academic pond compared to the Cambridge Technology Institute, but
Martin always got a charge from being the biggest fish, whatever the
pond. And it had been a good year, mostly. During the fall semester,
while he and Jenny were still getting settled into their new life, he
taught only his flagship Circuits and Electronics course, which allowed
him enough schedule flexibility to help with child care while Jenny
was getting her new business started. But in the spring, in addition to
developing and teaching his now much-revered version of Electricity
and Magnetism, he had taken over management of the three-plus-two
engineering program from the ailing Phelps Donahue, which meant
that in one stroke he had acquired almost sixty undergraduate advisees, all eager to optimize their three-year programs at Bottlesworth

before transferring to Dartmouth or the University of Maine. He liked these students, but they had consumed boatloads of hours in one-on-one counseling sessions. This required more on-campus presence each week, and even though the college was a good source of babysitters, Jenny had started complaining that they needed a more stable and regular solution to daytime child care. What would they do this summer?

Ah yes, summer. Summer starts the day the grades go in, and this summer would be Martin's first unscheduled block of time since the August before his junior year in college. Unscheduled time. Time to think, to write. Time to do battle with those nuts who push online education as the next great thing for universities. Imagine. Totally canned courses with hundreds, even thousands of online students, and no live contact between teacher and student. Ridiculous. Opens the door to serious and irreparable erosion in the quality of a college education. Someone has to call out that this particular emperor has no clothes.

Martin had left CTI with his eyes wide open. While he did occasionally miss the adrenaline rush from life in the academic fast lane, particularly those high-profile international conferences where he had so often been the kingfish, he didn't miss the stress, the catch-as-catch-can home life crammed between trips to conferences and sponsors and consulting clients, the intense competition for research grants, and the unpleasantness of journal authors whose papers he had rejected in his role as editor. And he certainly didn't miss the lawsuit-poisoned atmosphere that had followed CTI's decision, over his strong objections, to deny tenure to Kat Rodriguez. That, and being kicked off the Personnel Committee, had led him to leave CTI. Bottlesworth had its own attractions. Things were calmer. Less jumping about from one task to another. More time to spend with his children. Even his ulcerative colitis, which seemed to have been aggravated by that high-intensity CTI lifestyle, was now in abeyance. He took his meds on schedule, and his gut was behaving normally. Best of all, and best by far, the move to Bottlesworth was giving him this precious open summer. Finally. Time to write.

As he crossed the Quad back to his office, he began to compose the opening of what he could already visualize as a finished product, its snazzy dust jacket reading "*Education as Conversation* by Martin M. Quint." The blurbs on the back cover would hail it as a groundbreaking synthesis of linguistics, psychology, and sound educational practice. And when the second printing came out a few months later, it would be further embellished with snippets from glowing reviews in *The Chronicle of Higher Education* and *The New York Times*.

When he reached his office, he couldn't resist scanning his email for what must have been the seventh time today. The thought that someone out in cyberspace might need him trumped almost everything, even putting pen to paper, or, as in this case, fingers to keyboard. There was one newsworthy item, an email from Win Henderson, the Provost, alerting him that within a few days, possibly as early as next week, Bottlesworth College would be welcoming a Visiting Professor of Psychology from Oxford University named Glenda Aldrich, who would be spending a sabbatical year here. Her specialty was conversational comprehension. She might be a good resource for his book. Martin sent an appreciative response and then mercilessly deleted the rest of the messages. Time to get to work.

His opening paragraph took more than two hours to write, and rewrite, and rewrite again. It was something of a manifesto, and while he knew it was a bit pompous in tone and would need more editing, it made his point:

> I am a teacher. For more than twenty-five years, I have
> been in the trenches, working with real students. I find
> ways to burrow into and expand the cognitive structure
> within each student's head. While psychologists study
> cognition together with learning theory, and linguists
> study cognition and language, I am neither psycholo-
> gist nor linguist. I am a teacher. I have an intensely prac-
> tical view of how to connect the psychology of learning
> with the cognitive study of concepts as represented in

the human brain through language. The connection is made with conversation. My goal in these pages is to demonstrate how and why live conversation, with its salient content and embedded cognitive signals, is essential to the effective transfer of a concept from one brain to another — the essence of both teaching and learning.

Martin basked only briefly in self-congratulation. After a trip down the hall for a coffee refill to accompany his sandwich lunch, he returned to his desk and worked away until his head began to spin. The result? Almost eight pages drafted, words and ideas that had been simmering in his brain for years now erupting out of him in spurts, like the water bubbling from the top of a percolator spout. Enough for today. He saved the file, backed it up on a separate hard drive, and collected his backpack. Before leaving for home, he looked up Glenda Aldrich on the internet. Interesting person. Could be helpful.

At the second-floor landing, he bumped into Steve Wang, his Department Chairman and the one member of the Physics faculty with whom he had a sense of personal connection. Relations with his new colleagues were cordial enough, but making friends — real friends, personal friends — was never easy for Martin. With Steve, Martin hoped that over time, a real friendship might develop. Too bad his kids were so much older than JJ and Ellen.

"Grades in?" asked Steve with a grin, as they descended the stairs together.

"First thing this morning. Free at last, free at last. You?"

Steve gestured at his backpack. "Twelve exams left. Mine'll have to go in tomorrow. Going anywhere unusual or exciting this summer? Vacation or otherwise?"

"Book, book, book," said Martin with his own grin. "Just drafted the opening of chapter one."

"Good grief. Don't you ever slow down?"

"Can't afford to. I checked. Not counting the Memorial Day and

July Fourth weekends, there's just over one hundred days until Labor Day. If I can average a thousand words a day, I'll have a book draft by summer's end. Every day counts. Every hour, even."

"Did you get your thousand today?"

"Twenty-three hundred and counting," said Martin.

"Well done," said Steve. "Impressive."

As they exited through the revolving door and waved their good-byes, Steve called back over his shoulder. "And as they say in the theater, break a finger."

It was slightly less than a mile to the unspectacular three-bedroom house he and Jenny were renting just off the Harpswell Road, and Martin preferred walking to all other forms of transportation, even in the rain that had greeted him earlier in the day. He liked the exercise, and as long as he avoided oblivious pedestrians immersed in their smart phones and looked both ways before crossing streets, he could retreat into a Zen-like zone, a meditative Japanese garden, a place to think about whatever he wished, ignoring the college buildings, dorms, and sports facilities along his route. As he reached the edge of his neighborhood, his restless ruminations about the book outline began to recede, replaced by a gnarly reminiscence of his growing-up years. They were spent in what was now his sister Helen's house, only a handful of blocks from here, with a very strict but caring father and a mishmash of daycare providers and sitters, not one of whom had earned a favorable spot in his memory. His mother might be alive somewhere, but Martin didn't know where and kept telling himself he didn't care.

- - -

Jenny was at her desk in their shared study, a sunroom open to the living room through a rectangular archway that at some time in the past may have held French doors. A vase of tulips on her desk blazoned with a rainbow of spring color. She waved in acknowledgment of Martin's arrival, but remained focused on her computer screen. He leaned in to give her a kiss, eager to report on his day, but she offered only a cheek, saying, "Hiya, Goofus. Busy, busy. Updating the website. Can't stop until it's posted. Maybe ten minutes."

"Ellen?"

"Napping. Need to get this done while it's quiet. A client in Portland just bought one of Pierre's pieces, a terrific Chippendale replica. I took a bunch of photos before he delivered it. Putting 'em up on the website."

"Glad you had a sale," said Martin. "All sales welcome." He headed for the kitchen, but hearing a squeaking call of "Mommee" from upstairs, he turned back and went upstairs to find curly-headed Ellen, a miniature version of her mother, standing in the crib holding her stuffed dachshund by the tail, her mood halfway between a teary awakening and delight at seeing Daddy. Martin hoisted her up, planted a kiss on her belly, and took her to the changing table.

On her back with a dry diaper and a big smile, Ellen gurgled and laughed as Martin tickled her. Much as he enjoyed JJ and was proud to call him his son, it was Ellen and her infectious giggle that would send him over the moon, almost bringing tears to his eyes. Thank goodness he had found Jenny, and thank goodness she had finally been able to conceive and carry Ellen to term. A child he had fathered, the fruit of his loins. Pride beyond pride and delight beyond delight.

He brought her downstairs, filled a sippy cup with apple juice, and deposited her and the cup in the living room play area littered with foam blocks, wood blocks, toy animals, a little wagon, and two piles of books. Jenny emerged from the study, muttering. "I wish I had a web person. I just hate the editing part. I'm always afraid I'm going to post some godawful mistake that will shut us down."

"So hire a student. They've got the web in their genes."

"That takes money. And anyway, the students have left for the summer."

"Okay, okay. Let me tell you about today. I finally started the—"

"Can it wait? Sorry. I really need to go the market before picking up JJ. And there's news. I've got to go to Chicago early morning on Monday, back Tuesday night. It's a great opportunity. I figured that since classes are over—"

Martin cut in. "Since classes are over? Since classes are over I can manage the kids? Is that what you were going to say?"

"I wasn't going to put it as crassly as that, but yes, I'm assuming you have more time. We can talk later. This trip is important."

Martin watched in silence as Jenny grabbed her purse and went out the door, wondering about this first assault on his hundred days.

-   -   -

After the usual evening bustle — dinner at the kitchen table with conversation focused on JJ's report from his school day, their short family sing featuring nursery songs and some of JJ's favorites from the movies, then bath time, story time, and bedtime — Martin came into the living room where Jenny had set out their decaf. She was paging through an issue of *Architectural Digest* seated on her carved and cushioned settee, an exquisite Pierre DuChamp copy of a piece in the Victoria and Albert Museum.

As Martin plopped into the light brown overstuffed chair that used to be his father's, Jenny closed the magazine and looked up, expectant. She barely got a word out, "Let me tell—" before Martin said, "I actually got a piece—"

"Hey, Goofus. I was first."

They both laughed. Martin, still chuckling, said, "It's not often we both have news. Can I go first? Mine's short. Then I want to hear about Chicago."

"Okay. Brawn before beauty. Your turn."

"Today. Finally. Breakthrough. I actually got a piece of the first book chapter written. A big, bleeping deal."

"That's great," said Jenny, putting down her magazine. "One of the reasons we came here, after all. So is that it? My turn now?"

"One more. We're getting a visitor from Oxford who's an expert on conversation. I don't know her, but it might be neat to have a partner, somebody to talk to."

"It's a her?"

"Yes, she's a her. Most women are," said Martin.

Jenny mocked a grimace. "Jesus, Martin. Must you, with the nonsense?"

"Sorry. Bad joke. Anyway, I'll give you a full report when I meet her, and then we can invite her over for tea and crumpets. Now, tell me about Chicago. What's this about?"

Jenny sat up straight, her voice suddenly animated and nearly breathless with excitement. "Remember that last big job I did in Cambridge?" Martin nodded. "Well, the client has a sister in Chicago and this sister wants me to come see her place so I can recommend furnishings. She'll pay my travel. Isn't that fantastic?"

"Are there no suitable decorators in Chicago?"

"C'mon, Mr. Goofus." Jenny's tone suddenly turned gravelly, even a little threatening, setting the small hairs on the back of Martin's neck — his little seismographs — tingling with that infinitesimal crescendo that seemed to appear more often these days, like the gradual filling of a magma chamber deep beneath the surface of a volcano, the prelude to an eruption that he hoped would never come. "It's no different from your consulting in Silicon Valley. Do you think that when they hire you for this or that, they would accept a substitute? The west coast has plenty of semiconductor experts, some right in their backyard at Stanford. But you still get called out there once a month."

Martin interrupted. "But not this summer. I've cut out my consulting trips so I can write."

"A good decision, and I'm sure they'll miss you. But décor is like your consulting. The high-end furnishings business is all personal, word of mouth. I was recommended, and I need to be there in person if I want the business. It would be a big boost for my guys to expand beyond the New England market. Maybe a six-figure order, some serious income for me and for them. So unless you happen to have a current crisis that would interfere, I'm going to Chicago on Monday."

"Okay, okay, Mrs. Goofus. Calm down. Enough already. I'm convinced. And you'll be back by Tuesday night?"

"Yes. United has nonstops from Portland."

"And is the child swap on for Tuesday morning?"

"Unfortunately not. Paula says Roger is pretty sick with a cold, maybe even flu, and Edith's Jimmy is sniffling. Better not to spread it, so you'll have Ellen both days."

Martin sighed. "I guess I can write at home for a few days if Ellen will let me. But now, to celebrate a good day's work, it's music time." He relocated to the living room piano bench, turned on his Yamaha keyboard with its physically precise action and donned the headphones so Jenny would not be disturbed. He warmed up with Bach's first *English Suite*, then shifted to the massive Brahms *F Minor Piano Quintet*, a piece he dreamed about performing someday with the college's resident string quartet.

- - -

At six o'clock Monday morning, Jenny gave Martin a quick kiss and with a "Wish me luck," took off driving Martin's Honda, leaving her Toyota van with its car seats for Martin, a powerful metaphor for the transfer of child care.

After delivering JJ to school, he tried to write, but Ellen's need for book-reading time, blocks time, outdoor running-around time, lunch time, diaper time, and just plain playing-with-Daddy time made it pretty hopeless. When she was an infant, he could plunk her in a playpen and get some work done. No longer. Finally, during her naptime, Martin began to face the fact that it was time to make a child-care arrangement of some kind, much as he hated the idea. He turned to the family finances, paying this month's bills and reconciling their joint bank statement. It was not a pretty picture, with or without the $1500 a month it might cost for full-time child care. He and Jenny needed a revised cash plan before the end of May, possibly even redrawing the agreement that had served so well since their wedding. But how to raise such a prickly subject, what with Jenny keeping her inheritance from George separate? And here she is running off to Chicago. Chicago, of all places. Goddamit, why does it have to be Chicago?

- - -

Martin managed to keep up with his email in Jenny's absence, but not much more. Boiling with ideas that needed quiet writing time to consolidate, he could hardly wait for her return. Two precious days down the drain.

By the time she did arrive, JJ and Ellen were asleep. She wheeled her overnight bag over the crunchy crushed shells of the driveway and dragged herself up the three stairs to the front porch. Martin came out and they folded into each other with a hug and a long humming kiss, their special way of saying "I'm with you, and I love you."

Jenny drew back from the embrace. "Sorry to be so late, love. There was an accident just past Yarmouth."

"I saved you a chicken leg and some salad. Want some wine?"

"Yes, yes, yes. Red. But let me hit the bathroom first."

Jenny went to get settled while Martin got out the wine, warmed the chicken in the microwave, and put it and a plate of salad on the kitchen table.

As Jenny sat and took her first bite, Martin asked, "How was it? Was it worth it?"

With her mouth still full, she waved her hand and muttered, "Wait a minute." She took her time to chew and swallow and took a drink of wine before continuing. "That's better. Okay. The report. You wouldn't believe it. It's a mansion. I mean a freaking mansion. Evanston. In a historic district. Eighteen rooms, five bathrooms. She's hired me to create a plan."

"You mean do the design?"

"Everything, except for the bathrooms and the kitchen, just like the Cambridge job, but with an important difference."

"And what's that?"

She held up her hand as she took another bite of chicken. "God, I was famished. Okay. The Cambridge people were collectors of genuine antiques. Remember how they spent over $200,000 for a Roentgen card table? These people are different. Their house is so big, they want the look of the antique collector without paying those kinds of prices. It's perfect for my guys. Sarah — that's her name — loved our portfolio of replicas and will probably order as many as ten pieces, maybe more. And for whatever I purchase elsewhere, like the lamps and carpets, I'll get my usual designer commission. It's a dream job."

"Well, some income from your side, one of these days, woul tainly be welcome. We actually need to have a money talk."

Jenny looked up sharply but Martin continued. "Not tonight. I know, I know. Not tonight. You're tired. But Chicago, for God's sake? Gimme a break. You shut down your Cambridge business because you couldn't manage two kids. And now you take a job in Chicago?"

"Yes, but you were working ninety hours a week then. Now you're not. It makes a difference."

"But couldn't you have asked my opinion before agreeing to do this? I need time to write."

"Your opinion?" Jenny paused for a sip of wine, then another. "You'd have probably just told me not to do it. But you — you take consulting jobs without asking me. You announce that you're going to San Jose or Minneapolis or Phoenix on such and such a day. This is the same thing."

"It doesn't feel the same, and I told you, I cancelled those trips for the summer."

"Yes, my love, it may not feel the same to you, but it should feel the same. This was part of the promise of our move to Maine. Less pressure on you. More time for sharing of the kids and a chance for me to develop a real business."

"But not more travel, for God's sake," grumped Martin. "My writing clock is ticking."

"So let's get Ellen into daycare, and JJ too, once school is over. I can never understand why you're so opposed. Bill and Helen have Angela at The Kiddie Korner, and she seems to like it. Maybe they have a space. Anyway, I'm sorry if I sound crabby, but I'm really tired. I need to get some sleep. And I really do appreciate your taking the kids. And the dinner." She gulped the rest of her wine, got up, came around behind Martin, kissed him lightly on the side of his neck, and went upstairs. Martin touched the spot she had kissed, a unique Jenny kissing spot, one that said, more than anything, how much she wanted him in her life, in her bed. So, yes, maybe she was a bit crabby tonight, but she was still Jenny. His Jenny.

- - -

The next morning, Martin walked to campus and was in the midst of replying to an email from Peter Dempsey at CTI when there was a knock on his office door.

"C'mon in," said Martin, his back to the door as he typed. He heard it open and said, "Just a second, please. I'm almost done with this message."

When he finally turned around, he found himself looking at a woman he didn't recognize standing patiently by the open door. Mid-thirties, he guessed, straight brown hair with a hint of gold earrings peeking out, an alabaster face blazoned with a bright red lipstick, narrow shoulders and broad hips. Black slacks and a heavily patterned, overlarge black and white sweater. Icelandic, perhaps. And as he always did when meeting a woman of a certain age, admittedly a churlish habit, Martin looked for, but did not see, a wedding ring.

"Yes, come in. And you are?"

"Glenda Aldrich. I'm sorry for stopping by without notice, but I had an open interval before my meeting with the Human Resources person, so Professor Henderson pointed me in your direction."

"Ah, yes, the much heralded Glenda Aldrich. How nice," said Martin as he rose from his desk, offered a handshake, and gestured her into a chair at his round four-seater conference table. "Win alerted me. Welcome. And do call me Martin. We're pretty casual about names and titles around here."

"Thank you, uh... Martin. I'll try to remember. Not the British way, of course. As for me, perhaps Henderson explained?"

"All I know is that you're visiting with us and I've scanned your web page. Actually, I didn't expect to see you until after your exams. Aren't they in late May?"

"Yes, exactly. But the exams are all prepared now. I came over to get things settled. I'll go back for grading."

"And after that you'll be with us for a year?"

"That's the plan, at least for now. My father's health is failing, and instead of making emergency trips back and forth from England, I decided to resettle for a year, get him properly placed in an extended-care facility, that sort of thing. I'm staying with him in Freeport."

"In Freeport? I thought you were British."

Glenda laughed. "Yes and no. I'm actually a dual citizen, or as some have put it — in jest, usually — an American with a British accent. The short version is that my father was raised in Freeport and returned there after his retirement from a long career in England. Family ties."

"Well, I'm sorry that he's having health issues, but I'm pleased by the side-effect — having you here. You spent some time in Clark's group at Stanford? How did that come about? I mean you're in psychology and he's a linguistics guy."

"Yes. That was an odd chance. You see, I'm something of a hybrid. My undergrad at University College London was in a combined psychology and linguistics program. I went on to Oxford for a PhD, and while I was writing my thesis, I was introduced to Herbert at a conference. One thing led to another. I won an overseas fellowship, good for two years, and I spent those years in Clark's group, a self-funded postdoc, if you will. You've read Clark, I gather?"

"Indeed, I have. Some of it, anyway. He puts the finger on what I believe is the centerpiece of effective education, the two streams that make a conversation: content and signaling. I've finally managed to start a book about the role of conversation in education. I'm looking forward to picking your brain about all this."

"A delightful prospect," said Glenda, checking her wristwatch and standing up. "But just now, I'm afraid, I need to find my way to the Human Resources office. There's paperwork, apparently."

"Of course," said Martin, as he rose. "It's just behind the brick building that's straight across the Quad from here. Have they found you an office yet?"

"I'm not sure. This is actually my first day here. But Henderson did point at that big edifice next to yours. Said I'd be located there. I'm supposed to meet Dean Fruborg later today, and also Professor Pomeroy."

"Pomeroy? Don't think I've met him. Her?"

"Him. Department Head. We've met by Skype, but not yet in person."

"Well, do let me know when you get settled. I'm looking forward to hearing your take on my ideas."

Glenda laughed. "That presumes that my take, as you put it, will have value. Well, perhaps it will. I'll be awfully glad if it does." She got up, offered a handshake, and departed.

* 2 *

Jenny yawned as she entered the kitchen, her pink quilted bathrobe belted at the waist, uncombed waves of light brown hair flaring about her roundish face in a Medusa-like dishevel. Martin cherished that frowsy-yawny look, remembering the morning after their first full night together and how lucky he had felt that this amazing woman, ten years his junior, had somehow fallen in love with him. Martin reached out to collect Ellen from Jenny's hip. He planted a farty kiss on her belly that drew the usual infectious giggle, her hands tangling in his shock of brown hair. A joyful start to a big day.

"Will you be marching today, or just watching?" asked Jenny.

"Fred asked me to march," he said as he kissed his daughter one more time before handing her back to Jenny. "Apparently one of the Trustees wants to meet me — he didn't say why — and said it would look better if I marched, so I'll march."

"Do you mean march like soldiers, Daddy?" splurted JJ, already dressed for school, his mouth half full of cereal. "With uniforms and everything?"

Martin laughed. "We don't exactly wear uniforms, but we do wear long black robes with a special hood. You've seen my hood before, haven't you?"

"Yeah, but I didn't know you marched. That's awesome. Is there a band playing, like a parade?"

"There's a parade, and there's music, but it's very slow. Fred, I mean President Walsh, goes first, then Provost Henderson, then the Deans and Professors, and finally the students. Would you like to go?"

"Could I? I mean, can I miss school and go?" He looked to his mother, who arched her eyebrow. "Please, Mommy, please, please,

please. I wanna see Daddy march."

"Well," she said, "I'm not sure Miss Philips would be happy for you to miss school, but since this is your father's first graduation at Bottlesworth, I guess we can bend the rules a little. I'll call the school to let her know."

"Thank you, thank you. That's so awesome. And Sister too? Can Sister come? To see Daddy march?"

"Sure thing. We'll all go."

-    -   -

The Bottlesworth campus began at the southern end of the Maine Street shopping district, just past the spire of the First Congregational Church. Well-endowed and well-supported by its alumni, it displayed a sweeping history of institutional architecture. College Hall, the one remaining 1820-era Georgian-style brick-and-stone structure, and the only building where ivy was allowed to adorn the walls, now served as office space for the President, Provost, Registrar, Dean of Students, and the Office of Development and Alumni Affairs. The three-story gabled brick Science Building, dating from 1875, sat across the Central Quad from College Hall, and had office space for most of the School of Science faculty, several fully renovated classrooms, and two ground-floor instructional laboratories now used by the Physics Department. The other two sides of the Quad were filled by a pair of double-width gray limestone 1890s behemoths, Kent Hall and Corey Hall, eponymous gifts from a timber baron and a railroad baron. Kent, with a plain façade, was home to the School of Social Science. Corey, deeply sculpted with floral plinths set at the corners and along the eaves, held the School of Humanities. South of the Central Quad was the much larger Arts Quad, anchored by the Curtiss Library, a red-brick rectangular hulk with rows of narrow windows set in mostly blank walls, and beyond that, two quads of dorms, a new science building, and sports facilities. A nice compact campus.

For today's ceremony, the Central Quad was filled with hundreds of chairs arranged in blocks facing a flag-and-banner-festooned podium structure large enough to seat the officiants, the speakers, and that fraction of the faculty who had agreed to march. The student brass ensemble, seated on the steps of Corey Hall, was playing Corelli-like fanfares as the solemn procession filed in from the Arts Quad, the Marshals directing the order of the filling of seats.

As Martin's faculty contingent entered, each person's black robe sporting a brightly colored hood from the school that had awarded their post-graduate degree, he forced a happy smile and waved to Jenny and the children. But Martin actually hated commencements. Not the celebration part. He was proud of every student who made it through and he delighted in the throngs of graduates and huggy parents as they sipped lemonade and ate the little chicken-salad and tuna sandwiches put out under the tent in the Arts Quad during what by tradition was called "the foregathering" even though it happened after the ceremony. In Martin's mind, it should have been called the "after-gathering." What he hated was the tedium of watching every student walk across the stage. At Harvard, where Martin had gone to college, the degrees were handed out in the residence halls after the main ceremony in the Yard, a smaller and more intimate way to confer dignity and status. But Bottlesworth, with only three hundred graduates, did them one by one. At his previous school, CTI, they also did them one by one, but there could be up to fifteen hundred graduates at all degree levels. That's where he had learned to hate commencements. He almost dozed off during the ceremony, but like all such agonies of finite extent, the tedium did eventually come to an end.

Martin had taught only sophomores and juniors during his first Bottlesworth year, so his social duties with parents and graduates were minimal. As the crowd foregathered under the big tent, he found his way to Jenny and the children. Fred Walsh, still in full academic regalia, his wooly gray hair spraying out from under his mortar board, approached with a tall and young-looking blazingly blond man at his elbow — slender, sharp-featured, and dressed in a snappy black pin-stripe suit with a floral necktie. After a nod to Jenny, Fred said, "Martin, let me introduce the donor of your chair. This is Charles Caldicott."

Martin thought him awfully young to be endowing anything, but he reached out for a handshake and simply said, "Ah, Mr. Caldicott. A pleasure. This is my wife, Jenny."

Charles shook hands with Jenny as Martin added, "I'm more than thankful for the donation, and I'm honored to be the first chair holder."

"It's more of a pleasure than you think," said Charles, with an unsettling glint in his eyes. "I think you know I was planning to put this chair at CTI, but I was so irritated that they failed to give Professor Gillespie tenure, I decided to put it here, having no idea that they would bring you up from CTI to fill it. A real coup for Bottlesworth, in my opinion."

"Well, thank you for that," said Martin, "but events made it attractive for me to move." Turning to Fred, he asked, "I understand that the official appointment has now gone through. Is that right?"

Fred confirmed. "Yes, the Trustees voted yesterday, and you are now the Charles Caldicott Professor of Applied Physics. And, by the way, Charles is now one of our Trustees. That became official yesterday, as well."

Charles beamed. "Martin, I want to talk to you about a new project, one that I hope you'll like. I'll be around all next week. Can we schedule something?"

"Sure," said Martin. "Classes are over, and summer beckons. How about lunch on Monday?"

"Sounds good," said Charles. "Barnaby's at noon?"

"Barnaby's it is," said Martin.

Fred, putting a hand on Charles's elbow, said, "Please excuse us now. I need to introduce Charles to some of the others." They drifted off toward a cluster of celebrants just as Bill Engle, looking so trim and professional in a dark gray suit, waved from across the lawn.

JJ spotted his uncle, gave out a yelp and ran across the twenty yards of grass, tackling Bill and almost knocking him down. Ellen, who followed JJ everywhere she could, reached them just as Bill grabbed JJ by the waist and hoisted him over his shoulder. She reached up, and Bill bent down to toss her onto his other shoulder.

"Quite a load you have," said Jenny as she and Martin got close enough to be heard. "Anyone I know there?"

"No, not me," screamed JJ, laughing, echoed by Ellen's "No, nommee."

Bill let the two children down, and they started running in circles around the four grown-ups, Ellen falling down about every half turn. "These rascals are getting heavy. I'm not sure I can keep doing two at a time."

"Better you than me," said Jenny with a grin. "How's Helen?"

"Doing fine. Just now ending the fourth month, and the morning sickness has finally faded away." Turning to Martin, he said, "I saw you speaking with Fred and our new Trustee. Glad you could meet him."

"Yeah, he mentioned that he has a new project. Any idea what this is about?"

"Actually, I do, but it's officially under deep wraps until CC talks to you in person."

"CC?"

"He likes CC better than Charles. He's the one with the big bucks, so we call him CC." "But," said Martin with a chuckle, "aren't you the leech whose job is to extract those bucks? Can't you tell me what's up?"

"No, no, no. I'm just the associate leech. That's why I can't talk. The head leech said no leaks, and when Jeremy says no leaks... no leaks."

Ellen suddenly took a running tumble that landed her face down in the grass. She started shrieking, more out of shock than hurt. Jenny picked her up, kissed the tip of her nose, and got her calm enough to be heard. "Did Helen say anything about a sitter for the opera on Saturday? Our student regulars have already scattered for the summer."

"Oh, yeah," said Bill. "I forgot. She got Susan what's-her-name, the nurse from the college. I said we'd leave at five. That right, Martin?"

"Yeah," said Martin. "I chose the sushi place out of respect for Cio-Cio San. Dinner's at six and curtain's at seven-thirty. We're bringing the kids to your house?"

"Yes. Carlo really does better there. He likes to control his space."

- - -

The Saturday night performance of *Madame Butterfly* came to its predictably tragic end, Cio-Cio San taking her own life after releasing her young son to Pinkerton's wife. As the four left the Merrill Auditorium, Bill and Martin trailed a few steps behind Jenny and Helen, whose black French braid swayed gently from side to side with each step. Bill asked, "What did you think of Cio-Cio San?"

"I'm astonished that Portland's little opera company could get somebody so good. She really fit the role — from China, isn't she? And she could act. Jenny and Helen were both in tears at the end."

"I liked Pinkerton's acting, too, but were my ears wrong, or was he out of tune in places?"

Martin chuckled. "Your ears weren't wrong. The role is really a tough one. He's the tenor, but he's also a prick."

They reached Helen's van and climbed in for the drive back to Brimfield Junction, Bill at the wheel, Helen riding shotgun. Jenny leaned forward from the back seat and asked, "Here's a question for the ride home. Did Pinkerton do the right thing, demanding to take the child?"

"He never should have pretended to marry the geisha in the first place," Helen said, turning her head to be heard in back. "It was a cynical, creepy thing to do. Just like a man. Go for sex regardless of the consequences."

"Present company excluded?" said Bill with a smile.

Helen laughed. "Of course. You guys, I mean you gentlemen, would never have done anything like that. Right?"

"Right," said Martin. "As Jenny will attest, I was a perfect gentleman when we were courting."

Jenny laughed. "I attest. Almost too perfect. But really, was Pinkerton right to take the child?"

Martin said, "I think he should have provided support for Cio-Cio San and her boy and left them to live in Japan."

"But," said Bill, "the dishonor of Pinkerton showing up with an American wife was too much to bear. Her Japanese family had disowned her, so her only source of dignity was a continued affirmation that he would return. And he did. But with a wife. Something she hadn't figured on. If she's going to off herself anyway, it was humane for Pinkerton to take the child."

Jenny said, "Y'know, before I met Martin, I had never been to an opera. Now, thanks to all those Met performances in the movie theaters, I've seen enough to know that the plots, no matter how melodramatic or silly, can raise real questions. We once had a huge fight over *Cosi fan tutte*. Do you remember that, love, when we went to see the Met in New York?"

"Do I remember?" said Martin. "How could I forget? A nightmare. Our first real fight. I was scared I was losing you. We're not going to fight about *Butterfly* are we?"

"Absolutely not," said Jenny, with a wry smile, as she leaned over and planted a light kiss on her husband's cheek. "We can find other things to fight about."

* **3** *

Martin managed to ignore his email and churn out most of the rest of his first chapter before it was time to walk over to Barnaby's. Not knowing what to expect from Mr. Charles CC Caldicott, he had opted for safe academic attire — khaki slacks, a blue blazer, a white shirt, and his Eliot House tie.

Barnaby's was the closest thing Brimfield Junction had to a New York-style delicatessen. Located on Maine Street halfway between the campus and Route 1, it featured a series of booths with padded faux-leather seats along its right-hand wall, an array of square tables in the central space, and on the left, a large deli case filled with cold cuts and a dizzying selection of prepared dishes — everything from chopped liver to platters of stuffed cabbage. The walls were in dark wood, decorated with gracefully framed posters from past seasons of the Bottlesworth Chamber Music Festival.

It was the booths, with their implied privacy, that made Barnaby's the place of choice for a power lunch, and it was here that Martin found himself seated in the rearmost booth opposite Charles, who had dressed casually, also in khaki slacks but with a navy blue golf shirt that set off his ash blond hair in stunning fashion. Their server, a slinky dyed redhead with her left temple shaved to fuzz, her bare arms covered with red and green undecipherable tattoos, and a blue enameled stud pierced into the right side of her nose, had brought water and taken their orders.

"Tell me about your family," said Charles. "I saw two children. Is that the lot?"

"That's the lot," said Martin, taking a sip of water, recognizing that such small talk was a necessary ice-breaker. "The boy — he's six

— that's JJ, from Jenny's first marriage. Her husband died when he was a baby. A tough situation."

"JJ. I like double initial names. People who know me call me CC, and you should, too. What does the JJ stand for?"

"Jonathan Jefferson. And he's officially a Quint. I adopted him when we were married, and we all agreed he could take my last name just like Jenny did."

"All? You mean JJ got a vote?"

"Absolutely. He liked having my name. Emerging man of the family, and all that."

"And the girl?"

"Ellen. That little mop-head is ours. Year-and-a-half. Light of my life."

Just then, the slinky redhead brought Martin's Reuben sandwich and CC's Cobb salad, asked if they needed anything, and hearing "no thanks," slinked away.

Between bites, CC asked, "What really got you to leave CTI for Bottlesworth?"

"Didn't Fred tell you?"

"Fred told me his version, but I want to hear it straight from you. He said you contacted him, not the other way around. Is that right?"

Martin took a deep breath to suppress his irritation at having to retell an overtold story. "Okay, if you insist. Things were getting ugly at CTI. At the graduation, you mentioned Sharon Gillespie not getting tenure. I was sick about it, because she was probably the best teacher at CTI. Anyway, her decision came down just at the time I was put in charge of mentoring Kat Rodriguez through tenure. On the very day when Kat's case was to come up, my casebook with the letters got stolen — not just Kat's letters, all the letters from four tenure cases — and the letters showed up on the internet the next day."

"My God," said CC. "Who would do that?"

"Nobody knows. Someone with a bogus user account did the posting, and they never found him. Or her. I tried like mad to get her through, but she didn't quite make it. I even fought with my rtment Head about it. He kicked me off the Personnel Committee and Kat sued CTI. That made it even uglier. It wasn't just the stolen letters. There were allegations of sexual misconduct involving two members of the Personnel Committee. It was unpleasant even to go to campus. So with Jenny's blessing, I contacted Fred to ask for suggestions, and a few weeks later, Win Henderson showed up in my office and offered me a slot here. That's the story."

CC pressed on. "That's the outline of the story, but not the heart of the story. The real question is why'd you leave a hot-shot research career for a small college? That's what fascinates me. You're an international superstar. I was astonished and delighted that Bottlesworth got you, and I'm excited."

"Actually, I've got a serious book to write — about the role of live conversation in education — and Bottlesworth is giving me the time to do it. That's a pretty significant attraction. I never had the time at CTI."

"I do want to learn about your book project, but I'm interested in a different option."

"A different option?"

"Yes. Let me tell you a bit about me. I'm based in the Boston area, and I've done three companies, bing, bing, bing. The present one is called Autobot. It's in Andover."

"What do these companies do?"

"We're in the commercial-robot space, sourcing a mix of hardware and software solutions that can be retrofitted into the established market."

Martin couldn't quite digest that, so he asked, "Retrofitted solutions? Like what?"

"Sorry," said CC. "Bad habit. Talking like a venture capital guy. They say things like 'sourcing solutions' all the time. It's mostly bull. Anyway, we've had a very successful run creating add-ons to industrial robots. Our first company made a suite of software tools that improved the ability of pick-and-place robots to handle misaligned objects. After I sold that one, we got more into the hardware side, providing computer-vision add-ons for the robots that run around warehouses filling orders. They're now putting our systems on drones to fly around the warehouses and check inventory. That company hit big and I still own a decent piece of it. But Autobot is really my home run. We've found that adding a third computer-vision camera, what we call trinocular vision, allows a thirty-percent improvement in the accuracy of face-recognition software."

"So who buys that?" asked Martin.

"Think Department of Homeland Security. Commercial surveillance. Airports. Border crossings. Police."

"You mean you sell to the government?"

"Big time."

"How does it work?"

"I can't tell you. Not allowed. It's enough to say that our customers include all the usual suspects: FBI, Homeland Security, Immigration and Customs Enforcement, CIA, some of the larger city police forces. A lot of the commercial security firms, as well, although that market is slower to open."

"Wow. So this must be one of those start-up wonders — what do they call them?"

"A unicorn. Yup. It's already a unicorn, and when the valuation crosses two billion or thereabouts, I'll probably be ready to sell to one of the big companies. For now, though, I'm still building it up."

"Two billion? Wow. And you own it?"

"Most of it. I funded the second company with the proceeds from the first plus some venture investment. But I financed the Autobot startup myself, and when we landed TSA as a customer, we went cash-flow positive right away, so I didn't need any venture money. I own it all except for the stock options I've given to key employees. I think that about twenty of my folks are already paper millionaires."

"Why not go public and keep it going?"

"Not my style. The goal of most entrepreneurs is to create something, build value, and then sell it at the right moment. A few, like Zuckerberg, go public and then stay on and stay in charge, but most of us cash out and go on to the next big idea. And for me, actually, I'm beginning to feel that I've made enough money. I'm more interested in making an impact on education. Which leads me to a question."

Martin looked up, waiting.

With that curious sparkle in his eyes, CC asked, "Do you think you could entice Sharon Gillespie to Bottlesworth?"

Martin could barely conceal his shock. "Gillespie? Here? But we don't have a real engineering program. We have a three-plus-two with Dartmouth and Orono. So I don't see how…"

"Suppose Bottlesworth *did* have a real engineering program?"

"Well, it would have to be a pretty good one. I don't know her, but she was famous at CTI. She went to that new place, right?"

"Yes. Camberton College. In Needham."

"Well, she certainly wouldn't leave that for here unless we had something similar."

"Yes. Something similar. That's what I have in mind."

"But the Camberton Foundation put millions into starting that. Where would…" Martin stopped mid-sentence.

"Yes. You understand me," said CC. "I had no idea that putting this chair at Bottlesworth would attract someone of your caliber. And now that you're here, I asked myself why not get a half-dozen Martin Quints and combine their engineering expertise with some new people in economics and business. I want to establish a fifth school at Bottlesworth." Raising and spreading his hands as if holding up a banner, he intoned, "The Caldicott School of Engineering and Entrepreneurship — a mix of the two."

"Sounds overwhelming. And you're telling me because… because why?"

"Because I want you to build it. Hire the people, design the curriculum, be the dean."

"I'm thunderstruck. It would never occur to me to be a… to be a dean."

"You know that big old warehouse on the Clements Corner Road just beyond the pines? The one where Cabel Construction used to be?"

"Yes, why?"

"I can lease it. Twenty thousand square feet of high-bay space on the first floor with a full second floor. It's big enough for a bunch of labs, several classrooms, and plenty of offices. And it's only five minutes from the campus. The owner will sign a lease with an option to buy and allow us to do whatever buildout we want."

"We?"

"Yes. Are you on board for this?"

"Well, I'm not sure. It sounds amazing, but it's not what I thought was going to be doing here. I can't digest it. Who knows about this idea?"

"Fred, of course, Henderson, too. And the senior development people."

"Which is why Bill knew. He wouldn't tell me anything, though."

"Bill?"

"William Engle." CC nodded at the familiar name. "My brother-in-law. Do the deans know about this? Dean Kim in particular?"

"No, and I suggest we keep discussions to just us for now. I understand that the suggestion of a fifth school might ruffle some feathers."

Martin nodded and focused on finishing his lunch, his heart thumping. Was it excitement? Was it fear? Or was it irritation at seeing his precious summer disrupted?

As CC called for the bill, Martin asked, "What kind of a time scale are you on? I mean, how soon do you need—"

CC cut him off. "Take it easy, Martin. This is no bum's rush. What I would like to do over the next month or so is have access to enough of your time to talk this through properly and see if my ideas make any sense. I've rented a house in Harpswell for the summer, and I'll be around a fair amount. We need to consider scope, size, budget. All of that. And I want your input before I make a definite commitment, one way or the other."

"And am I your only candidate to run this thing?"

"For the moment, yes. But even if you eventually turn me down, I want your criticism of the plan. Can you at least to help with that?"

"I guess so," said a still stunned Martin, thinking that it would be stupid not to.

Back at his desk after parting ways with CC, he tried to focus on his book, but it was hopeless. He kept imagining a tornado sweeping across the landscape, buoying CC's gleaming face at the top of the funnel cloud, with buildings, cars, road signs, and, especially, drafts of books, being torn up in its path, pages flying off in all directions.

-    -   -

That night, after Martin had settled the children into bed, he joined Jenny in their study. She was staring at her computer screen filled with what looked like floor plans. Martin wasn't sure she was listening when he reported on his lunch, but when he finished, with her eyes still locked on her screen, she asked, "Would you want to do it? Be a dean?"

"I haven't the slightest idea. I mean, my instinct is no, I wouldn't. But when he said we could aim for first-class people, like Gillespie, it gave me pause. He seems a little bit like a wild man, impulsive, some wild gleam in his eye, a Mephistopheles type. Or maybe it's that look of people who claim to be born again — you know what I mean. The earnest evangelicals, the proselytizers. I have to see what CC really wants to do, and whether he'll put up enough money to make it possible. I can't decide anything on the basis of one lunch."

"It doesn't sound like you," said Jenny, still intent on her work. "You belong in the classroom."

"I know, I know," said Martin. "You're right. I shouldn't do it. I can't do it. This summer, it's just gotta be the book."

-    -   -

The next morning found Martin sitting with Glenda at his conference table, Martin with coffee in a CTI mug, Glenda with tea in a Bottlesworth mug, both beverages long since gone cold. He had been explaining the key points for his book and was currently ranting — with more vehemence than usual — about why online courses failed to meet his quality standards. Was this a boyish attempt to impress Glenda, this hot-shot Oxford person? Perhaps, but he would rather have her be impressed than the alternative. He flamed about how poor the student-support process was, with online chat rooms that were inefficient and largely useless, and Glenda agreed. But then she asked quietly about the flipped classroom. "Have you considered trying it?" she asked.

Brought up short, he asked, "You think it's a good idea?"

"I don't really know," she said, "I've never tried it. My teaching is mostly by tutorial. But I've seen news articles where online lectures worked rather well when combined with the use of class time for discussion and student interaction."

"But," he replied, suddenly feeling pushed in an unwelcome direction, "this would require a complete redesign of my class."

"Maybe so," she said. "Aren't there suitable lectures from that consortium, whatever it's called?"

"You mean FIE, the Free Internet Education outfit?"

"Yes, that one."

Martin laughed. "Oh, yes, they have lectures. Based on my class, in fact. They wanted me to do the online version, but I refused. So they got Harry Huang. It nearly wrecked his life for more than a year."

"But aren't the lectures done now? Couldn't you use them?"

Feeling a visceral urge to change the subject, Martin said, "Maybe I should take a new look. Hadn't thought of—"

Just then, Glenda's mobile phone chimed.

"Sorry. Text message," she said. "It might be my father. Give me a moment, please."

She rummaged in her purse for the phone, looked at the screen, and her normally pale face paled even more.

"Something wrong?" asked Martin.

"It's from Oxford. I'll…"

"Go ahead and reply. I can wait."

"Actually, I need to telephone. I'll have to…" Glenda got up to leave, but Martin offered her the privacy of his office for her call. He left to hit the lounge for another cup of coffee. As he approached his office, he heard her voiced raised in what sounded like astonishment.

"He said what?"

Martin paused, torn between curiosity and his offer of privacy.

"It's all stuff and nonsense. And I'm sorry, Professor Cavendish, but I just arrived in Maine a few days ago to tend to my father's illness, and it is not at all convenient to return for a hearing. It will have to wait until I return for grading."

At this point Martin was hooked. He listened.

"Well, the poor sod is lying. He broke down in my office, devastated over the accident, and all I did was give him a shoulder to cry on."

Glenda's voice level calmed to the point where Martin could no longer hear, so he waited, far enough from the door to avoid an accusation of eavesdropping. Within a minute, Glenda opened the door, a bright flush in her face.

"Something wrong?" asked Martin as he returned to the conference table.

"Yes, I'm afraid. Stupid, stupid, stupid. I would like to say it was nothing. Stiff upper lip and all that. But I'm too furious. A student, for God's sake. Bleeding furious."

"What happened?" asked Martin, eager for more. "I don't want to pry, but…"

"It's one of my tutees. He's invented the notion that I made improper advances. It's all rot, and deep down he knows it, but he's too upset to think clearly. The kid's mother was killed in a horrible bicycle accident in London. Horrible. She was crushed by a lorry making a turn. Grisly pictures in the press, the works. When he showed up for tutorial, he was a mess, a completely understandable mess. I was amazed he showed up at all, and I said so. That broke him into tears, and I offered a hug. That's it. A hug. Now he's complained to the Master of my college, and the whole pack of them are running around, wringing their hands."

"I'm sorry," said Martin. "Do you need to go back?"

"I'll be back soon enough for the exam grading."

"And he said okay to that?"

"She did. I think she understands, and even agrees with me, but she is required to follow up. And I'm required to cooperate. We have procedures. Ugh. What rot."

"Can I — I mean we, at Bottlesworth — help in any way?"

"Well," with a bit of a smile, "perhaps the best thing would be to get me a good internet connection so I can Skype back and forth. And, if you don't mind, I would ask you to stay mum until I know more about the situation. I'm a bit sorry to have even told you, but I guess when you're angry…"

"Yes, I understand. My lips are sealed. Should we continue this another time?"

"Yes. I need to cool off. And contact my solicitor. More nonsense for him to deal with. Y'know, we're all at the mercy of the accuser these days. When I was a student…" Glenda got up and started toward the office door.

"When you were a student, no one would have listened if you had a complaint?"

"Exactly. They would laugh it off. Pinch a titty, write a ditty. After all, boys will be boys, ha ha."

"Well, let me know when we can continue our discussion. In the meantime, you've got me thinking. About that flipped classroom idea."

"Good. And do send me your book draft. I'd love to see it."

After Glenda left, Martin emailed her the first chapter draft and a sketched outline for the rest, wondering all the while whether this suddenly arrived Oxford person would cause a flood that would breach the levee protecting his summer and wash away his book outline. How should he respond?

She may be right about the flipped classroom, but good grief — a complete redesign of my course? More work, just when I need to write what I already know? But she's right. My diatribe against online methods might sound shallow without having tried the flipped version. And what if it works, and works well? I would have to admit it, even become an advocate? Anyway, lecturing is getting stale. Students already register for the FIE version just to have access to the materials, so should I make a virtue of this new reality? Having her participate and criticize and annotate might make the effort worthwhile. She has chops in psychology and linguistics and knows way more of the literature than I do. A new buddy. A partner. A pushy partner, perhaps, but a partner. It might be fun, a pleasure. What a pity about that student.

* **4** *

On Friday afternoon, Martin loaded the groceries for the Memorial Day weekend into the back of Jenny's van, buckled Ellen into her car seat, picked up JJ at school, and drove the twenty miles to the cottage. He unloaded everyone and everything and checked the tide chart. A good swimming day. Helen and Bill would arrive just in time.

The water on the Maine coast is cold, almost always. The tiny ocean beach on the east side of Sagadahoc Point, some fifty yards from the cottage, is swimmable only in late July and August unless one has the constitution of a polar bear. In the bay on the west side, it's different. A sunny day warms the water in the marsh at the head of the bay, and when the ebb tide carries the warm water down into the bay, there can be delightful swimming for an hour or so during the narrow window between too-cold and too-shallow.

Helen and Bill arrived at 5:30, an hour after the tide had turned, so Helen immediately took all four children for a splash, now visible as specks to Martin and Bill, sipping their beers on the cottage deck.

"I'm glad you guys could come for supper," said Martin. "With Jenny gone again, I've had only the kids for company since yesterday morning. And I can't leave the kids and go running, so I'm feeling flabby."

"Where'd she go this time?"

"Just to Boston, but she went a day early to see her parents in Worcester. Her father's been sick and she hasn't seen them in a while."

"When's she getting back?"

"Traffic will probably be dreadful, so I don't expect her much before 8:30 or so, after dinner in any event. Speaking of which, I better start the coals. We're going to have a hungry army pretty soon."

Martin stood up to fuss with the charcoal grill down by the driveway, got it lit to his satisfaction, and rejoined Bill on the deck. "What does it feel like for you, becoming a father? Are you nervous?"

Bill took a sip of beer. "It's not so much that I'm nervous. Helen seems strong and healthy, and I've been with Carlo and Angela long enough to get a sense of what kids can be like. What I wonder is how the newcomer will fit in. Will they resent the intrusion?"

"I don't know about your kids — Carlo, especially — but JJ was mostly thrilled when Ellen arrived. He sometimes pouts out of jealousy and occasionally gives her a whack when she meddles with his books, but he's mostly gentle. And, you're right, being a father feels different."

"You mean from being a stepfather?"

"Yes. Holding her that first day absolutely blew me away. Such a little miracle."

"I wonder whether stepfathers are always jealous of the natural father."

"Jealous? You mean because of the sex? Are you jealous?"

"Just uneasy. This other man slept with my wife and the result was these two kids who aren't really mine. I mean, I don't have any doubts, or anything, but just thinking about it… I don't know… I'm just uneasy sometimes."

"But that other man is long gone, and good riddance. I could never understand why she married that bum in the first place. They were fighting all the time. Felipe would get drunk and go out driving, sometimes staying out all night. Helen finally threw him out and filed for divorce. It was a mess, a painful mess."

"Yeah. She said it took quite a while to heal up. Apparently I showed up at the right time, long enough after. How do you deal with husband number one? Did you know him?"

"Didn't know him and didn't really have to deal with him," said Martin, remembering their first time, the breakthrough, starting with that gentle kiss on the side of his neck. "Jenny did it — totally cleared the air. She loved George deeply, and his death left her feeling like she'd been knifed. But when she was ready, she took the lead. She made it…

uh… clear she was ready to move on, and we're fine. I think she still loves him, loves his memory, anyway, but we're fine. Fine. I better start the burgers."

Martin went into the cottage wondering how fine he and Jenny actually were, what with all the fussing over child care and travel. True, he was delighted by, even chauvinistically proud of the emerging success of her business, but he didn't like the side effect — leaving him alone with two children as she tripped off to Boston or, now, of all places, Chicago, with its grisly distinction as the last place he had visited before his first marriage exploded in a lipstick-stained mushroom cloud.

He returned with a platter piled with hamburgers and hot dogs and loaded up the grill just as Helen arrived with the passel of young cousins. Helen was carrying Ellen while JJ, skinny and shivering in his wet bathing suit, was carrying towels. Seven-year-old Carlo, taller than JJ and pudgier, with black hair like his mother, had two buckets of sand toys. Four-year-old Angela, a tow-headed blond with straight wispy hair that reminded Martin of his father, was crying because, she said, Carlo had hit her.

"Did not," said Carlo.

"That's enough fussing," said Helen. "Time for a quick shower for the lot of you, and then hot-dog time."

"And chips?" asked JJ.

"Yes, chips," said Martin. "And carrots and some fruit."

"I hate carrots," said Carlo.

- - -

An hour after Helen and family had departed for Brimfield Junction, Martin heard Jenny drive up. He had just made it to the cottage door when she burst in carrying her portfolio, muttering "Goddam traffic. Even Route 1 through BJ was a mess."

"And a sweet hello to you, too," said Martin with a smirk, as she rushed past him.

"My bag's still in the car. Gotta pee."

Martin collected Jenny's suitcase and put out dinner leftovers on the round oak dining table. Jenny emerged from the bathroom and wrapped Martin in a hug that evolved into that humming kiss they both relished, at the end of which she said, "Hello, love. You feel good. Nice to be home. And it's nice to be done with those, those… whatever. Kids in bed?"

"Kids in bed. Hungry?"

"Hungry." Jenny sat, shifted a burger and veggies to a dinner plate, poured a glass of wine, drank more than a polite sip, and picked up a carrot stick with which she pointed at nothing in particular. "These consignment deals are getting tougher and tougher. They're now pushing for sixty percent, some even asking sixty-five. We can barely make costs at those rates unless we boost the prices so high that we lose the economy of the replica. At fifty percent we can manage, which is what I told them."

"So you didn't sign up anyone new?"

"Nope. But the four places all agreed to have our literature on hand for prospective customers, and we'll give them a decent referral fee. On that, we could at least shake hands. But people have to see these pieces to believe how fantastic they are, and yet I can't price them out of range. I'm hoping that we get a few referrals. In the meantime, the Chicago deal looks huge by comparison. Anyway, sorry for ranting. How are the kids doing? Or, should I say, how are you doing with the kids?"

"Kids are fine. Ellen scraped her knee, producing wails of outrage, but it's nothing serious. Helen and Bill came for dinner and the swimming was good. Carlo was pestering Angela a lot, but he and JJ seemed okay this time. My biggest problem is that I get no work done when you're gone, and I'm losing my summer, one goddam day at a time."

"Well," said Jenny, "I get no work done when you're at the college, so you could say we're even, except that you're gone more than I am. And Ellen's really gotten too big to ignore. Requires real attention, minute by minute. Too bad all our student sitters have fled town. We should look for someone."

"Maybe we should, even though in my gut I hate the idea."

"Why do you keep saying that? Everybody but us uses some kind of child care."

"It just freaks me out, the idea of leaving Ellen with a stranger. And it costs money to boot, a lot of money. Anyway, how are your parents?"

"We've got money. Why does it freak you out so much? Weren't you and Helen in child care after your mother left? You survived."

"Actually, we need to talk about money before we can decide on child care. How are your parents?"

"Okay. I give up. You won't get daycare. You won't even talk about it. But you don't mind complaining about not having it. Jesus, Goofus, you're in such a rut. Anyway, Dad's finally getting better, which is a great relief. He's up and about. I would love to have them up for a decent visit once JJ's school is out."

- - -

Martin woke early the next morning, a shrouded dawn just beginning to crawl across the sky, and the familiar foghorn music, a mix of Charles Ives and John Cage, easing him out of an unsettling dream. This grinning blond-headed man had been pushing him toward the edge of the rocky promontory next to the beach, even though he was secured by a stout rope to the corner post of the cottage deck, creating a painful constriction at his waist. As he nodded himself to wakefulness, he recognized the pressure of Jenny's arm wrapped around his middle. He disentangled from her embrace without waking her and got up, looking forward to some exercise.

He threw on his running gear, went to the kitchen to start the coffee, and took off on his usual three-mile route, to the south past the beach all the way to the tip of the point, around to the bay side and back, then a final loop along the marsh road at the northern end of the bay. With the sky brightening, the bay shimmered with cloud-muted sparkles from myriad wavelets. Martin got his legs into rhythm and drifted into musing mode. Was CC pushing him toward a cliff?

He had come to Bottlesworth to teach and write, not build an engineering school. It didn't seem fair for Fred and Win and CC to pressure him. On the other hand, he had a nagging sense that, long term, he might not be satisfied just teaching and writing, so maybe CC was actually offering him a lifeline as well as the potential of adding colleagues who would share his interest in real-world applications. It was a conundrum.

There were so many positives in Brimfield Junction. Last fall, using some of the stock Martin had inherited from his father, they had added a second bedroom and guest bathroom to the first floor of the cottage and expanded the sleeping loft into a proper floor-wide bedroom with two sets of bunk beds, a big play space, now partly filled with a crib, and a full kid bathroom. The cottage now provided more living space than their Brimfield Junction house, and everything was weatherized for year-round use. Martin had even bought a second Yamaha keyboard, a duplicate of what he had at home, so he could accompany their after-dinner sings and both he and JJ could keep up with their practice. And there was Bill, a magnificent addition to the family, especially his ability to manage Carlo and his outbursts. Martin had no first cousins, and he wanted his own children to grow up knowing and liking their cousins. While Carlo had a knack for torturing JJ, things seemed to go better when Bill was around, and Angela was fascinated by baby Ellen. When the children managed to play together in peace, Martin basked in an inner glow of contentment. When things weren't peaceful — well, sometimes they weren't. Children fight. Children cry. It's what children do.

He returned via the loop road that cut across the peninsula north of the cottage, and as he was getting ready to pour himself a cup of coffee, a thump from above alerted him that it was time to make the pancakes. He hoped the children wouldn't wake Jenny.

-    -   -

Not long after breakfast, a familiar car pulled up to the neighboring cottage, thirty yards up the road, and JJ let out a whoop. "Gabriel's here." He dashed upstairs to get dressed, and within minutes, came pummeling down the stairs and out the door.

DeShawn and Tamiqua Washington had bought their cottage last fall. They were an odd couple. At six-foot four, he towered over his wife, who couldn't have been more than five-foot three. A Bangor native, he had played basketball for the University of Maine's Black Bears and then made it onto the Charlotte professional team as an undrafted free agent. The pay was good, and, as he liked to say with a wink, he had saved his money. After his retirement from the pros at age twenty-eight, he wanted to work with kids. He found a job as an assistant basketball coach at Cranborne Academy, a prep school thirty miles inland from Brimfield Junction. Cranborne might have been second-tier in the academic sense, but its high school varsity was the perennial basketball champion in the Maine Prep League. Their highly successful coach, Erskine Dennings, was getting on in years and his wife was slipping inexorably into dementia, so the school had hired DeShawn both as an assistant and heir apparent. He expected to be the head coach one year hence.

In addition to coaching basketball and helping out with soccer and lacrosse, DeShawn taught Health and Hygiene, a class he would describe with a sly smile as sex ed for boys, redecorated. Tamiqua, who had run track at UNC Charlotte, almost making the Olympic team as a distance runner, taught English, and when Cranborne went co-ed, she added an all-girl version of Health and Hygiene. She said the girls really didn't want to take sex ed with the boys. They had too many questions and were embarrassed.

The family lived in one of the school dorms as proctors, so they had no year-round housing expenses. This, said DeShawn with a character-istic wink, is why he was willing, on a prep-school salary, to sink money into a prime oceanside location. Martin suspected that after six years in the NBA, where average salaries were something like five million dollars a year, DeShawn could have made his seaside purchase with what amounted to petty cash.

The Washingtons' cottage was a small Cape Cod with naturally weathered gray shingles and a raised shed dormer holding two small bedrooms. Their son Gabriel was seven, and a perfect match for JJ.

When the Washingtons were at their cottage, JJ was mostly over there, leaving Martin free to care for and play with Ellen. A wonderful arrangement, all around.

As Martin was finishing up the breakfast dishes, JJ and Gabriel came running from next door. "Mom wants you to come for supper tonight," yelled Gabriel. "She said she's making gumbo."

"Happy to do that," answered Martin, wondering whether JJ would eat gumbo. "Tell her we'll bring hot dogs, just in case, and some wine, okay?"

"Ooo-kay," said Gabriel, and back they ran with the news.

-    -   -

The overcast lifted a bit, and with the tide out, Martin took Ellen to the ocean beach with her array of sand toys, leaving Jenny to enjoy her morning coffee in leisure. As he played with his daughter, each doing pat-a-cake on odd-shaped sand piles wetted down from the gentle tickle of the surf, Martin slipped again into pondering mode: Wasn't this what he had bargained for when he left CTI — time with his daughter, with his family, time to write, time to focus on teaching? Yes, it was, and yes, he enjoyed it. But he could feel that old energy coursing through his veins, urging him to be productive instead of sitting on the beach.

But isn't this productive? Being a parent? Playing pat-a-cake? Caring for my children? For my wife? For my family? The caring parent is usually the mother, at least in that deeply seated stereotype of the family life I never had. Sure, my father was a caring parent, but it was mostly through surrogates, and a tough kind of caring, at best. Maybe Jenny's right — maybe I'm still angry at him, more likely at my mother for abandoning us, or maybe both of them. But just playing with my daughter like this sometimes makes me feel guilty, a nagging sense of wasting time. I could be writing.

What do women professors do? Can they be caring parents and still carry the load? Based on some of my colleagues at CTI, the answer might be yes. Super-women. Running top-flight research groups while raising three apparently sane, bright, and capable children. But I couldn't manage it at

CTI. Always one more paper to write, one more conference to attend, and with Jenny running her decorating business from home, it was so easy to allow things to become unbalanced. It was only Ellen's birth that made me recognize how career-selfish I'd become. And thinking of careers for women, how is Kat going to manage? She married a woman. If at some point, one of them has a child, who will be the more caring parent? Can children ever be shared in a way that makes both partners happy? I hope so. I'm trying.

Martin gathered up Ellen to head back to the cottage. As they reached the steps to the deck, JJ and Gabriel came running up the road, JJ holding a huge razor clam in his hand. "I digged it up myself, Daddy," shouted JJ. "He squirted me!"

Tamiqua came by shortly after the boys, carrying a bucket of steamers, sloshing a bit of water with each step. "You want me to change the water?" asked Martin.

"Not yet," said Tamiqua. "I switch it to fresh water about a half-hour before cooking."

"You okay having JJ this afternoon? Or should they come over here?"

"Our place is fine," said Tamiqua with a grin. "They keep each other outta my hair."

Martin took Ellen in and turned her over to Jenny. With the sky lowering and threatening rain, it called for a quiet afternoon. Martin took advantage of the calm to get out his laptop and add the literature references and footnotes to his now completed first chapter. Breathing a sigh of relief with that job finished, he began paging through a new book on language and meaning, noting the citable text to support his next chapter, to be entitled "Concepts," a topic on which he expected little or no pushback from Glenda. He knew that between the way psychologists think about learning and the way linguists agonize over meaning and cognition, there was a connecting glue called conversation through which the active engagement of the mind permitted one to learn new concepts.

- - -

Martin helped himself to a bit more rice and covered it with a spoonful of Tamiqua's gumbo. "This is fantastic," he said. "Bay scallops. Never had that in gumbo. Is it from a family recipe?"

Tamiqua laughed. "Oh, no. In my family, you put whatever looks best in the gumbo. I stopped at Wilson's on the way through Bath, and he recommended the scallops. I like the big ones best, but all he had was the little ones. They cook, like, in two minutes so you don't put 'em in until just before serving. Jenny, you want some more?"

Jenny declined with a smile, but DeShawn followed Martin's lead, and took his own second portion. "You off for the summer?" he asked.

Martin held up his forefinger. "First time in living memory."

"So whatcha gonna do?"

"I'm working on a book about education. Part of my point is that online education suffers from a lack of direct conversation. Do you guys use any online stuff at Cranborne?"

DeShawn and Tamiqua looked at each other, their cheeks puffed out, and they started laughing. Martin was puzzled. "Did I say something funny?"

Tamiqua answered. "No. It's just that we argue about it at school all the time. Our headmaster wants us to experiment, but DeShawn and I, we like the old-fashioned way."

DeShawn added, "Actually, though, there's some fairly good stuff online about sex ed, allowing us to show photos — even videos — of body parts and some basic functional stuff. The kids tend to giggle a lot, but I can use the stuff to persuade the boys, if you'll let me put it this way, that size doesn't matter. I think it's good to fight the impressions the kids get from the X-rated websites."

"Kids watch those?" asked Jenny.

"It's impossible to stop," said DeShawn.

"Can we be excused?" said Gabriel. He and JJ left the table without waiting for an answer from the parents. Ellen climbed down as well and toddled after the boys, grabbing her stuffed dachshund by the tail and dragging it along.

"So how do you use the online material?" asked Martin. "The

good material."

"We assign certain segments for the kids to watch," said Tamiqua. "Then we discuss it in class. Works okay for something like sex ed, but there's nothing available for English that's any good, teaching kids to read critically and write decent essays, I mean."

Martin mused, "So you flip the classroom. That's a hot topic these days. We have a visitor from Oxford, and she's pushing me to try it in the fall."

"It's not great, but it can work," said DeShawn. "The kids like to watch videos on their own, especially about private topics like sex. But they don't like online reading if it's long. They prefer books, printed stuff."

- - -

After dinner, while Jenny was putting the children to bed, Martin picked up the book on semantics he was hoping to digest, but the foghorns had started again, their mournful reminder of the seafaring hazards of coastal Maine. Were they a warning to Martin, as well, to avoid the shoals of CC and his ego-driven enthusiasms?

His musing was interrupted by Jenny stealing up behind him, wrapping her arms around his belly, with hands descending seductively toward his crotch. "Both kids are sound asleep," she crooned as she laid her cheek on the back of his shoulder. "How about an early bedtime?" she asked, gently kissing the side of his neck and stretching to nibble on his earlobe. "I miss... uh... us."

"Best offer I've had all week," said Martin, getting up and drawing Jenny into a hug that evolved into their humming kiss that evolved further toward the start of unbuttoning.

* 5 *

As Martin walked toward campus on the Tuesday after Memorial Day, he was anxious about what would be his first-ever meeting with Jeremy Good, the legendary Director of Development and Alumni Relations who also doubled as an ex-officio chief financial officer, helping Fred with oversight on the Treasurer and the Comptroller to keep the place afloat. Martin recalled his father praising Jeremy to the skies with what he called a "Quaint Quint Quip," saying that Jeremy could charm the quills off a porcupine. He went on to say that they should name the Arts Quad for him when he died. A seventy-five-year-old rumpled, overweight gnome who favored jarringly colored bow ties, Jeremy had not only arranged for the Curtiss Library bequest, he had master-minded the arts campaign of the nineties that resulted in the spectacu-lar music, drama, and arts facilities as well as the necessary funds to relocate and improve student housing. In fact, the only recent building for which Jeremy had not been the prime mover was the Grantland Science Center at the south end of campus, which Fred Walsh had arranged over a handshake from an alumnus who ran a bond-trading firm in New York. While the faculty benefitted from Jeremy's mag-nificent efforts, they tended to resent his less-than-charming attitude toward them, implying that the faculty actually worked for him rather than the other way round. But given his extraordinary successes, when he issued demands to individual professors for assistance on this or that, the targets might grumble, but under no circumstances would they refuse to help.

Martin went directly to College Hall and up to the President's con-ference room on the third floor, where Fred Walsh, Win Henderson, and Jeremy were gathered around an oblong oak table, sipping coffee and nibbling from a bowl of donut holes from Dunkin Donuts. Jeremy looked up over the rims of his granny glasses and nodded a grunted greeting as if he were sizing up this new addition to his flock. Martin squeezed out an awkward hello, nice to meet you, and paused to pour coffee as Fred said, "CC called to say he was parking. He'll be here—"

"Right now," said CC, as he breezed into the room, waving his whole arm in a grand gesture and bowing to the table, reserving his one hand-shake for Martin. He poured himself a mugful of coffee, grabbed two of the donut bits and took a seat next to Martin, his left leg pumping up and down as if he were personally generating the energy to light up the room. "Can we get started?"

This conference room, with its dour portrait of Josiah Bottlesworth hanging directly across from Martin's seat, gave him the willies, nee-dling him with the distant memory of his mother, Josiah's seventh-gen-eration granddaughter who had deserted her family for the *avant-garde* New York art world. He barely heard Fred begin.

"Thank you all for being here. CC has given us a daunting proposal, and we need to look at all aspects before we can expand the discus-sion beyond this room. In particular, we are grateful to CC for offering to put up serious money to expand our presence in engineering and entrepreneurship, but we are mindful of the difficulties of making a change of this magnitude within an institution that has a well-estab-lished structure and traditions around governance. Win, you're first. What's the view from the Provost's office?"

Win, fifty-five years old, tall and broadly built, with a sun-browned fleshy face marked by bristly eyebrows over deep-set eyes, scanned the faces before speaking. "Well, I'm cautious. Right now, our four schools get along pretty well with one another. The deans and I share a common vision for the college, and even though every dean wants more money, more hiring slots, and more space, there's a certain level of mutual respect within which they compete, and we haven't had a serious fight since the completion of the theater. If we try to plunk a new school into the mix, I'm sure there will be disagreements, espe-cially over space, even though I can't predict the details. It depends, rse, on whether the new school creates budget pressures on the existing schools. And," as he look straight at CC, "that depends, I guess, on CC's willingness to lead a fund-raising campaign."

CC, dressed today in blue jeans, loafers, and a forest green polo shirt, responded. "My idea was not to do the campaign first. I'm prepared to put in twenty million up front, which would endow five chairs with enough left over to secure and renovate the space I've found, so there won't be any fights over space. If we can get really great people here, it will be easy to raise more money to build out the program."

"Hold on," said Jeremy, with the proprietary air of a lord speaking to his vassals. "There's a huge risk in taking that course. A school must be bigger than five faculty. Our schools have thirty faculty or so. If we're going to create a named school, we need a plan to get at least to fifteen faculty. Twenty million, generous as that is, won't get us there. I think we need to get more like eighty million pledged before we could start, and then only if we can see our way to sustainability."

Fred added, "I tend to agree with Jeremy. A new school must have both the ring and promise of permanence. We can't rush headlong into such a venture without a long-term plan for financing it."

CC pushed back his chair, his fidgety leg suddenly quiet. "Remember that old Chinese proverb? About how predicting is difficult, especially the future? When I set out to endow a professorship, I went first to CTI, not here. When I changed my mind and brought it to my dear alma mater, was that part of your long-term plan? Of course not. And then you landed a world-class individual to fill that chair. Was that part of your long-term plan? No, indeed. Events make their own future. No one has the ability to map out a plan that anticipates the synergies when new things happen. A Bottlesworth chair plus Martin Quint changes the landscape, at least for me. We need to change it some more. Adding applied science and entrepreneurship to a Bottlesworth education will inject new energy into the place."

"But," said Martin, with a cautious glance in CC's direction, "we can't reasonably expect to cover engineering and entrepreneurship with even fifteen faculty, much less five. Somehow, it has to be focused."

"Exactly," said CC, his leg starting up again. "Focus. On robotic systems for some aspect of medicine and microbiology, for example, things that will enable genomic medicine, or automate the CRISPR technology, stuff like that. Or machines that can read and react to human emotion — we could do that as an extension of what we've learned about face analysis at Autobot. These are really hot areas, cross-disciplinary, good new business opportunities all over the place. Even with only five faculty, plus Martin, of course, we could mount a terrific program, attract a different mix of students, make an impact."

Fred spoke up. "I like the idea of attracting a different mix of students, getting some of those entrepreneurial types who are both intellectually and personally ambitious, having them share meals with the history majors, making them argue with each other over life priorities. It would enrich our education. But I share Jeremy's concern about size and finance." Turning to Martin, he said, "I would like to ask you, Martin, if you're willing, to help CC create a multi-stage plan — five faculty growing to something like fifteen, an outline for an academic program and a high-level budget to get us there. Then we can evaluate the options. Until that happens, I don't want any discussion of this beyond us five. So, Martin. Will you help?"

Martin felt his face flush as he suddenly got the message. This meeting was a set-up, a genteel and polite set-up, but a set-up, nonetheless. A choreographed charade to get him on board, and even though he liked Fred and Win as colleagues, he felt used and angry. Was this to be his future at Bottlesworth? As Dean of the Charles Caldicott School of Engineering and Entrepreneurship? A manager of budgets and space, a mediator between fractious faculty? He had a book to write, dammit! But as the brand new holder of the Charles Caldicott Professorship in Applied Physics, he felt forced to keep it together. Staring at his ancestor's portrait, he turned to Fred and said, "Yes. It seems to be my destiny."

The assembled parties got up, and amid handshakes, CC said to Martin, "I'll get my finance guy to put together a business plan. I'd prefer to send it to your home. Don't want copies floating around campus."

Martin wrote his address and handed it over. On the way out, Win asked Martin, "You got a minute?" Martin nodded, and followed Win down to his office on the second floor, a gracious, bookshelf-lined space with two large windows overlooking the Central Quad.

As they sat, Win asked, "Have you met our visitor?"

"You mean Glenda Aldrich? Oh, yes. We're having our second meeting today."

"Good. I wanted to be sure that you've gotten connected because you're actually the reason she chose to come here instead of to USM in Portland. We need her, or someone like her, to cover for Cynthia Collins's anticipated maternity leave in the fall. When I told her about your interest in conversation, the book you wanted to write, she did some homework on you and decided in our favor. Just the kind of magnetism CC was talking about, I guess."

"That CC. Is he nuts, or not?"

Win chuckled. "Oh, he's nuts, all right, but it might be the right kind of nuts. Jeremy estimates his net worth at about six hundred million, so when he says he could put up twenty, he means it. He could probably just write a check."

"He's gotta be worth more than that. He told me that his third company is a unicorn, which means it's already worth more than a billion, and he owns almost all of it. When the value reaches two billion, he plans to sell. But what makes me nervous is that he doesn't seem to think long term. His view is to start something and then exit. How do we know he would stick to a plan?"

"We don't," said Win. "We're all worried about that. But he has an amazing track record in business, so for now, we're taking it seriously. If his plan passes muster, how could we pass it up?"

-    -   -

On returning to his office, Martin found an email from Peter Dempsey suggesting that it was time for a thesis-committee meeting with his final PhD student from CTI, Natasha Pribikov, now jointly supervised with Peter. Martin telephoned Jenny, who answered after three rings. "Hey, love," said Martin. "I've got to pop down to Cambridge for Natasha's thesis committee this Thursday. Any conflict with that?"

"Not at the moment. I'll mark it down."

"And if I can set up a chamber music session with Horatio and Sumner that night, could I stay over, return Friday mid-day? I really miss those guys."

Martin could hear Jenny exhale over the phone. "Well, at least you're asking before committing, which I appreciate. Yes, it's okay. And can you pick up milk on the way home? And a cantaloupe or honeydew, whichever looks best?"

"Sure, but I've got one more meeting. The tea and crumpets lady."

-     -   -

Just before Glenda arrived, the sky opened up, with buckets of rain pummeling the windows. Martin looked out to see her angling across the Quad from Kent Hall, her umbrella being tossed in the wind and blown inside out. She struggled to straighten it, without success, so she made a dash for the entrance to the Science Building.

She appeared at Martin's office door a minute later, wet and bedraggled, her slender face resembling an afghan hound emerging from a bath. "Feels like the coast of England," she said, with a chuckle. "The brolly couldn't take it, and I'm afraid I'm a bit soaked."

"Do you need a paper towel or something?" asked Martin.

"I guess I do. And I'd fancy a cuppa. Warm me up."

They walked to the kitchenette at the end of the hall where Glenda got her paper towel, and while they brewed tea for Glenda and coffee for Martin, he asked about the student situation. "Well, it's not any worse," said Glenda with a wry smile. "Master agrees that the boy is overwrought, and she has done two things. She referred my 'case,' as she calls it, to my Department Head, as per procedure, and she's connected the student with a counsellor. Grief counselling. It was her subtle way of declaring a cooling-off period."

"So no trip back to England?"

"Only at grading time. The Oxford procedures allow the

Department Head to mediate, so maybe this will just go quietly away. But it does worry me. Others in my department will surely hear about it, and then what? I get labeled as a tea and sympathy type?" She shuddered at the thought.

"And how's your father doing?"

"Rather well, actually. I don't recall if I told you. He has Parkinson's. That means he will go through a gradual but inexorable downhill. So far, he still has decent mobility and, thank goodness, is fully lucid. We've talked through the options, and he's agreed to go into assisted living. Now it's just a matter of finding the best place. In the meantime, I've connected with a home health agency in case he needs more assistance than I can handle."

The pair returned to Martin's office with their hot mugs and took seats at the round table. Glenda began. "So let's talk about talk. A conversation about education. I've read your draft about the teacher needing to create a model of how the student thinks in order to be effective, and I'm much taken by it." She chuckled as she said, "Are you sure you haven't been reading the psychology literature about human communication?"

"No, it's just based on my teaching experience. If you make a good model, you can connect with the student. Is this idea in the psychology literature somewhere?"

"Goodness yes, but not in that form. It's called by various names, such as the ostensive-inferential model of communication, but when you boil it down, it's exactly as you say."

"So everybody already knows this? I'm preaching to the choir?"

"Not at all. The people who study conversation and communication have agreed, generally, that there are two basic communication modes: one based on codes, like the way computers communicate, and one based on inferences about what the other person intends by speaking."

"Sure. Clark talks about the need for common ground, sort of a shared code. The inferences rely on the common ground. Isn't that right?"

"Sort of. But common ground is not a shared code. A code is like a

The social hall in the basement of the church had a wonderful Baldwin piano, a five-foot grand, regularly tuned and tweaked by Eddie Plunkett from Plunkett Piano Techs in Portland. The span of the program was enormous. The beginners had selected one-minute songs from their lesson books, while the teenagers and adults were to play chestnuts of varying levels of difficulty from the classical or show-tune literature.

JJ was scrubbed up for the occasion, with crisply creased brown slacks, a white buttoned shirt, even laced dress shoes, something Jenny had insisted on. He was eighth on the program, playing the second of Bach's *Little Preludes* from memory. When his turn came, he got up with a bold stride toward the front of the hall. Ellen stood up and started to follow him, since she always went wherever her big brother did. Jenny grabbed Ellen, who shrieked in protest, refusing all attempts to quiet her. JJ stood waiting as Helen came to the rescue, taking the bawling child from Jenny's arms and removing her to the entry hall, almost out of earshot. JJ resumed his erect and formal walk to the piano, bowed stiffly to the audience, positioned the piano bench to his liking, and sat at the keyboard. He hit all the notes without a single error. Fantastic! The rhythm? Well, that was a bit shaky, but it would improve with time. Martin was thrilled. So was JJ. He bobbed up from the piano bench and bowed twice to the applause of the parents and other students before resuming his seat next to Martin. For the rest of the program, he fidgeted.

Ellen eventually calmed down, and after the final chord had sounded and all the performers had been called to the front for a final bow, the two families went to McDonald's over at Clements Corner — JJ's choice — followed by ice cream at The Lickity Split on Maine Street.

Later that evening, Jenny came down to the study where Martin was slumped into his easy chair, immersed in Langacker. She came up behind him, wrapped her arms around whatever of him she could reach, and whispered in his ear, "Thank you, love, for opening up the world of music for JJ. It would never have occurred to me that he could do it so well and so young. You're a gem, and I love you."

Martin decided that the money talk could wait 'til after his trip to CTI.

* **6** *

Martin hit Portland just as morning rush hour was building to its peak, but Portland is not Boston, and with less stop-and-go than he expected, he got through town to the Maine Turnpike, heading south. His overnight bag was in the trunk along with a folder of music for clarinet and piano. Horatio Billingsworth, his old college roommate, would be out with his wife at some shindig with the President of Boston University where Horatio taught linguistics, but Sumner Collingsworth, his other roommate, was free. They were planning to work on the sonatas by Poulenc and Hindemith. Lovely stuff.

As the miles went by, Martin savored the memory of last night's glorious love-making, yet worried about this new grittiness in Jenny, as if she were developing a coating of pumice atop the smooth skin he so much loved to touch. It dredged up the decline of his first marriage, before the affair with Camille had surfaced.

But this isn't the same sort of thing. First off, I'm not having an affair. I'm as committed as I can be to Jenny and our family. And we still have these wonderful moments — like last night, like our early courtship. Katie was different. She was chronically depressed and refused to have children, while Jenny dotes on JJ and Ellen. But she's gotten so impatient with me now, outspoken, won't yield on simple things — family expenses, travel. Well maybe travel isn't that simple. I can't work anymore when caring for Ellen, and now that Jenny is doing her own travelling, I can see what I'm leaving behind when I go off on my consulting gigs, or even just to my office. So, yes, it's time to hire a child-care person and I hope it won't wreck our children, but not a daycare center, for God's sake — a person, someone who becomes part of the family. That will take money, though, and regardless, she's pushing back more and more often in a way that signals a deep anger.

- - -

There was no family sing that evening. JJ needed to do his final piano practice for tomorrow's recital. After supervising JJ's run-through, Martin ran the children's communal bath, supervised the splashing from JJ's boats and Ellen's yellow rubber duck, assisted with soaping and rinsing, got them out and dry, and with teeth brushed, helped them into their pajamas, JJ's covered with dinosaurs, Ellen's with baby rabbits.

With Ellen on one side and JJ on the other, Martin cuddled with his charges on JJ's bed. They started with Ellen's favorite storybook about bunnies, Ellen insisting on turning each page. When they reached the end, he said, "Time for beddie-bye," and Ellen flopped across Martin's belly to hug her brother. Martin was astonished at how affectionate JJ was with his sister, remembering his own childhood battles with Helen. JJ not only accepted her hug, he gave her a goodnight kiss on the cheek. How long would that last, he wondered.

After lights out for both kids, Martin went downstairs. Jenny was already at her computer, her screen showing house plans. "Chicago job?" asked Martin.

"Yup," said Jenny without looking up. "Scoping out the size of the job. How was the tea and crumpets lady?"

"Very good actually. She's rather forward — suggesting things like redesigning my entire course — but I think she knows a lot and will be a terrific resource. And the Chicago job?"

"It's going great. Have to go there in a week or so. This time with Pierre."

Martin hadn't paid much attention to Jenny's team of artisans, or for that matter, to what Jenny said was their astonishing artistry. Yes, the replicas were nice, but Martin's taste was more to stark Danish modern, which was how his Cambridge home had been furnished before he met Jenny. She, over time, with his love-besotted blessing, had gradually transformed their décor, one piece at a time, into a gracious mix of the modern with the best of the eighteenth and nineteenth centuries, and Martin had slowly grown to like the different look. As for the artisans,

Pierre was clearly their leader, the most experienced and the most creative. But traveling with Jenny?

"Again?" he asked. "And with Pierre?"

"Yes, again. She wants to meet Pierre. Get his opinion, and I can use his help to take more detailed measurements. There's also a big furniture show in Chicago, so if we can schedule to hit that, too, we'll do it. It's too late to get a booth, but we can walk the floor and distribute our handouts in person."

"With Pierre?"

"Sure. Why not? He's very presentable. Is that a problem?"

"The problem is having you away, with or without Pierre. This is prime writing time, and I get almost nothing done when Ellen's awake."

"Tell me about it, you Goofus," said Jenny, with less humor in her voice than the affectionate nickname might imply. "Guess who's given the primary privilege of trying to get things done with Ellen around? I'm an authority on that subject. I've said it 'til I'm blue in the face. We need to get Ellen into daycare. I've started making calls. The Kiddie Korner, where Helen has Angela, has no spaces for the summer so I'm looking for other options."

Martin forced his tongue into silence, sensing that this was not the time to bring up the money issue. Maybe tomorrow night. He picked up Langacker's book on *Cognitive Grammar,* and skulked his way in. After a half hour, Jenny announced she was going up to bed.

- - -

Bethany Stewart, the aging organist at the First Episcopal Church and an Adjunct Professor of Music at the college, had eighteen private piano students, ranging in age from six to sixty. She organized two student recitals a year, one before the Christmas holidays and this second one before everyone scattered for the summer. Martin had wanted to find JJ a local teacher other than himself, but it had taken a few months of settling in before getting referred to Bethany. JJ started with her in January, so today at five o'clock would be JJ's first performance ever.

The whole family came — Bill and Helen, their kids, even Ellen.

The social hall in the basement of the church had a wonderful] piano, a five-foot grand, regularly tuned and tweaked by Eddie] from Plunkett Piano Techs in Portland. The span of the program was enormous. The beginners had selected one-minute songs from their lesson books, while the teenagers and adults were to play chestnuts of varying levels of difficulty from the classical or show-tune literature.

JJ was scrubbed up for the occasion, with crisply creased brown slacks, a white buttoned shirt, even laced dress shoes, something Jenny had insisted on. He was eighth on the program, playing the second of Bach's *Little Preludes* from memory. When his turn came, he got up with a bold stride toward the front of the hall. Ellen stood up and started to follow him, since she always went wherever her big brother did. Jenny grabbed Ellen, who shrieked in protest, refusing all attempts to quiet her. JJ stood waiting as Helen came to the rescue, taking the bawling child from Jenny's arms and removing her to the entry hall, almost out of earshot. JJ resumed his erect and formal walk to the piano, bowed stiffly to the audience, positioned the piano bench to his liking, and sat at the keyboard. He hit all the notes without a single error. Fantastic! The rhythm? Well, that was a bit shaky, but it would improve with time. Martin was thrilled. So was JJ. He bobbed up from the piano bench and bowed twice to the applause of the parents and other students before resuming his seat next to Martin. For the rest of the program, he fidgeted.

Ellen eventually calmed down, and after the final chord had sounded and all the performers had been called to the front for a final bow, the two families went to McDonald's over at Clements Corner — JJ's choice — followed by ice cream at The Lickity Split on Maine Street.

Later that evening, Jenny came down to the study where Martin was slumped into his easy chair, immersed in Langacker. She came up behind him, wrapped her arms around whatever of him she could reach, and whispered in his ear, "Thank you, love, for opening up the world of music for JJ. It would never have occurred to me that he could do it so well and so young. You're a gem, and I love you."

Martin decided that the money talk could wait 'til after his trip to CTI.

* **6** *

Martin hit Portland just as morning rush hour was building to its peak, but Portland is not Boston, and with less stop-and-go than he expected, he got through town to the Maine Turnpike, heading south. His overnight bag was in the trunk along with a folder of music for clarinet and piano. Horatio Billingsworth, his old college roommate, would be out with his wife at some shindig with the President of Boston University where Horatio taught linguistics, but Sumner Collingsworth, his other roommate, was free. They were planning to work on the sonatas by Poulenc and Hindemith. Lovely stuff.

As the miles went by, Martin savored the memory of last night's glorious love-making, yet worried about this new grittiness in Jenny, as if she were developing a coating of pumice atop the smooth skin he so much loved to touch. It dredged up the decline of his first marriage, before the affair with Camille had surfaced.

But this isn't the same sort of thing. First off, I'm not having an affair. I'm as committed as I can be to Jenny and our family. And we still have these wonderful moments — like last night, like our early courtship. Katie was different. She was chronically depressed and refused to have children, while Jenny dotes on JJ and Ellen. But she's gotten so impatient with me now, outspoken, won't yield on simple things — family expenses, travel. Well maybe travel isn't that simple. I can't work anymore when caring for Ellen, and now that Jenny is doing her own travelling, I can see what I'm leaving behind when I go off on my consulting gigs, or even just to my office. So, yes, it's time to hire a child-care person and I hope it won't wreck our children, but not a daycare center, for God's sake — a person, someone who becomes part of the family. That will take money, though, and regardless, she's pushing back more and more often in a way that signals a deep anger.

I don't like the feeling and I've got no one to talk to except Jenny, and that seems to lead to upset these days. I wish... oh well.

Martin reached the CTI campus a little before eleven, parked in the underground garage, walked two buildings over to the Semiconductor Technology Laboratory, and climbed the four flights to his office suite. The desk in the outer office was now vacant. Felice had moved over to a two-office suite down the hall as assistant to Peter Dempsey and Tony Fiorello. Martin felt a little guilty still holding down this prime office space, but at least until Natasha graduated, he was entitled to such luxury. The axe would fall soon enough. No need to rush it.

Martin logged into his email account. Forty new messages since yesterday. He had almost an hour before his lunch meeting with Bill Burke, the Associate Department Head. Time enough to clean most of it out. But before starting — on a whim he couldn't explain — he sent an email.

To: volleyballgina@cti.edu

Gina—

I happen to be in town for a thesis committee meeting and wanted to catch up with you. Are you in town? If so, are you free for an early dinner? My treat.

-- Martin

By the time he had worked his way through the email stack, he had a reply.

Hi, Professor Quint—

Yes, I'm in town, working in Andover this summer. Excited to hear from you. Early dinner would be great but driving in is slow. I could do something in Medford at 5:30 or Cambridge near CTI by 6:15. Text my cell, 617-897-1676.

Gina

Martin made a 6:15 reservation at the nearby Legal Seafood and sent Gina a text, wondering if she would still look like the vision of

loveliness he remembered. He exited his office for the maze of corridors that would lead him to the faculty lunchroom, three intercon-
nected buildings away. Bill Burke was already seated when he arrived,
a short, slight figure with thick glasses and the perennial look of an
earnest puppy, wagging a hand from a corner table. Martin collected
his lunch at the buffet line and joined him.

"How's tricks? We miss you here," said Bill, as Martin took his seat.

"Tricks are good," said Martin. "It's very different. My classes have
only twenty students and I get to know their names."

"And are you enjoying it?"

"The pace is wonderful. This spring, I revised their E&M class.
Made it more like the CTI version, and it was a hit. Best ratings they
had ever seen."

"How's the family?"

"We're doing well. Jenny has a new business, selling replicas of
antique furniture made by Maine craftsmen. You'd be amazed at the
prices people will pay for a high-quality fake. And it's nice living in the
same town as my sister and being so close to our beach cottage. So yes,
the family is good, the children."

"Sounds pretty idyllic. I know you left because things were unpleasant here, but we've been hoping, now that Kat is gone and her lawsuit
is settled, that you would want to come back. Can we expect you to
return when your leave is up next June?"

"That's why I wanted to talk with you. There's news. I'm no longer
a visitor at Bottlesworth. A few weeks ago, they finalized the endowed
chair, and I've accepted it. I figured I should tell you guys so you can
make plans. I don't expect to come back to CTI."

"Wow," said Bill, who sat silent for more than a moment before
continuing. "I have to talk to Morris about this. Our inclination, and
hope, for that matter, has been that you would be back. Our faculty
hiring plans… I mean we haven't attempted to replace you with
someone junior."

"And I'm not saying you should… yet," said Martin. "But I don't
want to be a dog-in-the-manger. What I'm trying to tell you is that it

wouldn't be unreasonable to add a slot to this year's search targeted in my general area. I can't say right now, definitely, that I won't be back, but I'm leaning pretty hard toward Bottlesworth and it feels dishonest to string you guys along."

"Well, I appreciate your candor, Martin, but I just don't get it," said Bill. "How somebody playing for a pennant-winning team in the major leagues seems content to shift to a double-A minor-league team. Is there something besides the Kat thing driving all this?"

"Oh God, Bill, where do I begin? Of course the mess with Kat's tenure contributed. But when Morris kicked me off the Personnel Committee, it woke me up to the idea that I might have been following false values here, trying to impress everyone around me rather than satisfying myself. At Bottlesworth, I have the respect of the leadership, my colleagues, and my students. I can spend real time with my daughter and help her grow up. I don't have to travel somewhere every week, coming home late reeking of the de-icing fluid that sprays on the plane when you're stuck on the tarmac in Minneapolis. And for the first time in living memory, I have a summer in which I can actually think about ideas instead of just responding to sponsors, students, conferences, journals. I've even drafted the first chapter of my book. It might look like double-A baseball to you, but it has its merits for me. At least so far."

"But don't you miss the research? The action?"

"Actually, less than I thought I would. I'm plenty engaged thinking about the book, pushing into the linguistic aspects of conversation. And try to imagine a life in which you don't have to raise any grant money. Think about that, if you can."

"But the grad students? Don't you miss them?"

"You got me there. Not having any grad students is the price of my move. And no TAs either. I grade my own papers, for God's sake. But I've got access, really close access, to some pretty good undergrads and a blood-pressure level that I'm sure my doctor would like."

"Oh, well. Maybe we really have lost you to the other side. But please keep in touch. We want you back."

"Thanks, Bill," said Martin as he got up from the table. "Give Morris my greetings."

Martin went back through the maze of corridors to the third-floor conference room in the Semiconductor Technology Lab, where his one o'clock thesis-committee meeting was about to convene.

— - —

Natasha had made excellent research progress and, in discussion with Peter Dempsey, Tony Fiorello, and Martin — the thesis committee — all had agreed on a final list of three experiments before she could begin writing. When, at the end, she asked whether it was reasonable to expect graduation by the following June, Martin said yes. "Great," she said. "So can I start job-hunting this fall?"

"Why not?" said Martin. As they got up to leave, Peter asked if Martin could join him for a few minutes. Something to discuss, he said. They took the elevator to the fifth floor and entered Peter's outer office.

Felice, delighted at seeing her former boss, jumped up and insisted on a hug, cooing with her Sierra Leone lilt, "You're a sight for sore eyes, Martin. We never see you anymore. When you coming back?"

Martin untangled from the hug and said, "You'll certainly see me until we get Natasha out of here. Beyond that? I don't know yet."

"You mean you might be gone forever?"

"As I said, could be."

"Don't you get bored?"

"Oh, Felice. Boredom is the least of my problems." The two men went into Peter's office where Peter settled his roundish body into one of his standard-issue tube-framed chairs with brown upholstered cushions, the kind that Martin hated and had replaced in his office at his own expense.

"So what's up?" asked Martin, taking his seat.

"I just wanna know. Are you planning to come back next year?"

Martin laughed. "You're the second person to ask me that today. The third, actually, counting Felice."

"Yeah, well, I'm chairing the faculty search committee this fall, and we can't make plans if we don't know whether we have a vacancy in semiconductor materials."

"I just told Bill Burke at lunch to assume that I'm not coming back."

"No shit," said Peter. "You amaze me. No one quits CTI for a small college. I mean no one."

Martin, with a huge grin on his face, said, "You are now speaking to the Bottlesworth College Charles Caldicott Professor of Applied Physics. They gave me an endowed chair. And I said yes."

"Well I'll be fucked," said Peter. "It's too bad. We miss your teaching talent, and I miss our squash games. Tell me, old buddy, do they have enough of those moon-eyed freshman girls up there, the ones who keep falling for you?"

"Jesus, Peter," said Martin, with a grimace. "Don't you ever give up? If the ombudsman heard you talking like that, you'd be up on charges. For the record, all my students last year were sophomores or juniors, so I can guarantee that no freshman girls fell for me."

"Okay. Sophomore girls. Or junior girls. Or next year, maybe, senior girls?"

-   -   -

Martin arrived at Legal Seafood before Gina did, a bit curious as to whether Peter's teasing, if applied to Gina, had even a whiff of truth to it. He doubted it. She attracted boyfriends like a flower attracts bees and had even gone off to a summer job after her freshman year to be near one of those boyfriends.

He left Gina's description at the reservation desk and was seated. No way the maître d' would fail to note her arrival, so tall, with that glowing auburn hair, athletic. She had been his most promising undergrad advisee, exceptionally motivated and competent. And he just plain liked her — her spunk, her smarts, her looks, her blushes as she battled with innate shyness. But why this dinner? They had never shared a meal except for that pizza, once, in his office, while working together on the MOOC project report, and he'd made dozens of trips to CTI during the past year without contacting her. Was this just an end-of-school thing? Time to take stock? See how his favorite CTI student was doing? Or was there another agenda? He didn't know, but he felt eager to see her.

He saw Gina making her way through the tables, her sunset-colored hair set off by a pale green blouse decorated with her work ID on a lanyard around her neck. He got up to greet her, holding out both hands. Half a head taller than Martin, she reached out to take his hands in hers, and the two of them froze, eyes locked, unsure of the degree of formality this occasion required. "I've missed you so much," she said. "Thanks for asking me."

Martin disengaged, stepped back and said, "I guess I've missed you, too. Come. Sit. Let's talk. Much to catch up on."

The intensity of their greeting hung like a cloud over the table as they looked at each other, uncertain as to which should speak first. Martin finally found his tongue. "You look great. Are you still part of the C&E teaching staff?"

"Yes, with Professor Campbell. He took over for you. I'm now the head grader, for next year, that is."

Their server brought water, rolls, and butter, and took their orders.

"And do you still want to be a teacher?"

"More than ever. I wanted to ask you about grad schools. Now that I'll be a senior. I have to decide whether to take the deal at CTI."

"What deal is that?"

"You know. The work-study program through a master's? But I'm wondering about other grad schools, maybe getting a teaching assistantship somewhere. I mean like Stanford or Berkeley, but..."

"Well, what are you interested in?"

"I guess it would be called complex systems, like robotics, things that mix hardware and software and applications. I got a great job this summer."

"Really? Where?"

"It's a company called Autobot, in Andover. My father bought me a car so I could take the job. They make these incredible vision systems. I was amazed to even get the job, because a lot of what they do is classified. They're asking me about whether I would do the CTI work-study program, and they're talking to CTI about joining up."

"What an odd coincidence," said Martin, *sotto voce*.

"Did you say coincidence?"

"Yes, a coincidence. The owner of that company, a guy named Charles Caldicott, has just become a Trustee at Bottlesworth. I met him a few weeks ago at commencement. Seems like an interesting guy. Driven."

"I haven't met him, so I don't know, but the company is great. Neat people. I'm working on a software module to add some new camera control functions. That's all I'm allowed to say."

"Can you do that without a security clearance?"

"They said I can. But they've started getting me one anyway, which kind of surprised me since it takes so long."

"That means they want to hire you when you graduate," said Martin, with a grin.

Gina glowed. "In fact," she said, "I had to put your name down on the clearance application because you were my advisor. You'll say nice things, won't you?"

"Don't be ridiculous," laughed Martin. "I'll tell them you work for Al Qaeda."

Gina giggled and blushed, fiddling with her name tag. "What's it like at Bottlesworth?"

"Compared to CTI? Peaceful. I like it."

The conversation bounced back and forth, between Martin's platitudes about Bottlesworth and Gina's enthusiasm for her job. When the food arrived, Martin asked about volleyball. Yes, she said, still on the team, and when he asked where she was living for the summer, she said on campus. Martin tried to slip in a query about the boyfriend situation, but she breezed past the bait. Suddenly, as if a bulb long planted in the soil had chosen this moment to sprout and blossom, Martin felt an erotic rush, a fantastic need to be inside her skin. He thought of Rodolfo, smitten with his Mimi. Every time she fiddled with her work ID, and even knowing that such thoughts were taboo, Martin couldn't suppress his curiosity about what was under the blouse that was under the name tag.

In a swerve away from the forbidden, Martin asked whether there had been any progress on the MOOC front, the Massive Open Online Courses that had been the subject of their first project together. "Well," she said, "Professor Huang is still in charge of the MOOC version of C&E, and he's redone some of the lectures. Students in the dorm say they're quite good. And CTI is now giving credit for students who get an A in the MOOC version."

"Do you think they learn the stuff?" asked Martin.

"Some of them really do," said Gina. "Others? Well, not so good."

Their server asked about dessert, but they both declined. Martin paid the bill, Gina thanked Martin for the dinner and for thinking of her, and they fumbled their way through a departure, with more grasping of hands and uninterpretable looks, the hint of a perfume of mutual admiration lingering in the air.

-    -   -

Martin parked in front of Horatio's house, extracted his bag and, using the hidden key as per Horatio's instructions, let himself in. Shortly thereafter, Sumner Collingsworth, III, arrived. Six feet tall and hatchet jawed, with straight almost tan hair framing a hawk-bill nose and wide-set blue eyes that could be gentle or could bore right through you, he greeted his old friend and music buddy, and began setting up his stand. "Which first?" he asked. "Poulenc or Hindemith?"

"Let's start with Poulenc," said Martin, "but I want to ask you something. Have you heard of an entrepreneur named Charles Caldicott?"

"The guy who calls himself CC? Oh, yes. A Boston legend. Something of a wild man. Does robotics and hits one home run after another. Some of the Boston venture capital guys I know wanted to fund his latest company, but he wouldn't take their money. Funded it himself. Why do you ask?"

"Do you have any business relationship with him?"

"We'd probably be happy to take him public, if that's what you mean, but we're in investment banking. We don't do venture stuff. Why do you ask? Sounds ominous."

"He's the guy who funded my chair at Bottlesworth, and now he's got a wild idea about dumping significant money into a new program and he wants me to head it. I can't provide details, but I really want to know as much back-channel info about him as possible before I commit to anything. He makes me nervous."

"So what do you want to know?"

"Two things, I guess. Does he honor his commitments, and, as a philanthropist, is he ready to dig deep if necessary to make a program into a success? Maybe a third thing, too. I already know he's impulsive, but what's his track record? Have his impulses been right?"

"I'll see what I can find out. I know someone at Penrock Ventures who funded his first company, and he can lead me to others. May take a week or so. You ready for some music now?"

Martin took a seat at Horatio's refurbished upright Steinway, noodled a bit to warm up while Sumner did some long tones and scales and tuned to the piano's A. They opened their parts to the Poulenc and with the clarinet's opening lick, the pair vanished into their music.

-   -   -

Just as Sumner was leaving, Horatio and his wife, Blanche, returned from their dinner. Once the greetings and goodbyes had been said, Horatio got out a bottle of Dewar's, glasses, and ice, and the trio sat around the kitchen table, enjoying a nightcap.

Horatio, paunchy and graying, with a round face, a happy smile, and wild curly hair, asked Martin how the end of the school year had gone. Martin enthused about his successful teaching year and progress on the book. "And," he said. "we have a visitor from Oxford, a psychologist who studies conversation. She spent some time with Clark at Stanford, and she wants to help."

"What's her name?"

"Glenda Aldrich. You know her?"

"Never met her, but she's visible within the linguistics community. Her work on extracting meaning from conversation using psychological clues is pretty good, at least based on the two or three of her papers I've read."

Blanche, thin and angular in all dimensions, with straight, honey-colored hair cut in a short boyish mode, asked about Jenny and the children. Martin reported on JJ's recital, Ellen's love of bunnies, and Jenny's expanding business, including the excitement over her new Chicago client. He then pleaded fatigue. The group dispersed to bathrooms and bedrooms, but Martin's sleep was wrecked by Morpheus, who dragged him through an oft-recurrent nightmare, the exposure of the Camille affair and his return from a conference in Chicago to find Katie gone and "Fuck You Martin" written in red lipstick all over their house. He woke in a sweat, his pulse heavy in his chest. He got a drink of water, used the toilet, and returned to bed and sleep, but that sleep, too, was destined for disturbance. As the sky was brightening, he dreamed he was submerged in frigid surf, unable to breathe, clawing his way to the surface, finally rescued by a tall, faceless woman who dragged him to safety. He woke with a start.

-    -   -

That afternoon, as Martin and Jenny were unloading groceries and starting food preparations for tonight's dinner with Glenda and her father, Jenny asked about his day at CTI. He ticked through the meeting with Bill Burke, Natasha's progress toward her PhD, the music with Sumner.

"So Horatio didn't play?"

"No, he and Blanche were out at a BU thing. It was just me and Sumner."

"So what did you do for dinner?"

"I went to Legal."

"Poor Martin. No company at dinner, no one to impress," said Jenny with a teasing smile.

And Martin, with a flash of Gina and her name tag clouding his vision, simply asked which of the cheeses she had bought were for tonight's appetizer.

- - -

Glenda arrived while Martin was setting the table. Jenny was busy in the kitchen feeding JJ and Ellen, so he dropped his fistful of cutlery and went to answer the door. Glenda, in brown slacks and an attractive tan jacket, blurted out an apology.

"I'm sorry I didn't call ahead, but my father decided at the last minute not to come. He's a bit reluctant to socialize because of the tremors."

"Tremors?" asked Martin as he held the door for Glenda to enter.

"Yes. His hand tremors tend to make him a messy eater, so he is... I guess... somewhat shy about meals out."

"I'm sorry he felt that way. Let's get him out to the cottage next time, where he can be as messy as the rest of us tend to be. Or arrange a visit not involving a meal. I'm looking forward to meeting him."

Martin led the way into the kitchen and introduced Glenda to Jenny and the children. Ellen looked up in silence from her fistfuls of mac 'n cheese, but JJ charged right in.

"Are you really from England?" he asked.

"Yes, really," said Glenda.

"I know which way England is. At the beach, I can point to it."

"But it's very far. You can't see it, can you?"

"No, but I know where it is. Daddy's been there. He says they drive on the wrong side of the road."

Glenda looked to Martin with a smile. "Well, young man, we like to think that it's everyone else who drives on the wrong side of the road."

"No, no, no. The right side is the right side. You drive on the left."

Glenda responded with a chuckle. "True enough. Actually, though, quite a few countries do as we do, and some of them are large countries like India and Japan. We may be different but we're not alone."

"And you talk funny," said JJ, covering his mouth with his hand as he snickered.

"Now that's enough," said Jenny. "The British spoke English long before the Americans ever did, so it's we, not they, who speak funny, if anyone does."

"But I must confess," said Glenda, "that American television has outdone British television in spreading the speaking style, so much of the world would agree with JJ. People around the globe enjoy British television, but when they speak English, they sound like Americans."

Jenny said, "I need to take the children up for a quick story and bed. Get out the nibbles and drinks. I won't be long."

Martin offered a choice of Chablis or a pinot noir to accompany the cheese platter, a display ornamented with fresh figs and dried apricots and supplemented with Carr's assorted crackers, an obeisance to British authenticity.

Before relocating to the living room, Martin put water to boil for the noodles and set the kitchen timer. As they were getting seated, Glenda on the small loveseat and Martin in his father's old chair, she remarked on the astonishing settee. "That's an antique, isn't it?"

Martin laughed. "That's the idea, anyway. It's actually a copy of a museum piece made by one of Jenny's crew of artisans. She has a business selling replica antiques."

"Well, it's gorgeous. I'm impressed."

"Jenny will be pleased to hear that. Her stuff is pretty amazing, but I guess I see it all the time so I'm used to it. Have you made any progress in getting your father settled?"

"Actually, yes. We've found two retirement homes, one in Freeport and one in Portland, both anticipating that spaces will open in the next several months. They have three tiers of care, including full nursing care, which is what he will eventually need." Glenda fell silent.

"This must be so difficult for you," said Martin. "I'm really sorry."

Glenda exhaled a large breath. "It is difficult, but being here is much better than getting panic calls from Dad when I'm in the midst of an Oxford tutorial. If I could find a suitable position around here, I might actually relocate altogether. He really needs me."

"Really? Relocate? You mean leave Oxford?"

"Yes, possibly, especially if they throw me out over that hug."

"They could do that?"

"Who knows? In the present atmosphere, anything can happen."

Just then, Jenny came in, wineglass in hand.

"What hug?" asked Jenny.

"A bit of nonsense with an undergraduate. He lost his mother in a horrific accident, broke down in tears in my tutorial. I gave him a shoulder to cry on, and now he's filed a complaint of improper touching."

"Sounds like displacement," said Jenny.

"You mean displaced grief?" asked Glenda.

"Or displaced anger. He's angry at his mother for deserting him, and he's taking it out on you."

"Oh. I hadn't thought of it that way. It might be helpful in my forced mediation of this mess. But to change the subject, if I may, I just love that settee."

"Oh, thank you," said Jenny. "It's one of Pierre's best pieces. He's a fantastic craftsman."

The kitchen timer rang, and Martin excused himself to go finish the dinner preparations.

Glenda asked, "And you have this as a business?"

"Yes. Replica antiques. The look of the real thing at a fraction of the price. Maine attracts craftspeople. Artisans. Tremendously skilled, but cut off from the national market. I do the publicity and the selling, which gives them a visibility they would have trouble getting on their own, and we share the proceeds."

"Forgive me, but I'm curious," said Glenda, "How did you get into this business? Seems a bit unusual."

"An odd story," said Jenny. "I did both art history and psychology in college."

"Where you learned about displacement?" asked Glenda, with a grin.

Jenny acknowledged the grin with a smile of her own. "That, and from life, too. Once you're aware of displacement, you can find it under every rock. As for my business, my father is a furniture retailer, so after college, sort of on a whim, I took an internship in the furniture department of the Boston Museum of Fine Arts. I fell in love with antiques and eventually moved to one of the Boston antique restorers where I learned enough to begin operating as a decorator for the high-end market — especially collectors. When we moved to Maine, I already had contacts with a few of the local craftsmen who did both replicas and restoration, so I shifted to concentrate on marketing replicas. We're making good progress after only a year. People are starting to notice us."

Martin called from the kitchen. "Time to finish setting the table. Dinner in a few minutes."

As they went into the dining room to complete the arranging of utensils on placemats, Glenda commented on the table, how beautiful it was.

"We call it the Queen Anne," said Jenny. "I bought it shortly after Martin and I were married. It's genuine, but it's been so heavily restored, it wouldn't garner a high price on the fussy authentic market."

"It's just lovely, the depth of color. Is it oak?"

"The table top is oak and the legs are walnut. The color contrast is part of what I like."

"Soup's on," said Martin from the kitchen.

Plates were filled with a savory beef and onion stew served over noodles with green spears of broccoli. The pinot noir was poured, and the trio began to eat.

Amid murmurs of praise for the tastiness of everything, Martin asked, "So, tell us, how is it that you are a dual citizen?"

"Okay," grinned Glenda, "you asked for it. Here goes." Between bites, she told her story. "My grandfather on my father's side was an American. From Freeport. A GI brought over for the invasion. He married my grandmother, a Londoner, a few months before D-Day. It was a short marriage, albeit fruitful. He was killed in the initial surge onto the beaches, and some months later, my grandmother gave birth to my half-American father. Things in Britain were dreadful after the war, and as the widow of an American GI, she was able to bring the baby here. They lived with my grandfather's twin brother, Uncle Timothy, who was, in effect, my father's father. After high school, my grandmother took Dad back to England for university, after which he got a business degree and stayed in England to work for Marks and Spencer. My mother was British and they brought me up there, but because my father had claimed dual citizenship, I could also, and I did. Whew. Long story."

"And your father came back to Freeport?" asked Martin.

"Indeed. My mother passed away four years ago, just about the time my father was planning to retire, so he returned to Freeport to reconnect with Uncle Timothy and to care for him in his old age. And now here I am, coming to Freeport to take care of my father in his old age. The cycles of life, I guess."

"Is Uncle Timothy still alive?" asked Jenny.

"I'm afraid not. He died a year ago, and I came for the funeral. It was clear then that my father was beginning to develop health issues. And now..."

After some embarrassing dead air, Jenny asked, "Do you still have family in England?"

Glenda emitted a sound somewhere between a grunt and a chortle. "A few cousins on my mother's side with whom I have rather poor relations, and a husband with whom I seem to have even worse relations."

Martin's attention drifted back to his ghastly breakup with Katie, leaving it to Jenny to apologize. "Oh dear," she said. "I didn't mean to—"

"Perfectly all right," said Glenda. "We're negotiating a divorce, or trying to."

"Are there children?"

Glenda went silent and her mood turned somber. Looking down at her half-empty plate, she finally said, "That's the real issue." She paused, thinking. "I don't usually talk about these things. Certainly not with my Oxford colleagues, some of whom are bloody busybodies and gossips. The answer is no. There are no children. I wanted at least one child, but my husband turned out to be infertile. He blamed me until I insisted he be tested. After that, he refused to allow me to find a sperm donor and would not consider adoption. So things sort of fell apart."

"I'm so sorry," said Jenny. "I wish I could say something of use, but it's just sad. I'm really sorry."

"I'm still young enough, at least in theory," said Glenda, but with a wry smile added, "but there is the issue of a mate. I'm not sure I'm brave enough to have a child on my own."

"And no prospects?" asked Jenny.

"None whatsoever. While I was busy commuting from West Kensington to Oxford, managing my research, my lectures, my tutorials, and also, by the bye, managing our household, my dear husband was in the process of 'falling in love,' as he says it, with one of his graduate students at Imperial College. When he announced his intentions, I was caught flat-footed. And now, in my absence, he's moved her into our flat. I dread the process of throwing her out, and him along with her, but I've got my solicitor engaged in doing exactly that."

No one said anything. Jenny and Glenda resumed eating, while Martin was catching up with what Glenda had said — that it was her husband, her husband's refusal to accept help in having children combined with her husband's infidelity, that was leading them to divorce. Glenda was the victim, not the cause. Katie had been the victim of his infidelity with Camille, but she had also been part of the cause — her refusal to have children. Marriages can be such a mess. He wished he could do something for Glenda, something to help her, making amends, if possible, for his having been such a prick in his first marriage, not that it would make any sense to Glenda.

When plates were eaten clean, Jenny asked, "Should I get the salad?"

* 7 *

The weather forecast was for a rainy, chilly weekend. At breakfast, Jenny suggested they pass on the cottage. She wanted to work on her Chicago project. Martin answered, "Fine by me, but before you get started on that, we need some talking time. June starts on Monday, and we don't have a workable money plan at this point."

"You mean our budget?"

"I mean our budget."

"Okay, love. If we must."

"We must."

Martin went to the study to get their financial plan and budget up on the computer while Jenny got JJ settled at the piano for his practice and plopped Ellen in the living room play area, where she began pulling her stuffed bunny around in a little wagon through a sprawl of blocks.

"Here's the short version," said Martin, pointing to the screen as Jenny pulled her desk chair over next to Martin's. "A year ago, you had been putting in eight hundred a month from your business, I had a thirty-percent summer salary supplement through CTI, and I had some consulting income. So it was kind of a shock when I did the bills last week and looked at the bank balance. We need to dig into savings, yours and mine, starting now."

"Or maybe sell the house in Cambridge?" said Jenny.

"The Cambridge house is not the problem. We get enough rent to cover the mortgage and taxes with a small balance left over, just like in our plan, and we get a sweet tax deduction from the depreciation."

"Then what about Katie's alimony? Isn't that what makes it tight?"

"And what about the money you have that you're sitting on?"

"George's money? My business money? I'm more than thirty

thousand in the red at this point, and I still have to pay for my travel and publicity and sales materials. Things are slowly improving, but I'm not yet at break-even."

"But you still have over two hundred thousand in the bank, don't you?"

"And you have what, eighty or ninety thousand in stocks from your father?"

"So what happened to our agreement?"

"It's still in place. Your money is yours, my money is mine, and our money, including the Cambridge house is ours. I put decent money toward that mortgage when we got married."

"But it's not the house, it's the cash part of our money that's the problem. We agreed we would each put in toward joint expenses. I put my entire salary in and right now, you're putting in nothing."

"Your entire salary? Less three thousand a month for Katie? That's not exactly putting in your entire salary, is it?"

"But that was written right in our plan. Eyes wide open. I haven't changed that."

"And you're forgetting the child care I put in. Suppose we had to hire someone to take care of Ellen all day while you went off to campus. How much would that be? A thousand a month? Maybe twice that?"

"That's true. I agree. Child care is valuable. But we have a cash problem, and taking care of Ellen doesn't fix that."

"But George said…" and Jenny went silent.

"Yes, I know. I know. We've been over and over this. George said the insurance was so you would be able to stand on your own two feet in case anything happened to him. We've honored that to the letter. But that doesn't mean you can't spend some of it on the family."

"And you even stash your invention royalties away. Also for Katie, for Christ's sake."

"Yes. That's in our plan, too. I've just got to get Katie out of my life. I'm almost there. I still owe just over a hundred and forty thousand and I'm within twenty K of having that saved. Seven more months of payments, and I can buy her out with a lump sum and be done with it."

"What's so holy about seven months? Why not a year? Two years? I can do the math. You've saved up something like three years of alimony payments, sitting like food in a hamster's cheek. You could draw out three thousand a month to pay Katie until my business starts making a profit. Then I can contribute again."

Martin shouted, "Why is it always on me? You have money. We need money. For God's sake, why can't you unwrap a few hundred each month?"

Jenny started crying, and Ellen ran into the study also crying.

"Now you've upset Ellen," said Jenny, in a hiss. "And don't shout at me." She picked up her daughter and said, "Daddy was upset. It's okay, honey. We're fine."

But they weren't fine. Martin agreed to pay the monthly alimony from his saved royalty receipts instead of from his salary, deferring the day when he would be free of Katie. It alleviated the present cash problem without solving it. And if Jenny wouldn't put in any cash, he certainly shouldn't feel guilty about leaving her with Ellen and going to his office to work on the book. Jenny was the one who brought it up, after all. Child care was, for now, her contribution to their joint equity.

- - -

That evening, when normally he and Jenny would have shared a movie on television or gone to bed early enough to enjoy the touch of each other's bodies, Martin was in his study in the comfortable chair, reading more about the difference between the speaker's intention when making an utterance and the hearer's understanding of that utterance, and how much depends on the degree to which the speaker and the hearer share common ground, a shared set of concepts about the world and how it works.

Jenny came in after getting the children settled into bed, going directly to Martin's chair, pushing aside his book, and plunking a yellow card onto his lap, their caution signal borrowed from soccer. At least it wasn't a red card, the sign for serious trouble.

"What the fuck? I was reading."

"Yes, but we need to talk."

"Okay. If we must talk, let's talk." Martin scowled and dropped the yellow card and the book on the floor, at which point Jenny deposited herself onto Martin's lap. He squiggled his legs so that Jenny's weight was distributed less harshly on the tender parts in his crotch. "What is it? I thought we decided everything this morning."

Jenny put one arm around his shoulder and leaned into his chest. "I hate it," she said, "when we fight like we did this morning. It scares me."

"Well I hate it too, but..."

"But what?"

Martin looked across the room at his desk, inhaled, and blew out through flapping lips, a sound that would send Ellen into giggles were she not upstairs and asleep. "It still doesn't feel right to me," he said.

"So you're still angry?"

"Angry? I don't know, angry. Disappointed is more like it."

"Because?"

"Because it feels like we've lost our balance somehow. When we were in Cambridge... well, things seemed more balanced, more fair."

"More fair? Why? Because I was putting some money in each month?"

"Not just that, although that's part of it. But when we moved here, I thought we would keep sharing—"

Jenny sat up straight. "Sharing what? Expenses? Child care? Or is it suddenly my Chicago job that's put a bug up your butt?"

No, thought Martin, not a bug up my butt. The travel is bad enough, but every mention of Chicago is like a needle under my fingernails, reminding me of the ugliest day in my life. He struggled to keep to the subject. "It's a mix, I guess. This summer is my first ever chance to write, and I get the feeling that you want to unload the kids on me so you can go off on your adventures."

"Unload? Unload? Jesus, Martin, you go off to the college almost every weekday. I manage Ellen, laundry, half the shopping, most of the cooking, and JJ's after-school time. It's you who's doing the unloading. Not me."

"Listen, during the semester, I did my share of ⸻ school day."

"That's true, and until his school is out in two weeks ⸻ available for you. But you're using your book as an e⸻ everything back on me, just when my business is fina⸻ ⸻g to show real signs of life. That's what's not fair."

"I thought your business was going to be an internet business, not a business that takes you to Chicago for days at a time."

"Hey, I didn't solicit that Chicago job. It fell in my lap, but it's too good an opportunity to pass up. Do you realize that if we get as much out of this as I'm projecting, my little fledgling business will be in the black for the first time since startup? What do you want me to do? Turn it down? You're the one hung up on money, so you should want me to get profitable."

"No. Don't turn it down. I don't know. It just seems that we're going off the rails. Squabbling over time and priorities and money. I sometimes wonder if you regret coming here."

Jenny got up and walked over to her desk and sat down. She turned her desk chair to face Martin and said, "Perhaps I do. I mean, I really like being so close to Helen and her family, and I love the cottage, how close it is, but when we were in Cambridge, I had a few women friends, my clients were all local, my parents were much closer, and on the few occasions when I did have to travel, I could get to the airport in twenty minutes and the flights were nonstop. It's just harder here."

"Well, until that CC thing came up, I thought it was easier here, even though I also have to deal with the Portland airport when I go out west. But now, I'm not so sure. His big project is a huge distraction."

"It's another case of displacement," said Jenny.

"What? Did you say displacement? Your favorite explanation?"

"Yes. You're pissed off at CC and the college for pushing you into this new school thing, and you're taking it out on me by complaining about something we agreed on before we ever moved here, even before we ever got married."

"That's psychobabble bullshit. If I'm pissed off at you, it's for cause or pulling back on money when you should be chipping in, and putting more kid care on me just when I need the time to write."

"So you are pissed off at me."

"Yeah. I guess I am."

"Well, that makes us even. When you brought up that money stuff this morning, I almost blew my stack. We had agreed before we ever got married about what our financial priorities were, and you, because you say you need to write this book — which means you can't take any summer job — you expect me to dig into George's money to support the family even though you're sitting on a big stash so you can pay off your first wife in some kind of grand fuck-you gesture."

"But writing the book was also part of our agreed priorities, dammit. And if I'm going to write, I need time, big blocks of time. No teaching. Nothing else."

"Then tell the Bottlesworth people to stuff their engineering school thing and leave you alone!"

"I can't do that."

"Why not? You supposedly have this priority to write a book. Then tell 'em, and stick to your plan."

"But I can't. I just can't."

"And because you can't, I now have to use up George's money? And you talk about fair? Is this all about you, or is it about us?"

"About us? What do you mean?"

"Is this about us?"

"I should ask you that? Are you sorry you married me?"

"Don't go there."

"Why not?"

"Just don't. It's horrible."

"What's horrible? Am I horrible?"

"Mostly no."

"Mostly no?"

"Mostly no."

"But sometimes?"

"Sometimes I miss George so badly it eats at my gut. I get stomach aches. Don't even want to eat. He would never have fought with me about money."

"And would he have fought with you about child care? Or travel? Or was he just the perfect husband for you all the time?"

"That's nasty. And you know it." Jenny began to sob. "We were never together long enough to find out."

Martin sat silent, looking at the floor. After what felt like many minutes, Martin said, "I'm sorry for that crack. You're right. It was nasty. Should we head to bed?"

Jenny, still sniffling, nodded, and while they shared a bed that night, it was as if there was a bundling board laid down its center.

-   -   -

Both the weather and the mood at home stayed gloomy on Sunday and into Monday morning. Martin and Jenny barely spoke while getting the children's breakfasts, and Martin's walk to campus, normally a time for preparing his day, was focused on the nightmare — the daymare — that some irreconcilable argument with Jenny would blow up and wreck his life, their lives. It wasn't like with Katie, was it? No reason for jealous rage. No third party, no infidelity, no trips to Troy with Kat, which, however innocent, could look compromising. Just the two of them, needing to find a new way as the roadway of life took new turns. He hoped they weren't skidding into a ditch.

When he reached his office, he put his anxieties aside and focused on the FIE online version of Circuits and Electronics. Watching video lectures can be a tedious, even mind-numbing experience, especially when one knows the content of those lectures inside and out, but Martin had to confess that Harry Huang's presentations were actually pretty good. The idea of having students view them and converting the class time into problem-solving sessions, maybe even in-the-lab sessions with challenging design problems for the students, started to appeal to him. He began sketching what an outline might look like in this modified format.

After a lunch break, he turned to his book manuscript and made significant progress on the concepts chapter before calling it a day. As he was shutting down his computer, his telephone rang. It was Angelique, the Physics Department secretary. There was apparently a person from the Wilshire Private Courier Service standing at her desk with a package for which his signature was required. No she didn't know who it was from. And he should please bring a photo ID.

Martin went down a floor to the Physics office, verified his identity and signed beside the X, but was surprised when the Wilshire person insisted on photographing his ID, muttering that his boss required it. "Must be important," he thought.

He returned to the privacy of his office and opened the Wilshire envelope. Inside was a standard business-size envelope from Wilkins and Palmer, LLC, with offices on Grant Street in Pittsburgh. Heavy cream-colored bond paper and a nicely embossed crest logo next to the return address. It contained a single page, typed on matching cream-colored stationery emblazoned with the same crest:

May 26, 2015

Dear Professor Quint:

If you are the Martin Quint who was a faculty member at the Carnegie Mellon University in 2002, it is important that you contact this office as soon as possible regarding an urgent estate matter.

Please call our offices to confirm whether you are the individual we are seeking.

Sincerely,
Sylvia Palmer, Esq.
Attorney at Law

Martin dialed the law firm's number and left a message for Ms. Palmer. Yes, he was that Martin Quint. He provided all three numbers: office, home, and cell.

— — —

When Martin got home, he was greeted not only by JJ launching himself at his legs with a hug that nearly knocked him over, but also by Ellen, who toddled her way into the hug until she was knocked over by JJ's wriggling. Jenny called from the kitchen. "Glad you're home," she said. "The kids need some outdoor play time and I need to run out to the market for a bit. And there's a FedEx packet for you on your desk."

As Jenny approached the front door with her coat, purse, and car keys, she gave Martin a quick kiss on the cheek. Martin freed himself from JJ's grip, asking "How long will you be gone?"

"Ten minutes. Maybe fifteen. I need eggs and some fresh veggies. Back soon."

Martin opened the door for her, then turned to the children. "Okay, kids. It started drizzling a bit, so is it drippy wet soccer or drippy wet stoop tag? Which is it?"

JJ wanted soccer, which was fine for Ellen, since she loved chasing the ball around the yard. After a few minutes of passing the ball back and forth, Martin got out the little soccer goal and played goalkeeper while JJ tried shots from six yards away. Ellen, running back and forth between JJ and Martin, finally tripped, fell over, bumped her face on the ground and began screaming in exaggerated pain. Martin swept her up, gave her nose a kiss to feel better, and brought her in just as Jenny returned from her shopping.

As he helped Jenny put away the groceries, Martin mentioned the strange letter he had received that afternoon. "I have no idea what this could be about. I was only in Pittsburgh for three years, and I certainly didn't create any kind of estate there. Why this lawyer wants me is a total mystery."

Jenny asked, "Did you do consulting or something, maybe a patent?"

"Sure I did consulting, but that was on the West Coast. And I don't remember any patents from my CMU days. They came later, at CTI."

"And you don't have any family in Pittsburgh?"

"Nope. They're all from Michigan. Or were, at least. Maybe some relative I don't know about — who knows? Maybe even my mother. Maybe she moved to Pittsburgh, and then died. Who knows?"

"Well, let me get dinner together. Fretting over it won't help."

- - -

The Fedex was from Autobot. Inside was a spiral-bound booklet, about forty pages thick, with the words "Confidential Business Plan" in bold letters on the cover, beneath which was the title, "Caldicott School of Engineering and Entrepreneurship."

"Anything important?" called Jenny from the kitchen.

He called back. "It's CC's plan for the new engineering school. That sly son of a bitch must have had this already written when we met last Tuesday. No way this got produced in a week."

"Watch your language, please," said Jenny. "JJ's home and Ellen has ears, too."

Martin flipped through the pages. He saw an Executive Summary followed by sections on Goals, Program, Staffing, and Finance, and an Appendix containing page after page of tables and charts. Martin was familiar with business plans for start-up companies. But he had never seen a business plan for a university program. At first glance, it looked very professional and very complete. What was under the hood? And while business plans for start-ups focus on an exit five years out, this one needed a long-term vision for sustainability. Did CC think that way? It was a lot to read. He would start after dinner.

* **8** *

Martin's office telephone rang at 9:03. It was Sylvia Palmer in Pittsburgh, who wasted no time getting to the point. "We have a difficult situation here, so thank you for your quick response. Since you are the Martin Quint we were looking for, I need to confirm, when you were living in Pittsburgh, did you know a woman named Frances Kaminsky?"

A flood of images hit Martin as he stumbled out a yes, of course, they had been close friends.

"The problem is that Frances was killed in a highway accident five weeks ago, and Andrew is now an orphan."

"How awful. I'm really sorry to hear that Frances is dead, but who is Andrew?"

"Her son."

"And what does this have to do with me?"

"Aren't you his father? We found a diary in Frances's apartment that suggested exactly that."

"She had a son? Well, not by me. We stopped seeing each other way back. It was before I moved to Boston, so that must have been the summer of 2002. And we've had no contact since then."

"When did you see her last?"

"Actually, I can remember, exactly. It was that July Fourth. We went to the fireworks."

"Andrew was born on April 5, 2003. Did you and she have a sexual relationship?"

Martin paused, dazed. His gut was suddenly roiled by cramps, reminiscent of the bad old days when he had to plan his days according to the location of the nearest toilet. Needing to buy some time, all he could think of was "Lawyer."

"Ms. Palmer, before I answer any more questions, I would like to consult my lawyer. This sounds potentially serious."

"Of course, but I need to tell you that Andrew has been temporarily living with the family of a school friend. That will not work long term. And our office is not suitable as a permanent guardian. We need to get him settled in a good home. He's been through hell."

After the call ended, Martin dashed for the restroom. It felt like his old nemesis, acute ulcerative colitis, was back for another visit. Dr. Feld, his Cambridge gastroenterologist, had told him that UC was a bit like a loaded gun, easily triggered, and either food or stress could serve as a trigger. He knew what the trigger was this time. An orphan boy, twelve years old, possibly his.

Once his rumbling gut was relieved, he called the office of Corey and Associates. Trevor would be able to see him the next morning, at nine. With that settled, he called the gastroenterology department at the Mid-Coast Medical Center and got an appointment for Friday afternoon at three o'clock with a Dr. Youssef Sharif.

Work on his book between excursions to the rest room turned out to be impossible. Images of his last boozy fireworks date with Frances crowded out everything else. Had there been sex that night, going-away sex, a final teary goodbye fuck? He wasn't sure. He'd been too drunk to remember anything except the terror of driving home that night, squinting as he drove, hoping to avoid parked cars and curbs and cops.

-   -   -

Before heading home, he took an extra dose of balsalazide and hoped he could manage the walk home without shitting his pants. He made it, but with not much time to spare.

Ellen and JJ greeted him at the door, but he shook them off, took the stairs two at a time and disappeared into the upstairs bathroom. Jenny came out of the kitchen, looking puzzled.

"Did I hear Daddy come in?"

"Yeah. But he said he was sick," said JJ.

"Why? What happened?"

"He just ranned up the stairs to the bathroom."

"Probably a tummy ache," said Jenny, recognizing Martin's urgency from times past. "Sounds like he'll need something besides meatloaf for dinner."

- - -

After broth for dinner and with a totally empty lower bowel, Martin could once again function. He put the children to bed and came downstairs, finding Jenny in the study, poking at her email. Without looking up, she asked, "Any idea what set you off? Did you eat something bad at lunch?"

"No idea at all," said Martin. "If I go back on liquids for a day or so, it should calm down."

"Do you need to see a doctor?"

"Already made an appointment," said Martin as he picked up Clark's *Using Language* from his desk and slumped into the reading chair. "This Friday."

"Did you learn anything about that mystery letter?"

"A little. Somebody I knew back in Pittsburgh died, and the estate lawyers are reaching out to any and all former acquaintances. I don't know how they found me, but Trevor Corey said he would help me take care of it. I'll be seeing him tomorrow."

"You need a lawyer? Are you in some kind of trouble?"

"Trevor felt that since it was a lawyer who called me, it would be prudent for him to be the one to call back."

"Sounds excessive," said Jenny, as she frowned at her husband before turning back to her computer.

- - -

Trevor Corey, Jr., was the great-grandson of the donor of Corey Hall. Amply supplied with conservatively invested assets from his father's estate, he didn't have to work a lick. A short, balding, but fit-looking man, he ran a small family- and estate-law practice in Brimfield Junction to keep himself from getting bored, but the pace of things gave him lots of time for his favorite activity, sailing his forty-two-foot yacht berthed in Harpswell. Trevor had handled Martin's father's estate issues with competence and courtesy, so Martin felt comfortable calling about this letter. They sat in his tidy office decorated with photographs of tall ships, part of a two-office suite above the Bank of Maine on Maine Street.

"I'm glad you stopped where you did," said Trevor. "Admitting to sex would have been equivalent to claiming ownership of the child. But I'm sure they will ask for a DNA test. Is it even possible you're the father?"

"Theoretically, I guess it's possible, but we always used condoms. She had genital herpes which would flare up from time to time, so we used condoms." But the memory of driving home drunk washed over Martin like the storm surge in a hurricane. If they had sex, did they use a condom?

"I suspect they could find a way to require you to supply a DNA sample. The laws on absent fathers who cross state lines can be troublesome. So my advice would be to stall for a while, if you want, but be prepared to be required to give in."

"But I'm not an absent father, dammit. She was absolutely not pregnant when I left. And she never contacted me to say she was having a child. Absolutely never. Over however many years. Twelve, thirteen years."

"Okay. Okay. Calm down. I'll write a response on your behalf, denying responsibility, and see what happens. The worst outcome, I guess, is that they could file a child-support suit here in Maine, and we'd have to respond."

"I think the worst outcome would be to find out that I am this kid's father. I've got a happy family. I don't need this."

-    -   -

Martin put Sylvia Palmer out of his head, and between too many trips to the restroom managed to write like a demon all morning, eager to get a draft of the chapter on concepts in Glenda's hands before her departure for England. They had scheduled a send-off lunch meeting at Barnaby's.

Martin waved to Glenda from the back booth when he saw her enter dressed in a lightweight tan sweater that made her brown hair look richer in color than it actually was. She looked and looked and finally caught sight of him. "Sorry for being late. It must be tourist season. I couldn't find anywhere to park. I ended up back in the campus lot, and it's a fair walk to here."

"Not a problem. I've been thinking about our last conversation. Are things settled at home?"

"You mean with my father? Not yet."

"I meant…"

"Oh, yes, my huggy student and my not-so-huggy husband. I'll have a mediation session with the student when I get back, and my solicitor has pried my husband's girlfriend — along with my husband — out of our flat in preparation for my return. It's all very unpleasant, but it will eventually pass. In the meantime," and here Glenda looked up with a sly smile, "What can you tell me about a colleague named Abe Goldberg? Do you know him?"

"No. What department?"

"Economics. Very nice fellow. He's in the office next to mine and we've chatted a bit. Just curious. Now, may I try out an idea on you?"

"Let's order food first. Tummy before brain."

"Good point," said Glenda. She picked up a menu and flipped over the brightly colored pages. "We have things in England that are called delis, but, trust me, they're nothing like this. Tell me about the chopped liver."

"Chicken livers, cooked up tender in butter, then mashed with various tasty enhancements. They serve it with raw onions and black bread, some salad on the side. Thoroughly recommended."

The slinky redhead appeared with water for Glenda, took their orders, and glided away.

"Okay," said Martin. "Try your idea."

"When two people have a conversation, I can suggest a simple five-part taxonomy that I think will help you organize your thoughts. You ready for this?"

"Fire away."

"Imagine person A starts a conversation with person B. There are five ways B can respond. B can ignore A or walk away, which is totally antisocial. Or B could respond trying to change the subject, control the conversation. That's options one and two, both on the antisocial side. At the other end, option five, B can encourage A to go on without adding to the substance, or, option four, can respond right on subject and engage in meaningful conversation. Okay so far?"

Martin nodded and asked, "And option three is in the middle?"

Just then, their food arrived, and Martin urged Glenda to dig in. "So I spread some on the bread, with onion on top?"

"Exactly."

Glenda did as suggested, took a bite, and broke into a smile. "You're right. Lovely. Or as we say across the pond, smashing."

Martin took a sip of broth from his matzoh-ball soup before continuing. "Is the middle option where B tries to answer A in a positive way, but doesn't understand what A wanted to talk about?"

Glenda said, "Exactly. Put more formally, the responder wants to have a constructive conversation but can't overlap with the common ground of the signaler."

Martin thought awhile, and then with a broad grin said, "Eureka. You're a genius."

Glenda sat upright. "Genius?"

"Genius," said Martin. "Get this. The middle option, option three, is where the teacher gets the data to create his model of how the student thinks. Let's say the student understands what the teacher says and responds appropriately. That's your fourth option. But if the student's response is well-intended but off target, that's option three. Option three gives the teacher data about how the student thinks, so the teacher can try another statement, and by gradually testing responses, he can build up his model to the point where he can find a pathway for passing the concept he's trying to teach into the student's brain. This is super."

Glenda was delighted. "Well done. What's interesting is tha psychologists don't think of it this way. They think of options and five as primarily ostensive, delivering intentional content rather than substance, but you're saying that option three is heavily ostensive because it shows the signaler both the intention to respond and also the inability to land on the common ground."

"Well, I'm not sure I could write all this down to have it make sense, but I get the drift and I find it tremendously exciting. It places the model-building part into the formal structure of what a conversation is. Terrific."

When they got up from lunch, Martin was so excited, he gave Glenda a big hug, saying, "Thank you so much. You've made my day. My week. My month."

"Oh, bosh," she said, chuckling, as she unfolded with some haste from Martin's arms. "Got to watch out for hugs these days. This is just standard stuff in a different context. It's your context that makes it interesting."

They walked together back to the campus, Glenda asking Martin for more and more details about his family — about Jenny, about JJ, about Ellen, even Helen and Bill and their kids. Martin responded to each inquisitional escalation, but as he skipped from JJ's piano lessons to how Angela liked to play with baby Ellen, it suddenly struck him: Were he and Jenny stuck in Glenda's option three? At cross purposes? Talking past one another instead of connecting? Had their common ground eroded away? And when he had declined to tell Jenny about that dinner with Gina and, worse still, had been unable to tell Jenny about Andrew, what option were those? Falsehood by omission? Option zero?

- - -

On Friday morning, he went to Trevor's office to hear the report. "I had a nice talk with Ms. Palmer," said Trevor, leaning back in his desk chair. "Of course, she didn't like the letter I faxed, but she seemed pretty sensible, not spoiling for a fight or anything. It's pretty clear they have the boy's best interests at heart. Here's the story. First of all, their top priority is to settle the permanent guardianship for the boy, Andrew. His full name, by the way, is Andrew Quint Kaminsky. Pretty suggestive, don't you think?"

Martin felt his bowel once again rumbling. "It's more than suggestive. It's accusatory. I had no idea."

"Anyway," continued Trevor, "Ms. Palmer was the attorney who drew not only Frances's will but also the wills of her mother and her aunt, all three of whom, turns out, were killed in that crash. Andrew was spending the afternoon with a friend. The three women were on the Pennsylvania Turnpike, heading back from some kind of garden show when they got plowed into, flipped over, and their car caught fire. Really ugly scene."

"Awful," said Martin. "How awful."

"The aunt had no children, and Frances was an only child, one of those odd cases where the family tree is shrinking instead of growing. There aren't even any cousins out there, at least none Ms. Palmer could find. Andrew is now the sole heir for all three estates. But he can't inherit in Pennsylvania because he's a minor, which creates a guardianship issue. And to the extent that there is any good news here, it's that Ms. Palmer, just as careful lawyers are likely to do, put into the wills a full set of what-ifs for executorship and for guardianship of Andrew in case of disaster. And, indeed, disaster happened, so she is now the testamentary guardian, which means the Orphans' Court—"

"Orphans' Court?"

"Yeah. In Pennsylvania, the name of the probate court is the Orphans' Court. Anyway, the Orphans' Court doesn't have to appoint a guardian, which keeps the members of the old boys' club out of the pockets of the estate. It also keeps Andrew out of the foster-care system for now, which, in my jaundiced view, is a blessing. By the way, Andrew stands to inherit about three hundred thousand from various life insurance policies — that money doesn't have to go through probate — maybe an additional twenty thousand from the combined assets of the three women and as much as another sixty thousand in equity from the mother's home, and possibly another thirty thousand from Frances's condo, about four hundred thou' less taxes and legal fees."

Martin let out a low whistle. "In a situation like this, what happens to the boy?"

"Well, he has to live somewhere, and as testamentary guardian, Ms. Palmer is responsible for finding and approving such a place. I can't imagine her doing this forever — and if she did, her fees would eventually drain the estate to zero. It's a real pickle for her. She doesn't want the responsibility for the boy, but she's an honest, earnest type, and will do whatever is needed. The problem is, there aren't many good choices. Andrew is living with a friend, but Ms. Palmer says it won't work long term."

"So what should I do?"

"The lawyer in me says keep denying everything, but the human being in me says you should agree to a DNA test without fighting, and not a quickie test — the right kind, done by a hospital lab with appropriate security, producing evidence admissible in court. I can arrange it if you want. This poor kid needs to get settled. If you're not the father, no problem, but if you are and you fight it tooth and nail, you'll have made an enemy of the kid, and unless you turn a complete cold shoulder — and get another lawyer, by the way — he'll become your responsibility."

"But I don't want the kid. It's scary."

"Yup," said Trevor. "Scary is the right word. But please let me arrange for the test. You have to face this with dignity."

"How long does it take to get results?"

"Maybe two weeks. Something like that. We'll need to agree with the Pittsburgh people on a suitable lab, but I'm pretty sure I can arrange that this morning. So be prepared for a summons from me to go to the hospital to have your sample taken."

"Actually, I have a three o'clock appointment this afternoon at the Medical Center, so if you can set it up before then, I'll go to the lab, or wherever, and get it over with."

On exiting Trevor's office, Martin dashed to the restroom down the hall.

- - -

Martin made the terrifying trip to the lab at the Mid-Coast Medical Center where he allowed a witnessed and certified cotton swab of his saliva to be sent off to the designated facility in Pittsburgh that would decide Andrew's fate, or at least Martin's role in that fate.

He then found his way to Dr. Sharif's office, where the woman at the check-in desk copied his medical insurance cards and gave him a clipboard with a stack of pages to be filled out: his medical history, medications, something about patient privacy, and a financial responsibility guarantee. Then, a bubbling nurse named Nancy invited him to a tiny exam room, where she took his vital signs and sent him back to the waiting area. And he sat. And waited. And brooded.

How much do I tell Dr. Sharif about my history? The real history. The personal history. Do I share the horrible details, how it was the stress in my first marriage that set off my irritable bowel, aggravated by alcohol and poor eating habits? And how, just when I was up for my Associate Professor promotion at CTI, the shit hit the fan about Camille, and how all through the subsequent divorce process, I was losing weight and sleeping badly? Just reliving those days, sitting here in a doctor's office, sets my gut rumbling. But I did reform, better eating, regular exercise, and there were no serious problems for years. It was when Jenny accused me of an affair with Kat that my gut blew up big time. It wasn't true. There was no affair. But Kat and I did go off to Troy together after the Istanbul conference, and, mea culpa, I did forget to send Jenny an email with contact information, and when Jenny finally found and called the right hotel, it was Kat who answered the phone in my room. It was all innocent, but it didn't look innocent, and Jenny, caught up in the fear of abandonment during her pregnancy, went ballistic. She insisted on staying at the cottage instead of returning to Cambridge, and this meant I had to commute to Boston from Maine, three days a week. It was during one of those commutes that UC hit in all its fury, and it took Dr. Feld's diagnostic colonoscopy, regular doses of balsalazide, and weeks of loving patience with Jenny to get things back to normal. And now it was Andrew, who had, without any ill intent, fired another bullet from that loaded gun in my gut.

Dr. Sharif turned out to be a pleasant, balding, round-faced man who spoke in a gentle, soothing manner, as if calming patients and calming irritable bowels required the same set of skills. In reporting his medical history, Martin described the post-Troy episode as being triggered by a lunch consisting entirely of grapefruit, which was true in the narrow sense, but he did add that his marriage was a bit "under stress" at that time. Yes, things had improved, and the meds were working, until recently.

"Do you have any idea what set this latest episode off?" asked the soothing doctor.

"I suspect stress," said a subdued Martin.

"Some specific event? Or stress in general?"

"I just learned that I may have fathered a child twelve years ago. I think that's what set me off. It was like a bomb in my belly."

"And this was Tuesday?"

"Yes."

"And have things settled down?"

"A little. I'm still on a liquid diet, and things are getting better."

"Sounds like you did the right thing. I was considering whether you should try one of the steroids, budesonide, that can treat sudden flare-ups, but it can have side effects. Under the circumstances, I'm going to give you a prescription that you should fill and have on hand if you have a sudden recurrence of bad symptoms. Otherwise, the balsalazide is the appropriate treatment. If things don't get back to normal, we'll have to do another colonoscopy."

With that, they shook hands, and Martin went forth, prescription in hand, wondering how he would handle things with Jenny.

- - -

At dinner, Martin opted again for clear broth and confirmed that, yes, he really was having a flare-up of the UC. He would have to stay on a bland diet for a week or so. And he had a prescription in case of things getting suddenly worse.

"I'm so sorry," said Jenny. "You still don't know what set it off? Was it something from CC, or from that letter?"

"I have no idea."

Martin knew he was once again crossing a red line, dissembling like this with Jenny, and he also knew it would come back to haunt him some day, but what could he do? Just blurt out over dinner that maybe he had son he hadn't known about? Impossible.

-    -   -

That evening, Martin used the reading of CC's business plan as a mental diversion, at least until bedtime. Sleep, however, was elusive. He could barely visualize Frances after all these years, but he could certainly remember what it felt like to share her bed, her touch, her taste — and this with Jenny asleep at his side. Had Frances actually borne his child in silence? Why the silence? How could he tell Jenny? And what of the boy? Would he have to take him in? Could Jenny even bear that? Or would she pull a Katie, write "Fuck You Martin" all over the house in red lipstick, and vanish with JJ and Ellen?

* **9** *

CC's amazing rental in Harpswell was located on a rocky ledge above a small inlet, an angular cedar-shingled sculpture, with a steeply sloped roof section creating space for high windows that flooded the oversized living room with northern light. On the twenty-five-minute drive from Brimfield Junction, Martin, in his sleep-deprived and Andrew-distracted state, had missed one of the turns and was now arriving fifteen minutes late. CC came out to the front steps as he drove up.

"Any problems getting here?" asked CC, in jeans and sandals.

As Martin climbed out of his car, he said, "Missed one of the turns and had to backtrack. Sorry I'm late."

"Well, c'mon in. It's just us. Phyllis and the kids needed to stay home to register for the summer soccer league."

CC offered a beer, but Martin declined in favor of plain water. He didn't want to risk either his touchy gut or any compounding of Andrew-induced muddle-headedness.

"How about the back deck?" asked CC. "It's on the shady side of the house."

The pair went through the sliding door to a mahogany deck furnished with an oval iron mesh table and six floral-padded wrought-iron chairs. Mottled sunlight reflected from the water below imitated the glint in CC's eyes. "So whaddya think?" asked CC as they took their seats, CC's left leg pumping away.

"It's a bit overwhelming," said Martin, struggling to focus, "and I want to be sure I understand your concept. If I have it straight, your idea is to use your initial endowment to hire faculty and use them as a recruiting tool for a development program funded by an industrial consortium. Independent of whether we can get the people, do you really think you can bring in a million a year from industry? What's the draw? Why should they contribute?"

CC beamed. "Yes, that's the plan. The draw? First of all, it's me. Second, it's you and the people who will join you. Third, it's the focus on biogenetics, or whatever else we choose, and the pre-competitive sharing of results. And fourth, it's access to great students."

"But I've done consortia before," said Martin. "We were never able to get more than a hundred K per company. I don't think there are ten companies out there to put up that kind of money."

"Sure, there are. The drug companies and the genetic engineering companies all have huge research budgets, hundreds of millions a year. What they don't have is a long-term view because they spend most of their money satisfying the FDA. We provide the long view. We create an advisory board from these companies and define a research agenda that they can all buy into, the pre-competitive development of enabling technologies. Each company would have automatic licenses to use what we invent, and they would have first dibs on hiring our students."

"And once the consortium is in place?"

"Their one mil per year would allow us to hire research staff and technicians, pay the operating costs, and even hire one or two more faculty. Then we do the campaign."

"So you really think of this like a venture-backed business?"

"Yup. Think of the funding of your chair as seed money. The twenty mil I put in is the A round, and we get started. The consortium functions like a B round, creating a five-year runway, and we do the campaign as the exit — putting the school on a solid financial basis for an indefinite future."

"Has Jeremy seen this?"

"I'll send it to him as soon as you tell me that I'm not crazy."

Martin laughed. "But I think you are crazy. Totally."

"I know. You asked Collingsworth to check up on me, didn't you."

Martin blushed. "Yes, I did. I'm sorry. I just thought…"

"You did exactly right. It's called due diligence, and one can never do enough of it. You can be sure that once Fred told me who they were

proposing for my chair at Bottlesworth, I did my own due dilig(
on you."

"And I passed?"

"Actually, since you asked, I did have some concerns about why someone like you would choose to leave CTI, but that makes sense to me now. And I couldn't be happier that Bottlesworth got you, someone of your caliber. That's when this whole idea for the new school hit me. If Bottlesworth can get one Martin Quint, it can get many more. You can't build something great without great leadership and great people."

"You realize, don't you, that I've never had any administrative experience? Even turned down a request to become Associate Department Chair."

"Yes, I realize all that, but you've managed big grants and you could attract top people as colleagues. That's what we need. Great people. I've always run my companies that way, and it works. Get great people. And, speaking of companies, I want you to come down to Autobot one of these days. See a real company in action."

"Would love to," he answered, suddenly visualizing Gina at a cubicle desk, hard at work.

"So why do you think I'm crazy?" asked CC.

Martin banished the image of Gina and took a deep breath. "You're not going to like this, but I've gotta say what I think."

"Of course," said CC. "Lay it on."

"Okay." Martin paused looking down at his feet. Raising his head and looking CC straight in the face, he said, "I think you've got this completely bass-ackwards. The plan is completely wrong."

CC looked startled. "Completely wrong? You mean the idea of the school is wrong?"

"Not necessarily the idea of the school," said Martin. "The plan. Thinking of it as a business. It's not a business. It's a school."

"Yes, but—"

Martin cut him off, raising his hand like a stop sign. "Let me finish. The purpose of a school is to educate. The heart of a school is not a research consortium, it's a curriculum, with qualified faculty and real-life students. It makes no sense to talk about a school until the educational program is defined."

"Yes, of course. Part of our charge from Fred is to create a plan for the curriculum."

"Fair enough, but your plan assumes we can get great people here. We won't be able to get great people unless they're actively involved in defining the program. Once they buy into the excitement of the new program, then maybe, and only maybe, they'll decide to join us."

"So you're saying we start with the people?"

"The people and the program. Instead of jumping into a school, we should do serious brainstorming. Assemble a panel of top people as consultants, the kind of people we would ultimately want. Get them to work as a team to flesh out a program that would excite them. That's essential. And here's the thing. This is important. I don't know enough to define a curriculum by myself. We need experts from different fields."

"So, if I can slip back into my start-up analogy," said CC, "you're saying we should use some seed money to hire a panel of consultants to write the business plan for the A round of financing. And pick consultants who are also our targets for actually joining us. It might make sense. I did that with my second company."

Martin continued. "And I assume you did that planning in secret. But this is different. You can't operate a panel at a university in secret. A terrible idea. Much better to announce it so alumni can learn about it. Lay the groundwork for hitting them up in the eventual campaign."

CC blew out a long breath. "You may be right. I'm just not tuned in to the academic niceties like you are. I may have the vision, and," adding a chuckle, "the money, but I need a real educator, an academic leader type, to make it happen. It'll take me some time to digest all this, but I hear what you're saying."

"So what now?" asked Martin.

"I'll do some rethinking," said CC, "and, when I'm ready, some rewriting. I'll be in touch. As I said, you might be right. You're probably right. Glad to get your input."

- - -

Martin found his way back from the tangle of Harpswell roads without difficulty and drove to and through Brimfield Junction, heading directly for the cottage, deeply worried that CC's ego-driven push for a named school would lead to a train wreck. On the other hand, while CC might be crazy, he did appear to listen, and he even appeared to agree with what Martin said. It would never be boring working with somebody like him. As long as his life wasn't wrecked by Andrew. Or by Jenny.

He arrived at the cottage to find Helen resting in one of the deck chairs, a wide-brimmed straw hat shading her face. "Hi, big brother," she called. "Jenny and Bill are at the bay with the kids."

"You feeling okay?" asked Martin as he ascended the three short steps to the deck.

Helen patted her rounding belly, saying, "This little creature is starting to drive me nuts. He has a way of kicking my backbone that sends pain down my right leg. So I decided to flop out for a while."

"Yeah, Jenny had that kind of problem with Ellen. She would get sciatica."

"I don't know if that's what you call this, but it makes me want to drink some booze to put the little guy to sleep."

"Is it a guy, by the way?" asked Martin.

"Yup. We did the ultrasound yesterday, and there's definitely a little-boy thing."

"Neat. Have you picked a name?"

"We talk about it. I'm partial to Jeremiah, in honor of Dad. Would that be okay for you?"

"Of course. Does Bill like it?"

"Thinks it's a bit old-fashioned. But it's under discussion, at least."

"Speaking of Dad, can I ask you something?"

"Sure. What?"

"Do you ever think about our vanished mother?"

"Good grief, brother. What set that off? You've never said a word about her."

"Well, being back at Bottlesworth, and walking past old Josiah's grave every day and then having to stare at his ugly puss in the President's conference room, it makes me wonder why she left. Do you have any idea?"

"Only what Dad told us, that she wanted a life as an artist and ran off to New York."

"But do you believe that?"

"Why not? You're being spooky. Are you going to go looking for her, or something?"

"No. Just curious. I'm kind of surprised at how little I remember about her. Anyway, what did Jenny lay in for dinner?"

"Chicken thighs on the grill, corn on the cob, and I suspect Bill will bring back a bucket of steamers. JJ always wants to dig clams. You need help?"

"Not at all. Rest your bones. I can do this," and he went into the house to start on dinner, adding a can of chicken noodle soup to the menu for himself.

- - -

Martin and Bill were enjoying the after-dinner fire, pine and birch logs crackling and snapping, shooting occasional sparks that would flare like shooting stars into the screen. Helen and Jenny were upstairs putting the four children to bed.

"Are you allowed to talk about the CC thing now?" asked Martin.

"With you I am. But no one else."

"Okay, good. How much detail has CC given you and Jeremy?"

"Not much. He said he would give us a business plan — that's what he called it — but only after you had approved it. Have you seen it?"

"Yes, and it's complicated. We had a good discussion today. It needs pretty heavy editing before CC will be willing to share it."

"What's the bottom line?"

"I'm not sure I'm supposed to tell you, and that makes me feel really weird. But he is doing what Fred asked — looking to phase up to fifteen faculty. What I want to know is why Bottlesworth would buy the idea?

Seems awfully risky."

Bill chuckled. "Jeremy says that if you lose money on every transaction, it's hard to make it up with volume. And we do. We lose money on every student. That's why we need an endowment and why our Development staff has to keep the contributions coming in. If CC's new school is to pass fiscal review, we have to show that we aren't worse off than before in terms of fundraising, scholarships, that kind of thing."

"Sounds like a tall order. CC scares me a bit, but he also impresses me. Seems totally fearless. Or maybe reckless. Either way, it gets the juices going."

"Enough shop talk," said Helen as she and Jenny came downstairs. "Kids are all tucked in. Aren't we playing poker tonight?"

Bill got up to add a log to the fire while Martin collected the cards, the poker chips, and the scorecard. Rather than move money around within the family, the four played for free days. They kept a cumulative score sheet, game to game, and whenever someone was down by more than a thousand chips, the loser would get all four children for a whole day. The couple left childless would have the day free to go to Boston, or to Portland, or go hiking, or just spend the day in bed making love. The child-free spouse had most of a free day, but had to provide dinner, typically Chinese takeout followed by ice cream from The Lickity Split.

Tonight's game ended with Jenny as the big winner, Martin losing all his remaining chips to her on the last hand. But no one reached the minus-one-thousand cutoff, so a child-free day was not awarded. "Wait 'til next time," said Martin.

"In your dreams," said Jenny, her face softening into the grin of a victor. She got up from the table, went around behind Martin, and gave him a kiss on the side of his neck, a lovely reminder, thought Martin, of that night when she had yanked him out of his post-divorce gloom and, finally, made him her lover. And once everyone got settled into bed, Jenny took Martin on a sexual ride with an intensity that he found both overwhelming and delightful, washing away, for the moment, all memories of Frances and his worries about her son. Maybe he should let her win at poker more often.

* 10 *

Martin and Jenny were in the study at their respective desks as Martin tried to deflect his anxiety about Andrew by bitching that he still felt whipsawed by CC and Fred to help with what might be a crazy plan, and how, on the other hand, Glenda was not just supportive of the book, she was really helping, even leading the way in some areas. "We had such a great Skype call today."

"How's she doing?" asked Jenny. "Is her student thing settled?"

"Not yet, but she said she planted your idea about his accusation just being a stand-in for anger at his mother, for deserting him. We are making progress, even with her troubles at home and my interruptions from CC."

"Speaking of Mr. CC, I've been thinking. They should pay you."

"What do you mean, they?"

"The college. About the summer supplement thing and your worries over money. They should pay you for the time you put in on CC's project, solve your money worries. Then, if I could find a full-time daycare place, which I haven't been able to do yet, we could get the kids settled for the rest of the summer and stop fighting."

"The kid-swap isn't working?"

"Not really. It's only two kidless mornings a week, and then I lose the morning when I have all three kids, and, of course, when one of them gets sick, we tend to cancel. It would be so much better to have a regular arrangement, even if it costs."

Martin thought about mentioning George's money, but knowing where that would lead, he just said, "I don't think they do that. Pay, I mean."

"Well, it's time they started. Here you are doing the work of the

Development people, and getting no extra pay. It's not fair."

"It is a lot of pressure. Maybe I should, but…" Martin fell silent.

"My sometimes loveable dear Mr. Goofus who can never say no. Do you even hear yourself when you talk about pressure?" Jenny's tone was halfway between bland acceptance and sarcastic gouging. "You collect pressure situations like an opioid addict collects oxycodone. And like an addict, you keep on taking one more than you should. Even that classroom flipping, for example, sounds crazy. More work to do instead of the book."

"But the classroom flipping is part of the book. Maybe an important part."

"Well, if you don't watch out, you'll be just as overloaded as you were at CTI, except that you'll be underpaid in the bargain. Why can't you just tell Fred no? Or at least get paid for it, so we don't have to fight over money. I hate fighting over money."

"I could say no, I guess, but it would seem like a nasty retort to Bottlesworth after just being named to a chair. And, of course, CC doesn't make it easy to say no. He's boiling over with energy and enthusiasm, and he can put real money where his mouth is. What I'm hoping is that I can help get a decent plan in place, and then get someone else to actually run it."

Jenny emitted a soft laugh. "Lotsa luck. When were you ever happy with how someone else ran anything? Once you plan it out, you'll feel you have to run it. Anyone else would ruin your brainchild."

"But it's not my brainchild. It's CC's. It's him who'll worry about it being ruined."

"Which is exactly why he'll insist that you run it."

"Maybe you're right. It does worry me. On another subject, though, do you have dates for your Chicago trip yet? I need to know which days I'm on kid duty because I need to do another CTI trip. Gotta consult with Harry about his online version of my old course."

"I'm working on it. Looks like one day with Sarah and two days at the trade show, starting a week from next Monday."

"With Pierre?"

"Yes, with Pierre."

"Where will you stay?"

"Sarah's put us in a hotel. Why?"

"What's Pierre like?"

"Martin, you've met him. You know what he's like. Are you suddenly jealous? Is that what I'm hearing?"

"No, I don't know. This is just new to me, so much traveling. Makes me edgy."

And that made Jenny edgy, another surge in that magma chamber, leading this time to a minor eruption, a steam vent popping. "Do you know how long I've had to put up with you travelling to God knows where with God knows who? You just dump me with the kids and take off. Even when I was pregnant. Have you forgotten going off to Troy with that Kat woman, in radio silence? Relax, you idiot. This is business. Pierre is a very nice thirty-year-old boy with a wife, two children and a mortgage, and he does a great job with clients."

"I'm sorry. You're right. It's just—"

"It's just that you're jealous. Is it the travel, the supposed excitement of travel, which I've learned is greatly overrated, or is it some misguided concern about Pierre?"

"I'm not jealous." Martin turned to his computer. "I've got stuff to do." And as he tried to plow through the online FIE lectures he would need for the flipped classroom experiment, all he could think about was Andrew in Pittsburgh and Jenny and Pierre in Chicago.

* **11** *

Saturday afternoon. Martin and Jenny were dashing about the cottage, picking up toys, clearing the kitchen counters, getting lunch dishes into the dishwasher, cleaning the bathrooms, taking out the trash, and, finally, sweeping the floor. As the last dustpan of sweepings went into the outdoor trash barrel, Jenny said, "Okay. We're ready. Now remind me. Names."

"Well, you've met CC. His wife's name is Phyllis, and the three boys are Phillip, Edward, and Curtis, but I'm not sure which one is which. I'm hoping they like to swim. Otherwise, I'm not sure what to do with them. Maybe take turns in the canoe up in the marsh."

"I wouldn't worry," said Jenny. "We'll take them off to the beach or the bay, and leave you and CC to your talk. JJ will want to show them how we dig clams. And Ellen will be happy to have a toddler around. The youngest is two, right?" Without waiting for Martin's answer, she added, "And you can start the grill when it's time. I've got steaks for dinner. If you feel you can't eat steak, I made some chicken soup. It's in the red thing in the fridge. And I thought the children would enjoy corn on the cob. There are also fixings for a big salad. Do their kids eat vegetables?"

"I've no idea. They said they would bring some wine and not to worry about menu details. CC said their kids were omnivores. If so, they may be the only such kids on the planet."

A few minutes later, CC's black Cadillac Escalade pulled into their driveway. Phyllis was the first to emerge, brilliantly blond like her husband, her hair in a pony-tail. Slender and tan, she wore white slacks, sandals, a blue and maroon low-cut floral blouse, gold chains dangling in the low-cut place and gold loop earrings to match. Her narrow face was partially hidden behind oversized sunglasses with blue frames that matched the color of her blouse. She pushed the sunglasses up onto her head, and stretched out both hands in greeting, three different rings blazing in the sun. "You must be the famous Jenny," she announced as Jenny came down the steps from the deck with JJ and Ellen.

"Definitely Jenny, but hardly famous. Welcome," she said as two blond boys scrambled from the back seat and came over to stand beside their mother, each with a rolled-up towel and swimsuit under one arm. "Now tell me which is which."

"Sure," she said, her hand on one head, then the next. "Phillip here is eight, Edward is six, and CC is untangling little Curtis from his car seat. Is this young man JJ? My husband likes double-letter people."

Not sure of what to say or what to do, JJ just stared at the two boys. "JJ, take Phillip and Edward inside," said Jenny. "There's lemonade in the fridge. And everyone should get into bathing suits."

"Did you ever dig clams?" asked JJ as the three boys went inside, Ellen tagging along as she always did.

CC came up to Jenny holding Curtis and Curtis's pacifier just as Martin came out to greet his guests. "Very nice of you to have us over like this," said CC. "We may be on the water in Harpswell, but we have no beach. The boys miss the sand and the surf."

"It's cold, of course," said Martin.

"My kids love cold. I predict that Phyllis won't be able to get them out of the water even after they start shivering."

Jenny and Phyllis left for the beach with the children, leaving Martin and CC sitting on the deck, CC with a beer, Martin with club soda. Martin asked, "Are we ready for Monday?"

"Absolutely. I can show you the slide deck if you want, but it's pretty much what you saw in the revised draft. In the meantime, I had my facilities guy put together some drawings of the warehouse space. I brought the plans. Should we take a look now?"

"Might as well," said Martin. "We can spread them out inside."

CC went to his car and returned with a rolled sheaf of poster-sized paper. Drinks in hand, the pair went inside to the dining table. CC explained as they paged through the drawings, "I asked him to sketch it up, assuming two classrooms seating thirty, a large general lab area, two smaller specialty lab areas reserved for maybe chemistry hoods or something like that, a computer server room, one office suite — that will be yours — six other offices, and some cube space for who knows what."

Much as he hated to admit it, Martin was impressed and excited by the drawings. They discussed options for the lab space and how much flexibility was needed, whether there were enough offices, what the trade-offs might be. After a half hour, CC said, "Do you think this is good enough to allow us to rough out a facilities budget?"

"As long as it can be changed later, absolutely," said Martin. "Looks really exciting."

"Great." CC rolled up the drawings, and without missing a beat, said, "Now, listen, you owe me a visit to Autobot. It's only two hours from BJ, down and back in one day. Send me dates."

With a hopeless grin, Martin said, "Okay. Okay. I'll visit."

"Good. Now tell me about this book Fred says you're writing."

-    -   -

While Martin was explaining his book plans, the help he was getting from Glenda, and his new teaching strategy, the afternoon had gone about as one might expect with three boys, ages six to eight. A loud game of tag on the beach, body surfing in the breakers, and climbing on the granite promontories resulting in Phillip getting a scrape on his left shin that required a trip with Jenny back to the cottage for first aid.

Martin made the dinner arrangements. He set up the folding card table for the boys while the grown-ups and the two toddlers sat on booster seats at the dining table. Everyone dug in, especially the children. Edward, in particular, polished off his plate in what felt like a split second and then asked for more salad, the first time in Martin's memory he had ever heard a child ask for more green stuff.

CC asked Jenny to describe her business, which she did with bubbling enthusiasm, especially when she described the Chicago job. It was part preening and part sales pitch, making Martin wonder whether Jenny was hoping to add CC as a client someday. Ugh, thought Martin. He's rich enough to afford her stuff, but don't we have enough entanglements with him just now?

Phyllis speared some salad with her fork and, making a sweeping gesture, said, "This place is just lovely. Did you decorate it?"

Jenny smiled. "Not this place. Martin's father set everything up and we've left it pretty much alone. It's homey. But I do have some of our special pieces in our BJ house. Next time, perhaps? You'd be amazed at what my guys can do."

"Do you spend much time here?" asked Phyllis.

"Ah, yes," answered Martin. "One of the perks of Bottlesworth. In my old job at CTI, we would have been lucky to get two full weeks plus a bunch of weekends. Now, what with the satellite internet we put in, we can spend big chunks of time here as long as we don't have to be at any face-to-face meetings. It's great."

"I thought I'd be able to do that with our place in Harpswell," said Phyllis, "but with summer soccer league and computer camp for Phillip and my dear husband's ninety-hour work weeks, it just doesn't happen."

"It's not just me," said CC. "Phyllis volunteers at the Peabody-Essex Museum in Salem, two days a week, so it's our nanny who does most of the chauffeuring and Curtis-minding."

"You have a nanny?" asked Jenny.

Phyllis laughed. "Actually, we do, a lovely woman named Anita from Guatemala. She lives with us. But her mother was ill, so we sent her home for a month. She gets back next week."

"A nanny?" muttered Jenny under her breath.

Martin stood up and asked, "Who wants ice cream?" A roar from the kids' table led to dessert. This was followed by a thank-you-filled loading up of the Escalade and the departure of the Caldicotts, but not before Martin had promised to visit Autobot the following Friday.

-   -   -

Once quiet reigned, with dishes done and children in bed, Martin and

Jenny sat together in front of the fire, relishing the calm, Jenny with a snifter of cognac, Martin with plain water. "He's really very nice," said Jenny, "but she seems a bit stuck up. What do you think?"

"You spent more time with her than I did, but it seems like a nice family. The kids are amazingly well-behaved. For kids, anyway. What makes you think she's stuck up?"

"Look at how she dresses. All that glitter, at the beach. And a nanny, for Christ's sake. Normal people put their kids in daycare. Who around here has a nanny?"

"Rich people," said Martin. "And they're plenty rich."

"We should get a nanny. We could use one. I know, I know. Money. So with Mr. CC Caldicott, disrupter of your life, did you have a good meeting?"

"Good enough, actually. We present his revised plan on Monday morning. You did find a sitter to cover that, yes?" Jenny nodded. "And we went over a preliminary layout for the new space. Then he wanted to know all about my book."

"You mean he was interested in all that conversation stuff?"

"Amazingly, yes, he was. Said he might want me to consult at his company."

"But I thought they did robots. What do you—"

"It's for his training program, not the robots. They hire an average of fifteen people a week, sometimes more, and organizing their new employee training is a big challenge. He thought I could help. I might want to."

Jenny shook her head, laughing quietly. "There goes my lovely Mr. Goofus, once again saying yes when he should be saying no. Think about your book. He's seducing you," said Jenny.

"Maybe he is, but it feels like fun."

"Watch out he doesn't screw you over."

"I'll watch, but speaking of screwing," sensing an urge that pushed aside his pervasive visceral anxiety over Frances and Andrew, "you feeling at all friendly tonight?"

"Are you?"

"You can't tell?"

"I can tell... just teasing. After spending our day with Mr. and Mrs. CC Snooty Caldicott, I'm feeling pretty good about my own Mr. Goofus, and that thought warms me in all the right places, the ones you know how to touch."

-    -   -

The next morning dawned bright and clear, but in spite of the passionate love-making the previous evening, all Martin could see as he emerged from sleep were clouds of anxiety, twisted like little spirals of DNA sitting in a lab somewhere in Pittsburgh. He put on a cheerful face, and drove the family to Brimfield Junction after breakfast.

Around noon, Pierre DuChamp arrived in his pick-up truck. A bit shorter than Martin at five-foot ten but equally square of face and frame, Pierre's straight black hair was pulled back in a ponytail, showing off his gold loop earrings. He was wearing blue jeans with a light brown sport coat over a dark blue shirt and work boots. An odd mix.

Jenny came downstairs with her suitcase, collected her marketing portfolio from the study, hugged her children while telling them to be good, and went out to where Pierre was standing. Martin and the children followed, and he and Pierre shook hands. "Good weather for flying," said Martin.

"Yup," said Pierre, a man generally of few words, which made Martin wonder how he could possibly be as good with clients as Jenny said he was. She gave Martin a hug and quick kiss, put her bag in the truck bay, and climbed into the passenger seat. Pierre got behind the wheel, waved, and off they went.

"When is Mommy coming back?" asked JJ, holding hands with Ellen, who watched in wistful silence as her mother vanished.

"Tuesday night," answered Martin. "We've got three days with just us. We can all go the park. How about that?"

"Okay, I guess," said JJ.

* **12** *

During breakfast the next morning, the sitter Jenny had hired to cover Martin's critical meeting at Bottlesworth called to say she was sick. With no time to arrange a substitute, Martin collected JJ, Ellen, her diaper bag, her stuffed dachshund and a canvas tote bag full of foam blocks, dropped JJ at school, and transported Ellen and her baggage to the College Hall conference room. Fred, Win, and Jeremy were already assembled. Fred and Win, at least, seemed amused and welcomed the toddler. CC arrived as Martin was bribing Ellen with donuts, then settling her and her toys into a corner behind his chair. CC connected his laptop to the projector while Martin distributed copies of a new Business Plan, this one titled: "Feasibility Study for a Program in Engineering and Entrepreneurship."

Fred said, "This looks interesting. We're all ears. Ready to go?"

CC showed his first slide and began. "Let me start off by saying that, thanks to Martin, we have a plan that I think everyone will like. He said, and I quote, that my original idea was 'bass-ackwards,' and I had to agree with him. His notion is to start with the people — have them define the program — then start in earnest toward building a school. I'll walk you through it."

CC's Business Plan now had four phases: scoping, initial hiring, consortium, and campaign. The slides were linked to the graphics and charts in the document, and his audience turned pages in sync with each new image.

When he finished, the three officials looked to each other, waiting for someone to start. Fred broke the ice. "This looks very interesting, and I like the idea of starting small. The notion of a new school could create all kinds of anxieties on campus, but a study group for a new program is always a suitable activity. What do you think, Jeremy?"

"Boom," said Ellen, as she knocked over a small tower of blocks, and everyone laughed except Jeremy, who grunted while still peering at the financial charts. Ellen decided at that point to climb into Martin's lap, and with more donut bribery, settled into the task of covering Martin's clothing with crumbs and powdered sugar.

Jeremy spoke. "Obviously, we need to study this stuff, so I'm going to reserve judgment until I've had time to read it all. But the basic outline does make some sense. The thing that I'm not sure about is this consortium idea. Looks risky. Hard to pull off."

CC answered, "If we get the right people, the consortium will be no problem. I have enough contacts to make it work."

Jeremy scoffed, "This is not venture capital, my friend, this is a college. A million-dollar consortium is a big deal. We've only done one so far, in forest-resource management. It was for membership at the 25K per level, six members, the paper and timber companies. We spent almost all of the first year's money in legal fees before we could find language that all ten companies could agree to. And then it fell apart after only two years. So I'm suspicious. Not opposed, mind you, just suspicious."

Win said, "I agree with Jeremy's concern, but the idea of a preliminary study group makes a lot of sense. How about you give us a few days to digest all this, and we get back to you?"

"Fine with me," said CC. "In the meantime, Martin and I will brainstorm a set of names for our panel and we can draft a prospectus. We'll need to have something for recruiting them."

"But no contact yet, right?" asked Fred.

"No contact," said CC.

After the meeting adjourned, CC packed up his laptop while Martin collected Ellen and her detritus. The three of them toddled at Ellen's pace across the Central Quad and up the stairs to Martin's office. The whiteboard still had Glenda's sample sentence written five times with a different word underlined.

"What's this?" asked CC.

"My Oxford person is teaching me how psychologists deal with conversation. It's done its job so you can erase it. But while you think, I've got a stinky diaper to take care of."

Martin took Ellen to the restroom and used the floor as a changing table, ending with a minute of the tickling and giggling game. This was more fun than CC could offer, but after the longest pause he thought his resident billionaire would tolerate, he returned to the office with Ellen. He dumped the blocks onto the floor and tried to deposit Ellen and a sippy cup of juice into their midst, but Ellen had a different idea. She demanded a pick-up to Martin's lap, and giggling with joy, she pushed her fingers into Daddy's mouth and tried to blow air through her lips the way Daddy could. Finally, Martin made a lip-fluttering exhale, and Ellen screamed with delight.

Standing at the now clean whiteboard, CC said, "She's cute. My youngest likes that noise, too. But can we proceed?"

Martin, with fingers once again in the way, laughed and said, "We can try. I can tell you that her giggles are better than some of the alternatives."

"I believe you. I've got three of my own. Anyway, here goes. I think we need something like six people, including you. Assuming you cover electrical, we need mechanical, computer systems, microbiology, biomedical engineering, and I think somebody from the economics and business side. Besides me, I mean. Somebody academic. And, given my expertise, perhaps, someone in computer vision. Not sure about that. The study panel may want to move in a direction that's not just genetic medicine."

Martin, removing Ellen's hand briefly, added, "I think we should get some of the present college faculty to participate. That would build some important bridges if we get this moving forward to the school level. Less fuss if it benefits people already here."

"Good point," said CC. "My first target, as you know, is Sharon Gillespie. She can do the mechanical side, and she sure as hell can do robotics." He wrote her name on the board while asking, "Do you know anybody good in computer systems?"

At this point, Ellen climbed down and walked over to her sippy cup, sat with a thud, took a drink and started pushing the blocks around with her free hand. Martin was relieved to be able to talk unimpeded. "Actually, there's a computer security guy from CTI. His name is Julian Kesselbaum." CC started writing. "Two esses in Kesselbaum. He's a real guru about computers. Like Gillespie, he didn't get tenure. Runs a consulting business in Cambridge and helps the CTI people when they need him. He's a great teacher. Kind of a weird guy, but he knows his stuff and loves to teach."

"Okay. Kesselbaum is on the list. What about the others? I think Pendleton at Harvard is good in computer vision. We could add him if we think we're going that way."

Martin shook his head. "I don't know him or anything about him. And I really don't know the Bottlesworth faculty well enough yet to suggest anyone else. Suppose I sit down with Win and talk it over? He'll probably be able to identify a couple of people from the biology side and somebody from economics, maybe even someone in computer vision."

"Great. You do that, and I'll get cracking on the prospectus. Well done, Martin."

CC shook hands with Martin and started to leave but Martin stopped him, saying, "By the way, if you're thinking of endowing professorships, you might consider one for Glenda Aldrich. She has family reasons for relocating to this area, and if you liked getting someone from CTI, you might also like getting someone from Oxford."

CC smiled. "Easy boy. One set of endowments at a time. Nevertheless, I would like to meet her. If she's as good as you say, I might want to hire her at Autobot." He zipped out of the room, leaving Martin wondering why he continued to get swept up into CC's fantasy. He had enough on his plate, what with Frances and her son and the detonation that would go off in his marriage if Andrew turned out to be his.

- - -

Jenny returned Tuesday night overflowing with enthusiasm. Pierre had been masterful in presenting the capabilities of her team, and the client was thrilled. Martin said all the appropriate things, but as much as he loved his wife and his little cherubs, he was happy to be able to go to his office on Wednesday morning without JJ and Ellen in tow. Among the usual flood of emails was one from Sumner that couldn't have been clearer. CC had a stellar record as an entrepreneur, had never defaulted on a promise as far as Sumner could determine, made good hiring judgments, treated his employees well, even generously, and, as a result, had very little turnover in his various ventures. His technical judgments and sense of market timing had been "exquisite," an unusual word for Sumner to choose. As for his philanthropy, this might be a new activity. The professorship at Bottlesworth seems to have been his first large gift, so the book was open on how he'd do in that arena.

Martin drafted an email to CC confirming Friday morning for his Autobot visit. But he paused before sending it. His head was suddenly awash with a collage of anxieties, starting with a quote he remembered from his high school English class: "Hitch your wagon to a star." To hear CC tell it, CC was hitching his Bottlesworth wagon to Martin, but to Martin, CC was the star and the owner of the wagon. His drive, his money, his vision, his daring. Martin had to concede that he was already hitched-up, but he felt more like the horse, yanked into position, laced into the traces, and directed to pull. Then a vision from one of his nightmarish dreams resurfaced, Martin on the cliff, looking down at the water below, but this time seeing CC swimming around saying, "C'mon in. The water's fine." Was CC a star worth following? Or was he Mephistopheles?

Returning to the email, he muttered, "What the hell," and added a comment that one of his former CTI advisees, Gina Farrell, was working at Autobot for the summer. You might want to keep an eye on her, Martin suggested. She's really good, and she wants to become a teacher.

And once the note was launched, he wondered what the fuck he was doing, dragging Gina into the CC mix. It's crazy. But deep down, he knew all too well what was going on. That image of Gina in the rant grasping both his hands with that look in her eyes. He knew, and he hated the fact that he knew, and he hated the fact that, forbidden or not, he wanted to see that look again. Was he really wandering? With Gina? No way. She's a student, for God's sake. Students are taboo. But was that why he was so worried about Jenny and Pierre? A displacement? Accusing Jenny of having wandering thoughts when he should be accusing himself?

-   -   -

A half hour later, Win was staring at Martin's white board. On the left were the names Sharon Gillespie and Julian Kesselbaum written in CC's bold lettering, one beneath the other, and a column of three question marks next to the cryptic words, bio, gen-med, and bus. Martin was bringing Win up to date on his progress with CC. "We have two outside names, but I thought if we fill some of the slots with people already at Bottlesworth, the whole project will seem less alien. So I want to pick your brain. I haven't met many people in the other departments."

Win stroked his jaw, scratched his head, and sat silent. Martin waited. And waited.

"So you don't like this idea?" asked Martin.

"No, the idea is fine," said Win. "I'm really worried about how to start something like this without the gossip mill creating a backlash before we even get it off the ground. Participation might look like an inside track to an endowed chair, and that is like dynamite with a lit fuse."

"Can I suggest something?" Win nodded a go-ahead. "Everybody already knows that I'm an oddball, brought here to do Applied Physics. Big headline in the campus newspaper and all that. How about you give me a list of, say, six or eight faculty members who have done some kind of applied work, and let me just go meet them to chat. No mention of a panel, just a get-acquainted talk. That way, I can explore their interest in expanding the applied side of Bottlesworth, independent of CC or any project."

Win exhaled in a big puff. "Great idea. Just what the doctor ordered. I'll email you a list of suggestions later today."

As Win got up to leave, Martin said, "Can I ask you about something else?"

Win paused to listen. "This CC thing is taking an awful lot of my time. At CTI, if I had a summer task that took time, my department or my research grants would pay a summer salary, a supplement. I'm not getting anything from CTI this summer, and my book is getting drowned by the CC project. I'm willing to do it, I guess, but my question is, can I at least get some salary aid in compensation?"

Win's look was not encouraging. "What you're saying sounds reasonable, but we don't have funds for that kind of thing. If a faculty member has a grant, we can pay supplements out of that. There's no budget for this kind of speculative development activity. But I'll talk to Fred and Jeremy and see what might work. How much are you thinking about?"

"Somewhere around a third of my monthly normal seems fair, based on the time I'm actually spending on it."

"I'll let you know," said Win, heading for the door.

Martin turned to his email. The only useful note was from Steve Wang asking about trying a squash game. He answered in the affirmative and turned to the FIE website to poke around in the online version of C&E, preparation for Friday's flipped-classroom discussion with Harry Huang at CTI.

-     -   -

Steve Wang, it turned out, had played varsity squash at Princeton, and he was quite a few notches better than Martin. Martin did his best, but ended up losing three straight games, by nine, eleven, and twelve points.

As they headed to the locker room, Martin asked, "Where did you learn to play like that? I thought only Indians and Pakistanis could play pro-level squash."

"What? You think because I'm half-Asian, I play only badminton or ping pong? I grew up in Brooklyn Heights. I played tons of tournaments as a kid."

"Well I'm such a hacker, is it any fun to play with somebody like me?"

"Sure is. I can't push you around in the academic world, so maybe I can push you around a little on the squash court."

"Very funny. Don't you control budgets? You can push me around that way, can't you?"

"Bottlesworth is funny. Our tiny departments are more like divisions of a bigger department controlled by one of the four Deans. Evelyn Kim controls the School of Science budget, and she can be a tough bitch at times, if you'll pardon my French. I mean she's honest and fair, but tough, tough, tough. Department Heads here are just like petty functionaries. We manage our specific educational programs and make recommendations on hiring and promotion, but we have no real power. We don't even own our space. It's all with the Schools and the Deans."

"Ah, well," said Martin, as they emerged from their showers and were getting dressed. "I'm allergic to Deans. But I do have a budget question, and maybe I have to talk to Evelyn Kim, but I thought I should start with you."

"And?" asked Steve.

"I'm going to try a huge experiment in the fall with C&E. It's called flipping the classroom, using the FIE lectures as homework and using class time for group problem-solving."

"Well, I'll be damned," said Steve, with a wry smile. "The conversation guru using FIE?"

"Glenda Aldrich — you know, our visitor from Oxford — she pushed on me to try it and it makes sense. It allows more student-to-student interaction and actually expands their total class time to six hours a week from four."

"Sounds good. But what's the question?"

"Can I get a teaching assistant of some kind? I'm worried about handling twenty students by myself for group sessions, where each group is four or five."

Steve laughed. "Yes, you have to talk to Evelyn. I don't have any money for TAs. I would support your request, but it's her call. Getting a budget for that kind of thing is like sucking your Kool-Aid through a pinched-off soda straw. On a totally different topic, though, I really want you and Jenny to come to dinner sometime soon. We have some friends who are not part of the college. Thought you might enjoy meeting them."

"Sounds terrific. We'd love it."

"And I forget. You've got two kids, right?"

This gave Martin pause. How many kids did he have? He took a deep breath and answered, "Yeah. A boy six and a girl going on two. Too young for your girls."

Steve laughed, "Yeah, my girls. My young women. Twelve going on sixteen and fourteen going on twenty-one."

* **13** *

Autobot headquarters was located in a matched set of four build-ings just off Interstate 93 between Interstate 495 and the Merrimac River. Martin arrived on the dot of ten and parked in front of the main entrance in a space marked "Visitor," pausing to take a look before going in. There was an eerie similarity to that warehouse on the Clements Corner Road, with a high-ceilinged first floor and a normal-sized second floor above, but these were spiffy modern build-ings, windows gleaming in the sunshine, walls of red brick sprinkled with occasional light-colored bricks to break up the uniformity of the façade. A blue and orange sign above the main entrance read "Autobot — Seeing the Future."

Martin entered the main lobby and was greeted by a video display reading "Autobot welcomes Professor Martin Quint." He was struck by the size of the security desk, its broad, chest-high front panel, easily fifteen feet wide, presumably housing video monitors for closed-circuit surveillance of the premises. The two uniformed security guards behind the desk were occupied with telephones, one of whom gestured for Martin to wait, giving him a chance to look around. The lobby had a seating area tucked behind the front windows, with three pale green upholstered chairs arrayed around a black metal and glass coffee table next to a magazine rack with literature about the company. A pair of steel double doors with a key-card entry lock was just beyond the secu-rity desk, next to an elevator and a staircase to the upper floor.

The guard finally completed his telephone call and waved Martin over. Yes, Mr. Quint was expected and Mr. Caldicott's assistant would come down to get him, but first the guard needed to copy his photo ID, taking Martin's driver's license into an office behind the desk. A copy.

Of course, for security, a paper trail in case of problems, a stark and needling reminder of the Wilshire man photographing his ID when he had dropped that letter into his life. In hindsight, he understood why Sylvia Palmer had insisted on it. But what if he had refused to sign for the letter? Would he now be in court? In a paternity suit?

The guard emerged some four minutes later with Martin's printed name badge on a lanyard. As the guard returned the license, he said, "You will need to be escorted everywhere, Mr. Quint, as I'm sure you understand." Martin nodded, and the guard picked up the phone and dialed.

Five minutes passed. Martin finally sat down in one of the chairs by the coffee table and began leafing through the promotional materials. Some of the systems looked like they could be mounted on the metal detectors used in airport screening lines or in those new systems being installed in passport-control centers. Others were wall-mounted, all boasting exceptional face-recognition capabilities. The graphics were slick, as was the paper on which they were printed. Slick. Yes, CC was slick. And boastful. It fits.

A young man in navy slacks and a plain light blue shirt appeared at Martin's elbow. "Professor Quint?" Martin turned to him, noting a cherubic face surrounded by brown Botticellian curls. "I'm Kenneth, Mr. Caldicott's executive assistant. If you will come with me, we'll go to his office."

Martin rose and followed Kenneth up the vinyl-tiled staircase to a heavy door with a large, metal-grilled window. Kenneth used his badge to release the lock, and they entered a sunshine-filled atrium with a kitchenette visible to the right and a half-dozen tables and chairs spread out toward the windows, some of which were occupied by pairs of nerdy-looking young men in T-shirts, deep in conversation. The atrium gave way on both sides to a long corridor, with windowed offices to one side and an array of cubicles to the other. Five doors down to the right was CC's office suite. The outer office had two desks, at one of which was a brown-haired young woman who smiled and said nothing. On the left-hand wall was the door to a conference room; on the other,

CC's private office, out of which he popped. "Hello, Martin. Glad you found us okay. I've got my guys in the conference room, eager to meet you. Come on in."

Autobot's conference room was no different from the dozens of such spaces Martin had visited over the years. A long oak table surrounded with nondescript speckled gray upholstered swivel chairs, windows with drapes that could be closed, a projector suspended from the ceiling, a white board and projection screen at one end, and a sideboard on which were a coffee urn and trays of fruit and pastry. Standard issue, all of it.

Three of the chairs were occupied, and CC made the introductions around the table. "This is my team," said CC, "or at least part of it. I've asked them to give you the unclassified intro to the company, with emphasis on our hiring and training needs." Turning to the VP of engineering, he said, "Kaspar. Can you start us off?"

The next ninety minutes were spent in a criss-cross between three PowerPoint presentations on the company's technology, marketing strategy, and personnel plans, punctuated by CC's interruptions to comment on details and a few questions from Martin about scope, and numbers, and growth. Through it all, Martin could feel the excitement and enthusiasm of CC's team, their belief in his vision, and their commitment to success. It was clear, also, that none of his expertise in semiconductor technology would be relevant to Autobot's mission. So what, exactly, did CC expect him to do if he became a consultant? Was this just going to be more seduction on CC's part, or was there substance to it, something Martin could get excited about?

At noon, CC thanked his team members, who shook hands with Martin and departed, leaving CC and Martin alone. "Very impressive," said Martin. "You clearly have a touch for this stuff, and your team loves you."

CC beamed. "I hire very carefully, and then I support the people I hire. It builds loyalty. I haven't lost a senior person since Autobot was started. And when the members of the team really get to know each other, they work better together, and our bottom line benefits."

"So what on earth would you expect me to do to help here?"

"Let's discuss this after lunch," said CC. "We have a cafeteria in the next building, the one where we do most of our engineering development, and a private dining room we use for important visitors like you."

Martin laughed. "You mean important customers, don't you?"

"Yes, actually. Customers. Sort of. We have to be careful with our government customers because they have strict rules about accepting gifts, and meals are considered gifts. So we have a printed menu with prices, prices that fit into their per diem, and they actually do pay us for their lunches. We even create an audit trail in case of questions. We issue receipts in duplicate, and keep our copy attached to a signed chit. It's a bit of a hoot, such fuss and bother over lunch, but we follow the rules to the letter. Anyway, our chef is quite good, and he's expecting us at 12:15, so we should head over. You are allowed to accept our lunch without paying for it."

They left CC's office, went downstairs and followed a path across a small lawn area to the neighboring building. The lobby was less elaborate than in the headquarters, but the security desk was similar and similarly staffed by two guards who waved to CC as he and Martin went up the stairs and through the security door. Instead of a modest atrium, this building's upper floor held a sunny cafeteria with tables for perhaps a hundred diners, half of them full. A number of hands were waved in greeting. "I usually eat with the troops," said CC, as he escorted Martin along the hallway toward the private dining room. "Good for morale. But today, we'll do the upscale thing."

The private dining room had dark wood paneling with brightly colored photographs of New England landscapes adorning the walls and three round tables that Martin guessed could each seat eight, only one of which was set for a meal, with three places. "Who's joining us?" asked Martin.

CC's eyes twinkled. "Someone you know."

Just then, there was a timid knock on the door, and CC went to open it, looking up at his tall guest. "Ah, you must be Gina Farrell. Please come in. I'm CC. CC Caldicott," and he reached out a hand. "A pleasure to meet you."

Gina was baffled, blushing bright red as she accepted the handshake, and with the look of a startled deer, came into the room. Were she not already at maximum blush, she would have blushed even more on seeing Martin. "Professor Quint? I'm not… I mean, I had no idea…"

CC laughed. "Please forgive the surprise, Miss Farrell. Martin had told me you were working here, and I thought it would be fun to get acquainted over lunch, so I'm responsible for the summons you got. Martin has spent the morning learning all about Autobot, and we're now going to enjoy a nice lunch. So please come join us. Have a seat. I want to know all about what it's like to have Martin for an advisor."

Martin was irritated at CC for pulling this kind of stunt, but he managed to keep his composure, banishing as best he could his ridiculous fantasy. "I had no idea, Gina," said Martin. "Really. But I'm always happy to see you, so I can forgive CC for his mystery invitation, if you can." Gina smiled, still hesitant, but she seemed to accept that, at least at lunch, she, and not Martin, was the guest of honor.

A waiter appeared with water and menus as they took seats. There were three seven-dollar entrees: grilled steak tips, a Caesar salad with chicken, and a vegetarian plate with quinoa, grilled Portobello mushrooms, and tomatoes. CC said, "It's on the house, Gina. Order whatever you want."

Gina seemed to catch her breath and restore her composure. She selected the vegetarian plate, with a Diet Coke. Martin followed Gina's lead, but asked that the tomatoes be left off his plate. CC went for steak tips. As the waiter left, CC asked, "So tell me, Gina, how did you manage to get Martin so enthusiastic about you?"

A blush once again colored her face, but she stayed calm enough to answer, telling about how she had been impressed with his lecturing during her CTI admissions tour, and then as a freshman asked him about teaching, and this led to her first project. Once she got this far, she relaxed, began fiddling with her name tag as she spoke, and told the rest of the story more easily, including the report on MOOCs that went to that faculty committee and her work for Martin as a grader during her sophomore year.

"So he's a good teacher?" asked CC.

"Hey, that's enough, CC," said Martin. "It's not fair to put Gina on the spot like that with me sitting here."

"Okay," said CC. "You don't have to answer, but I really would like to hear what you would say."

Gina looked sideways at Martin and said, "He's the best. The best I ever had, anyway. I'm working with Professor Campbell now, and he's okay, but he's not like Professor Quint."

"So you really want to be a teacher? A teacher like him?"

"Absolutely," said Gina, with growing confidence. "But I'm not sure how to get real experience. I do grading now, but I want to try classroom stuff. And if I do the Autobot project for my master's, I won't be able to be a Teaching Assistant in grad school—"

CC interrupted. "So you're the student with the project we're using to apply to CTI?"

"Yes, that's me," said Gina, looking up, smiling and finally fully calm.

The food arrived, and conversation drifted onto less charged topics, such as what Gina did for fun, and what was it like in the dorms at CTI, and was she enjoying her job. Martin was mostly silent as CC and Gina chatted, his eyes following every seductive twitch of that name tag, listening for clues about her private life and hearing none. It was when CC returned to the subject of graduate school that Martin got a hint. "I can go pretty much anywhere," said Gina, "and that's the problem. How to decide. CTI with the master's plan looks really good, but I want to teach, and I'm from California, so maybe I should go back there, maybe Stanford or Berkeley."

CC said, "Well, there's no one better than Martin to advise you about that, so I would encourage you to keep in close touch with him as your plans develop. That's okay with you, Martin?"

"Of course," said Martin, as blandly as he could manage. "My CTI email address still works."

Gina declined dessert with thanks, saying she had a 1:30 meeting with her team. She bid a hasty goodbye, exchanging a handshake with

CC and a look of uncertain meaning with Martin.

CC and Martin returned to CC's office. "Let's talk turkey," said CC. "I want your advice about our training program for new hires and for individuals who are eligible for major promotions. I know you've never done this before, but you have no idea what a natural you are for this kind of thing."

Martin was doubtful. "I can't see what I can add to what you're already doing, and I'm plenty busy. Pardon my French, but your goddam school and my goddam book are already in direct conflict for my time, and I'm planning to try the flipped classroom in the fall and I'll need planning time for that as well, and I also need to find some kind of assistant for the fall class. I'm really reluctant to take on more stuff. And Jenny would kill me if I did."

"I hear you," said CC, "but I'm also persistent. So think about it this way: If you are really committed to understanding how conversation impacts education, you need to step outside the normal classroom environment and test your ideas in an industrial setting. I'm offering you that opportunity, and at a rate you will enjoy. Our usual for someone of your caliber is three thousand a day plus expenses. I'm going to get my contracts guy to draw up a letter agreement that you will get in a few days. In the meantime, think about it, not just as an added job, but as an enrichment to the context for your book."

"Enrichment," thought Martin, doing a quick calculation about what three thousand a day would do for his money problems, for daycare, and for finally getting rid of his obligation to Katie. Suddenly eager for the money if not the work, he fumbled over his words. "I must confess that I hadn't thought about it that way, as an enrichment for the book. But I will... think about it, that is, even if don't know how I could manage the time. Would I have to travel?"

"We've got almost four thousand employees now, sixteen hundred spread around the Boston area, most of the rest at our factories in Kentucky and Ohio, and sales teams, of course, all over. Is travel a problem?"

"A big problem. I might be able to help you here in Andover, but

I really don't want to take on travel commitments. I've got a book to write."

"Of course. We'll manage just from here, at least for a start."

"Okay. I'll think about it. But right now I've got to head into town before the traffic arteries clog up. I'm meeting someone at CTI at three."

Suddenly CC said, "Would Gina do?"

Martin said, "What? Do? What do you mean?"

"How would you rate her as a potential Teaching Assistant for your course in the fall?"

"That's ridiculous. She's going to be a senior. She needs to graduate."

"What if she took a leave and came to Bottlesworth to help you teach? You could give her classroom experience and get some badly needed help, killing two birds with one stone. We could defer her CTI cooperative program for a year, so after the term with you, or even a full year, she could come back to her senior year, and then her master's program. She'd be in great shape and with terrific teaching experience. Win, win, win. Whaddya think?"

"Why do you do this stuff? Push on other people's lives? First my life with the new school, now Gina's life?"

"Hey, don't get angry. I just see opportunities where other people see problems. I've always done that. And mostly, my ideas are good ones. So give it a thought. I won't mention it to Miss Farrell or anyone else unless you approve of the idea."

With a promise that he would think about the suggestion, Martin said his thanks and goodbyes, and left for his meeting with Harry Huang in Cambridge.

- - -

Late that evening, Jenny and Martin were sitting side by side at their desks. Jenny suddenly looked up from her email and announced that her next Chicago trip wouldn't be until after July Fourth.

Martin, his voice dripping with irony, asked, "So we have, what, three weeks with you at home? Good news. Great news."

"Martin, there you go again, bitching about my travel. For the zillionth time, it's time to hire somebody. I've found two other daycare centers in BJ that have space. We can visit first thing next week, check them out."

"It's not in our budget."

"Pardon my French, love, but that's bullshit. You have this hang-up about daycare, and how it will do damage. Get over it. And that CC guy. He's throwing money at you. What did you say he offered today? Three thousand a day for hand-holding their training program? You could drive down in the morning, drive back at night, pay for a sitter for a whole month, and have change left over. Do you realize how hard I have to work to bring in three thousand net?"

"So you're suggesting that I take his job? For the money? Add to what you call my overload?"

"I'm not suggesting anything. But don't use money as a reason for peeing and moaning about child care. We can afford a sitter when we need one. You're just too damned hung up on leaving your kids with someone other than their mother."

"So where are we with all this?"

"We're both pissed off, that's where we are, and I don't like it any better than you do."

-   -   -

The next morning, right after breakfast, JJ was helping Ellen with her build-and-smash-the-blocks routine by making super-tall towers, the two of them exploding in laughter after Ellen's "Boom." Jenny and Martin had stayed at the breakfast table.

"I know I was scornful last night about taking CC's job for the money," said Martin, "but in the cold light of morning, it might make some sense. If I do the consulting thing, once or maybe twice a month, we could hire a regular child-care person, five days a week if needed, and we could stop fighting about travel. Provided we could find someone we trust, of course."

"You mean it? Really?"

Martin looked up. "I guess I do, but here's the deal. I really hated the daycare crap Helen and I were dumped in. I want Ellen to have a real family experience growing up. So — and this is the point — if we're both gonna be able to work, I would prefer we get our own sitter, somebody who becomes a regular part of the home environment."

"So you mean a nanny, right?"

"I guess that's what I'm saying. Hire a nanny. If I'm bringing in another six thou' a month, we could certainly afford it. Did I tell you about Gounod?"

Jenny shook her head. "You mean the composer?"

"Yeah, Gounod. When I was driving to CTI the other day, they were playing his *Faust* opera on the radio, and all I could think of was that CC was the devil, tempting me, and not just with money."

"I thought Faust was tempted by a woman," said Jenny with a crinkly smile. "Did he dangle a babe in front of you?"

"No, no, there was no babe. I mean … He's so fucking quick, and he just bubbles with ideas. It's intriguing. But getting overloaded? Yeah, that worries me."

"Well it worries me, too … a lot … so a nanny. Yes, a nanny. The fact is, neither of us really wants to be alone on double-kid child care for days at a time. Maybe I should ask around?"

"Yes. Do that."

"I'll ask Helen. She knows everybody, or at least more everybodies than I do. And I'll be shopping today for the party. Anything special—"

"Party? What party?"

"My staff party. Did you forget? They're all coming to the cottage on Sunday. Six adults and maybe four kids? Weather forecast is good. Noon cookout."

"It's probably on my calendar, but yes, I forgot. A Freudian forgot, since I was hoping to do some writing this weekend."

"Freudian or not, they're coming and you're the grill master. Any special orders?"

"No, just the usual. Burgers, dogs, chips, potato salad, slaw, beer, watermelon, you know."

- - -

Martin sat by the fire, listening as Jenny reported to her mother about the party.

"Yes, Mom, JJ and Ellen are just fine.... When did you say? July Fourth? That might work. Is Dad well enough to travel?... No, I have to go back to Chicago and I'm not sure of dates yet, but it won't be over July Fourth.... Yes, we're getting close to a furnishings deal. A big one. My team is so excited. Our first shot at a big sale. They're collaborating really well on the various designs of... Yeah, we had the party. Yesterday. And the best news is that I found someone to do regular child care.... At the party. The wife of our upholstery guy.... No, no. Not him, we changed. Her name is Kuc. Kuc Diem. No, not Thailand. Vietnam. Her husband — his name is Van — he has the furniture maintenance contract from the college. But he's a genius with leather and silk and brocades, so we don't use the Portland guy anymore. They're both refugees, boat people. Can she drive? Of course.... Yes, we're going to watch her drive and verify. Don't worry.... Two high-school-age children. No, they didn't come. Just Kuc and Van. But Pierre and Anna brought their kids, a boy four and a girl two. So cute. I put JJ in charge of keeping them happy. He decided on a game of follow the leader, and... yes, Mom, follow the leader, and he marched around, and waved his arms, and jumped and rolled on the ground and each of the little ones did their best. It was a riot.... Martin's fine. Too busy, though, and seems down in the dumps sometime, drifting off to somewhere else. I'm worried that he's getting overloaded, but you know him, can't say no to anyone. Anyway, I'll check with him about July Fourth for a visit and let you know. That's good. G'bye. Love you."

Down in the dumps, am I? Only if the DNA comes out wrong. Then, "the dumps" won't come close to describing it. More like the seventh level of Dante's inferno.

- - -

On Tuesday morning, Jenny and Martin, each separately, accompanied

Kuc driving Jenny's big van, and they agreed that even with her small stature, she could handle it just fine. A deal was struck, with scope and timing details still somewhat vague, but Martin and Jenny now had a nanny, starting that very moment.

Martin left for the campus to meet with Evelyn Kim, both to explore her level of interest in expanding programs directed toward engineering and entrepreneurship, and to test the waters about support for a teaching assistant. She responded with enthusiasm about the new program, adding her view on how it should be organized. But she poured ice water on Martin's hopes for a teaching assistant. "If you have a grant, it's fine, but without, I'm sorry, we have no such budget."

"Even for an important experiment?" asked Martin.

"Even for an important experiment," answered Evelyn.

Returning to his office, he found an email from Glenda. She was back in Freeport, exams completed. Could they meet tomorrow?

* **14** *

"So how was England?" asked Martin as he and Glenda went down the hall for Martin's coffee and Glenda's cuppa.

"Blustery," said Glenda with twinkling laugh, "and I don't mean just the weather. My soon-to-be ex-husband, somewhat under protest, has taken his own flat where he can shag his lady love *sans interruption*, and my solicitor is drawing up our financial settlement. He's actually being very generous, which is, I guess, a measure of how quickly he wants me out of his life."

Martin grimaced, as an image of Katie's red lipstick calligraphy and her demonic divorce lawyer drifted before his eyes. They started back toward his office, drinks in hand.

"I'm glad it's getting settled, and I'm really sorry that he... that you're going through—"

"Oh, no," said Glenda. "Sorry is the wrong word. I'm finally free to look for a better man, someone who wants both me and a family."

Did Katie find a better man once she had freed herself from Martin and his infidelity with Camille? Martin had no idea. He sent his money each month and never heard anything back. But he had, for sure, found a better woman. How odd that committing the sin of adultery could have opened the door to a better life. But this nonsense about Gina simply had to end. That would be the road to hell, for sure, and Andrew was already providing enough options for ending up there.

"And the student situation?" he asked as they got seated at his conference table, an image of Gina floating in front of him.

"Blustery, too. Or rather, chilling. As I suspected, at the height of his upset he told other students who ended up telling their tutors and now the whole college looks at me askance. My Dean is sympathetic, but..."

"I know what you mean. We had a nasty case at CTI. Facu faculty — not a student thing — but nasty. Probably affected a t case. I'll tell you about it sometime. For now, though, I'd rather talk about how on earth we're going to evaluate the flipped-classroom experiment."

"I've several ideas," said Glenda, and they dove into the subject. An hour later, the white board was full of notes; the progress had been immense. They were about to take a coffee break when Martin's phone rang. It was Trevor. "You've got news?" asked Martin.

Trevor didn't mince words. "The DNA test was positive, my friend. Andrew Quint Kaminsky is your son. Just got the report faxed to me, certified by the lab that did it, and even a technical summary supporting the conclusion."

"I'm just finishing up a meeting. Can I call you back in a few minutes?"

Glenda took the hint. "An important call?" she asked as Martin hung up the phone.

"Yes, very," said Martin. "I guess we should pick this up later. I'm not sure when, but I'll let you know."

Glenda left and Martin dialed Trevor's number.

"So it's true?"

"It's true."

"Shit. So what do I do now?"

"I suggest we both get on a plane and go to Pittsburgh. Meet the boy. Meet with the lawyers. Get an agreement on how to proceed."

"How soon?"

"Yesterday," said Trevor.

"I could go on Friday. Jesus. The last thing I need right now is another child."

"How soon can you confirm plans?"

"I'll have talk to Jenny tonight, and it could get ugly. You should listen to police radio in case of a homicide."

Then he ran for the men's room.

- - -

Martin spent the rest of the afternoon rehearsing the speech he was going to have to make that night, unable to find a pathway to the truth that wouldn't set off dynamite. Through dinner and the kid-to-bed ritual, that was all he could think about. Bombs going off. No way to prevent it.

Once the house was quiet, Martin suggested they take their decaf to the living room. They got settled, Martin took a deep breath, and started. "Okay. I've got something important to say, and you're not going to like it. That mysterious letter from Pittsburgh that came a few weeks ago? It's a mess. You remember when we went to see *Madame Butterfly* and you asked about Pinkerton?"

"Yes, about taking the child. Why?"

"It appears that I may be a Pinkerton." And Martin, in spite of his many rehearsals, couldn't manage to keep from weeping.

Jenny sat bolt upright and stared at her husband with an expression halfway between fear and disgust. "What? What are you saying?"

It took a full minute for Martin to regain enough composure to continue. "Here's the story," he said, choking through more tears. "It seems that just before I left Pittsburgh to come to Cambridge, I made a woman, my girlfriend at the time, I got her pregnant."

Jenny was a sphinx, waiting.

"I had been dating her for half a year, a little more maybe, but when I decided to move to Cambridge, she didn't want to leave her family, so we split up. I never heard from her after that."

"Until now? Is that what the letter was about? She's suing you for support?"

"I wish it was that simple. I'd happily pay support, use money from Autobot, and be done with it. But it's more complicated. She and her mother and her mother's sister were all killed in a horrible car crash some weeks ago. There's a surviving boy, now a complete orphan, named Andrew. He wasn't in the car, not hurt. But apparently, in one of Frances's diaries — that was her name, Frances Kaminsky — there was a note that says I'm Andrew's father, which is how they found me. And she gave him Quint as a middle name."

"My God, Martin. What are you going to do?"

"Trevor said I should take the DNA test, and I did."

"And it says you're the father?"

Martin couldn't hold it together. He once again wept with his head in his hands.

"How could you not know?" Jenny shrieked. "That's impossible."

"She never told me. That's how. We had already decided to split up. It must have happened on that last—"

"You're a grown-up. Didn't you use birth control, for Christ's sake? How can you tell me..."

"I was drunk. It's as simple as that. We went to the fireworks, then to her apartment, and then we got drunk. I don't remember anything else except driving home."

"She wasn't on the pill?"

"No."

"Drunk. A drunk fuck. Holy smokes." A silence descended on the unhappy pair, the way the fog creeps across Sagadahoc Bay, except that fog is peaceful. This was just plain scary. Jenny continued. "That poor kid. Left alone like that. I know something about being left alone. What do you know about him? Do you have to take him?"

"I've never met him, so all I know is that he exists and he's mine. As for taking him, it's not clear," said Martin, sniffling his way back to control. "That's certainly one option. The alternative would be to find a family in Pittsburgh to take care of him until he's old enough to take care of himself."

"And he's how old now?"

"He's twelve."

Jenny's jaw trembled, fighting back tears. "I feel really sorry for this kid, this drunken-fuck child of yours, but how could we take him, a twelve-year-old, into this family? JJ would be crushed."

"Don't call him a drunken-fuck child," said Martin. "He's a child. He's my child. He has a name. It's Andrew. I didn't intend to start his life, but apparently I did. We've gotta deal with it. As for JJ, we don't know what it'll do to him, but you're right about one thing. I don't want to take him either."

"This just isn't fair," she moaned, finally losing her grip and going over the cliff. In between her sobs, she choked out her words. "I've had enough goddam wrenchings in my life. So now what? A son? Jesus, Martin. It's enough. I'm not ready for a teenaged son. Not yet, anyway, until JJ grows up."

"Trevor says I need to go to Pittsburgh right away. On Friday, if possible. I've gotta meet the boy. Talk to the attorneys. Do you want to come? We could leave the kids with Helen. Or Kuc, maybe?"

"Not me. No way. It's your mess to clean up."

"Okay, I'll go alone, but I am going."

-   -   -

Early Friday morning, Trevor picked up Martin and they drove to Portland to catch their flight to Pittsburgh. Wilkins and Palmer was located in one of those buildings on Grant Street that simply teemed with lawyers. Close to the courts. The offices were on the fourth floor. A glass door opposite the elevator with the firm name and logo painted in gold leaf led to a receptionist's desk staffed by a nameless woman with dark brown skin and elaborately braided long hair. She took their names and asked them to take a seat, gesturing to the chairs. "Would either of you gentlemen like coffee, or some water, perhaps?" Martin and Trevor declined and settled down to wait, Martin's chest tight, and his pulse racing as if he had just completed one of his three-mile runs.

A few minutes later, Sylvia Palmer, middle-aged and middle-shaped, in a skirted navy business suit with a frilly-fronted blouse, came to greet them. "Very nice to meet you both, and I'm pleased you could come so quickly. Andrew is expected in about half an hour. He'll be accompanied by his friend's mother. In the meantime, perhaps we can talk about options?"

She led the way to a conference room that looked out toward the south, the river glistening in the distance through a crevice between two buildings. "I'm not sure how familiar you are with Pennsylvania law, but there are two guardianship issues here. One is the guardianship of the person, of Andrew. That's the most important one to settle first, because right now, in the eyes of the State of Pennsylvania, I'm his guardian, a situation I want to make as temporary as possible. But as Andrew's biological parent and with no other claimants on the scene, it will be very easy to get you certified as his guardian in the view of the state. He can then live with your family or with anyone else you approve of."

Martin asked, "Aren't I automatically the guardian, though? As his biological parent?"

Sylvia smiled. "According to the terms of Ms. Kaminsky's will, with his grandmother and great aunt both dead, I filed paperwork to become Andrew's testamentary guardian. I'm also executor of the estate, all three estates. I'm eager to transfer that guardianship to you. It would require suitable filings in Orphans' Court, and possibly an appearance."

"Who's he staying with now?"

"He has a friend from school, Lavelle Walton. But his mother made it clear that we can't plan on them long term. She's a single parent, doesn't really have room for him, and has an ailing relative to care for on top of everything else."

"Aren't there other families where he might be welcome? I mean really welcome, not just dumped?"

"That's a problem," said Sylvia. "Andrew hasn't suggested anyone. He doesn't seem to have many friends. And since his mother is no longer with us.... We could certainly help you look, if that's what you want us to do, but we felt that it would be best to get your input before taking such action."

Trevor spoke up. "What's the second guardianship? I assume that's the estate?"

"Exactly," said Sylvia. "There's actually quite a lot of money here. Until the estate is settled, we maintain fiduciary responsibility. But if Mr. Quint becomes Andrew's guardian of the person, an accompanying request to have him become guardian of the estate would be natural. Oddly enough," turning to Martin, "since you're already a natural parent, it's only the estate guardianship that will require us to gather references of your good character, that sort of thing. Given your professional stature, though, I doubt that the court would refuse, but we would still have to file a proper dossier and motion."

The telephone on the sideboard buzzed, and Sylvia got up to answer. "He's here? Good. Please show them in."

The conference room door opened and in walked a half-boy, half-man, temporarily trapped in that imponderable purgatory of early adolescence, about five foot four, square shouldered and square jawed like Martin, with brown straight hair like Martin, but with cautious, almond-shaped eyes that reminded him of Frances. A young-looking, narrow-featured black woman, no taller than Andrew, came in behind him, and was acknowledged by Sylvia and Martin in silence.

"Hello, Andrew," said Sylvia. "This is Martin Quint. He's your father."

Martin reached out a hand and Andrew, still with cautious eyes, shook it, but said nothing. "I'm sure you find this strange," said Martin. "I certainly do. Until a few days ago, I didn't know I had a son. And I was really sorry to learn that Frances, I mean your mother, had died. It must be awful for you." Andrew remained silent.

Sylvia did introductions for Trevor and Janet Walton. There followed an awkward pause as the five took seats around the conference table.

"I'm curious," said Martin. "Did your mother ever tell you anything about me?"

"Nope," said Andrew.

"So what did she say when you asked about your father?"

"She said that he went away."

"It's true. I did go away. I loved your mother, very much, but we decided not to get married because I was going to leave Pittsburgh and she didn't want to leave her family. But she never told me she was going to have a baby. I guess she decided . . ."

"Last year, I asked her, but she said she didn't want to."

"Contact me? Is that what you mean?"

"Yeah. I asked her. But she wouldn't even tell me your name."

"Did she say why?"

"'Cause you left her. That's what she said."

"Well, I'm very sorry. I can't say now what I would have done if I had known your mother was pregnant. We're not smart enough to be able to figure those things out. But this is today. You need a family, and I'm going to do whatever is necessary to help you get on with your life. Do you understand?"

Andrew nodded, but said nothing.

Sylvia said, "May I suggest something? Andrew doesn't know you and you don't know him. Can you stay in town for a few days? Spend some time with him? We've done enough homework about you to know that you would be a responsible host."

"But would Andrew like that?" asked Martin, looking directly into his son's eyes.

Andrew nodded, but again said nothing.

"We were planning to fly back tonight. I'll have to call home, but I should be able to stay at least for the weekend, maybe through Monday."

Phone numbers and contacts were exchanged, Martin shook hands with Andrew again, saying he would see him again soon, as soon as he could change his travel arrangements, and Andrew and Janet departed.

Before he and Trevor left, Martin asked Sylvia about getting school and medical records. She said she would collect them for him, possibly before he went back to Maine.

"Grab some coffee?" asked Trevor, as they exited the building.

They walked around several blocks until they found a Starbucks and were lucky to grab an open two-seater table.

"You handled that well," said Trevor. "You said you would do what he needed without promising to take him in personally. Exactly right."

Martin had a distant look in his eyes. "Just before my father died, which was before little Ellen was born, he said that something special happens when you have a child of your own. At the time, of course, I didn't know what he was talking about, but when I picked up Ellen for the first time, it hit me like a hurricane. I was overwhelmed. And just now, up in that office, it hit me again. That's my son. He looks like a son of mine should look. I'm not gonna let him down."

"Does that mean you'll take him to Maine?"

"That depends on Jenny. She's really upset just now. Blaming me for messing up, even though I had no idea."

"Were you surprised that Mrs. Walton is black?"

"A little."

"So I have to ask. Was Frances black or even part black?"

"No. Polish descent and thoroughly Caucasian. Why?"

"Odd that a black family would be the one to step up to take him in."

"Maybe, but these days, kids make friends more easily than when we were in school. JJ"s best friend at the beach is black. Nice kid. Nice parents. It all feels perfectly normal."

They sipped their coffees in silence. Then he called Jenny.

"Hello, love. I've met him. Yes, he looks sort of like me. No, he hasn't said hardly anything, but... Can you wait a minute?... No. They're going to arrange for me to spend some time with him over the weekend, so I'm staying in.... Until Monday afternoon.... Well this time, dammit, you'll just have to reschedule whatever it is.... I can't leave here without... Okay, we'll talk tonight." Martin looked at the now silent phone.

Trevor said nothing other than a goodbye as he headed for the airport.

-    -   -

Martin changed his return flight, booked a room at the Wyndham near his old haunts at Carnegie Mellon, picked up a rental car, and did a little shopping — toiletries, a spare shirt, socks, underwear, and a small overnight bag. He called Janet to schedule a pick-up of Andrew in the morning. For dinner, he decided on La Cucina, one of Frances's favorites. It was a way to connect with her memory, to reconstruct the good part of their togetherness. Maybe her son — his son — would do that, too. Time would tell.

After dinner, he called Jenny again. This time they were able to have a conversation. Jenny apologized for blowing up earlier. She had been unable to believe that Martin didn't know about the child, even in the face of his persistent and consistent denials, and she was absolutely furious that Martin had kept it secret for so long. She felt betrayed, as if Martin no longer trusted her, hiding things from her, not sharing, a transgression Martin had to acknowledge, which he did. Jenny said she was conflicted about the boy — very sorry for him and his situation but not at all eager to take him in. And after thinking about it, she could now believe that he didn't know about him because, said with a tiny giggle, he just wasn't that good a liar. This brought a laugh from Martin, scattering at least some of the shards from her earlier explosion. Jenny asked what he was like. Quiet. Probably still in deep shock. So what's going to happen next? Martin confirmed that he was obligated to get Andrew settled — no, not legally — morally and emotionally. He would spend a few days in Pittsburgh to get to know him a little, and see what made sense. When Jenny repeated that she hoped they didn't have to bring him to live with them, Martin agreed. He was going to meet as many friends as Andrew had and see what might work. But he made it clear that, yes, Andrew was his son, and strange as it sounded to Jenny's ears, she was his *de-facto* stepmother. "I know," said Jenny. "I know."

After the call, he checked with the hotel concierge about getting tickets for a Pirates baseball game, went back to his room, and did a Google search for things to do with kids in Pittsburgh.

* 15 *

The Waltons lived in the lower floor of a two-family house toward the east end of a gracefully aging neighborhood. Martin was greeted at their door by a lanky, chocolate-colored boy with a high-top fade haircut. He looked a bit taller than Andrew. "Are you Lavelle?" asked Martin.

"Yes, boss," he said, half smiling. "That's me. Andrew's coming. So you his dad?"

"It seems that I am. It's a surprise for me as much as for Andrew, but yes, I'm his dad. Is your mother home?"

"She's at work already. Me and Andrew is all that's here."

"And you'll be okay alone after we go out?"

Lavelle laughed. "Yes, boss. I'm used to being home by myself."

Andrew came to the door with a small backpack and those cautious eyes. Martin asked, "Hey, Andrew. You ready to go out for a bit?"

Andrew nodded, and with his head hung down ever so slightly, followed Martin to his car. As they were getting ready to climb in, Martin asked, "Do you like baseball?"

Andrew looked up quickly. "You mean to play?"

"Or watch. Either one."

"I don't get a chance to play much, but I like the Pirates."

"Would you like to go to the game tonight?" Andrew nodded, and for the first time showed the hint of a smile.

Martin got out his phone as Andrew opened the car door and got in. "The concierge, please? Hi, Martin Quint here, room 305. I spoke to you last night about Pirates tickets? Yes, please. Two tickets. Best seats available." There was a long pause while Martin shrugged and waved the phone while Andrew watched. At last the voice on the other end returned and Martin responded. "Behind third base? Great.... No, we

can pick them up at the will-call. The game's at seven? Okay, thanks."
Martin hung up and got behind the wheel. "We're in luck. Two box
seats behind third base. Is there a place near the ball park that you like
to eat?"

"I don't know. Only been to one game before, with my school, and
we didn't eat there. Mostly, I just watch on television."

Martin said, "We have a wide open day. Your choice. There's the
IMAX at the Science Center, a trampoline park, the amusement park,
or take a walk along the river, or the zoo. Whaddya like?"

"I dunno. Do we hafta go somewhere? What I really want is to
go home."

"You mean your place? Your mom's place?"

"Yeah, but the lawyer lady said I shouldn't go there by myself. It
would get them, and maybe me, in trouble. So I haven't been."

"Do you have a key?"

"Yup."

"Let me make a call. I want the lawyer lady to know, so there's
no trouble."

Martin dialed Sylvia Palmer's cell phone and left a message. "This
is Martin Quint. I wanted to let you know that Andrew and I will be
heading to his apartment in ten minutes. If you object, call my cell."

Andrew sat in the front seat of the car, immobile, while Martin
waited. A few minutes later, the phone range. "Hi, thanks for getting
back to me," said Martin. "Andrew said what he wanted to do was go
home, and I want to take him.... Yes, he has a key. I was just being
careful about protocol. So it's okay? ... Great, thanks."

"We're good," said Martin. "You can navigate."

- - -

Andrew's home — Frances's home — was a tall-windowed condo on
the first floor of a converted lime-green Victorian-style house, its steep
roof interrupted by dormered windows on the third floor, poking their
way out as if gasping for air. The neighborhood was two notches more
upscale than where Frances lived the last time they were together, but

the furnishings were the same — what Jenny would call "colonial precious" — neat but unspectacular, a mix of ivory tones and darkly finished oak and maple, lightly colored and understated floral upholstery and wallpapers, oatmeal-colored wall-to-wall carpeting, frilly semitransparent curtains. It was a shock to Martin to see these furnishings with new eyes, with Jenny's eyes.

As soon as they entered, Andrew headed for his bedroom in the back. Martin did not follow, preferring to absorb the atmosphere of his former lover's space, asking it to speak to him about the years in which she had raised their son. But it wouldn't speak. It was just as silent as Andrew, as silent as Frances had been all those years. He was not welcomed; he was tolerated.

Andrew came out and asked, "Would it be okay with the lawyer lady if I stayed here while you're in town? And you, too? Both of us?"

"You really want to do that?"

"Yeah. I miss my stuff."

"And your mom?"

"Yeah. My home."

Once again Martin called Sylvia Palmer, and, once again, she approved.

"Listen, Andrew, I need to check out of the hotel. Come with me. It won't take long. Then we can get a pizza and come back here for lunch. Okay?"

For the second time today, Andrew cracked the tiniest smile. "Okay," he said, quiet, with cautious eyes. "I like pizza."

-   -   -

Over lunch at Frances's kitchen table, Martin tried to get Andrew talking about school, about sports, about his friends, but he deferred and dodged. School was okay, he did some sports, mostly basketball although he preferred soccer. Lavelle was his best friend, but he wouldn't elaborate. Instead he said, "I got a lot of stuff to ask you. Stuff I wanted Mom…" Andrew clammed up.

"It's okay," said Martin. "Ask away."

Andrew looked Martin face-on and asked, "Why'd you leave

"A fair question. First of all, and I said this yesterday but it' times hard to believe. I didn't know when I left that your mom was pregnant. We had decided, both of us, that we were not going to get married. It wasn't just me. It wasn't just your mom. It was both of us. So when I left, I thought your mom and I had an agreement."

"But why'd you leave Pittsburgh? If you'd stayed…"

"You're right. If I stayed, I might have married your mom, and her life would have been different, and my life would have been different, and, for sure, your life would have been different. I left to take a job at a different college. That's why I left."

"So your job was more important than my mom?"

Holy shit. Tears started down Martin's cheeks. This unknown twelve-year-old kid had pierced his armor, cutting through to his essence with one simple question. Yes, his job was more important. His job had always been more important. Ask Frances. Ask Katie. Hell, ask Jenny. At least with Jenny, he was trying.

Andrew sat quietly as Martin gradually recovered his composure and rambled his way through to an answer. "This is hard for me, Andrew, very hard, and I hope you'll try to understand this. Grown-ups have to make a lot of difficult choices in life. Who to marry. Where to live. How to live. Some of us are fortunate enough to have some kind of special talent. Some are musicians, some are artists, some are actors or even politicians. I'm one of those people. I have a special talent for doing science and for college teaching. Some people with a special talent waste it. They do drugs, or drink booze, and then their talent is destroyed. But most of us feel a compelling need to put it to work, to make something out of it. In my case, this meant going to the most intense, the most competitive, the absolutely toughest scientific professor job I could find. I was here at Carnegie Mellon. That's where I met your mother. And we loved each other. We truly did. But when the Cambridge Technology Institute in Massachusetts offered me a position — a better, tougher, more competitive position at a school with even more brilliant students — I felt a strong need to take that job. So

I agreed to move. But your mother didn't want to move. She had to make a hard decision, too. She wanted to be with her family. Her family meant more to her than I did. And, I guess the way you asked, my new job meant more to me than she did. We agreed. We didn't fight. We each made a choice not to marry. She chose her family over me. I chose my job over her. We both chose. Can you understand that? We both chose. Not just me."

Andrew sat motionless for a long time, staring at his feet. Then he took a long drink of his Coke, finishing it off with the whistley gurgly sounds of his straw sucking out the last drops.

"Can I ask you a question?" asked Martin. Andrew looked toward Martin and nodded.

"Do you have any idea why your mom never told me about you? Did she ever say…"

"All she would say was that you left."

"Was she angry at me?"

"I dunno. Maybe. Would you have married her if you knew? About me, I mean?"

"I don't know. Honestly, I don't know. We can't go back and fill in things that didn't happen. That's why life is different from science."

Andrew looked up sharply. "What does that mean?"

"Well, in science, you get to try things and change the conditions and then try them again. In life, you get only one shot each time. You marry or you don't marry. You stay or you leave. There's never a way to figure out what would have happened if you made the other choice."

"So you wouldn't have married her?"

"I don't know. I might have. But she might have not wanted me to marry her, even though she was pregnant. Maybe she felt that if she told me about you, I would feel I had to marry her, and then we wouldn't be happy. Maybe she thought it was better to raise you by herself than to be married to me. I just don't know. And we can never know."

"So is it always like this?"

"You mean, you get one choice and can't go back?"

"Yeah. That."

"Yes. It's always like that. I always felt sorry that your mother and I split up, ashamed in a way because I had disappointed her. I never found out how she felt about it because I never spoke to her again. Neither of us tried to go back."

Andrew took a big breath and blew a long whoosh of an exhale. "So what's gonna happen to me? Am I gonna have to leave Pittsburgh too?"

"We need to talk about that. A lotta talking."

-    -   -

After lunch, Martin and Andrew drove to the trampoline place a few miles outside the city. Since Andrew was under eighteen, Martin had to sign a release for him, and it said, in large italics, *"Must be signed by the parent or legal guardian appointed by the state."* Martin took a deep breath, signed in the space, and wrote "parent" after his name. When the attendant asked whether he was really the parent, since the child's last name was Kaminsky, not Quint, Andrew spoke up and said, "My middle name is Quint. This is my dad."

Andrew, it seemed, had been there before with several friends from school, and knew what to do. He could go sky high on each bounce and do somersaults and various kinds of roll maneuvers. Martin pulled out his iPhone and took a video of his acrobatics to send to Jenny. Then he decided to risk it himself.

Trampoline was a completely new experience for Martin, and his floppy style got Andrew laughing. They spent another half hour, at which point Martin called a halt, claiming risk to his back if they did anymore. Martin suggested they go directly to the ballpark and get there early enough to see the players take batting practice. Andrew smiled. "Never been to batting practice," he said.

The Pirates' game was a big hit. The Pirates were playing the Philadelphia Phillies. Martin, as a fan of the Boston Red Sox in the American League, wasn't familiar with the players on either of the two National League teams, but Andrew was. He knew the entire Pirates lineup, even the batting averages of some of players, and most of the Phillies as well. He ate hot dogs and popcorn and lemonade and cotton candy and kept score. When the Pirates got a runner on base and the count went to two balls and one strike, Andrew said to watch for the hit-and-run.

Martin asked, "You know the difference between a hit-and-run and just plain stealing the base?"

"Yeah. They do it on a count where the pitcher pretty much has to throw a strike, like two and one. The runner takes off so the second baseman runs over to cover the base. That leaves a hole on the right side where the hitter tries to place the ball. He swung all right, but he missed, and the guy was thrown out. If it was a straight steal, the hitter wouldn't have swung 'cause the pitch was really low."

Martin heard all this with amazement, with respect, and with the half-dawning of affection, suggesting that behind that sphinx-like mask, that quiet born of shock and tragedy, was a real live boy, with interests and passions and brains and personality.

The Pirates won the game in the most exciting fashion possible, with a walk-off home run in the bottom of the ninth inning. Andrew cheered, and as they were walking toward Martin's car, he recapped the game, commenting on each of the players' performances. The trampoline park and the ball game had clearly swept away, at least temporarily, the cloud of caution in Andrew's eyes.

When they got home, Martin had a haunting sense of Frances's presence in spite of the sterility left behind by the lawyers, who must have gone through the apartment and arranged for it to be thoroughly cleaned. The beds were not made up and there was not a shred of food in the kitchen. He guessed that they had taken an inventory of the contents, the kind of thing that, at some point, had to be done. Andrew located the sheets and towels, and they made up the beds together, laughing as they flipped out the folded sheets and got mixed up over which way to hold them. Andrew said he didn't want to take a shower, but Martin did, so Andrew went off to bed, leaving Martin to his nighttime preparations. It was too late to call Jenny, but he sent an email with a report on the day and attached the video of Andrew doing trampoline. Then he lay down to sleep in Frances's bed, imagining her body next to his but still unable to recall their last night together.

-    -   -

Martin didn't sleep well and awoke early. He called Jenny. She had viewed the video, and asked what Andrew was like. "He seems like a nice kid," said Martin. "Not sullen or especially angry, although he nailed my butt yesterday, asking whether my job had been more important than his mother."

"He asked that?" said Jenny. "As direct as that?"

"Yeah, as direct as that, and as you said, I'm not a good liar. I had to answer yes. But then I tried to explain that we both decided, together, not to marry. It wasn't just me leaving her. That's a tough thing for a kid to digest. He's gotta feel that I abandoned him, regardless of the facts. And I can't tell how bad he hurts inside. But mostly, he seems scared about what's gonna happen to him. I'll be talking to Mrs. Walton tonight. But I haven't been able to extract names of other friends or other options. Maybe things will loosen up today, and he'll talk more."

Just as Martin ended the call, Andrew came into the living room in his pajamas, yawning. "We'll have to go out for breakfast," said Martin. "You have a preference?"

"Is IHOP okay?" asked Andrew.

"Sure. You have a favorite thing there?"

"Blueberry pancakes."

-    -   -

It was a day of activities — the Science Center, an IMAX movie about pandas, lunch at a neighborhood deli, and some quiet time at home during which Martin told Andrew about his family, but just the highlights: a wife, two kids, living in a college town, the cottage at the beach. But he made no mention of George's sudden death and did not share his own experience of growing up without a mother at home.

It was time to go to the Waltons' for dinner. The minute they arrived, Andrew disappeared with Lavelle, leaving Martin with Janet, who was putting the finishing touches on a dinner of meatloaf and mashed potatoes. He asked if he could help and she directed him on setting the table and cutting up a cantaloupe for dessert. As these preparations were underway, Martin tried to test the waters.

"I must say how impossible it is for me to thank you enough for taking Andrew in."

"He's a nice boy," said Janet. "And he's good company for Lavelle. My hours at the hospital keep changing, and I don't like leaving Lavelle alone so much. So having Andrew here is helpful, at least in that way. But I can't do it much longer. It's just too much."

"I understand you're also caring for an elderly relative?"

"Yes, my aunt. She's getting along in years and is doing poorly. I'd like to get her out of her apartment and into assisted living, but we can't afford it."

"Is she close by?"

"It's only six blocks, but sometimes it feels like six miles. I would take her in here, but we ain't got the space unless Lavelle sleeps in the parlor."

"Can I ask? How's Andrew's mood been since... I mean, lately."

"With me, he's silent mostly. Poor child, losing his momma and grandma like that. But with Lavelle, they yakking all the time, and doing that computer thing, whatever it is."

"Are there other friends? I mean do you know of any? You have a lot on your hands, but it would make sense to find a real friend and a home for Andrew."

"You mean you ain't taking him home with you?"

"Not right away. This is all very new for me, there's a lot to straighten out."

"Yeah, but ain't you taking him when all that's done?"

"I'm not sure yet. Part of it is what Andrew wants. I'm not sure he wants to leave Pittsburgh. And it would be a big adjustment for my family."

"You mean more than the adjustment I've made to take him in?"

"No, but similar."

"You married, Mr. Quint?"

"Yes, and—"

"So it ain't similar. You got help."

"True, but I've got two children at home, six and almost two, and they're a handful."

"Your wife work?"

"Yes. We both work. Are the lawyers helping you out with some money while you've got Andrew here?"

"They give me eighty a week, to cover food and all. It helps."

"Would it make a difference to you if the amount were larger?"

Janet had finished her dinner preparation. She stood up as tall as her five-foot-four frame would allow and said, "Mr. Quint. Sounds to me like you're trying to sell your son. That boy belongs with his father, with his natural family."

Martin felt his face redden. "I'm sorry if I gave that impression. That's not at all what's happening. The most important thing is a good living situation for Andrew. But there is some insurance money, and if money can help, it should be used. I'm not trying to sell him." But of course, he was, and he knew it. And was ashamed of it.

Janet called the boys in for dinner, and during the meal, Martin managed to get the two boys to talk about their school, who was cool, who were jerks, which teachers they liked, what sports they did. Lavelle liked to play pick-up basketball games at the local park. Andrew preferred soccer, but it was easier to join Lavelle's games than to find welcoming soccer teams, so he struggled with basketball. He said he usually got picked last when they made teams. *Ouch*, thought Martin.

After the meal, Martin and Andrew returned home, where the silence of the unspoken filled the rooms. Martin tried to find a pathway into conversation. "I'm going back to Maine tomorrow, so this is probably your last night here for a while. Is there anything special you'd like to do?"

"No. I just wanna know what's gonna happen to me."

"Do you like living with Lavelle and Mrs. Walton?"

"It's okay."

"Don't you have other friends?"

"Not really. Most of the kids in my school, they leave us two alone."

"Why is that?"

"Well, we like computers and math and stuff, and most of the kids, they just goof off."

"And you and Lavelle don't?"

"No. Lavelle talks a lotta trash, especially with the black kids, but he's really smart. The other kids don't get it. I like school. We both do."

"How did you manage after school, with your mother working?"

"Grandma or Aunt Flora, they take me — took me — after school, a lotta times with Lavelle too, even for supper some nights."

"Of course. I'm sorry. I forgot," said Martin.

"And she, I mean Mom, she had regular hours. Mrs. Walton, we just don't know when she's working and when she's home. It's crazy sometimes. Me 'n Lavelle, we have to make our own supper. Stuff like that." Martin's imagination leaped ahead to the fall, to school, wondering who would supervise homework if Andrew stayed with the Waltons. Unease was creeping across his consciousness, an inexorable tide of responsibility gradually lapping its way across the bay of uncertainty into his heart. He was having trouble visualizing a family situation in Pittsburgh that he would find satisfactory. Like Jenny had said, he was not often pleased with how others ran things. So who could run Andrew's life — his son's life — in a manner he would approve? Perhaps Janet was right. Andrew needed to come home with him, whatever that might do to the rest of the family.

- - -

The next morning, after breakfast at the local deli, Martin delivered Andrew to the Waltons', greeted by Lavelle. He wanted to hug his son, but that was not to be. Andrew said, "Bye," and ducked into the house, leaving Martin on the doorstep.

On the way to the airport, he stopped by Sylvia Palmer's office to pick up a thick envelope with Andrew's school records, but Sylvia herself was in court. He left her a long note, reminding her that he also wanted medical and dental records, adding that he needed to consult with his wife about next steps, and could they please increase the support payments to Janet Walton to one-fifty a week.

* **16** *

Martin had to take the bus from the Portland airport. He reached home in time for dinner, but until the children were in bed, there could be no conversation about Andrew. Martin came downstairs after tucking in the kids and found Jenny sitting stone-faced in the living room, holding a mug of decaf. "Okay, Mr. Pinkerton, where are we? What's the situation?"

"I'm sorry I ever raised the Pinkerton analogy," said Martin. "I really prefer Mr. Goofus. That, at least, sounds friendly. So if you're going to call me names, call me that, okay?"

One corner of Jenny's mouth curled into a mini-smile. "Okay, Mr. Goofus. Same questions, though. Where are we? What's the situation?"

"The situation, which is very different from Pinkerton's, is that Andrew's extended family was apparently very supportive and loving until that crash. Frances wasn't alone. Her mother and aunt helped a lot. Andrew had a real family. And he's a nice kid, a scared kid, and, right now, a kid adrift."

"Through no fault of yours."

"True. When you don't know about something, you sure as hell can't do anything about it."

"But now you know."

"Yes, and if I don't step up, no one will. Or at least no one I've been able to find, so far."

"Tell me about him. Is he smart? Is he healthy? Is he polite? Tell me."

Finally given an invitation, Martin went through a complete review of their two days together, Andrew's questioning about Martin's leaving, his worries about what would happen, his enjoyment of the baseball game, his claiming Martin as his dad when signing in at the trampoline, Janet's acid comments about Martin's intentions, and ending with a description of that haunting look in his cautious eyes and how quickly he ducked away from Martin when he was dropped off.

"It sounds to me like you've made some kind of decision."

"I would like to make a decision, but I can't do it without you."

"So you want to take him in?"

"Yes, assuming he's willing. Which I don't know yet."

"Even if it produces terrible stresses here at home?"

"I can't predict the level of stresses. For example, we don't know how JJ and Ellen would react, but I don't agree with your instinct that it would be bad. If he were a troubled kid — a delinquent type — well, maybe. But he's not. I read his school reports on the plane home. He's an A/B student, best in science and math, less good in English and history."

"You realize we can't fit him here, don't you?"

"Why not? We could double up JJ and Ellen in the bigger bedroom and give Andrew the small one, at least short-term. And we're not wedded to this house. At some point, we could move a bigger one."

"For more money?"

"Money's not the issue. His estate has money if we need it, and CC's consulting is providing more than we need for Kuc. We could afford a bigger house now."

"It makes me nervous. Would you agree to be the guardian if I say no?"

"I'm hoping you don't say no. And we certainly couldn't have him here if you say no."

"So, you're saying it's up to me?"

"In a sense, it is. I know what I want to do, but I can't force this child on you. We need to be in this together."

"You know, love, this is just one more example of how you never want to disappoint anyone. I'm not convinced you really want to take this kid in. But I'm very sure, knowing you, that you feel bad about the fact of him and what it means — that in a drunken stupor you left behind a pregnant woman when you moved to Cambridge. This must be eating you raw."

"Why all the emphasis on being drunk? Haven't you ever gone over the edge when you had too much to drink? Or are you too perfect for that?" Jenny sat mute. "And you're right. It is eating me raw, and has been since that lawyer told me he was mine. But please, try to hear this. He's a nice kid. I actually like him. So it's not just guilt about Frances. It's about this kid's life."

"Your son's life."

"Yes, my son's life. I do care about my son's life. Is that so odd?" The snarl in Martin's voice made Jenny jump.

"No, but I'm stunned at how quickly you bought into him."

"You're right. I bought in quickly, and I'm stunned by that, too. That first time, seeing him in the lawyer's office, I got that gut sense that this was my kid." Jenny shook her head in disbelief. "I know, I know. It's fast and hard to believe. But my gut knew. This was my kid. And when he told the trampoline guy that I was his dad, I almost burst into tears."

"But if we bring him here, it could destroy our family, our children."

"How can you be so sure?"

"I just have a sense of doom. JJ, for example, would be crushed. And maybe the boy has learning problems, or health problem, or God knows what."

"I told you his school records are okay. I've asked the lawyer for his medical records. We should have those soon. And as for JJ, can I make a suggestion?" Jenny waited. "I think one of us, or maybe both together, should talk to JJ and tell him he has a brother we didn't know about. See how he reacts. Play it slow."

"Don't you dare mention this to JJ or anybody else until I've had a chance to digest things."

"Okay. Okay. But do your digesting. Suppose we stall a lot, and then end up taking him anyway. Andrew will know. He'll resent it — the stalling, I mean. And how can I explain it to him? That you were against it? What would that do to your relationship with him, long-term?"

"You're right about the risks of stalling, but just now, we have to stall. I'm just not ready, even to talk to JJ."

- - -

The next morning, Martin went to his office and tried to think about the book, but between his wretchedness over Andrew and the wretchedness still roiling his gut, he was making no progress at all. A mysterious email from Jeremy Good asked that Martin please come by his office at his earliest convenience. Knowing Jeremy's reputation for summoning faculty, Martin wondered what more he was going to be asked to do. CC's project was already taking way too much time, and now he had a new son to deal with.

It was a cool and foggy day, so Martin elected to grab his windbreaker before crossing the Quad to College Hall. Jeremy's office was in the rear of the second floor. Martin knocked, and hearing "Come in," opened the ornately paneled door and entered.

The view from the office windows was mostly of two administration buildings, but the space itself was attractive. An oversized dark wooden desk with claw-foot supports — in an antique-style that Jenny would probably recognize — sat at one end of the room behind two brown leather chairs. A six-seater teak conference table was centered on a maroon-and-white Bokhara rug at the opposite end. Jeremy was seated behind the desk, peering over his glasses.

"Ah, Martin. Do come in. Have a seat," he said, gesturing to one of the leather chairs. "We have an odd situation here." As Martin hung up his jacket and went to sit, he noted a cupboard built into a portion of the floor-to-ceiling bookshelf behind Jeremy's desk. It included a coffee maker, what looked like a liquor cabinet, and a refrigerator below. Martin guessed, with a guarded smile, that Jeremy's set-up could provide whatever beverage his guests might prefer to lubricate their funding decisions.

Once Martin was comfortably settled, Jeremy was more abrupt. "It's Bottlesworth policy that the solicitation of major gifts be done through this office."

Martin was puzzled. "Of course. That's what I would expect. What's this about?"

Picking up a letter from his desk, Jeremy said, "Did you solicit this gift from Mr. Caldicott?"

"Me? I don't understand. He's the one who's pushing the new school, not me."

"I don't mean the new school. I mean this fifty-thousand-dollar grant."

"I'm sorry, Jeremy. I have no idea what you're talking about."

Jeremy waved the letter. "Mr. Charles Caldicott has just sent us a grant of fifty thousand dollars to set up a fund to support, and I quote, 'the educational initiatives of Professor Martin Quint,' close quote. What educational initiatives do you have that need this kind of support? Was this your way of getting support for a summer supplement, what Win asked about?"

Martin's jaw dropped. "I never asked him for anything. He asked me about my book, and then I told him about my plans for the fall. That's it."

"Did you ever mention being short of funds?"

"I did say that I wasn't sure what kind of teaching assistance I might get in the fall, since the Dean said she had no budget, but I never asked him for help. It was just a conversation."

"Well, whether you asked or not, you did convey a need. These kind of things need to be coordinated with this office. People like CC are major targets, and we could miss out on serious support when individual professors go into fundraising mode."

Martin felt his bile rise. "Look, Jeremy. I understand what you're saying, and I now want you to understand what I'm saying. I did not solicit a gift. The only reason we even had this conversation was that we had a meeting to talk about plans for his new school. I thought he was just being polite."

"No reason to get heated up," said Jeremy. "But you do need to understand that if he's willing to make a fifty-K gift, he's probably equally willing to make a one-hundred-K gift, so it's possible you left fifty K on the table."

"This is nuts." Martin felt his fury growing. "I know how

money-raising works at a university, for God's sake. We had the same policy at CTI. And I would never do anything to undercut your office. My father told me you were, and I quote, 'legendary,' close quote. CC decided this on his own, with no input from me, so stop lecturing me like I was a child. He put up fifty-K without a request. I assume that if we needed it, he would put up another fifty-K. He's talking about twenty million, for Christ's sake. This is peanuts to him."

"If I accept the gift," said Jeremy, "what would you do with it?"

"You mean you might turn it down?" asked Martin, aghast.

"If you don't have a suitable use, I might prefer he save his fifty-K for something we really need."

"Since I just learned about this three minutes ago, I think I'm entitled to think about it — if you're serious about needing an answer, that is. The summer supplement does come to mind, and a teaching assistant of some kind for the fall. Seems like he wants me to have some grant support for educational stuff and you should just say 'thank you.' That's certainly what I plan to do unless you step in and impose your agenda on his generosity. I don't have to spend my summer on this new school thing, you know. I could do what I came here to do — write my book and teach."

Jeremy sat silent, staring at Martin over the rims of his glasses. After half a minute, he asked, "Do you think he would have made this gift if he wasn't already convinced that you were committed to the new school?"

"Maybe not," said Martin, nearing the boiling point. "But all I've agreed to do is help formulate the plan. I'm honoring that agreement, so far on a volunteer basis, and it takes a shitload of time. You can refuse the gift if you want, but since he's offered the money and I could use it, I'm making no promises about what I'll do if you turn it down."

"Okay, simmer down," said Jeremy. "I'm going to accept the gift. Hell. I'm not stupid enough to turn it back. But please, if in the future you have discussions with CC about anything that might lead to a grant of this kind, get me in the loop. We need to coordinate all contacts with major donors."

Martin scoffed, "Perhaps you should tell that to CC rather than me. It would give him a good laugh." He was beginning to enjoy both his win and his windfall.

As Martin walked back across the Quad to his office, his pulse coming back down toward normal, Jenny's words about being seduced rang in his ears. First the consulting, now this. The traces hitching Martin to CC's wagon had just gotten a notch tighter.

\- \- \-

"I heard about CC's grant," said Win with a chuckle as Martin spread his notes out on Win's conference table. "Jeremy was bullshit. He's convinced you asked him for it."

"C'mon, Win. For the record and under oath, no, I didn't ask him. You've seen him in action. He's the kind of guy that just steps in and interferes."

"True enough. Anyway, we're going to approve a thirty-percent summer supplement for you from the grant. So now that you're officially hired, let's get to work."

Martin turned to his notes. "Thanks. Jenny, especially, will appreciate that. And, just so you know, having Glenda Aldrich here has been a blessing. She's really helping me move the book along. Did she tell you that she might want to relocate to Maine?"

"You mean leave Oxford? I had no idea. But we've got other fish to fry just now. What have you come up with?"

"Okay, on the people thing, I think we're close. I'm assuming we're going for Gillespie for robotics and Kesselbaum for computers, and I've got four internal candidates gleaned from your list of suggestions. An odd mix."

"What do you mean odd?" asked Win.

"Well, Abe Goldberg in Economics seems like a good choice. He teaches both microeconomics and finance and was actually in a start-up for three years. Mehmet Kiraz also fits. He works in genomic medicine, right down CC's sweet spot. Has a cooperative research program with folks at Harvard Medical School but he has absolutely no commercial experience, zilch. Then there's Siobhan O'Hara. Works on sequencing of viruses and has won an NSF career-initiation grant, a real plum. But she's just finished her first year, and like Mehmet, she has no business experience. Given her new-hire status, it might be risky for her to get involved in a new enterprise."

"Actually, I'm not so sure about that. Bottlesworth takes a broader view than you might think of what an academic contribution is, and making an impact on a new program could be an important boost for her eventual promotion. So I think this sounds terrific. Who's the fourth?"

"Your Dean of Science. Evelyn absolutely lit up when I asked her about more applied opportunities for students. She's a biologist, of course, and that's relevant, but she hasn't been active in research for at least five years. She reacted positively about a program expansion, but I suspect she would only be happy if she could run it. She seems pretty autocratic, and CC might not like that idea so well."

Win stroked his chin, thinking. "Yes, that's how Evelyn is, but I like the mix. A Dean, a junior faculty member, two outsiders. Sounds good. I'll talk to CC and Fred about the compensation for the outside experts. CC would be inclined to pay them a lot of money, and Fred will be opposed and want small honoraria. But I'll handle it, somehow. In the meantime, you can discuss the list with CC."

As Martin was about to leave, he asked, "Can I bring up something else? Another CC crazy idea?"

Win laughed, "Whose life is he messing with now?"

"Actually, he's messing with one of my former students who wants to be a teacher, even worked with me on my course at CTI. She's about to enter her senior year and has a summer job at CC's company — pure coincidence. When I was down there last week, he invited her to lunch and peppered her with questions. After that, out of the blue, he suggested that she should serve as my assistant for my fall course, take a leave and spend it here. She doesn't know anything about this idea, but I wanted to see if it would even be possible to hire someone like her to be my Teaching Assistant. I'm really going to need help, because I'm doing an experiment with flipping the classroom, using the FIE lectures outside of class and discussion and problem-solving in class. She has a head start on all this, because she's familiar with both versions."

"You'd pay her out of CC's grant?"

"Exactly, but I don't want to pursue it if it would mean a fight with the administration."

"How much?"

"It seems fair if we make it comparable to the base Teaching Assistant stipend at CTI, something like two thousand a month. I can check the amount. It needs to be enough so she could rent a room somewhere and feed herself and her car."

"CC really does stir the pot, doesn't he? He seems perfectly willing to push into other people's lives, his eyes blazing."

"So you've noticed that?"

"How could I miss it? I'll add this to my list when I talk with Fred."

* **17** *

JJ and Ellen knew how to milk the special privileges that always accompanied a visit by Jenny's parents, the only grandparents they had, since even if Martin's mother was still alive, neither he nor Helen had shown any inclination to go searching for her. It was almost a taboo subject, the missing grandparent, so the children made the most of the ones that weren't missing — with ice cream and trips to McDonald's and the toy store and the book store, core activities of the July Fourth holiday weekend. For Martin, though, July Fourth was an anniversary of the wrong kind, the annual dredging up of shame over having dumped Frances for the sake of a job, made staggeringly worse this year by Andrew — not his person, just his existence. But July Fourth had arrived and Martin was determined to make the best of it. Jenny had insisted that no mention be made of Andrew to her parents, which lowered the visible tension level enough to make the children the center of attention.

JJ and Carlo loved parades, and Brimfield Junction put on a pretty good show. The Quints, the Engle-Mourinhos, and Jenny's enthusiastic parents, Grace and Harvey Hewes, assembled to make a day of it. The weather was dry but it was windy, with puffy clouds skidding across the sky, looking just like the cotton candy that the kids absolutely had to have or the world would end. Grandpa Harvey took remedial action, and the world didn't end.

The sheriff's cruiser, its lights flashing, kicked things off promptly at two o'clock, followed by all the usual accoutrements: the VFW post marching in formation, the high school band, the Mayor and City Councilors shaking hands with the crowd as they ambled along, and a few floats, with one from the Lobstermen's Association promising availability of live or steamed lobsters after the parade. It ended with a set of seven vintage cars, some with ooga horns that made Ellen laugh. Finally, the town fire engine came through with sirens in full voice. This frightened Ellen into a fit of shrieking. Carlo taunted her, calling her a fraidy cat, prompting JJ to yell directly into Carlo's face to leave Sister alone. Helen stepped in to separate the combatants before blows were struck while Jenny and little Angela got Ellen restored to her normal good nature.

After the street was clear enough, the family moved over to Riverside Park for a kids-versus-grownups soccer game and picnic. As dusk settled in, the family relocated to the grandstand of the high school sports field for the fireworks display, and with that first detonation, Martin found himself back in Pittsburgh, reliving the pain of having to tell someone he felt he loved that they were not going forward together. It was stupid to feel this way so many years later, especially with his wonderful new family all around him, but he couldn't help it. Guilt of this kind and the attendant shame never go away. But some decisions, no matter how painful, just have to be made, and that meant moving on without Frances. What would be the decision about Andrew? Just asking the question sank Martin into a funk.

-   -   -

With Andrew now out in the open, at least with Jenny, and with his colitis finally calmed enough to be considered under control, life settled into a new metastable — albeit tense — normal. Jenny and Martin went to Freeport one afternoon to have tea and scones with Glenda and Cecil, her father, and were surprised to see Abe Goldberg there, as well. Round of face and round of belly, but not at all fat, he stood a few inches shorter than Martin, with curly brown hair and dark eyes that projected a firm persona, happy with the world, and, apparently, quite happy with his new female friend. Glenda's normally pale cheeks flushed just a bit as she did introductions. Cecil looked like a male version of Glenda, straight brown hair over a narrow face and shoulders, and wider at the middle. His tremors were nowhere near as disabling as Martin had imagined, and conversation — centered around Cecil's questions about the book project — sparkled. Abe joined in, adding his two cents whenever he could find an opening.

"I like her," said Jenny on the way home. "She seems bold and capable. And working with her makes you happy."

"I'm actually thrilled. She knows the literature much better than me. I'm considering asking her to become my co-author."

"And is this Abe Goldberg someone you know? He seems nice, too."

"Just met him recently. Seems like a happy guy. Doesn't know it yet, but he's a candidate for CC's Task Force."

"Is Glenda's divorce final? Or is she, as we might say, jumping the gun?"

"So you think that too? It's not yet final, but as you said, she's bold. And I presume that Abe is not married. It would be out of character for her to take up with someone else's husband after what she's just been through."

\- \- \-

It felt good to once again be able to work, first on class plans for the upcoming semester, then in a cordial but disputative session with Glenda who, now with the proprietary rights of a co-author, disagreed sharply with the approach Martin had taken in his draft of chapter four. Their back and forth excited Martin, even as she convinced him that he had been wrong. Yes, Glenda was bold, and he loved it. Working with her was simultaneously energizing and humbling. It was clear that, with her help, the book would go faster and, with her expertise, would be a much more solid contribution to public discourse on education than he could have created on his own.

He also had a sense that Jenny was slowly coming around. All he needed was patience. And for CC's project, it was time to recruit. This had provoked an intense meeting convened in Win's office. CC wanted to be the one to contact Sharon Gillespie, but Win, supported by Martin, was firm that CC should remain in the background until the Task Force was assembled and had a chance to develop a program.

He was to be described as an anonymous donor who was prepared to support the initiation of the new program once it had been defined. This meant, of course, that Martin had to be the one to ask Gillespie to help out, and he had never met her.

It proved easy to find her via the web. She was amenable to a meeting at Camberton on Friday morning, and Julian Kesselbaum was free for lunch that day, as well. The timing was arranged to pack everything into one Boston run: Martin's first consulting day at Autobot, an overnight with Horatio for an evening of music, the Gillespie and Kesselbaum meetings, an in-person visit with Natasha, and one more session with Harry Huang. This flurry of engagement reminded Martin of his overscheduled life at CTI. It made him feel whole again. And this layer cake of appointments had a tasty icing — another chance to see Gina in private. Rather than attempt to fit her into his consulting time, he arranged another dinner at Legal Seafood.

- - -

Martin left for Andover at seven. In the solitude of his car, all he could think about was his Pittsburgh past, the good times with Frances — dinners, theater, arguing over whether Faulkner or Steinbeck was the best American writer, and, of course, the bedtimes, her touch, her feel, her intensity — then the painful breakup, and now what, a child? What if Andrew came to live with them? Or if he didn't? What might it do to his marriage, his family, either way? Wouldn't he resent Jenny if she said no, and wouldn't she resent him if he guilt-tripped her, or just pressured her, into saying yes? He was reminded of a saying he had heard from one of his professors in graduate school — he couldn't remember which one — that you know you are making an important decision when you are very sure that you lack the essential information. Boy, was this ever such a case.

He reached Autobot at nine and tried to clear his head to prepare for immersion into his as-yet ill-defined mission. He got signed in, and Kenneth escorted him to CC's office, where he was presented with his schedule for the day: six ninety-minute timeslots with the key personnel, starting with Alice Yee in Human Resources. Alice's office was just down the hall. CC deposited him there, saying he would catch up at lunch.

It was a blizzard of information for Martin, a thorough orientation to the ins and outs of a fast-growing company. After HR, it was Engineering, a quick lunch with CC to talk about his upcoming visit with Sharon Gillespie, then Marketing, Sales, Technology, and Facilities. By five, he was wiped out, but he was beginning to see a few opportunities where he might have constructive input. When he left, he told CC he would think about what he had learned and send some notes in a few days.

- - -

The traffic into Boston was horrific. He used the Sullivan Square exit and his knowledge of the back streets to get to Legal Seafood by 6:15. Gina had beaten him by a few minutes and was already at their table.

This time it was Gina getting up when Martin arrived, holding out both her hands in greeting, saying how happy she was to see him again, and this time it was Martin who clasped those hands with a fond smile, a smile returned by his companion in full measure, an enigma of meaning hovering like a butterfly gently flapping its wings above the table. Sobered by the reality of Andrew and all his attendant baggage, Martin did his best to ignore that imagined butterfly, whatever it meant, and stick to business. She's a student, for God's sake.

As they got settled, Gina, with a new hint of confidence that caught Martin's attention, said, "I heard you were at Autobot again today. Is that right?"

Martin responded with raised eyebrows and a shrug. "Yeah. CC thinks I can do something constructive out there, and today was my first official day, learning the ropes."

"He's an amazing guy," said Gina. "He just boils with energy."

"Indeed. And he's perfectly willing to use that energy, and the money behind it, to intrude into other people's lives."

"Like yours? Your consulting is an intrusion?"

They were interrupted by their server, who brought water and rolls and took their orders.

"Intrusions," said Martin, pausing, musing. "CC seems to specialize in intrusions. I guess you have to ask yourself, in situations like this, what is your mission and what, therefore, is an intrusion?"

"I thought your mission was to teach and write your book. Has that changed?"

"Let's just say that things have been added to the list — some by CC, some by others. That's what I wanted to talk to you about."

"Me? You want to talk to me about something? I thought we were going to talk about my grad school plans."

Martin smiled. "I'm happy to discuss grad schools, maybe even today, but I actually have something important to suggest. It's a bit of a story."

Gina, rapt and focused, listened.

"A colleague at Bottlesworth, a psychologist visiting from Oxford, suggested I do a flipped-classroom experiment with C&E in the fall. I decided she's right, so I'm gonna do it."

"You mean use the online lectures?"

"Exactly. And use the class sessions for team problem-solving."

"Sounds worthwhile. Maybe the best use for those lectures. I think they should do it at CTI. The kids don't come to lecture anymore, less than half. The others are watching the online stuff."

Their food arrived, Martin's swordfish and Gina's cioppino, and they shared small tastings across the table. Martin was startled, and a bit chagrined, by the internal surge this moment of intimacy produced.

As they started to eat in earnest, Martin, with a tight throat, asked, "How would you like to be a pioneer?"

"Me? How could I do that?" asked Gina, gathering a spoonful of her fish stew.

"Okay. This is a radical suggestion, so don't jump out of your skin." Gina looked up, spoon suspended. "How would you like to take a term off from CTI and come to Bottlesworth as my Teaching Assistant? Help me get the flipped classroom launched and make it a success."

The spoon went back in the dish. Gina's face was a kaleidoscope of emotion, flipping between shock, admiration, embarrassment, and back to shock, perhaps even a bit of fear. "Could I do that? Really?"

"I'm pretty sure it will be approved at Bottlesworth, and we have the funds to pay you the same as a TA at CTI."

"You mean you've already talked about this with them?"

"I had to. I couldn't even suggest it to you if it was going to be shot down at Bottlesworth. But with your experience as a tutor and grader and your knowledge of the online version, you could step in faster than anyone else I could think of."

"Except for one of the CTI TAs. Why not ask them?"

"A good question. And I don't have an answer other than that this is a real suggestion that you should consider." And, thought Martin, one you should accept. Come to me in BJ. Help me. Comfort me. Pull me from the surf.

"What made you think of this?"

Was this an accusation from the seemingly more confident Gina? Or, worse, was it a request to hear what could not be spoken? Martin's voice cracked a little. "It wasn't my idea," he said. "It was CC's. His intrusion. Now into your life. He suggested it right after our lunch meeting a couple of weeks ago. He knows I need an assistant at Bottlesworth, and he even made a grant to the college to provide the funds. And when you said you wanted classroom experience, he put two and two together."

The two turned back to their food, using eating as an excuse for a breather.

When Martin finally spoke, he said, "When I left for Bottlesworth, you wanted to transfer. Remember?" Gina nodded. "And I talked you out of it?" She nodded again. "I felt you would get a better education at CTI than Bottlesworth could provide, and I continue to think that way, but for you to get real teaching experience... that might be a reason for spending some time with us."

"It's a lot to think about," said Gina, her complexion suddenly bright, an enigma. "How soon would I have to make a decision?"

"I would need to know fairly soon, certainly by early August. I know this is sudden, and it's a big deal. But talk to your parents, your friends, your advisor. Scope it out. I'd be delighted if it works. And if it doesn't work, I'll go to Plan B."

"And you have a Plan B?"

"Not yet. But if you say no, I'll think of one."

The conversation drifted to Gina's summer, her successes at Autobot, trips to the Cape Anne beaches — amiable chatter, all of it. Martin kept up his half by asking polite and appropriate questions, but he kept visualizing Gina at the beach in a string bikini while simultaneously searing his brain with the mantra, "She's a student, she's a student, she's a student." The dinner ended with more grasping of hands, more impenetrable looks. They agreed to talk by phone in a week and went their separate ways.

- - -

Martin reached Horatio's just as Sumner was arriving. Martin brought in his overnight bag and his folder of music, and with minimal time spent on greetings, the trio focused on music. They warmed up with the Beethoven Opus 11 *Trio*, always fun and relatively easy, and then worked on a new piece by the contemporary American composer Rick Sowash. It was a first reading, and therefore splotchy in places, but they agreed it might be worth working up for performance at some point in the indefinite future.

Afterward, they gathered with Blanche at the kitchen table. Sumner asked how things were going with CC. Martin was circumspect, talking only about his support for the flipped-classroom idea, which drew a disbelieving laugh from Horatio. "I thought you hated that online stuff?"

Martin said, "It's not that it's online, it's that there's no conversation. If we flip the classroom, there will be more opportunity for conversation, not less. But now it's time to hit the sack. Busy day tomorrow."

That night, Gina figured directly in his dreams, this time erotically. He was embarrassed to find semen stains on the sheet and hoped that Blanche wouldn't notice on laundry day. But this was totally crazy. Gina wasn't doing anything to lead him on other than be her gorgeous self. He was a happily married man with a loving family and a wife who was a stunning partner, both in life and in bed. But something was driving him into this fantasyland. He had to get a grip on it before they tried to work together. One false step, one mistake, and the consequences would be unthinkable.

At breakfast, Martin went into more detail with Horatio about ostensive-inferential communication and the five options for conversation that Glenda had suggested. Horatio expressed encouragement about the progress Martin was making, suggesting that perhaps this move to Bottlesworth would prove to be a boon, after all.

"One is never sure," said Martin, "but it feels pretty good just now." As he said those words, he hated that he was dissembling with his oldest friend, failing to mention his newfound son. Another sin of omission, an option zero silence.

* **18** *

Murdock Hall was easy to find. Professor Gillespie was in her second-floor office and got up from her desk when Martin knocked and poked his head in. Five feet tall, wiry, with a pointed nose in a narrow face, curly brown hair cropped almost into an afro, and metal rimmed glasses that projected the intensity of her posture. She wore jeans and a checked shirt discreetly open at the neck. No wedding ring. Martin flashed an image of a speedy mongoose, ready to flee or to pounce, depending on the situation. Was he a visiting cobra? No way. He came in peace. They shook hands and took seats at a round oak table.

"I was surprised to see your email," said Sharon, "since I knew your name at CTI. Mr. Super-Teacher is what my students said. When did you move to Bottlesworth?"

"A year ago," said Martin. "And you've been here since … ?"

"Since CTI kicked me out, so that's two years," she said with a laugh. "It wasn't fun at the time, but they actually did me a favor. I absolutely love it here. We get kids involved in projects the minute they step on campus, and we don't let up until they graduate. So how can I help you? You said you wanted to draw on my expertise?"

"It's a funny thing, actually. Bottlesworth is thinking of creating a program that combines engineering and entrepreneurship, and based on what I've learned from the Camberton website, that's what you folks do. Am I right?"

"Totally. Having Babson next door helps on the business side. But yes, we do both, more on engineering though."

"Well, Bottlesworth would like to hire you as a poorly paid consultant to serve on a task force we've set up to define a program of this type within our college. It would have to be smaller than what you've got here, but it sounds like the direction and focus are so similar, your experience would be of immense value."

"Really? Sounds interesting. What kind of time commitment?"

"Maybe a meeting a month for the next six months. Something like that. The goal is to create a white paper defining a program that makes sense for a school our size but big enough to have an effective educational program. We thought of you immediately as a resource."

"Why me?"

"I know we never met, but I followed your activities at CTI from a distance, and I'm appalled that you didn't get tenure there. We were thinking of making robotics a focus of our program, and that's right up your alley. And with you having experience at Camberton, that sealed the deal for us. You are number one on our list."

"And who else is on your list?"

"I would prefer you keep this quiet, since I haven't spoken to him yet, but our other outside candidate is Julian Kesselbaum, another CTI castoff with exceptional credentials. Do you know him?"

"Oh yes. Computer systems and security. Julian was very supportive when CTI dumped me. Sent me a nice note and we had lunch. A strange guy, but a dedicated teacher."

"Yes. And we have four quite good folks at Bottlesworth, one in economics and three in some aspect of biomedical engineering."

"Is bioengineering the planned focus?"

Martin nodded.

"So let me ask, what if this task force comes up with a good plan. What then?"

"We have a donor with big bucks salivating to give us the money to start it."

"Do I know this donor?"

"I'm not sure, but our administration has been sworn to silence on the donor's identity. If we can't create a good plan, it won't matter. But we're talking real money. Twenty million in seed funds is what our Provost said."

"Sounds interesting, especially since it involves two former CTI colleagues who share my distinction of no longer being there. I'm still pissed off at how they handled my case, even though it has turned out okay. Let me think a bit and check out the Bottlesworth website."

"That'll be fine. How about I call you in a week?"

They shook hands, and Martin left for Cambridge and his lunch meeting with Julian Kesselbaum.

-    -   -

Julian, looking as owlish as ever, met Martin at The Brewer's Friend, a pub not far from Julian's Central Square office. Lunch started with some swapped information-security stories, Martin reliving the agony of Kat's stolen tenure letters, and Julian bragging about neutralizing a bogus intruder buried within the CTI computer user accounts. Julian was still teaching as an Adjunct at UMass Boston and Bunker Hill Community College, and his consulting business was doing well.

"Are you still the hotshot computer security guru at CTI?" asked Martin.

Julian laughed. "Except for the US government, CTI is probably the primary target for hackers worldwide. Penetrating CTI is like a hacker badge of honor. So, yes, I get called in from time to time. But my consulting business has taken off — I've got more than a dozen banks as clients now — so I only come in when stuff gets really bad. CTI is such a strange place. Supposedly the best engineering school in the world, but all they care about is research."

"Well, they do try to do a decent job of education, don't they?" said Martin

"Not when they fire their best teachers."

Including you, thought Martin. This led him to explain the reason for his visit, and he was startled by how quickly Julian leaped at it. Martin had worried that Julian might be insulted by the "poorly compensated" component of the consulting offer. But, no, once Martin said that Sharon Gillespie had already been asked, Julian agreed to help, and said he would even do it for free. "She's one of my idols," said Julian. "The most creative teacher ever at CTI. Never should have let her go." They parted with more shared enthusiasm than in any previous encounter.

Martin went on to his CTI meetings, first with Natasha to review progress, then with Harry Huang to finalize the transfer of teaching materials he would be able to use in the fall. On the drive back to Maine that afternoon, Martin felt the familiar flush of having had a horrendously busy two days, with one success after another. That latent enthusiasm for operating at full capacity burst forth, and he sang along with a Met rebroadcast of *The Elixir of Love*, interrupted briefly as he passed the exit for Autobot by a ghostly image of Gina, floating in the space between his eyes and the road.

-    -   -

By the time he got home, the apparition of Gina had long since faded. He wrapped Jenny in a hug and crowed about the fantastic two days he'd had, the consulting, the success with CC's plan, his meeting with Harry. Jenny, in turn, crowed a bit about what Sarah might purchase from her team. Pierre had assembled drawings from every team member, and Jenny had prepared a multipage quotation. She could barely contain her excitement. "It looks like Sarah will order as many as eleven pieces in total, with a price tag over ninety thousand. I get thirty percent, so I'll inch into the black for the first time."

"Congratulations. Black beats red every time. So when is this trip?"

"We fly out Tuesday morning."

"We?"

"Yes, Pierre and me."

"Well, thanks to Kuc, Tuesday morning will be fine."

"Oh, and a FedEx for you came this morning. From Pittsburgh. I left it on my desk by mistake. It's thick."

Martin went into the study and picked up the packet. "From the lawyer," he called out. "Probably medical records."

But it was much more than that. It included an inventory of the merged estates and a draft petition for guardianship of the person. A copy of the petition had also been sent to Trevor Corey. Martin put the petition aside, figuring that was Trevor's to review, but he flipped through the listing of the two homes, the two cars not involved in the wreck, and the furnishings and personal effects of the three women. At the back was a financial summary, showing the insurance proceeds, preliminary appraisals of the two pieces of real estate with the two mortgage balances, status of the various bank accounts that were now held for Andrew's benefit, and a listing of other liabilities, some real estate taxes and utility bills. There was also an accounting of Wilkins and Palmer's financial actions on behalf of the estate, paying off credit cards, hiring the people to clean up the homes and do the inventory, the money for Janet, and their own fees, which by this point were already in the eighteen-thousand-dollar range.

It was pretty clear that Sylvia Palmer was pushing him to get herself out of the loop, with the not-so-subtle message that the status quo would continue to drain funds out of Andrew's stake in life. He turned to the medical records. He was relieved to find nothing serious: no history of seizures or mental illness or childhood leukemia. No surgeries or hospitalizations. Vaccinations up to date. One broken finger at age ten, cause not given. The dental record showed a few cavities and no need for orthodonture. As close to a clean bill of health as one could hope for.

After dinner and kids' bedtime, Martin found Jenny at her desk in the study. Picking up the packet, he asked, "You wanna see this? His medical record?"

"Might as well."

Jenny turned from her screen as Martin gave her just the medical record. "What's the rest?"

"Estate inventory and finances. It seems to be a net of somewhere north of three hundred and fifty thousand, but it's being drained by the ongoing payments to Janet Walton and by legal fees."

"So you're telling me to get on with it?"

"In a gentle way, yes. You can look through the medical stuff if you want, but I can tell you that there's nothing in there to worry about."

"And you want to take him in."

"I do. But we need to talk to JJ first. I'll do it, if you'll let me."

Jenny sat silent for a long time, the medical papers in her lap. "It's so unfair," she said. "I feel sad for Andrew, but I didn't bargain for this."

"And neither did I. Life happens. George died. That wasn't fair. When I got Frances pregnant, she never told me, and that wasn't fair, either. And the car crash, that also wasn't fair. It was cruel. Life isn't fair. But life is life. Andrew is my son. Can you imagine living with me if we don't take him in? Him going to some foster home? Me worrying about him and then resenting your refusal?"

"That's what's not fair," said Jenny, her voice suddenly gnarly. "If I want to stay married to you, which I do, I don't actually have a choice. Just like when George died. No option but to get on with it. I understand, at least intellectually, that you couldn't live knowing he was not cared for in the way you would approve, and there's no guarantee of that unless we take him in. But everything was getting better here — my business, JJ's school and music, your book. This feels like someone dropped an anvil on my head, on our heads. It could be a disaster."

"But it also could be wonderful. Can't I at least talk to JJ? I think he'll surprise you."

Jenny took a deep breath and exhaled slowly. "I guess that's the next step. I don't like it, but it's clearly inevitable. Can you wait until I'm back? Okay?"

"Okay. I'll do it Saturday."

-    -   -

Jenny and Pierre left for Chicago on Tuesday morning. Martin kept a watchful eye on Kuc and the children and was delighted not only with what he saw, but also with what he managed to get written, even working at home, now with a nearly fleshed out outline for the flipped-course version of Circuits and Electronics and a revised version of the first five book chapters ready to pass back to Glenda's critical eye. He was also delighted with what he ate. Kuc, all four foot ten of her, loved to cook — pho with chicken, lettuce-wrapped spring rolls, marinated grilled salmon, jasmine rice — and she insisted on cooking dinners for the family before she left for the day. To Martin's amazement, the children loved the food, even the lettuce wraps.

On Wednesday morning, Martin received an email from Win that his request to hire Gina as a teaching assistant had been approved up the ladder by Steve Wang, Evelyn Kim, and himself. Martin called the Physics Department office to confirm that Steve was in and hurried over to campus. With Martin sitting in his office confirming the details, Steve drafted and signed the requisite appointment letter while sniping with a bit of envy at Martin's unique status in having the resources to do this, but he also suggested, once again, a get-together dinner at his home. Martin consulted his iPhone calendar, and they set a date, subject to Jenny's concurrence when she returned from Chicago.

Martin almost clicked his heels as he walked back to his office. He made a scan of the letter and emailed it to Gina, following it up with the signed original in the regular mail. He also suggested she come up some weekend to look for a place to live.

There was progress on other fronts, as well. Fred, Win, and Jeremy had finally approved CC's revised four-stage entrepreneurial plan, so Martin and Win, with CC's editorial heckling, had crafted a mission statement for the Task Force on Engineering and Entrepreneurship. Dean Kim and Professors Goldberg, O'Hara, and Kiraz had been notified that they would be asked to participate once the outsiders had been identified and signed up. A modest compensation package for the outsiders — an honorarium of eight hundred a day plus travel expenses — had been deemed academically dignified and appropriate, with CC chafing for more. Ever eager to move ahead, CC gave in, and then made a gift of fifteen thousand dollars to cover the costs.

- - -

When Martin got home that afternoon, Kuc called from the kitchen. "Jenny call," she said. "She ask you call." He untangled himself from the children wrapped around his legs, saying he had to call Mommy.

Jenny was higher than high. "Can you believe what Sarah decided to order? Pierre was masterful. He presented everybody's work in the best possible way, and she's taking a total of eighteen pieces, including several big ones. Each one of my guys sells at least three pieces. A complete dining set, with eight of Suzanne's distressed chairs and a period-piece table replica from Pierre. Two sideboards from Bart with intricate wood inlay, a matched pair of sofas from Pierre, end tables, a wood-inlaid coffee table, and more — a dish cabinet for the buttery, a little room between the kitchen and dining room, and two wardrobe-dresser pieces for the master bedroom. The rest would be regular commercial purchases that I can work on from home. It's like a dream come true. A fucking breakthrough."

Martin, startled by the intensity of Jenny's f-bomb, echoed her enthusiasm. "Fucking fantastic. Congratulations. I couldn't be happier. And I have some news, too. My teaching assistant thing is sorted out."

"You found someone?"

"Yes. One of my former advisees from CTI is taking a leave and will come here to help me teach."

"What's his name? Did I ever meet him?"

"It's Gina. Gina Farrell. That incredible freshman I told you about who did such a spectacular job with the MOOC thing. She's a senior now, and she wants to become a teacher. So we worked it out. Bottlesworth will hire her, at least for the fall."

"Well good for you. A big relief. Kids okay?"

"Kids are fine. Kuc is a treasure."

"Listen, we're going out to celebrate. We're probably coming home tomorrow unless Sarah needs us for something. I'll let you know. Will you be at the cottage?"

"No. Here at home. I'm getting too much done to risk going to the cottage."

-   -   -

The next day, Pierre dropped Jenny off at five o'clock. Martin came out to offer congratulations, but Pierre drove off. "What's with him?" he asked. "Not even a hello?"

"It's nothing. Just in a hurry to get home, I guess."

Martin wrapped Jenny into a hug, but she barely responded. "You okay?" he asked.

"Exhausted. I need a shower and a lie-down before dinner. I'm hoping you're cooking tonight."

"Kuc did the cooking. She insisted."

Jenny focused entirely on the children during dinner and did the dishes while Martin took care of kid bedtime. When he came down, he found her sitting at her desk, staring at her computer screen.

"You okay? You should be celebrating."

"I'm sort of in shock."

"A good kind of shock, right?" Jenny nodded weakly. "Did you pick up a bug or something?"

"No. Just worn out. I'm going to bed early."

"Okay, love. Glad you had a good trip." Martin went to the Yamaha, put on the headphones, and practiced for more than an hour before turning in.

* **19** *

On Saturday morning, Martin took JJ for a day at the cottage, just the two of them. The Washingtons' car was not in sight when they pulled up — a relief for Martin, who wanted JJ's undivided focus. They put their cold chest with the picnic lunch in the cottage and walked the half-mile around to the bay side, where the canoe was stashed. The tide was coming in, the perfect time for a quiet paddle up the channels in the marsh. Around the first bend, they startled a heron, who took off with a squawk.

They reached a biggish pool where birds liked to feed and allowed the canoe to drift up against the reeds. Even though it meant disturbing the quiet, Martin decided that it was now or never. "I've got some important news for you," he said.

"Cool," said JJ. "What is it?"

"I just found out that I have a son, someone I didn't know about. This means that you have a brother."

"A brother. Where?"

"He lives in Pittsburgh now."

"With his mommy?"

"His mommy is a friend from many years ago, someone I knew long before I met your mother."

"How old is he?"

"He's twelve."

"Wow. That's old. But why didn't you know?"

"It's hard to explain. But you know that when a mommy has a baby, like with Ellen, the baby lives inside before it comes out?" JJ nodded. "A mommy sometimes doesn't know right away when a baby is started, and if the mommy doesn't know, the father doesn't know either. When

I lived in Pittsburgh, his mommy and I thought we might get married. But I was moving to Cambridge and she wanted to stay in Pittsburgh, so we decided not to. I didn't know that a baby had already been started when I left, and she never told me."

"She had a baby and didn't tell you?"

"That's right. I just found out last week."

"Why didn't she tell you?"

"I have no idea. She could have, but she didn't."

"How did you find out?"

"This part is very sad. The boy's mommy — his name is Andrew — was in a car crash and she died. She didn't have a husband or any other family members, so Andrew is alone now. He's temporarily staying with a friend from school. His mother had left my name in some papers, and the lawyers found them and called me."

"Wow. A brother. I've always wanted a brother." Before Martin could say anything, JJ added, "But I like Sister, I do, really. I like Sister."

"I know you do. I'm very proud of you and how nice you are to Ellen."

"And he's twelve? Is he gonna live with us? In our house?"

"That's what we're trying to decide, your mom and me."

"Well, I think it's awesome. To have a brother. A big brother. Awesome."

-    -   -

"You can ask him," said Martin that night. "He said, and I quote, 'I think it's awesome to have a brother.'"

"I will ask him. I want to be sure. He's..." Jenny sputtered out the words. "He's all I have left of George, and I won't do anything to..." Martin wrapped Jenny in a hug, a silent warming hug, her limp in his arms.

-    -   -

In spite of Jenny's huge success in Chicago, her mood remained sullen. Martin presumed it was about Andrew, her internal debate over taking him in, a debate in which he could not really participate. So he did his best to wait on her decision and to focus on work. The work paid off. He was delighted with the speed with which he and Glenda had drafted, at least in rough form, almost all of the sections of the book that didn't depend on the flipped-classroom experiment, and he had a mostly complete syllabus for the fall class, which he emailed to Gina for comments. He had also signed up Sharon Gillespie and Julian Kesselbaum, requesting their August schedules in the hope that they could convene a first meeting of the Task Force before school began.

After several days of tiptoeing around Jenny's uncertain state of mind, he took a deep breath and once again broached the prickly subject of meeting Andrew. This time Jenny said okay. This weekend, after Martin's day at Autobot.

-   -   -

Martin was surprised to run into Julian Kesselbaum at the Autobot security desk turning in his badge. "What are you doing here?" asked Martin. "Are you part of Autobot?"

Julian smiled his wispy smile. "Not yet, but Mr. Caldicott wanted to talk to me about computer security, said he needed a consult. He told me that you're consulting on education and training. A good choice, in my opinion."

"Well, thank you for that, but it's odd."

"Why odd?"

"Just odd," said Martin, as he completed his sign-in and was escorted by Kenneth to his meeting with the HR staff.

At lunch with CC, in the private dining room, Martin asked about Julian, and CC replied, "You told me what a guru he was, so I thought I would get his opinion on our security systems."

"C'mon, CC," said Martin. "Don't bullshit me. You hired him because he's on the Task Force. Isn't that it?"

CC laughed. "I guess you now know me well enough by now. Yes, I want to know the people on the project and what's going on, and, for the record, I haven't hired him yet."

"But haven't I kept you up to date?"

Martin stared at CC, who stared right back, eyes ablaze. "Yes, as far as I know, but as you are aware, I always do my due diligence and I like multiple channels."

"But Julian thinks our discussions are confidential, so he won't tell you anything unless you tell him you're planning on being the donor."

"I already told him when we met this morning and I swore him to secrecy."

"Jesus," said Martin. "You just can't keep your mitts out of things, can you?"

"It's a failing, I admit," said CC. "But the slow pace of academic decisions drives me nuts, and Julian is out in the business world now."

"Well, just so you know, this really pisses me off."

"I don't mind that you're pissed off now, but I think you'll see your way to get over it. This project is a big deal for me, and I gather intelligence from as many dimensions as possible. Remember how you checked me out? Well, I check out everything. I already know Sharon Gillespie, but Julian is new to me. I want—"

Martin interrupted. "So how do you know Sharon Gillespie? Where did this fascination with her come from?"

"We were students together in the robotics lab at CTI. I was finishing my master's just when she was starting her doctorate."

"Was it personal?"

CC smiled. "Okay. You got me. I wanted it to be personal, but she was so focused on her studies I ended up looking elsewhere."

"So you were in love with her. Does that explain—"

Now CC interrupted. "Not in love, Martin. Attracted. Surely, you know the difference. Call it a crush. A temporary crush. Haven't you ever had a crush on somebody?" An image of Gina's lithe body in that string bikini flashed into Martin's head as CC continued. "Anyway, I kept track of her career, and when I went to CTI to offer them a chair, my hope was that they would give it to her. She's pretty phenomenal."

"Okay," said Martin, recovering from his reverie. "I get it. And she's clearly worthy of that kind of support. Actually, quite nice of you.

When you shifted the chair to Bottlesworth, did you think she would fill it? Instead of me, I mean?"

"Not really. I knew she was well suited to Camberton."

"And you didn't know Julian?"

"No. Just met him today. If he's an important part of this program, I need to get to know him. And even if you are pissed off, which I understand and for which I apologize, please don't quit us here at Autobot. Our HR team is really excited about your suggestions."

"No, I'm not gonna quit, but I am gonna sit down with Julian and read him the riot act on secrecy. I will keep you informed, as we agreed, and you will please not ask him to break his confidentiality."

"Okay, okay, peace already. I'm not even sure I'll retain him. I'd have to get him a security clearance."

"What you do with Autobot is your business. Did he tell you his stories about the fake logon IDs at CTI?"

CC laughed. "He sure did. He's very proud of having fixed that."

-   -   -

Martin and Jenny left the children with Helen and Bill and flew to Pittsburgh on Friday night, staying at the Wyndham. The next morning, they went to pick up Andrew and were greeted by Lavelle, with his twinkling "Yes, boss," when Martin asked whether Andrew was ready.

Jenny said, with a big smile, "You must be Lavelle. I've heard a lot about you — all good." She extended a hand for a handshake.

"So you his stepmom?" asked Lavelle, holding her handshake gently, and for longer than Jenny expected.

"Since I'm married to his father," releasing her hand, "I guess I'm his stepmom. Yes."

Cautious-eyed Andrew appeared behind Lavelle. Jenny stepped forward, again with an outstretched hand. "Hi, Andrew, I'm Martin's wife, Jenny. It's a pleasure to meet you." Andrew accepted the handshake but said nothing.

"My mom's home," said Lavelle. "C'mon in and say hello."

As they entered the living room, Janet came out of the kitchen drying her hands on a dish towel. Andrew and Lavelle escaped to a room in the back. "Hello, Mr. Quint," said Janet, "nice to see you again. And you must be Mrs. Quint?"

"Yes, I'm Jenny."

"And I'm Janet. You come to collect Andrew?"

"I came to meet him."

"That boy needs a family. When you gonna collect him?"

Martin said, "There's things to sort out first. I hope you can manage a bit more."

"You know that if you folks don't collect him soon, he's got no place else to go. You know that, doncha? He's a good boy, but we can't keep doing for him this way."

"Yes, we understand," said Jenny.

"When his ma was killed, I didn't have no time to sort out anything. I just took him in."

"And we really appreciate that," said Martin.

"But you still waiting. Whatcha waiting for?"

"Lawyers," said Martin, getting a sharp sudden look from Jenny.

"We'd like to go out for a while with Andrew," said Jenny. "Could you let him know?"

Janet muttered something too low to be heard, but went into a back hallway and called to Andrew, who appeared a moment later. "Ready to go out?" asked Jenny. Andrew nodded.

Once they got in the car, Jenny said, "If it's all right with you two, I'd like to drop Martin off at the hotel so Andrew and I can spend some time together. Is that okay?"

Martin, surprised, nevertheless said, "Fine by me. How about you, Andrew?"

"Sure, I guess. It's okay," said Andrew, so quietly he could hardly be heard.

"Since I don't know Pittsburgh," said Jenny, "you'll have to navigate, but we can go anywhere you want."

- - -

Martin never did find out in detail what Jenny and Andrew did that day other than that, among other things, they had spent an hour or so in Frances's condo. When they returned to the hotel late in the afternoon, Andrew seemed to have relaxed a little, those cautious eyes less suspicious. Martin had made a dinner reservation at La Cucina, where Andrew ordered spaghetti and meatballs but declined the offer of a salad to go with it. Jenny selected mushroom risotto and Martin took the veal scallopini, happy to be able once again to enjoy real food. Dinner conversation was guided by Jenny. It was a repetition of much of what Martin had already heard over dinner with the Waltons, but now Andrew was talking, really talking, not just answering with minimum words. Jenny convinced Andrew to try tiramisu for dessert, and after his first tentative taste, decided it was good, and polished it off. They dropped Andrew off at nine, greeted by Lavelle. His mom, he said, was working.

Back at their hotel room, Martin asked Jenny to report. "We had a nice day together. That's as much as I want to say. But you're right. He's yours, and that means he's also mine. We need to get him settled."

Martin, both surprised and pleased, asked, "Should we see if he can come back with us tomorrow?"

"What the hell," said Jenny. "We're going to be in tumult no matter what, so the sooner we get him settled, the better, especially so we can have relatively open time with him before school starts."

"The lawyer gave me her home phone. Let me give her a call."

- - -

Sylvia Palmer heartily approved of the move and said so, but nevertheless asked, "Does Andrew agree?"

"We haven't told him yet," said Martin.

"Call me again when you have. I'm pretty sure he'll agree to go with you, but… Anyway, assuming he agrees, I'll send you written confirmation that, as his official guardian, I approve." She added that they might be able to get a court date on the guardianship within a month, or maybe sooner if there was a cancellation on the docket. She even offered to pay Martin and Jenny's travel expenses from funds already in hand, but Martin declined.

"That's Andrew's money," he said. "Best to keep it separate for now. But I would like to get Frances's old diary, if I could, the one with my name in it."

"Officially, the diaries — and there's quite a stack of them — those are Andrew's property now, so until you're the official guardian you'll have to ask him about it."

"Really?"

"Really, but I'm sure he'll say it's okay."

"Where are they?"

"We have them. Needed the 2002 one, at least."

"In case I fought reality, right?"

"Right. They'll be released to Andrew and you once you're the official guardian. Until things are signed on the dotted line, I think I'll hang on to them."

"No need to push it. But I am curious about what she said."

After Martin ended the call, Jenny asked, "How are you going to tell him?"

"Go over there in the morning, take a deep breath, and tell him. I'm his father. He should be with me, with us. You have a better suggestion?"

"Sounds forced, and might freak him out. Can't you be a little more positive? Tell him we both want him to come, and that JJ is excited about having a big brother. Something for him to look forward to?"

"Good point. We'll need a suitcase for his stuff. Should we show up with it, or tell him first?"

"Better tell him first. Then deal with suitcases."

-    -   -

Martin and Jenny arrived at the Waltons' at nine and were greeted by Janet. Andrew and Lavelle had gone to the playground for some basketball.

"You come to take him with you?" asked Janet.

"Yes," said Martin. "It's time."

"I'm gonna miss that boy. He's good for Lavelle. But I can't keep doing for him. He needs to be with his family. I'm sure you understands that."

"We do," said Martin. "You've been amazingly helpful, and we can't say enough thanks. Can you tell us where the playground is?"

"Turn left outta the house and go three blocks. It's on the left. You'll see them."

It was a short walk. Andrew and Lavelle were in a game with six other boys, mostly black, shooting and jousting. As they approached the court, Lavelle noticed and stopped the game. He said something to Andrew, who left the court and headed toward his new parents. The game resumed in his absence.

"Sorry to interrupt the game," said Martin. "You having fun?"

Andrew shrugged. "It's okay."

"Well, it's time to talk seriously. Can we sit?"

The trio walked to a nearby wooden bench under a maple tree and got settled, with Andrew between Martin and Jenny.

"We want you to come home with us," said Martin. "It's time."

"Now?" asked Andrew, his eyes suspicious, his lips tensed. "Today?"

"Yes, now. Today."

"Do I have to?"

"We can't force you," said Jenny, "but we're your family now. Even JJ is excited about having a big brother."

"But, but…" Andrew tried to keep it together, but couldn't. "But things are okay here," he sobbed. "I like living with Lavelle."

"We know you do," said Martin. "Having a friend like Lavelle is important, and he'll still be your friend. But you need to be with your parents, with me, with us. Lavelle's mother has been amazing in caring for you, but you know it can't go on like that. She's overloaded, and we have a good home for you."

"But do I have to?" wailed Andrew.

"Eventually," said Jenny, "you will have to. We want it to be now so there's plenty of time to get settled with us before the end of the summer. You'll like where we live. And you'll find lots of new friends."

"Not like Lavelle." Andrew's wailing reduced toward sniffling. "He's special."

"Yes," said Martin. "I agree. He's special. But we're pretty special, too. We can give you a good place to live, with both a father and a mother. We want you to find your way forward, and we can help."

"So I have to go today?"

"Yes. It's time. We need to tell Lavelle. Or would you rather do that?"

Andrew took a deep breath, wiped his drippy eyes and nose on his sleeve, and with despondency resonating in his semi-deep adolescent voice, said, "I'll do it."

- - -

Martin called Sylvia to confirm that Andrew had agreed and went to buy a carry-on suitcase, while Jenny helped Andrew select enough clothing to last him until he and Martin could drive back together and collect the rest of his things. The packing-up was quick. The departure was not. Janet, for all her firm composure, was the first to break down in tears, hugging Andrew to her bosom saying how much she loved him, how he needed a real family, and that she would miss him. He wrapped his arms around her, trying to hide his sniffling, but said nothing. Jenny's eyes were moist, too. Martin's face was a stoic enigma, wondering what this new life would be like for all of them as he waited for Andrew and Janet to unwrap from each other. As they went out the door, Lavelle and Andrew shared a fist bump and hand clasp, but Lavelle was silent, his usually ebullient self stilled as he watched his closest friend ever disappear.

- - -

Andrew's tears stopped when they got in the car, but he remained subdued as they drove to the airport, looking at everything with those cautious eyes, apparently afraid. Martin asked, "Have you ever flown before?"

"No. We never did. Is it loud?"

"When you take off, yes, but then it settles down. And the view from up there is absolutely amazing. We'll get you a window seat if you want. Do you like geography?"

"You mean like maps and stuff?"

"Yeah. Maps and stuff."

"Sort of. I know the map of Pennsylvania, anyway. We studied it in school."

"So you can look down and follow the rivers, pick out the cities, the mountains. It's pretty neat."

This seemed to relieve some of Andrew's hesitancy. They checked in, went through security and boarded their flight. Andrew turned his head away from the window as the plane accelerated for takeoff, and his hands gripped the armrests, but once they were airborne, he seemed to relax. He started sneaking peeks at the ground, got a bit bolder, and then spent the rest of the flight with his nose almost pressed to the window, catching glimpses of the ground between puffy blobs of cloud drifting below them. When they descended through the cloud layer, he muttered, "Awesome." The thump of the landing and the sudden deceleration on the runway startled him, but he said, "This is totally awesome. I wanna learn to fly a plane."

When they reached the car, however, Andrew once again hesitated, "How far is it? To your house."

"About an hour, a little less," said Martin.

"Do we have to go fast, like on a highway?"

"Well, we do have to go on a highway, but I won't drive fast. Does it make you nervous?"

"It's just… I don't…"

Andrew's jaw wobbled as he tried, without success, to hold back tears. Jenny wrapped him in a hug and whispered to Martin, "Let's move the car seats to the wayback and I'll sit with Andrew in back."

"Will that be okay?" asked Martin. "I'll drive carefully. I promise."

Andrew didn't say anything, but he did stop crying as Jenny and Martin wrestled the car seats into the cargo space, piling them on top of the suitcases. Everyone climbed in and they departed, with Andrew leaning up against Jenny in the back seat all the way to Helen's.

When they arrived, Andrew clambered out just as Helen, Bill, and all four kids came out on the front porch. JJ ran down the steps, right up to Andrew, and said, "Hi. I'm JJ. You're my brother."

Andrew said, "I guess so. I never knew I had a brother."

"And this is Sister. Her name's Ellen but I call her Sister. And that one is Carlo. He's my cousin, and that's Angela. She's Carlo's sister. And this is Uncle Bill and Aunt Helen. They're so cool."

It wasn't clear to Martin how Andrew was taking this blitz of an introduction, but he was as proud of JJ as it was possible to be. What a kid, he thought, doing in twenty seconds what adults would have fussed and fumed over and then mess up by being too formal. Bill came to shake Andrew's hand and Helen, being Helen, swept him into a big hug that clearly embarrassed the boy. "Do you folks want some refreshment, or would you rather head home?"

"Home, I think," said Martin. "We've got some furniture moving to do before bedtime," smiling at his new son.

-    -   -

Martin explained that the plan was to move Ellen's bed into JJ's room, and let Andrew have the smaller bedroom to himself. JJ objected. He wanted to share his room with his brother. Martin looked to Andrew, who shrugged as if to say, whatever you want. So Martin rolled out the futon in JJ's room. Jenny, in the meantime, had gone to pick up a take-out dinner.

The expanded family was too large for the kitchen table, so they got out the protective pads for the dining table and ate at the Queen Anne. "I guess, now that we're five, we've got a lot of rethinking to do about furniture," said Martin.

"And about whether this house is big enough," murmured Jenny.

JJ didn't want to let Andrew out of his sight, but Jenny said that he needed some privacy for showering and getting ready for bed, so she bathed JJ and Ellen as usual, then gave Andrew unfettered and uncrowded use of the kids' bathroom.

Martin had been worried that there would be lots of awkward times with Andrew's insertion into the mix, but JJ kept peppering him with questions about his school, and what grade he was in, and what it was like in Pittsburgh, and did he know how to dig clams because that was so much fun, and he would show him, and did he ever go in a canoe, and what was his favorite sport. When Andrew said soccer, JJ said, "That's mine, too. How cool."

JJ finally yawned, and Jenny took that as a sign that it was bedtime. She took the boys upstairs, tucked them in, and gave each of them a kiss.

As Martin and Jenny got themselves ready for bed, they heard muffled sobs. Martin started for the boys' bedroom, but Jenny stopped him. "He needs time to cry," she said. "He's trying to be tough, but let him cry. I just hope it won't frighten JJ."

✳ **20** ✳

The next morning, Martin loaded the children into the van and drove to the cottage, giving Jenny some child-free time to work on a plan for refitting their house for three children while managing the increasingly urgent requests from her Chicago client. The Washingtons' car was parked at their cottage when they arrived, and JJ ran next door, with Andrew following, but no one was there. "Probably over at the bayside," said Martin. "Let's go to the beach. Bathing suits, everyone!"

Andrew had never been to the ocean. He was shocked at how cold the water was and seemed stunned the first time he and JJ scrambled up onto the tallest promontory, standing silent a long time, staring at the undulations of water and light and the eider ducks swimming in the backwash around a small island just offshore.

"Wanna dig some clams?" asked JJ.

"I guess so," said Andrew. "You do that here? On the beach?"

"Oh, no. We go around to the other side, the mudflats at low tide. Great clams. The tide's going out now. It's fun. I'll show you."

Martin took a deep breath and agreed to let them go by themselves. He was reasonably sure that Andrew was not reckless, but he told both boys no swimming without an adult, and they promised.

An hour later, Andrew and JJ returned to the cottage with an empty bucket and thoroughly soaked bathing suits.

"I thought I told you no swimming without an adult."

"There was an adult," said JJ. "The Washingtons were all there, and me and Gabriel and Andrew went swimming. They want us all to come for supper tonight. The water was perfect."

"So what do you think of the coast?" asked Martin, looking at his oldest son.

"Pretty nice. Never seen anything like it. I bet Lavelle would like it."

"Who's Lavelle?" asked JJ.

"My friend. I stayed with him after…"

"Yeah, him," said JJ.

"And you met the Washingtons?"

"Yessir," said Andrew. "The man, is it DeShawn? He said he used to play pro ball? For Charlotte?"

"True. He did. Now he's a coach."

"Maybe he could teach me to play better," said Andrew.

- - -

Martin suggested that the Washingtons come to the Quint cottage for potluck, since he had more sitting space for meals. He set up the card table for the boys, with Ellen at the big table on a booster seat. Tamiqua brought slow-cooked spare ribs and corn, plus some steamers. Martin supplied the wine, a salad, and ice cream for dessert.

Over dinner, Martin did a trial run of what would be the official Andrew story: Yes, Andrew was his son. He had been living with his mother, a previous partner and, no, they had mutually decided not to marry. When his mother died, the obvious choice was for Andrew to come here. The telling barely raised an eyebrow. Andrew seemed to know not to chime in with any details.

After dinner, the three boys started a game of Monopoly, and Ellen dragged her stuffed dachshund to a corner of the living room with a pile of books.

"What's the school situation?" asked Tamiqua.

"He'll be in seventh grade. We'll register him next week."

"You gonna send him to the public school?"

"Sure. Why not?"

"Just wondering, with everything he's been through, how he'll fit in."

"Time will tell. Seventh graders can be cruel, but they can also be okay. We need to find him some local friends his own age. Best way is through the school. And maybe through soccer. He likes soccer."

"Yeah, he said that," said DeShawn. "But he also asked me a lot about basketball."

"His best friend in Pittsburgh, a kid named Lavelle, is pretty good in basketball, and Andrew kind of suffered when the two of them would go to the playground. He said he was always picked last."

DeShawn chuckled. "There's always a kid picked last. Maybe," he added, with one of his patented winks, "I can give him a few pointers. Can I take the boys to the playground tomorrow?"

"It would be a blessing," said Martin.

-    -   -

That night, Martin insisted that Andrew be allowed to sleep in the guest room. JJ pouted, wanting him upstairs in the loft, but he was so tired out from the day's activities, he put up only a minor fuss. Once Ellen and JJ were bedded down, Martin and Andrew had some quiet time together, sitting in front of the fire.

"How're you doing?" asked Martin.

"Okay, I guess."

"You miss your mom a lot?"

"Yeah. A lot. But Jenny's nice. She really is. It helps."

"Jenny's a dream. I'm lucky. We're all lucky to have her. Can I make a suggestion?"

Andrew looked up, expectant. "When someone experiences a sudden tragedy, which you certainly have, it can be helpful to talk to someone about your feelings. Not a family member, a counsellor, someone to help you through the grieving."

"You mean a shrink?"

"Or a psychologist. Or a pastor. Anyone who has experience helping people cope with such a big loss."

"I don't need a shrink."

"I agree. You don't need a shrink. But you might need someone to talk to anyway. Think about it. Experience says it's best to talk things out sooner than later."

"I don't need a shrink," said Andrew, shaking his head.

- - -

The next morning, DeShawn took Andrew, JJ, and Gabriel to Bath, the closest place with a park that had regulation-height basketball hoops, while Ellen stayed with Martin. They started on the beach, building and wrecking sand castles, followed by lunch. During Ellen's nap, Martin wondered what had become of his life. The book had been effectively farmed out to a partner, an intrusive and sometimes pushy partner, whose highly relevant knowledge and strong ideas were a plus, even in the face of the extra work that would be required to turn his teaching structure upside down. CC's intrusion was looking less ominous now that the Task Force was set up, and his funding of Gina's position was a blessing. His only concerns were, first, putting his Gina fantasy to rest, which he vowed to do now that her teaching position was a certainty, and, second, healing his relationship with Jenny, who had seemed increasingly tense and remote since Andrew entered their lives — no more warm and cuddly moments, no soft kisses on the side of his neck, not even a hint about sex. Was it just having Andrew in the house, a change in her sense of privacy? Or the stress of the Chicago job? Or did he do something else to set her off?

Martin's cell phone interrupted his musing. It was Sylvia. "Can you get on a plane tomorrow? I got us a court date on Friday morning. There was a cancellation and we were next in line."

"I have to confirm with Trevor Corey that the petition is okay, and I'll need to cancel some stuff," said Martin, "but it should be all right. Does Andrew need to be there?"

"It'll be best to have Andrew there. He's old enough that the judge may want to see his demeanor. The estate thing will take longer, but getting Andrew's guardianship situation settled is my top priority."

"Fair enough. Maybe we can bring his stuff back over the weekend. And could I have a sit-down with you about the estate when we're there? I have a lot of questions."

"Absolutely. I'll fax you directions to the court."

After ending the call, Martin called Trevor, who said the petition looked fine and that Trevor did not need to be in court to represent him. All he needed to do was confirm to the judge that he was Andrew's father and wanted custody. Martin then asked him about the estate part, and Trevor said he would email him a list of things to ask about later that day. His next call was to Jenny, who said they might as well get it over with. Finally, he had to call CC to cancel his scheduled consulting visit.

-     -   -

"You said you had just two," said CC's voice over the phone.

"I thought I had just two," said Martin. "But it turns out — surprise, surprise — that I actually have three. And I've been summoned to Pittsburgh tomorrow for a court hearing to settle official custody."

"So he's with you now?"

"Yeah, we brought Andrew here last weekend. And I need to ask a favor."

"Sure. What?"

"The official story I'm putting out is that I knew about this boy and that he was living with his mother by mutual agreement. I prefer that the surprise element be suppressed as much as possible. It's just too embarrassing."

"You'll never manage that. People will figure it out."

"I don't care if they figure it out. I just don't want to be the one announcing it."

-     -   -

That evening, Jenny and Martin were on the way home from the long-promised dinner party at Steve and Susan Wang's beautiful old farmhouse home a mile north of the river, one of the few occasions they had to mix and meet beyond the command-performance college functions and occasional cookouts with Jenny's kid-swap friends.

"It was refreshing to meet some more people who are not at the college," said Jenny, "but that guy, Gordon what's-his-name, does he really support Donald Trump?"

Martin laughed. "No way to tell whether he liked him or warning us against him. I liked his crack that Trump could sell icebergs to the Eskimos. But Trump'll never get the nomination. Too vulgar. I mean, coming down that escalator? Ridiculous. And he's too racist, too narcissistic. And a bully."

"I hope you're right," she said. "He scares me."

"Did you hear Susan say that her younger daughter will be in seventh grade in the fall, same as Andrew? She seemed like a nice kid."

"Yes. Maybe they can be friends, although friendships between seventh-grade boys and girls — well, I'm not sure how that works these day. Seventh grade can be so miserable, with the girls growing up faster than the boys. It was nice to meet another teacher from the middle school, but she painted a somewhat scary picture. I'm worried about what Andrew will find there."

"Yeah, Susan has always said it was a decent school with dedicated teachers, but Allyson was going on and on about the oversized classes and the pot and the ecstasy."

"Well, that's what schools have become these days."

"I'm glad we could mention Andrew without incident. Everyone seemed just to accept the fact that we added a kid over the weekend."

"Easier for them than for us," said Jenny.

When they got home, they thanked Helen for sitting, offering to do similar duty at their house should the occasion arise.

"Well," she said, "I thought it best for Andrew to have someone familiar here rather than a new person. He's so quiet."

"Yes, he is," said Martin. "He's still in shock. It worries me."

* **21** *

Martin and Andrew flew to Pittsburgh on Thursday, stayed at Frances's condo, and met Sylvia Palmer at the courthouse at nine o'clock on Friday. They had to wait an hour before the case came up, but it took only ten minutes for the judge to agree to Martin's replacing Sylvia as Andrew's legal guardian.

The trio left the courthouse and went a few doors down the street to grab a take-out lunch before going up to Sylvia's office to talk estate issues. Sylvia suggested that Andrew and Martin go through both homes very carefully and take anything that Andrew wanted, large or small, even favorite furniture, which could be set aside and shipped. All she needed was a listing of what they took or wanted sent.

Andrew asked, "You mean I can take whatever I want? To keep?"

"Whatever you want," said Sylvia. "While you can't officially inherit yet because you're too young, this is really your property, your family's property, and no one is trying to take it away from you. But once you collect whatever you want, we will have to decide what to do with the rest. Do you understand?"

"I guess. But do I have to decide today?"

"Not this minute," she said, "But since you're both here, maybe you could stay for the weekend and take your time. Does that sound all right?"

Martin said, "We're already planning on that. I'll be renting a car, or maybe a van depending on how much Andrew wants to bring. By the way, is the diary at the house?"

"No. We have a box with all the diaries here. You can take them."

The subject shifted to the homes themselves. Sylvia suggested selling them using the public sale procedure, which would usually take two months or so. Andrew teared up. "You mean sell my home? And Grandma's house, too?"

"Yes, Andrew," said Sylvia. "It costs a lot of money to own a condo or a house, so if you and your father want to keep it, you would either need to spend money on mortgages, taxes, utilities, and upkeep or rent it out—"

Martin interrupted. "I think Andrew and I need to talk some more about this. What do you say, bud? Can we talk about his while we drive back to Maine?"

"Yeah, I wanna think about it some," said Andrew, his eyes signaling relief.

"It's your call," said Sylvia, "but a decision, one way or the other, will figure into my final estate report for audit."

"Do you know any property managers I could talk to?" asked Martin.

"I'll have to ask one of my associates, but I think we have a few names. I'll email them."

Martin thanked Sylvia for her help, and, before he and his son departed for the emotionally wrenching task of parsing possessions, he asked whether Frances had any documents that he should get from her, property deeds or the like.

"The property deeds are registered." said Sylvia. "I got them from the family's safe deposit box along with the condo documents and car titles. I'll need to keep them until we finish off with the estate."

"But I'll need the condo documents if I talk to a property manager. Can you make a copy?"

"It'll take a while. How about I messenger it over later this afternoon?"

Martin noted privately that a messenger was an unnecessary added cost, but he agreed. Time mattered more than money just now.

- - -

They stopped at Staples on the way to Andrew's home to pick up some packing boxes. Andrew emptied the clothes from his dresser and set aside his books, a few games, and a small pile of what he called "just stuff" — his pocket knife, a framed Pittsburgh Pirates poster, a baseball glove, the growing-up photographs of him from the mantelpiece, some with his mother, a little snow globe and a print of a Degas dancer, which he said was his mother's favorite. When they were going through his mother's room, they found a box of family photographs, and Andrew picked out three pieces of his mother's costume jewelry to take with him. There was nothing in the kitchen that Andrew wanted, but he did ask Martin if they could bring his mother's small writing table and computer with them. Martin laughed and said, "Okay, bud, I'll get a van, not a car, but absolutely we bring them," at which point Andrew also asked about one of the living room chairs and a floor lamp.

"That's where my mom would sit and read," he said.

"We'll bring it," said Martin. "And, of course, we'll take the diaries."

"I guess so. Is it okay to read them? I mean she wrote them for herself."

"You can decide. But let's take them with us. And let's walk through one more time before we go to your grandmother's. We'll be back here tomorrow in case you think of something else you want to take. In the meantime, how about you use my phone and take photographs of everything we're leaving behind, so you'll have that as a memory?"

"Yeah," said Andrew. "I like that idea. And can I call Lavelle now?"

"Of course," said Martin. A visit was arranged for the next day. Then Martin called Jenny to report.

- - -

Martin got Andrew up early so they could go out for breakfast before their appointment with Edward Kowalski from Pittsburgh Property Management Services, who showed up promptly at nine and took a few photographs of the front of the house before ringing the bell. Edward was both friendly and efficient, walking through, taking notes, and promising to return the condo documents after he had reviewed them along with a proposal.

After Edward left, Martin encouraged Andrew to look around once more, which he did without adding anything to the piles created yesterday. Martin meanwhile opened the drawers in Frances's desk, but found them empty. "Okay," he said. "Let's go Lavelle's. We seem to be done here."

- - -

Janet answered the door and wrapped Andrew up in a smothering hug, calling, "Lavelle, get in here, boy." She then asked, "How you doin', Andrew? These folk treatin' you right?"

Before Andrew could answer, Lavelle popped up, saying, "Hey, daddy boss. Welcome back. C'mon, Drew," and the boys disappeared to a back room.

Janet expelled a large breath. "I gotta say, my boy do miss his Andrew, but I'm glad you got him now. It's God's plan. Is the legal stuff all fixed?"

"All fixed," said Martin. "I'm now the official parent. We're getting Andrew set up for school, and my wife is trying to figure out how to cram all five of us into our little house. Two of the kids will have to double up."

Janet laughed. "That's like fitting three of us here. Not much space. How long you staying?"

"We're driving back tomorrow with Andrew's stuff. He's picked out a few pieces of furniture to take, so I've gotta turn in my rental car and swap it for a van. How about I leave Andrew here while I do that?"

"Fine by me," said Janet. "I don't gotta work at all today. Next shift is tomorrow afternoon. It's nice to hear that chattering again."

Martin drove to the closest U-Haul depot, reserved a small van for the trip home, turned in his rental car and got a lift back to the U-Haul place. On the way to the Waltons', he pulled over and phoned Jenny.

"I have a hare-brained idea," said Martin.

"Compared to what? Compared to taking Andrew in the first place?"

"Maybe. I want to invite Lavelle come stay with us for a week — at the cottage. Andrew really misses him, and it would ease the loneliness for at least a while. Can we do that?"

Jenny was silent for what felt like a month, but then said, "I actually like the idea. I've been worried about Andrew feeling so alone. Yes. Bring Lavelle. It'll be like camping in our house, but the cottage can hold us all. Yes. I like it. Do it."

When he returned and told Janet about the invitation. She stiffened. "You mean take him all the way to Maine? How long? How's he get back?"

"It would be a week. We'll stay at our beach cottage, and both boys would clearly love it. As for getting back, we'll put him on an airplane in Portland next Sunday and you can meet him at the airport. Whaddya say?"

"He sho' miss his friend, so maybe."

"Can we ask him?"

"I'll get 'em," and Janet went to retrieve the boys, who were ecstatic with the idea. Andrew told him about the ocean and also about DeShawn Washington.

"You mean the pro? The guy who played for Charlotte?"

"Yup," said Andrew. "He took me and JJ and his son to shoot hoops. He's awesome."

And it was thus arranged. Lavelle came with Andrew and Martin to Frances's condo to help load the furniture and boxes into the van, after which Martin took the boys back to Janet's. Andrew stayed over with Lavelle, while Martin went back to Frances's condo for what he expected would be his last night there ever. An eerie reminder of times past.

-    -   -

Martin couldn't sleep. The diaries were irresistible. He got out of bed, slipped on some pants, went out to the van, and brought the box inside. He sifted through to find the one for 2002. The entries were cryptic, one or two lines, and only on some days. He flipped pages quickly, not so much reading as catching an entry here and there.

January 1. Martin watched football all day. Foo.

February 14. Valentine's dinner. Roses. Hot dessert between the sheets.

March 31. Leave CMU? Cambridge?
Massachusetts? Really?

April 27. Says he's going. Do I love him enough to leave
home, leave Mom, leave Aunt Flora?

June 15. I don't think I can become a Mrs. Quint in
Massachusetts and he hasn't actually proposed anyway.
Loves his work more than me. Would that ever change?

Martin flipped ahead to July.

July 1: It's over. We agreed. Fireworks is goodbye time.

July 5: Bad hangover. Shouldn't have invited him back here.

And then quickly to what he had to see.

September 7: Yup. Pregnant. Do I tell him? Do I want a
guilt-tripped husband who puts his work first?

Martin already knew her answer to that question. He returned the diary to the box, went back to bed, and tossed and turned much of the night.

- - -

Martin worried about Andrew's fear of the long road trip back to Maine, but with Lavelle around, Andrew seemed like a different kid, more comfortable, more confident. The front seat of the van was a bit crowded with both boys stuffed in next to Martin. Andrew and Lavelle jabbered about some computer game that Martin couldn't understand, about the Pirates, and about playground basketball. The real estate discussion with Andrew, of course, did not happen, but Martin was delighted with hearing Andrew so animated. Eventually, fatigue set in and both boys fell asleep, Martin hoping he could find a friend for Andrew locally, someone to fill in for and eventually replace the obvious companionship he so desperately needed.

Other than the grueling length, the fourteen-hour drive was

uneventful — intervals of jabber, of sleep, bathroom stops, food stops, fuel stops. They arrived in Brimfield Junction at ten-thirty. JJ and Ellen had been put to bed and, not wishing to wake them, Jenny had set up the futon and a sleeping bag on the living room floor for the boys. Were they hungry? Yes. Jenny brought out cheese sandwiches, carrots, and ice cream, all of which were attacked with gusto. Martin suggested they not unload the van until the morning. Jenny wondered where they would put the desk, chair, and lamp that Andrew brought, but agreed that they needed to be in sight, not dispatched to the basement. And then she tossed another complication in the mix. "I have to go to Boston tomorrow — actually, Worcester tomorrow and Boston on Tuesday. My dad got us a consignment referral in Worcester, and one of the Boston consignment shops wants to talk more. I think they learned that our stuff is unique. The owner said she'd be free on Tuesday morning, and there's an antique show I can hit on Tuesday afternoon."

"So I've got all four kids?"

"Unless you bring Kuc to the cottage, you've got all four kids."

Martin blew out a long breath. "Okay. Okay. I'll be a daddy this week, or at least these two days. Then you can maybe be a mommy?"

"Sure. I'll be back Tuesday night."

"Good, because I owe CC a consulting visit on Thursday."

* **22** *

The next morning was bright and sunny. JJ came galumphing into the living room at seven and woke the sleeping boys. "Hi, Andrew. Was it a long drive? And you're Lavelle? It's awesome you could come. We're going to the cottage today for the whole week. You can meet my friend Gabriel. And my mom is bringing Sister downstairs. Her name is Ellen but I call her Sister. She's nice, mostly."

By now, the boys were awake enough to stretch, and yawn, and slowly get vertical. Jenny came downstairs with Ellen just as Martin emerged from his basement treadmill and weight-lifting routine. The entire mob crowded into the kitchen, where the three boys and Ellen took the four seats at the kitchen table, leaving Martin and Jenny serving as cooks and wait staff. Toaster waffles proved a success, Martin popping them in and out of the toaster almost as fast as the kids could eat them. Not having anticipated teenage appetites, they quickly ran out, so Martin offered scrambled eggs, which both Andrew and Lavelle accepted and wolfed down.

Jenny watched this devouring, and said, "It looks like I didn't buy enough food for the cottage. You'll have to stop at Shaw's on the way to stock up. And I've gotta go by ten."

"So we better get the van unloaded now, because I'll need you to drive me back here when I turn it in."

Andrew and Lavelle hurried to dress and helped Martin, still in his workout clothes, to haul the boxes, the computer, the desk, the chair, and the lamp into the house. "We'll put it all in the living room for now and sort it out later. Can we leave you boys here while I turn in the van? Or do we all go?"

Lavelle laughed. "Sure, boss. Me and Andrew been left alone so

210   Stephen D. Senturia

much, we're used to it."

Andrew added, "And you can leave JJ and Ellen if you want. We'll keep 'em outta trouble."

Jenny said, "Well, JJ, you can stay if you want, but we'll take Ellen." JJ glowed with delight at being left with his older brother and his totally amazing friend.

After depositing the van at U-Haul, Jenny dropped Martin and Ellen at the house and took off for Worcester in Martin's car. Lavelle and Andrew had moved the desk into a corner of the living room and had set up Frances's computer. They had even linked it to Martin's wifi network using the password JJ dug out of Martin's desk drawer.

"Great," said Martin. "So now Andrew can have his own computer. But we should get going. The cottage beckons."

- - -

The sun was bathing the cottage with direct light from the southeast and speckled light reflected from the ripples on the bay to the west, creating a magical shimmer on the walls. JJ and Andrew took Lavelle to show him the beach while Martin unpacked and stowed the additional food, keeping half an eye on Ellen driving her dachshund in her wagon through piles of blocks. He then collected his daughter and toddled to the beach. The boys were on the top of the highest promontory, JJ pointing, apparently speaking with great authority about the ocean and which direction was England.

Martin called to them, and they started down toward the beach just as DeShawn and Gabriel showed up. Gabriel ran to the boys and Martin and DeShawn watched JJ do his master-of-ceremonies thing, introducing Lavelle to Gabriel, who turned and pointed at DeShawn.

As the boys crossed the beach toward the grown-ups, Gabriel shouted, "Dad, this is Lavelle. Andrew's friend from Pittsburgh. And he wants to shoot some hoops."

DeShawn laughed with a sly wink. "Sounds good, bro. You talk some trash, too?"

Lavelle, a bit overwhelmed both by DeShawn's height and the

radiance of his status as a real pro, still managed to sass back, "Sho' thing, boss. I talks trash with everbody."

DeShawn laughed. "Maybe after lunch, I'll take you two up to Bath for a workout. How would that be?"

"Awesome," said Lavelle.

"What about me and JJ?" said Gabriel.

"We can all go," said DeShawn.

Martin said, "I've loaded up on lunch supplies, so why don't I feed this army and then they'll come find you."

"Sounds good," said DeShawn.

-    -   -

Martin sent Glenda a message that he had his hands full of family issues just now, and hoped she could make progress on the book editing on her own for a few days. He had no doubt about the answer. She was, bit by bit, taking over the book from him. He resented Glenda's intellectual aggression, but he clearly needed her to give academic credibility to his point of view. The worry was that her scholarly focus would dilute the pungency of his message. For example, that glorious first paragraph of his, the manifesto written so many weeks ago, was no longer appropriate. Now, as co-authors, they were struggling a bit with how to open that first chapter, set the correct crisp tone, but she was definitely adding value and carrying the project forward while he dealt with the Andrew situation. And the Jenny situation. The remote Jenny, going through the motions of motherhood and wifehood and business owner, but emotionally and sexually withdrawn as if protecting herself from something. It dug up memories of his troubles with Katie's depression, and he wondered if Jenny were slipping into that hideous morass as well. The right answer was to pull out a yellow card, get her to talk. Maybe get her to a therapist. But these days, it wasn't clear that a yellow card would work. It might just start a fight, and he didn't want any more fights. He was functioning reasonably well, and his gut was still behaving, but as he had said to Glenda, he had his hands full, to the brink. Don't make waves.

- - -

Just before four, DeShawn returned with the boys, who headed directly for the ice cream in the freezer. "How'd it go?" asked Martin.

"We had a lotta fun," said DeShawn, then in a whisper, "and that Lavelle. He's something else. He's got spunk and some real talent. It looks to me, if he keeps at it, he might be able to play college ball. I'm impressed."

"Really? You joshing me?"

"No, I'm not," said DeShawn with a grin. "I would love to have a kid like him at Cranborne."

"Too bad he lives like seven hundred miles away."

"Yeah, anyway, we had a good time. Send Gabriel home for dinner, okay?"

"Will do," said Martin, as DeShawn departed.

"Hey, you guys," said Martin. "Clean up your dishes and the mess in the kitchen before whatever you're doing next."

Four bodies and eight hands, with giggles and a cry of "oof" as Lavelle dug an elbow into Andrew's stomach, got the dishes from the table to the sink to the dishwasher. Andrew wiped the ice cream drips off the counter.

"Let's play Monopoly," shouted JJ. Martin set up the card table, and soon there were the usual mutterings about whether to buy the railroads, the pain of landing on Broadway or Park Place, and "you lucky stiff." Ellen, meanwhile, wanted Daddy to read to her and was crabbily insistent about it, so Martin tucked his bundle of joy onto his lap, with a pile of books at his side, and went through them, one at a time.

As he read, letting Ellen turn each page, he drifted into an unfamiliar state of contentment. It took him by surprise. Always so busy, he rarely had the chance to feel anything but urgency and worry. Now, even with Jenny away and four children to manage, what with Glenda in charge of the book draft, Andrew's estate issues moving forward under Sylvia Palmer's steady hand, the first Task Force meeting set up for a week from Tuesday, Gina coming to visit the weekend after that to find an apartment, the syllabus for the fall C&E virtually done — wow, it was time to rest. And the warmth of love for these children just washed over him and brought a tear to his eyes. Ellen looked up as Martin paused, and reached up to touch the tear on his cheek.

"Daddy boo-boo?" asked Ellen.

"No, sweetheart, just happy."

- - -

Lavelle volunteered that he and Andrew would sleep on the bunk beds in the upstairs loft with JJ and Ellen. This was a surprise to Martin, who expected they would want to be free of the smaller children. But no, they would use the guest bathroom downstairs and would sleep upstairs. Martin felt something magical was going on. Having Lavelle here with Andrew softened everything up. He was less morose, noisier, more fun.

The next morning, Gabriel and DeShawn came over. "If it's okay with you boys," DeShawn said, speaking to JJ and Gabriel, "and with you, Martin, I'd like to take Andrew and Lavelle for some serious hoops. Is that okay with you guys?"

JJ whined, "But we were gonna do chess. Lavelle said."

Lavelle answered, "We will, but later. Okay, li'l boss?"

"Okay, I guess." Turning to Gabriel, he said, "Let's go outside. You can be the Martian this time."

DeShawn left with Lavelle and Andrew, and while JJ and Gabriel were on the deck engaged in some made-up game that involved a lot of shouting and running around, Martin was inside with Ellen. She was on the kitchen floor, surrounded by a mix of pots and pans and wooden spoons that she had hauled out of the bottom cabinet drawer. As she banged on the pots, making toddler music, her laughter was infectious, almost mesmerizing for Martin. He took out his cell phone and made a video to send Jenny. She would love it. Maybe cheer her up.

Martin heard JJ scream, and not less than ten seconds later, Gabriel burst into the cottage. "JJ's hurt. He tripped and fell off the deck. Come quick."

Martin dashed outside and found JJ on the ground beneath the corner between the deck stairs and the deck, screaming in pain. "Help me. It hurts. Help."

"Stay still, bud," said Martin as he knelt by his side. "Tell me what happened?"

Through gulped sniffles, JJ gasped out the words, "Me and Gabriel were playing Martians and Space Heroes, and he bumped me, and I fell off the deck."

Gabriel pleaded, "It wasn't my fault. We just bumped and he fell."

"Where does it hurt?" asked Martin.

"My arm. My arm."

Looking to Gabriel, Martin said, "Go get your mom. I need some help here."

Martin looked at JJ's left arm, which was swelling badly just above the wrist. "Did you land on it?" JJ nodded, his crying now reduced to occasional sobs, sniffles, and gasps of breath.

"Well, bud, it looks like you broke your arm. Don't worry, we'll get it fixed up. But I want to get another grown-up here, and then I'll call the doctor."

Tamiqua's shadow fell on the pair. "Hurt bad?" she asked, looking over Martin's shoulder. Gabriel looked almost ashen behind his mother and looked relieved when she said, "Honey, go inside and play with Ellen, so she won't get scared. Okay?"

As Gabriel went up the deck stairs, Martin said, "Looks like he broke it. What should I do? Try to splint it?"

"JJ, can you stay still for a while?" asked Tamiqua.

Stifling a sob, JJ said "I think so."

"Best not to move it until your dad talks to the doctor, okay?"

"Okay," said JJ. "I'll try."

"I'll stay with him. Go in and call."

Martin went in to call the Mid-Coast Medical Center Emergency Room. He emerged a few minutes later with a plastic bag filled with ice, a newspaper, and a roll of adhesive tape from the first aid kit.

"Here," he said, "put this ice on it. And here's an aspirin. It tastes awful, but if you chew it up and swallow, it will help with the pain. And they said to make two splints with rolled-up newspaper and tape them to the arm. You ready for us to try that?"

"Okay," said a sniffling JJ. He accepted the pill, chewed and swallowed, and watched his father fashion the splint.

"Now this may hurt," said Martin, as he prepared to tape the first splint, "but you're gonna be brave, right?"

"I'll try," said JJ, suddenly howling as Martin got the first piece of tape in place.

"Hang in there bud, just a bit more to go."

As Martin finally got the second splint secured, JJ relaxed a bit. "Would you mind watching Ellen while I take JJ to the hospital?"

"Better than that," said Tamiqua. "We'll come with you. It's better not to freak her out by having her daddy and brother disappear like that after all that screaming."

"Sounds smart. That's great. I'll collect Ellen and her diaper bag and we can get going."

-    -   -

"Yup. He broke it." The four children were all in bed and Martin was on the phone with Jenny. "He was very brave when they set it. It wasn't completely separated, so the doc said it would heal in about four weeks, maybe less. In the meantime, he's got a cast and is in some pain from the swelling, but we got a chewable painkiller and he's now pretty calm. A little proud, if I may say, lording it a bit over Gabriel, even over the bigger boys. What happened with you today? Was it good?"

"Yeah, I guess. The Worcester store will take two pieces. Mom and Dad send their love. How are you doing with Andrew and Lavelle?"

"DeShawn took them both all the way to Cranborne today for a serious basketball session. It's funny. I get the feeling that DeShawn is trying to recruit Lavelle."

"You mean to come to school here?"

"That's what I mean. I could see him almost drooling over Lavelle when he brought them back this afternoon."

"Well, that might not be a bad thing if Lavelle was close by. What do you think?"

"I hadn't thought about it at all. I've been too busy with JJ."

-   -   -

It was around midnight when Martin woke to JJ's crying. Martin went up to find JJ sitting up in bed, holding the cast in his free hand, sobbing uncontrollably. Andrew and Lavelle were both awake. "What do we do?" asked Andrew.

"Go down and get the bottle of pills from the kitchen counter, and a glass of water." Sitting on JJ's bed, he said, "I guess it hurts pretty bad, huh? We're getting you one of those pills."

JJ chewed and swallowed and took a drink of water from the glass Andrew had brought, snorting his tears back as he braved his way through the pain.

Martin said, "Andrew, you and Lavelle can move to the guest room downstairs if you want."

"Naw," said Lavelle through a yawn. "We gotta keep li'l boss company."

Three hours later, JJ was crying again, and this time he had wakened Ellen, who started shrieking, which woke Andrew. Martin was getting a new and humbling appreciation for what he had been dumping on Jenny whenever he went west for his consulting trips. He got another chewable tablet for JJ, picked up Ellen to calm her down, and told Andrew he could move downstairs if they were disturbing his sleep. He did, but said that Lavelle could sleep through a train wreck. On cue, Lavelle opened one eye, yawned, and drifted back into slumber.

-   -   -

The next morning Martin was on the phone with Jenny. "I'm totally exhausted. When will you be home tonight?"

"Actually, if you can manage, I'd like to stay over one more night."

"Really? Staying where?"

"With Charlotte. I have a chance for a late lunch tomorrow with representatives from an international association of antique replicas dealers. They're here for the Boston show, and…"

"Okay, okay," snapped Martin. "I'll manage."

"Hey, Goofus," said Jenny. "Don't be like that. I'm sorry you've had to deal with a crisis, but this is important, and it sounds like—"

"It sounds like I'm coping? Right?"

"Well, it does. And if you need help, you could go home and have Kuc come."

"Maybe, but something special is going on here with Andrew and Lavelle and DeShawn. I'm not sure what it is, but I've finally seen Andrew looking happy. I don't want to mess that up by cramming us back into the BJ house where we don't have enough space. What I'd like most is to get some sleep."

"Poor Goofus," said Jenny. "I'll be home, I mean at the cottage, by dinnertime tomorrow."

"Okay. I love you," said Martin. He waited for her response, but the line was silent.

Exhausted as he was, even with Jenny's delayed homecoming, Martin felt that same surge of contentment, that blanket of warmth that had caught him by surprise the day before. Taking care of children, nice children, was really quite satisfying. With each sound they made or action they took, he could sense peoplehood emerging, minute by minute in each of them, and its effect was electric. And sharing meals with neighbors was quite a nice thing to do. Having been disconnected from his work other than by email for more than a week, its urgency had seemed to fade a bit, making him wonder why he pushed so hard at it. He had to pinch himself to realize that this was not a dream. He was simply on vacation. What a concept, vacation.

* **23** *

By the next morning, JJ's arm had calmed down. There were no more tears. Tamiqua volunteered to take all five children to give Martin a break. He checked his email, where he found a proposal from Edward Kowalski on renting and managing the two Pittsburgh properties. The proposal included active rental management, maintenance supervision, and paying the taxes, mortgage, condo fee, insurance and utility bills. He sent a note of thanks and said it was under active consideration, recognizing that he couldn't discuss this with Andrew while Lavelle was still in Maine. He then picked up a new book on semantics, tried to read it, and opted instead for returning to bed for a catch-up on sleep.

After lunch, he went next door. DeShawn had taken Lavelle and Andrew to the beach for some ice-cold body surfing. JJ and Gabriel were doing a puzzle, and Tamiqua was reading to Ellen. When Martin poked his head in, she emptied a basket of Gabriel's action figures onto the floor and deposited Ellen in their midst, saying, "I've gotta talk to your daddy, okay?"

Ellen smiled and started picking up one toy at a time, admiring its colors and shiny surface, banging it a few times on the floor and putting it back in the basket, then picking up the next one.

"Want some coffee?" asked Tamiqua.

"Yes, yes, yes," said Martin with a yawn.

They took their steaming mugs onto the tiny front deck, where the murmur of the surf reminded Martin of the inexorable changing of the tides, the ebb and flow of life, sometimes depositing driftwood and the odd detritus. Andrew had been deposited into his life, but Andrew wasn't driftwood. Andrew was his son.

"These are such wonderful kids," she said. "That Andrew is a nice boy. It's so sad what happened."

"Yeah, and it's clear that Lavelle is an important friend. Andrew's finally smiling and laughing. I was so worried."

"Don't kid yourself," said Tamiqua. "He's still hurting inside. You gonna get him some counseling?"

"I would like to, but he says, and I quote, 'I don't need a shrink.' I can't imagine what must be going through his head."

"That's where we have an advantage."

"We?" asked Martin.

"At Cranborne. Every student is assigned to a counselor, and regular meetings are mandatory."

"But aren't your counselors just the teachers?"

"Yes, we're teachers, but we have a staff psychologist, and if we're worried about a student, we can get support and help."

"I don't expect the BJ schools have anything like that. But I have the name of somebody. As soon as we get through this week, I'll set up an appointment."

"They always say it's best to get help sooner rather than later, so I hope you find a path."

"Me too," said Martin.

"And you folks come here for dinner tonight."

"Again?"

"Again. Will Jenny be here by then?"

"She should be, and thanks."

-   -   -

Jenny rolled up to the cottage at five and unloaded her suitcase and portfolio. "Great day," she said, giving Martin a quick hug. "Made an important connection with that association of replica dealers. It helps me understand the international nature of the market." Looking around, she said, "The children?"

"Next door," said Martin. "We're invited for dinner."

"Wonderful. I'll get cleaned up."

"Want me to help you get cleaned up? The house is ours. We could…"

"Not now, Mr. Goofus, not now," said Jenny.

"But we're never alone anymore."

"Yes, I know, but not now. I just can't."

-    -   -

As soon as she had refreshed herself, Jenny and Martin went next door, Jenny focusing on the children — a big smothering hug for Ellen, admiration of JJ's cast, and questions to Lavelle and Andrew about how they were enjoying the ocean. At dinner, she commented with awe on the huge amount of food Tamiqua had put out. Tamiqua said with a laugh that Cranborne was a good training ground for adjusting to the explosion into teenage appetites.

"Speaking of that," said DeShawn, "I've been talking with Lavelle about his school, and I've planted an idea in his head."

Lavelle and Andrew grinned at each other while the table fell silent.

"Yes, I would like Lavelle to consider coming to Cranborne. And he likes the idea. So does Andrew."

"Is that possible?" asked Jenny. "I'm not sure Janet—"

"There's a scholarship program," said DeShawn. "I've spoken with Mrs. Walton, and she says we can talk more once Lavelle gets home."

"Wow," said Jenny. "It never occurred to me that—"

Martin cut in. "DeShawn just wants to win the state championship. Isn't that it?"

DeShawn laughed. "Of course I do, but I also want smart kids to get a shot at a good education. Based on what Lavelle has told me, his school is not that great, and we could—"

"Is that right?" asked Martin. "About your school?"

"Compared to Cranborne? My school, our school, sucks," said Lavelle. "When I saw that place, I just knew. And Coach can, I mean, DeShawn can—"

"He'll get a chance to develop his ball skills as well as his brain," said DeShawn. "Open the door to college. That's what I told his mother, and she's thinking about it."

"Well I'll be darned," said Jenny.

- - -

The following night, the last before Lavelle's departure, the two families gathered at the Quints' cottage for steamers and lobsters with cole slaw and corn on the cob, a buttery, drippy, finger-food dinner. Lavelle and Andrew seemed tentative about the clams, but with urging from DeShawn, tried one each, then one more, little dribs of butter dripping down their chins.

"They look gross," said Andrew, "but they taste good. Kind of a smoky thing."

Lavelle laughed. "Like that low-tide mud smells. What do I do with this lobster?"

Martin said, "If you're gonna come to New England to school, knowing how to eat a lobster is a necessity. Watch and follow." While Ellen and one-armed JJ needed help with their lobsters, Lavelle and Andrew followed Martin's lead and managed to extract claws and the tail, dipping in the drawn butter, and downing the sweet flesh. They even poked through to extract the little luscious bites of body meat.

After the Washingtons had left, after Jenny had put Ellen and JJ to bed, and after Lavelle and Andrew had finally gone upstairs, Martin once again tried to warm up Jenny toward an intimate bedtime, but she pleaded fatigue, and said no.

- - -

The next morning, the family drove to Brimfield Junction and unloaded Jenny, JJ, Ellen, and their bags. Martin, Andrew, and Lavelle continued to the Portland Airport. When they reached the security checkpoint and located the person responsible for getting unaccompanied minors onto the correct flight, Martin found himself giving Lavelle a huge hug, saying that he looked forward to his return in September.

"Me too, boss," said Lavelle. "Hey, Drew, be cool, okay?"

"Okay," said Andrew, and they executed a fast fist-bump maneuver that Martin couldn't follow.

They waved as Lavelle completed the security check and walked toward his gate. On the drive back to Brimfield Junction, Martin asked whether Andrew had enjoyed the visit. What he said surprised Martin. "I wanna go to Cranborne too."

-   -   -

When Andrew and Martin reached home, they were confronted by Jenny and JJ in the middle of an argument about sleeping arrangements.

"But I wanna share with Andrew," whined JJ.

"We have to fit in this house," said his mother, "and the only way we can do this is for Ellen to move in with you and give Andrew the smaller bedroom. We can—"

"But that's not fair," shrieked JJ, now almost in tears.

Jenny suddenly laughed. "It sounds like you think Andrew is somehow disappearing. He's not. But we need to get his desk and this chair out of the middle of the living—"

"The desk is in the corner," said JJ with a pout.

"Yes, but it can't stay there," said Jenny. "The only way we can fit in this house is—"

"Then let's get a new house," shouted JJ. "I hate this."

Again, Jenny smiled. "We might need a new house, a bigger house, but right now, young man, you are going to share your room with Ellen and Andrew is moving into her room. And that's it."

Andrew went over to JJ and said, "That's up to your parents, y'know. I'll do whatever..."

"And," said Jenny, "the whatever is that we're moving Ellen into—"

"It's not fair," wailed JJ.

Andrew, with a sheepish smile, said, "Actually, Jenny, I can do—"

"No," said Jenny. "It's the furniture. The only way I can manage to have the desk and the chair added to our household is if we put you and them in Ellen's room along with a single bed. They'll just fit."

"You mean it's my mom's furniture that makes the problem?"

Martin spoke. "Actually, it's now your furniture, and we want you to be comfortable here. We can fit the desk into the bedroom upstairs, which means you'll have—"

"It's not fair," screamed JJ, slamming one of Ellen's foam blocks to the floor.

"Actually, bud," said Martin, "sometimes life isn't fair. And this is one of those times. When we brought Andrew home, we knew it would be crowded, but we also knew that we would make him welcome. Do you want to make him feel bad?"

"No," said JJ, "but…"

"Then let's set things up this way. If, after a while, it looks like another arrangement will work, we'll try that. But right now, we've got to get our house in order, and this means moving the furniture like your mother says and finding a place for Andrew's clothes and the boxes of things he brought. This is his home now. Okay?"

"Okay, okay," whined JJ, crestfallen but no longer shrieking. "I'll share with Sister, if I have to."

- - -

An hour later, Jenny went online to order a bed, some linens, and a dresser for Andrew's clothes. Ellen was getting fussy, JJ was still silently fuming, and Andrew was upstairs, busy sorting out what he needed right away. Martin sniffed around for that sense of warmth and contentment he had felt at the cottage, but it eluded him. And he had serious work to do — the final preparation for the Task Force meeting on Tuesday.

Jenny called Andrew to come down and pick out a bedspread. He studied the options she had up on her computer screen, but then surprised Jenny by saying, "Is it possible to get some Pittsburgh thing? Like a Pirates bedspread?"

"You mean the baseball team?" asked Jenny.

"Yeah. I really like the Pirates."

"Where would I get that?"

"Lemme show you." Andrew took over the mouse and keyboard and within a minute, displayed a black-and-yellow patterned bedspread with the Pirates logo in the center. "My mom, she already had bed-spreads, so she wouldn't get me one."

"Sure, honey," said Jenny. "We'll do it. And I guess you want black-and-yellow sheets and pillowcases?"

Andrew smiled. "They make that?"

"I'll see," said Jenny.

Martin witnessed all this from his desk with wonder, wanting to wrap Jenny in his arms for this gentleness with his son. She had been so remote lately, even crabby. Days and days with no sex. Now, maybe, things were softening up. She was being a real mom to Andrew, and he loved her for it. He turned with enthusiasm to the plans for Tuesday. It looked to be an interesting day.

-    -   -

That evening after dinner and bedtime for the younger children, Martin asked Andrew to join him in the living room to talk about things.

"What things?" asked Andrew.

"Well, how are you feeling, for example," said Martin.

"Okay, I guess."

"Was it hard to see Lavelle go back home?"

"Yeah. He's my best friend. I hope he comes back here for school."

"These things are complicated, so—"

"I know. His mom may say no."

"It's not just that. Cranborne is expensive, and—"

"But DeShawn says there's scholarships."

"Yes, and maybe it'll all work out. I hope so. But there's something else important I need to talk about."

"What's that? About me going to Cranborne?"

"There's that, and there's also what to do with your Pittsburgh condo and your grandmother's house."

"Can't we just keep them?"

"If we do, we'll have to rent them out to pay the costs. Would you want us to do that?"

Andrew's face contorted, and tears appeared.

"I'm sorry," said Martin. "This is hard. Why don't we wait a while to decide."

Andrew nodded.

After Andrew went off to bed, Martin sent Sylvia Palmer an email saying that the real estate issue was going to have to remain open for a bit longer. If it costs money, so be it.

* 24 *

Martin waited for Kuc to arrive before he walked to the campus. While he had kept up with email during his ten-day hiatus from Bottlesworth, he was woefully behind with snail mail, now piled to a height of nine inches. Before digging into it, he telephoned Dr. Minna Schwartz, a psychologist he had found on a website listing of mental health providers. His only due diligence had been an innocent-sounding telephone call to the college medical service asking whether they knew anything about her. They confirmed that she was on their list of approved providers, which was good enough for Martin to try her out. He left a phone message asking for a consultation at her earliest convenience. Then he dug into the pile of mail, almost all of which went quickly into the recycle bin.

One letter from Stanford required a response. It was from the Faculty Search Committee in Materials Science at Stanford. Before he could even read it, his phone rang. It was CC asking to be filled in on plans for the next day's Task Force meeting. Martin talked through the agenda he had constructed, and reminded CC that his association with this was not going to be revealed. But CC proved, once again, to be irrepressible.

"I had dinner with Sharon Gillespie last Thursday," said CC. "She's going to be a terrific contributor."

"You mean you talked about the Task Force."

"I guess I did. Now before—"

"Jesus, CC, you wanna wreck this before it even gets started?"

"No, but before you blow up, she told me about the Task Force, not the other way around, and she's no dummy. She knew I was a Bottlesworth alum and asked if I knew anything about it. What was I going to do? Lie to her?"

"But why did you have dinner with her in the first place?"

"To talk about consulting with Autobot."

"Same excuse as with Julian."

"Listen, Martin, I value your wisdom about academic things, but I run a real business, and if I want to hire Sharon Gillespie or even the Pope as a consultant, I'm entitled to do so."

"No argument there, but if we weren't doing this Task Force, would you have approached her?"

"Maybe, maybe not. But it's my decision, in any event. When can I expect to hear from you about the first meeting?"

"You mean before or after you get reports from Sharon and Julian?"

"I want to hear directly from you. I haven't asked them for reports, and won't."

"But you won't stop them from volunteering, right?"

"Right," said CC. "Talk you to Tuesday night?"

"Sure. Tuesday night."

"And is the consulting on for Thursday?"

"Yes, it's on," said Martin.

Martin slammed the phone down, muttering to himself about CC's antics, then realizing that Jenny was right. He didn't like the way other people tried to run things — interfering with what he knew was the right way — even when, as in this case, the other person was actually the source of the thing being run. Oh, well. It's his money, his idea. If it implodes into a cloud of campus gossip, it'll be on CC's head.

He turned to the letter from Stanford.

> Dear Professor Quint:
>
> We are writing to request your frank assessment of Professor Katarina Rodriguez, who is being considered for a tenured appointment in the electronic materials division of our department...

Martin didn't need to read the rest. He knew this kind of letter by heart, muttering "Sonuvabitch, I knew this would happen." His response was short and to the point, drafted into an email and sent within minutes.

Dear Search Committee:

I am in complete support of Professor Rodriguez's candidacy for a tenured post at Stanford. As you are no doubt aware from my CTI tenure letter that somebody stole and posted on the internet, I consider her to be the real deal, absolutely worth tenuring.

The only thing I would add to what is already in the public record is that when CTI turned her down, I told Morris Wong that CTI was making a mistake, that her results would get confirmed and published, after which Stanford would make her a tenure offer. CTI didn't buy my argument, but I'm delighted to see my prediction come true. Hire her. Call me if you need more ammunition.

Sincerely,
Martin Quint
Caldicott Professor of Applied Physics

The rest of the day was reserved for catching up with Glenda, who had completed her edit and footnoting of now six chapters of the book, adding slews of new corrections to text that he thought had been mutually settled. They had agreed that Langacker's linked tree structures for representing concepts was a good basis for Martin's models of students' ways of thinking, but they had a disagreement on semantics. Martin felt that within the context of engineering, things could be precisely defined, whereas Glenda continued to stress the flexibility of interpretation of even quite simple utterances. She kept reminding him that in those critical option three conversations — where the instructor gets the data to build his or her model — it was important for the instructor to be able to gauge not just the correctness, or lack thereof, in the usage of technical terms, but also the student's state of mind. Curiosity? Frustration? Impatience? Even anger? They spent much of the afternoon seeking common ground around this issue, a stunning reflexive example of an option-three conversation. There was only one interruption — a call from Dr. Schwartz offering an opening at four o'clock that day. Through it all, Martin was beginning to feel trapped. Glenda had the domain-specific knowledge that he so badly needed, but her style was getting increasingly bulldozerish. Yet with Andrew's arrival, he didn't have the time or the energy to bulldoze back. He wondered what would happen when they got to the flipped-classroom trial. And whose book was it at this point? Had Glenda taken over?

-   -   -

"I've never consulted a psychiatrist before," said Martin, as he dropped into a puffy brocaded armchair opposite Dr. Schwartz. Faint sunlight filtered into her spartan office on the second floor of a shopping strip, one block off Maine Street. She was perhaps fifty, short, plump, with gray, curly hair framing a round and gentle face, rimless glasses perched on her nose. "And what prompted you to call?" she asked.

Martin paused before replying, staring at his feet. Without raising his eyes, he said, "I have a complicated situation at home, and I'm worried about my son, his state of mind."

Asked for more, Martin gradually spun out the story of Frances and the sudden and shocking revelation of Andrew's existence and predicament, and Jenny's initial reluctance around this new reality. He got as far as saying that he and Jenny had brought him home three weeks earlier, and except when Andrew's friend from Pittsburgh visited, he was mostly silent, seeming unhappy and morose.

Dr. Schwartz interrupted. "Obviously, this has been a huge and tragic disruption for Andrew, and I would expect him to have a period of intense emotional reaction. Has he talked to you at all about any of that?"

"It's pretty clear that highway driving in a car makes him nervous, which makes perfect sense to me. But when I suggested he speak with someone about his feelings, he got steely and said 'I don't need a shrink.' I don't think I can force him into counseling, but I would sure feel better if he had access to it. He's clearly very upset. I tried to talk to him about what to do with his mother's condo in Pittsburgh, whether to sell it, and he couldn't talk about it."

"You may have to wait a while for that issue to settle. After all, you're talking about his home, the home his mother created. If he were much younger, the estate executor would simply sell it, but Andrew's at that delicate in-between age, where he needs to be part of the decision, so I'm glad you asked him. It was very perceptive of you. As for not seeing a shrink, that resistance is perfectly normal, a denial of need. Don't let it stop you from encouraging him. It will help if you tell me more about your family as a whole."

Martin wondered, for what felt like interminable minutes, how to start. There was so much to tell, but what should he include? His first marriage and how it detonated in his face? Meeting Jenny, falling in love, her almost neurotic fear of abandonment when she was pregnant with Ellen? The joint decision to move to Bottlesworth? The edge around her business and money? Andrew, of course, but suddenly no more sex? The pluses and minuses of working with Glenda? The irritating crush on Gina he couldn't seem to shake off?

Eventually, Martin spoke. "I really don't know where to start."

"Start anywhere," she said. "Tell me about your parents."

"My father taught here, at Bottlesworth. Did you ever come across him?"

Dr. Schwartz laughed. "My professional ethics say I should remain silent, but since he is no longer alive and you are his son, I can tell you in confidence that he came to me for grief counseling when his second wife died. Over a period of three or four months, as I recall."

"I had no idea," said Martin. "He wasn't one to share that kind of thing. Always presented himself as self-reliant, tougher than nails. So then you must know about my mother?"

"I know about your mother."

"My absent mother..."

"Yes. What are your feelings about her now?"

"Feelings? Every day when I walk across campus and see the Bottlesworth gravesite, I get a reminder of how she left us, and I guess it makes me feel weird."

"Where is she now?"

"I have no idea."

"Have you ever tried to find her?"

"No. Why?"

"It's curious. It makes me wonder what feelings you have deep down about being abandoned."

"Having feelings, like anger, would make sense I guess, but mostly I just feel numb. She left, and I was too young to understand it. I still don't know why she left."

"And how does that affect your day-to-day life?"

"I don't think it does, really."

"But doesn't her absence during your childhood affect how you think about your own family? Do you and your wife ever talk about that? Tell me a bit about her."

Relieved to shift the topic away from his own mother, Martin lurched into a panegyric on Jenny, how amazing she was, how loving, what a good mother, smart in business, supportive of his career, comfortable with his spotted marital past, enjoyed music, on and on.

"And are you able to talk with each other?" asked Dr. Schwartz.

"Usually, yes. But she was really upset when I told her about Andrew, and I'm feeling that she's still angry at me. It scares me. And she was going to Chicago with one of her business associates. She seemed to delight in making me very uncomfortable. She teased me about being jealous."

"Were you?"

"I guess I was. Which is strange. I mean she's never before given me an ounce of a reason to be jealous. But something feels wrong, really wrong."

"Are you and she intimate?"

"Do you mean do we have sex? Until recently, the answer has been yes, and it's usually totally wonderful, for both of us. But lately, no."

"So you think she's angry? About Andrew?"

Martin tried — inadequately, he felt — to describe Jenny's initial anger at him for not telling her about the letter right away, and the contrast with her more recent welcoming behavior toward his new son.

"I'm so sorry to interrupt," said Dr. Schwartz. "These issues are clearly very important, but our time is up. I would like to see Andrew in person. This particular appointment time is presently open. Do you wish to schedule it for next week? Can you persuade him to come?"

"Do you want to see him alone?"

"Yes," said Dr. Schwartz.

Martin made the appointment and left for the Task Force get-acquainted dinner. As he walked down Maine Street toward the river, he wondered what it would be like to find his mother after all these years. Was he angry? Maybe. But what would he want to say to her, anyway? Why'd you leave? Like Andrew's asking him. Why'd you leave? Was it to get away from us, from Helen and me, from Dad? Or was your artsy career more important than your family? Which would make me your son, the son who abandoned Frances for his career, leaving behind another son.

On an impulse, he got out his phone and sent an email to Trevor Corey asking for an appointment.

- - -

The dinner for the Task Force was set in the private dining room at the Green Heron, a hotel on the north side of the river. It had a lovely formal garden, now richly adorned with splashes of color, and the most elegant restaurant in Brimfield Junction.

The assistant manager greeted Martin at the door and confirmed the arrangements — drinks and passed hors d'oeuvres at six, dinner at six thirty with a vegetarian plate for Professor Gillespie, dessert to be served after the speeches.

Abe Goldberg was the first to appear. As he approached Martin to shake hands, Sharon and Julian entered, whispering to each other like furtive lovers, Julian stooping as he spoke to the much shorter woman.

"Aha," said Martin. "Our distinguished visitors. Let me introduce Abe Goldberg from Economics. Sharon Gillespie of Camberton

College, and Julian Kesselbaum, computer guru."

Win Henderson was next, uncharacteristically dressed in jacket and tie, asking, "Can I meet the newbies?"

Martin shepherded him toward the trio, noting over his shoulder that Mehmet Kiraz and Siobhan O'Hara had just arrived together, laughing, sharing a joke of some kind. Mehmet was short, thin, and of dark complexion while Siobhan was fair, red-headed, womanly proportioned, and a full four inches taller than Mehmet. Another odd couple, thought Martin. He went to greet them just as Fred Walsh entered, and Martin took everyone over to meet Sharon and Julian.

The buzz of chatter, lubricated with wine and yummies, filled the room as six-thirty approached, but Evelyn Kim had not yet arrived. Martin asked the assistant manager if they could hold dinner a few minutes for the last guest.

By six forty-five, Martin said we might as well eat. Places had been set at a round table large enough to seat nine. Just as the group had tucked themselves into chairs, Evelyn Kim dashed in the door, the tail of a bright floral scarf flowing behind her black dress. She strode up to the table to introduce herself to Julian and Sharon, then took her seat as a waiter brought her a glass of red wine. "Sorry I'm late," she sighed. "Thanks for waiting."

Evelyn's arrival had draped a blanket of hush over the group, but as salads were brought in, forks lifted, bread passed, bits of conversation emerged like seedlings, some of which grew into the kind of small talk so typical of forced social situations — families, the weather, your academic focus — pairing off neighbor to neighbor, amiable, mildly informative, time-filling, tension-reducing.

After the main course, Martin asked Fred to say a few words of welcome, after which he gave the floor to Win, who scanned the faces at the table before speaking. "As the Provost, it's my job to keep us operating at an excellent academic level, with a happy, productive faculty, with smart, engaged students, and doing all this under budget and without turf wars between schools, departments, or individuals." Everyone laughed as Win continued. "Whenever we try to do something new, some faculty members get nervous, wondering what aspect of their perks and support will get cut back to make the new activity possible. This is understandable. I'm happy to report that in this instance, we are poised to be able to implement a new program without squeezing what we already do. It's an exciting time. All we ask is that you give us the benefit of your judgment, and do your best to come up with a consensus about what we might be able to pull off. Thanks in advance for agreeing to serve."

As Win ended his remarks, Martin signaled to the waiter that dessert could be served. Coffee was brought round to accompany the crème brûlée. Martin reminded everyone that they would meet at eight-thirty in the second-floor conference room in the Science Building. With the scraping back of chairs, the pleased-to-meet-yous and see-you-tomorrows being said, the group gradually thinned until only Evelyn Kim remained.

Evelyn approached Martin. "Can I ask you something?"

"Sure, what?"

"Do you already have in mind a structure for this group?"

"Well, the only structure so far is that Win asked me to chair it. Why do you ask?"

"It's just that my experience suggests that a clear structure helps guide deliberations, and your agenda seemed a bit floppy."

Martin forced a smile. "Tomorrow is just our first session. I'm sure that by the end of the day, we will have a more organized structure. And your suggestions on how to do that will be more than welcome."

"Good," said Evelyn. "See you tomorrow." She breezed out of the room, the tail of her scarf once again following the flow of her black-clad person.

- - -

"Any surprises?" asked Jenny as Martin arrived home.

"Only that Evelyn Kim — she's the Dean of Science — clearly wants to take over. And it looks to me like Sharon Gillespie and Julian Kesselbaum have a thing on."

"Really?"

"Who knows? Looks can be deceiving, but they came into the dinner looking like conspirators. So either they have plans for the Task Force, or they had just gotten out of bed."

"There may be other explanations, Goofus. Maybe they're just friends. Anyway, I also have news. Sarah has asked me for one more in-person consult. I could go Wednesday, back Thursday night?"

"Just you? No big sales job with Pierre."

"Just me."

"Is Kuc available?"

"She is."

"No problem then. By the way, what does Andrew do during the day? Do he and JJ do things together? Or what?"

"They play chess sometime, but Andrew spends a lot of time at the computer."

"With that awful game?"

"There's a lot of that game, but he says he also goes to sports websites. And he occasionally fools around with the kids and the soccer net. And he reads — mostly fantasy books — Harry Potter sort of thing, but with vampires. Kids are very big on vampires these days."

"I thought vampire books were mostly written for teenage girls."

Jenny snickered. "Is that your view of teenage girls? That they like vampires?"

"Well, don't they?"

"Maybe they do. Something wildly romantic about getting bitten on the neck."

"Can I bite you on the neck?"

"No. Not tonight, thank you."

Jenny went upstairs, and Martin brooded. What the fuck was going on? Was it time for a yellow card? Maybe even a red card?

* **25** *

Martin arrived at the conference room with Julian and Sharon a few minutes before eight-thirty. He surveyed the arrangements: a folded stand-up name card at each place, a printed agenda, one-paragraph bios of the participants, and a note pad and pen. A flip chart with colored markers next to the screen. On the sideboard, thermoses of coffee with fixings, donuts and muffins, a tray of fresh fruit, bottles of water, paper plates, cups, and napkins. He plugged in his laptop and started the projector as the four Bottlesworth faculty drifted in.

Martin stood at the head of the conference table. "Welcome. This is an exciting day. To get us started, I would like to go around the table and ask each of us to say a few words about our thoughts on this enterprise. Share your own experience that might be relevant. Let's start on my left with Evelyn Kim."

What followed was a predictable but necessary twenty minutes of introductions, more revealing in their style than in their content. Evelyn Kim described in somewhat braggy fashion how the School of Science had grown under her leadership. Abe Goldberg was excited about the prospect of teaching courses in entrepreneurship, to share what he had learned during his startup days about both the stresses and delights of small-company life. Mehmet Kiraz described his joint research program at the Harvard Medical School, wondering how it might mesh with a Bottlesworth program in biomedical engineering, possibly a good enrichment for the students. And Siobhan O'Hara evoked a laugh when she said she had no idea why she was on the Task Force, having only been at Bottlesworth for a year, to which Abe responded with a chuckle that we always need the unbridled energy of the next generation. Julian was next, and as the only person who was full-time in the business world and operating his own company, he carved out the elder-statesman niche on the entrepreneurship side.

Martin then gave the floor to Sharon Gillespie, who presented a thirty-minute talk with PowerPoint about Camberton College, their original mission as a school of engineering, their partnership with Babson next door enabling an entrepreneurial enrichment to their program, their focus on projects and team-building along with coursework, and a novel program of industrial internships. When she was finished, she was peppered with questions. How many faculty? What disciplines were emphasized? From Abe Goldberg, how much endowment did the Camberton Foundation put in? Sharon didn't know. What did she think was the minimum set of offerings that could make a difference? To Martin's delight, she said that in her mind, this was what the Task Force's job was going to be. How to get started.

Martin called a brief break for coffee and comfort, after which he moved to the "Mission and Structure" item on the agenda. "I think it will help us along toward creating a structure if we pose two questions and have a free-form discussion around them, brainstorming, if you will. Here they are:

"First, what absolutely must be in a curriculum that embraces engineering and entrepreneurship in a meaningful way? And second, since there are so many engineering disciplines, should a Bottlesworth program focus, and if so, in which application area? I'll take notes on the flip chart. Let's start with the first question: curricular essentials."

Everyone spoke at once, or it seemed that way to Martin. The usual disciplines came up: electrical, mechanical, chemical, economics, biomedical, Julian tucking computer systems into the mix, but Martin pointing out that these major disciplines actually had a lot of overlap — for example, mechanical and chemical and electrical all relied on linear system theory. He pushed them toward individual subject areas, frantically taking notes. When they got to thermodynamics, an argument ensued between Julian and Evelyn, Julian saying it was not essential and Evelyn almost shrieking that without thermodynamics, there could be no meaningful education. Sharon tried to lighten the atmosphere with a bit of wisdom from her thesis advisor at CTI, that thermodynamics was the only subject that one should never study for the first time.

Martin suggested they move to the second question, application areas, and ideas were again plentiful: robotics, prosthetics, virtual reality, gene sequencing and splicing. Martin filled a flip-chart page, and then called a halt.

"This is a great start," he said. "Now for the structure. I would like to propose two subcommittees, one on curriculum, the other on application focus. I'd like Evelyn to chair the one on curriculum, with Julian and Siobhan as members — but hold your fight over thermodynamics, please — and Sharon to chair one on application focus, with Abe, Mehmet, and myself as members. I'll be *ex officio*, to use a pompous phrase, on the curriculum committee, as well, and can coordinate between them. If this is agreeable, after lunch, I suggest we split into these two groups to have a two-hour planning session on how to proceed. Then we regather at around three, share notes, and construct a plan — and find a date — for our next meeting. Agreeable?"

The rest of the day was intense, broken only by sandwiches brought in for a working lunch. The application group emerged with a list of schools to survey about student project programs in the biomedical and robotic arenas, and the curriculum group with a similar list to survey on curriculum, including asking selected graduate schools what they would look for in admitting students from a primarily liberal arts college. As the final piece of business, a schedule of four more meetings was agreed to, one per month, with the target of having a draft proposal by the November meeting and a final draft by the end of the December meeting.

Thus was the Task Force launched. It was with a mixture of relief and raw pride that Martin reviewed the day. To his mind, he had just pulled off what initially had felt like "Mission: Impossible." CC would be delighted. But was he cut out to be the Dean? A manager of budgets and space? Would the proposed program be exciting enough to get him to cross over to the dark side?

- - -

Thanks to Kuc, Martin was able to spend much of Wednesday with Glenda, still sparring a bit over semantics but making great progress on how they would evaluate the flipped-classroom experiment. On Thursday, he made his down-and-back consulting visit to Autobot, where he presented his ideas on how to introduce more peer-to-peer conversations into the Autobot training program on worker safety. Alice Yee, CC's vice-president of human resources, was delighted.

Jenny was home from Chicago by the time he got back, and he reminded her that Gina was coming the next day and would be staying with them.

"Here?" asked Jenny. "And this weekend? We have JJ's seventh birthday party at the cottage on Sunday. Did you forget? We've invited everybody, the Washingtons, the Wangs, Glenda and her father, my kid-swappers, five of JJ's friends from school. It'll be about twenty-five in all."

"No, I didn't forget, but this is the best weekend for her, and I've lined up a real estate agent and everything. She'll be here just tomorrow night and maybe Saturday night."

"And where will she sleep?"

"I've already asked Andrew to camp for the night in the study, and he said it's fine. I'll take care of everything."

"Why don't you put her up in a motel?" snarled Jenny. "The school should pay for it."

"It's peak tourist season, love, the Chamber Music Festival. The motels are all booked up. Couldn't find a vacancy, even as far away as Freeport or Bath. It'll be okay. I'll be taking her apartment hunting on Saturday."

"Leaving me with the kids."

"I guess. Yes. Leaving you with the kids. Do you want me to ask Kuc to help?"

"No. I'll manage," said Jenny. "I'll manage."

- - -

Martin was actually relieved that Gina would be staying with them. Jenny's meeting her, welcoming her at their table, seeing her with their children, all of that would keep those idiotic feelings of his thoroughly suppressed. He hoped that as soon as they started working together, the fantasy would dissolve back into the proper kind of professional relationship they had always had, especially with Jenny watching.

Gina arrived while Martin was upstairs putting the younger children to bed. Jenny answered the door and welcomed her in, eyeing both her stature and her striking physique. "Welcome, Gina. Come in. Are you hungry? Thirsty?"

"Oh no, Mrs. Quint," said Gina. "I stopped to eat in Kittery. I'm fine, really. Is Professor Quint home?"

"He's upstairs. And please call me Jenny. Let me show you where you'll be sleeping." Gina picked up her bag and followed Jenny upstairs just as Martin was about to start down.

"Hey, Gina. Andrew's in there. Let me introduce you. He knocked on Andrew's door and poked his head in. Andrew was at the computer. "Gina's here. Come say hello."

Andrew got up and said, "Hey. I'll get my stuff so you can..."

"No hurry," said Gina. "Thanks for..."

"Whatever," said Andrew and he collected pajamas and a book and went downstairs.

Martin said, "When you get settled, c'mon back down. I'm going for a nightcap. You want anything?"

"No, I'm fine. Just some water, I guess."

"Jenny?"

"No. I'm off to bed early. Wiped out. So I'll say my goodnight now."

Martin descended the stairs and went to the kitchen to pour himself a Dewar's on ice and a glass of water for Gina. He took the drinks into the living room and saw Andrew, now in pajamas, unrolling the sleeping bag in the study.

"Will it bother you if we talk a bit?" asked Martin.

"No, I'm gonna read a while."

"Okay, thanks." He sat in his father's old chair, waiting. He heard the toilet flush, the water run, and footsteps on the stairs. Gina emerged from the stairway with her work badge still around her neck. She sat in the small loveseat next to the Victorian settee.

"This is a nice house. Thanks for putting me up." Glancing toward Andrew, "I know it's… uh… a disruption. What's the plan for tomorrow?"

"I've found four possible places for you to look at. The real estate agent is coming at around nine. Then I want to go over my plans for the lab sessions with you. Can you stay tomorrow night if need be?"

Gina said, "Sure. And I can make a quick decision on living space, since it's just for a semester. I'm really excited. This is totally cool, getting to do this."

"It's actually a bit scary, but I feel more confident knowing that you're here to help. Doing it alone would be just too much."

"You'll have to show me what you want, but I'll do whatever it takes."

They lapsed into an awkward silence, Martin thinking, *Whatever it takes? Whatever I want? What do I want? Her help? Yes. Her admiration? Yes. More than that?* Graphic images of what might be swirled in his head. *No, no, no.*

Gina yawned and said that the drive had tired her out. Martin asked if she had everything she needed — towels and things. Gina assured him that everything was fine, and went upstairs. Martin sat, thinking about auburn-haired young women and twelve-year-old sons, noting in passing that Gina was young enough to be Andrew's sister.

-   -   -

Gina liked the second place they saw. It was a fully furnished mother-in-law apartment above the garage of a house four blocks away — a modest living area with an adequate strip kitchenette, one tiny bedroom, and a bath. Cable TV and wireless internet. A parking spot. The owner lived on the premises and offered Gina such an attractive rent, she simply said yes.

With that settled, Martin took Gina on a walking tour of the campus, ending at the labs in the Science Building where their classes would meet, two open areas with moveable tables, a handful of oscilloscopes, signal generators, meters, test equipment, and a set of drawers with components for various kinds of student experiments in physics.

"Will the students have their own nerd kits?" asked Gina, referring to the portable electronic circuit boards used at CTI where students could assemble working circuits without having to do any soldering. "If we're going to do problem-solving," said Gina, "shouldn't they actually build the stuff? And be able to do it at home?"

"Of course. Since I wasn't sure we'd actually be doing this, I haven't ordered them yet. But we really should. Let's go to my office."

An internet search in Martin's office located two alternatives. Gina recommended the one exactly like the CTI model at $130 per. Martin wrote out a purchase requisition for twenty-five sets, charged to his CC fund. And with that, Martin felt he was once more working with a student assistant, a junior colleague, not the object of a childish fantasy.

They ordered takeout sandwiches at Brimfield Bagel and spent the afternoon reviewing the detailed lesson plans, Gina asking several probing questions along the way. When they had covered everything, Martin called home and offered to bring Chinese takeout for dinner, an offer that Jenny accepted.

At dinner, JJ asked, "Are you going to live with us when you teach here?"

Gina smiled her lovely smile, answering, "No. I'm staying just for tonight. I'll have my own apartment when I come in September."

"I wish you could stay with us," he said. "You could share with Andrew."

Gina laughed and Andrew looked at his feet. "Um, I don't think so. I'm going to be fine in my apartment."

"Too bad," said JJ. "I like sharing my room. I share with Sister. Or maybe we could switch. You could share with Sister and I could share with Andrew."

Jenny gave JJ a threatening look, but Gina just smiled some more. "I had to share a room with my brother when I was growing up, and I didn't really like it. He was a pest."

"Older or younger?" asked Martin.

"Two years older. And a pest. But then I got taller than him, and..." suddenly Gina blushed bright red, "anyway, my parents split us up. Then he stopped being such a pest."

Martin turned to Jenny, saying, "We got all our required stuff done today." And toward Gina, "I know you plan to go back tomorrow, but how'd you like to join JJ's birthday party before you go? At our beach cottage. At least for lunch and a swim."

"That'd be cool," said JJ.

"Oh. I didn't bring a bathing suit," said Gina.

"Okay, lunch and a wade," said Martin.

Looking directly at Jenny, Gina asked, "Are you sure that's okay? Not an intrusion? I don't want to mess up..."

Jenny, in a monotone, said, "There'll be enough chaos that one more won't matter. It's fine. Join us."

- - -

The birthday party was a great success, with a full day of swimming, beach tag, grilled chicken and hot dogs and unlimited chips and ice cream and cake. Martin, occupied as grill master, kept one eye out for Gina, who seemed to mix well, especially with the teenage contingent — Andrew and the two Wang girls. His other eye was on Glenda, who had brought Abe Goldberg along with Cecil. Cecil seemed to enjoy chatting up Steve Wang, and Jenny spent quite a while talking to Glenda and Abe, with much laughter in evidence.

After most of the guests had left, DeShawn took Martin aside and reported that he had talked to Janet Walton, and that Lavelle was applying to Cranborne. There was scholarship money and two spaces in the seventh grade class due to last-minute cancellations.

"Two spaces?" asked Martin.

"Yeah, why?"

"Andrew says he wants to go to Cranborne too, and I'm starting to wonder if it might be a good idea. I mean, being with his one friend from Pittsburgh might really help him adjust to his new life."

"You want me to make an inquiry?"

"I'll send you his school record. It's probably similar to Lavelle's."

"You do that."

"And I'll talk to Jenny about it. She doesn't know yet."

-    -   -

That night, Martin was in the study using Jenny's printer to make copies of Andrew's academic record. Jenny came in, saying, "I really do like that Glenda person. And her father. And Abe. Nice people."

"Did you learn any more about them?" asked Martin, feeding more originals for copying.

"She said her divorce will be filed soon. And Abe is a bachelor. A widower, actually. His wife died young — no children. She sure didn't waste any time latching onto an eligible. What on earth are you doing there?"

"Copying Andrew's record, and yeah, she charges right in. Not just with Abe. She's taking over my book."

"Is that bad?"

"It's frustrating and humiliating, that's what it is. I clearly need her, but she just charges ahead, dragging the subject away from what I thought was my key idea."

"Are you fighting?"

"No, not really. I do like her, but it's not easy getting to agreement on some things."

"So back to Andrew's record. Why are you copying it?"

"I'm sending it to DeShawn. To see if he would fit at Cranborne."

"Why are you even thinking about that? He's already set with school."

"Andrew said he wanted to go there."

"He said what?"

"That he wanted to go to Cranborne. That time when DeShawn took both boys to Cranborne — you were out of town. Anyway, on the way back from dropping off Lavelle at the airport he said he wanted to go to Cranborne."

Jenny slumped into her desk chair, almost frowning. Then she said, "It's so strange, you doing all this without me. And this is may sound horrible, but I have a feeling that sending him to Cranborne might make a lot of sense. It's not that I want Andrew out of the house, this overcrowded house — he's a nice boy and JJ admires him — but the link to his old home via Lavelle coupled with the oversight he would get from DeShawn and Tamiqua, maybe that's more important. How much does Cranborne cost?"

"I'll have to ask DeShawn. Or check the web. I didn't do that yet, but remember, there's a pretty fat estate that could pay tuition."

"Maybe so, but is spending it on prep school the right use?"

"I have no idea. I thought we would keep it separate and not touch it until he was ready for college, but..."

Martin finished his copying and tucked the sheaf of papers into an envelope, as Jenny sat, brooding.

"I'm taking him to see a psychologist on Tuesday."

"You're what?"

"Yes. Last week, I went to see a psychologist, Dr. Schwartz, because I was worried about Andrew, his grieving, that kind of thing."

"And you never told me? What's going on, Martin? You've been doing all these things without telling me?"

Martin hemmed a bit. "Well, I didn't know what would come of it, and you've been so distant lately, I wasn't sure..."

"Wasn't sure of what?"

"Well, how you're feeling about Andrew."

"I don't know what I feel about Andrew, but as I said, he's a nice boy and JJ admires him, and I'm doing my best—"

"But you've been so... I don't know. I feel that you're still horribly angry about the whole thing. You've been remote."

"Remote?"

"Suddenly no sex. Why is that?"

Jenny's eyes were glued to the floor.

"I don't know. It's just that things don't feel right."

"What things?"

"I don't know. Just things. I'm sorry, I'm just not in the mood, and I need to get to bed. We have a client meeting in Wiscasset at nine tomorrow."

With that, Jenny departed. Martin had a growing sense of panic, that Andrew was in fact wrecking their family, their marriage. *But what can I do about it? Andrew's my son, and she's being kind to him, acting like a loving mother. So what's wrong? What have I done to set her off like this? Will I ever get her to talk straight with me?*

* **26** *

Martin spent much of Monday morning responding to a blizzard of messages between various members of his Task Force. Worries about Jenny notwithstanding, it was exciting to see CC's brainchild in gestation via the ultrasound of email. The challenge of creating a new curriculum, fitting both engineering and entrepreneurship into an otherwise ivy-style college, now had real meaning for him. People he respected, like Sharon Gillespie and Julian Kesselbaum, were pitching in, helping, and he could sense a growing urge to get it moving, get it built, make a success. What would it feel like to build up a whole new school from scratch? Be a Dean? Hire people? Set program goals? Maybe, as the eighth-generation descendent of the college founder, this was indeed to be his destiny.

- - -

"Some snafu with your son?" Martin was just getting seated opposite Trevor Corey's desk.

"No. That's going along fine, as best I can tell. I think I want to hire an investigator."

"What on earth for?" asked Trevor. "You're not thinking of snooping into that lawyer's honesty, are you? Or Andrew's family history?"

"No, something different. I'm thinking it might be interesting to track down my mother."

"After all these years?"

"Yeah. Maybe I need to find out what happened to her. Why'd she leave? Andrew kept asking me why I left, and that got me thinking. Do you have an old address for her in my father's estate papers? Maybe in a copy of the divorce decree?"

"I'll have to check my files. You've already done the usual web searches?"

"Yes. Hilda Ann Philips Quint, in all possible permutations. There are a few Hilda Quints and dozens of Hilda Philips — even JJ's first-grade teacher was a Hilda Philips. But no artist popped up. I haven't got either the time or the skill to track down every one of them. I think I need a pro."

"Well, as you might guess, family law does tend to build connections to private investigators, so yes, I have two suggestions, one here in BJ and one in Portland. I'll send you their contact info along with whatever I can find in your father's old file."

- - -

Back in his office, Martin put in a call to Sylvia Palmer. He brought her up to date on the Lavelle situation and asked her opinion about Andrew's express wish to attend Cranborne.

"I hardly know Lavelle, but as I think about it, going to school with his best friend might be a real salve on the edges of his grief. How far is it from your home?"

"About thirty miles. Too far to commute unless we were to hire a dedicated driver."

"Aren't there other commuting students in your town?"

"Maybe. I'll ask them."

"And how expensive is it?"

"Expensive. Could be as much as thirty-five K per year for a boarding student — less, obviously, if he commutes. And my sense is that once someone goes to a prep school like this, the transition back to public school rarely works. So if he goes, it's like six years at thirty-five K, and that would mean spending up the money I thought would be saved for his college, for his future."

"Well, I can't advise you on that issue, but I can tell you that until you make a decision about the real estate, we're kind of stuck in limbo. I'm thinking I should just get appraisals under the assumption that the estate is keeping the properties."

"Not just yet. Andrew's starting to think about all this. But isn't there also money available from the insurance that wouldn't be tied up?"

"Yes. Quite a lot of money. But — and please forgive me if I'm sounding imperious — as executor, I can't approve this kind of spending without hearing directly from Andrew that he understands the implications. And he's only twelve. It's a problem. He's in between being too young and being of age."

"But once I become the whatever-it's-called, the guardian of the estate?"

"Then you make the decisions."

"So in terms of liberating all this, a decision on the properties would be important."

"One way or the other. Yes."

"Thanks, Sylvia. You're a big help. I'll have to talk to him about money and hope that he understands. And before we commit, if we do, I'll be sure to have you speak directly to Andrew."

-   -   -

On Tuesday, Martin came home from campus in mid-afternoon, and announced to Andrew that he was taking him to see Dr. Schwartz.

"But I don't need a shrink," protested Andrew. "I'm fine."

"I agree," said Martin. "You don't need a shrink, but that doesn't mean that talking with someone who's nice and caring wouldn't be good for you. I want you to go this once."

"But—"

"You don't have to say anything. You can just sit there if you want. Dr. Schwartz is a nice woman, and I think you'll find it good to talk to her. And just so you know, any conversation with her is confidential. She won't be reporting to me about what you say. So you can talk about your mom and your family and about us, about JJ, about Lavelle, about school. Anything. That's entirely between you and her."

"Well, I guess I'll go, but I don't see why."

"I'm not sure why, either, but I have a sense that you'll find it helpful."

250 Stephen D. Senturia

It was a mild, cloudy day, but with no rain forecast, Martin and Andrew walked to Dr. Schwartz's office. He left Andrew in her capable hands and went around the corner to Barnaby's for coffee and a pastry. He needed to think.

It's true, what Jenny said. I'm pushing ahead with Andrew's plans without consulting her. And this is new. We used to talk about everything. But a level of mistrust has slithered in between us. Is it because of me, my fuck-up with Frances, my having to bring Andrew into the family? Or is Jenny's still angry about my hiding him from her at first? Except for the Andrew issues, she should be elated. Her business is going into the black for the first time, thanks to Chicago. And without abandoning the family, I've managed to get the book going and the new course format, we have no more money troubles, and Kuc gives us both plenty of time to work. But when Jenny experiences victory, it usually makes her horny. Now instead of being hot and turned on by success, she's been cold and totally turned off. And it hurts. In my touchy gut. In my swollen balls. It's gotta be Andrew. But she's so nice to him. And then she says getting him out of the house isn't a reason, but maybe it really is a reason, maybe even for both of us. I miss my wife. If he goes off to Cranborne with Lavelle, maybe she'll come back.

His iPhone beeped, reminding him that it was time to reclaim his son, so he returned to Dr. Schwartz's office to find a smiling Andrew in the waiting room.

"So it was okay?" said Martin.

"Yeah, she's nice, like you said. We talked mostly about school. She said she wants to see us both next week to talk more about that."

"You mean you told her about Cranborne?"

"Yeah, I told her about Lavelle and everything. She said it's a big decision, and we should all talk together."

"Okay. Next week it is. In the meantime, I think we should visit Cranborne to talk to them. Whaddya say to that?"

"When can we do it?"

"Friday. I have to go to Boston tomorrow and Thursday. I'll call them."

And the pair, father and son, walked home.

-    -   -

On Wednesday, he drove to Andover for his consulting at Autobot, stayed with Horatio and Blanche, and the next morning went to CTI for a session with Harry Huang. He wanted Harry's critique of the set of team-oriented design problems he wanted to use in his flipped-classroom version of C&E. Harry skimmed through the sheaf of examples, liked the general idea, and promised to send more detailed comments within a few days.

In the faculty lunchroom at noon, Harry and Martin were joined by Peter Dempsey. As he had done before, Peter teased Martin about his small-college life, again joking about his access to admiring female students. But this time, Martin had a response. He described the Task Force and how exciting it was for Bottlesworth and he talked with gusto about the flipped-classroom experiment.

"I'll be damned," said Peter. "You've changed colors, like an octopus on the rocks — protective coloration. They giving you a TA for this?"

Martin chortled. "Give is the wrong word, but I got a grant, and I'm using it to hire one. A CTI student, actually."

"Really," asked Peter. "Which one?"

"Gina Farrell. The one who first helped me critique the MOOCs. Harry knows her."

"Yeah," said Harry. "She's super smart. Very capable. Knows the course well."

"And is she cute?" asked Peter.

"Cut the shit," said Martin. "Can't you for once consider a female without thinking of sex?"

Peter said, "It's hard," and laughed at his own lewd joke.

"You're hopeless," said Martin.

As they got up from the lunch table, Peter asked Martin if they could talk about something in his office.

"Not related to female students, I hope," said Martin.

"Nope. Female faculty," said Peter.

-    -   -

"So what's up?" asked Martin, taking his seat in Peter's office.

"It's Kat," said Peter. "I'm not sure I should be telling you this, but it looks like Stanford wants to hire her."

"Did they ask you to write?" asked Martin.

"Yes. You too?" Martin nodded. Peter continued, "So my question is, whaddya think?"

"Have you written already?"

"No. I wanted to talk to you first. I think she got a raw deal here, so I'm inclined to be positive, but when she was turned down, I figured there must be something wrong that I didn't know about."

Martin blew out a long breath. "I don't know how to say this, Peter, but I've got to ask you something, in strict confidence." Peter waited, so Martin went on. "Was there ever anything personal, I mean anything intimate between you and Kat?"

"Between me and Kat? Are you kidding? She was the ice maiden."

"Did you flirt with her, come on to her at all?"

"Well, I joked around, for sure, but I do that with everybody. Why? Did she complain or something?"

"You weren't asked to write a letter when she came up for tenure. I wish you had, because with your expertise in transistor physics, a letter from you maybe could have put her over the top. But she didn't want you to write. So I'm asking, in confidence, was there anything?"

"Jesus, Martin. You should have talked to me about it at the time. I would have written a strong letter. A super-strong letter. There was nothing serious between us, ever. I mean, yeah, I asked her out a couple of times, and yeah, she eventually started turning me down, but I didn't take it personally."

"Well, she wasn't sure. She said you had been socially aggressive. How many dates did you have?"

"Two, maybe three."

"And then?"

"She said no more."

"She tell you why?"

"Not really. Just that she wasn't comfortable what with me being so close to her field and being senior. But I didn't buy that. Now that we know she's lesbo, maybe that's what it was, although I never got any such hint."

"Did you pressure her for sex?"

"I guess I might have. Well, you know me. I kind of joke around a lot about sex, and I may have given more than one suggestion."

"Okay, I think I get the picture." Martin looked down at his shoes for a long breather, struggling to digest what he had heard. "Okay," he said, looking straight into Peter's face. "As for the Stanford thing, I see no reason not to write the letter you would have written at CTI. My letter, of course, was up on the internet, so they and anybody else who cares to look it up know what I think about her. And I haven't changed my mind. I wanted her tenured here at CTI and I already wrote to support her tenure at Stanford. But here's the thing that bugs me. Think about this. If she had been tenured here, I probably wouldn't have left. So maybe, just maybe, your joking around about sex with her, leading her to not want you to write, might be the reason she's going to Stanford and I'm now at Bottlesworth. Like chaos theory: the flap of a fucking butterfly wing that causes a hurricane."

"Jesus, Martin. I had no idea. If only you'd asked me at the time. You make me feel ashamed."

"That's not my goal. I was never going to mention this, but you asked. It's been eating at me for two years. I'm glad to get it off my chest."

"Better that, maybe, than keeping it buried. I wish I had written for her, really. I would have supported her to the hilt. And I'll make sure Stanford knows that."

The two friends got up, shook hands, and Martin headed for his car for the drive back to Brimfield Junction. He knew that Kat had been truthful about Peter being socially aggressive. That much came out during the deposition phase in her lawsuit. But Martin, hearing Peter's enthusiasm for her professional qualifications, was mortified that he hadn't confronted Peter at the time. He could have overridden Kat's list of names and specifically suggested that Morris ask Peter for a letter. He was too new to the process and didn't understand what his role should have been. He had maybe screwed up big time, not just Kat's life, but *his* life, his family's life. It really was like chaos theory. Shit. Beware butterfly wings and their consequences.

There's an optimist in each of us, at least those of us who are burdened with Type-A personalities. We think we do things right, for the best, and are admired for it. But in my life, anyone's life? Failures. I failed Frances building up my career. Hell, before that, I failed to make first-string center forward on the high school soccer term, and except for the way Helen used to throw that in my face when we were kids, I managed to keep my self-image as high as if I had made first string. But I felt I was failing my father all the time — never good enough. And my mother? Who in hell knows about her? Did we, I mean Helen and me, did we fail her? Why'd she leave? Should I find her and ask? And Katie. Jesus. I certainly failed Katie. But in that funny way of thinking about it, I had to fail Katie in order to save myself from a worse failure, the living hell of a failed marriage. Maybe that's how we work. We use the "save yourself" mantra to excuse our failures. And now I learn that I may have failed Kat as well by not asking Peter to write. Massive implications, a bomb thrown into our family. The one person I haven't failed is Jenny, but she's behaving like I have. I mean, yes, there was the stupid Troy thing, but except for that. Or maybe I actually fail her every day by not paying attention to what she needs, by going off to campus or the West Coast, or by not admiring the furniture her company makes, or taking enough time with the kids. But I cancelled all my West-Coast consulting and took the Autobot job to get a nanny, and I sure as hell have spent a lot of time with the kids this summer, so who knows? If she won't talk to me, I'll never know.

- - -

That night, with children tucked in, Martin started to tell Jenny about his conversation with Peter.

"Pardon me for butting in, love, but that woman is out of our life, so why do I have to hear about her again?"

"It's not about Kat. It's about me. I think I fucked up her tenure case, and it's eating my guts out."

"You mean when the letters were stolen?"

"No. Before that. When I gave Morris the list of names to write to. I left Peter off the list."

"Why would that matter? Weren't there plenty of people who could write?"

"He was the one person at CTI besides me who really understood the importance of her work. He could have written a really strong letter."

"So why wasn't he on the list?"

"Kat didn't want him on the list. He had, as she put it, been socially aggressive. He dated her a few times, but she turned him down. I should have probed Peter to see about that before I turned in my list to Morris. He was nothing but positive."

"What difference would it make? You mean one letter could make the difference?"

"Yes. That's how close it was. So here's the thing — and it's killing me — if I had recommended that Peter write, then maybe Kat would have gotten tenure and we wouldn't have moved here. Jesus. It fucking freaks me out."

"I think you're overreacting. If Kat didn't get tenure, she didn't deserve it."

"Well, Stanford wants her now, just what I predicted."

"So let her go to Stanford. Good riddance, as far as I'm concerned. And as for us — to use an overused phrase," the timbre in Jenny's voice rising and rasping, "shit happens. George drops dead, Prince Galahad comes along, tenure letters get stolen, we move, we add a teenage son, and here we are, like it or not. How are Horatio and Blanche?"

"You sound so angry."

"Don't talk to me about angry."

"Why not?"

"Just don't."

"This isn't like you. It hurts me when you talk like this."

"I don't like it either, but that's how I'm feeling these days. I need to go to bed."

As Jenny started for the stairs, Martin said, "I'm taking Andrew to Cranborne tomorrow."

Jenny paused, "Really? Are you serious?"

"Yes. We're having an admission interview."

"Well I'll be damned," said Jenny. "I'll be damned."

* **27** *

This was Martin's first look at Cranborne in many years. DeShawn gave them a quick tour. Martin was struck anew by how collegiate it looked, albeit on a small scale. Red-brick buildings arranged in three large quadrangles, a decent-sized library. Sports facilities that rivaled Bottlesworth, including a field house with a hockey rink, swimming pool, and basketball arena. Looking through Andrew's eyes, and comparing this scene to the Brimfield Junction Middle School where he had already taken Andrew to register for seventh grade, Martin could understand Andrew's wish. Five hundred students in all, roughly thirty per class in the middle-school grades, six through eight, expanding to one hundred per class in grades nine through twelve. Ninety percent residential. About twenty-five students commuted from Brimfield Junction. There was a bus.

DeShawn dropped Martin and Andrew at the admissions office after the tour. They had to wait a few minutes in the reception area before Stephen Bowditch, Director of Admissions, came out of his office. Taller than Martin, lanky, narrow-faced, with glasses and straight honey-colored hair, casually dressed in a sports shirt and khakis, he shook hands with Martin, then Andrew, and invited only Andrew into his office.

Martin spent the next half-hour doing email by phone. When Stephen did finally emerge, he invited Martin to join them. Andrew was smiling.

"We've had a nice chat," said Stephen, inviting Martin to join them in his office. "I'm pleased that Andrew is so interested in coming here. I think you already know that his friend Lavelle Walton will be coming as a residential student. And Mr. Washington told me that he had apprised you of our pair of last-minute vacancies in our seventh-grade class, so there is one space left. I'm going to recommend to our committee that Andrew be offered this space. I think he'll be a fine addition to our student body. Our committee will meet on Monday, so we'll have a quick decision for you."

Martin suddenly thought about Omar Khayyám's moving finger of destiny, which writes, and having writ, moves on. Andrew was the moving finger, writing turmoil into his life and especially into his bed, and maybe now Andrew was moving on, giving Martin and Jenny enough space to reengage with each other.

"I'm delighted," said Martin. "My wife and I are both products of public schools. The idea of sending Andrew to a private school is a bit jarring to our way of thinking, but given Andrew's situation and the fact that Lavelle will be here, we're inclined to support his wish. We are a bit concerned about cost, though, and we need to have some serious talks about it."

Stephen responded, "Andrew, would you be kind enough to wait in the outer office?"

Andrew left, now with a shadow of worry on his face. Stephen continued, "You need to understand, Professor Quint, that we have very limited resources for financial aid, and we prefer to use it for seriously disadvantaged students."

"Like Lavelle?"

"Yes, like Lavelle. Mr. Washington made a strong case for committing resources to get him here. I don't know your situation, but it's a fair assumption that your family is quite a bit better off than the Walton family. Our normal tuition plus room and board is thirty-two thousand for a full academic year. That includes texts and all fees, but it assumes that Andrew would have medical insurance from your family."

"And if he commuted?"

"The commuting tuition is eighteen thousand five hundred. That includes lunches."

"Okay. That's the data we need. One more question. What's the spectrum of college acceptance out of Cranborne?"

"I'm glad you asked. Out of our most recent senior class of ninety-eight, seventy-three are going to four-year colleges, nineteen either entered or are entering the job market, most in combination with some junior or community college, and six are going into the military."

"Any ivy league or equivalent schools?"

"Two Harvard, two Brown, one CTI, seven Bottlesworth, three Colby — you need more?"

"No, thanks. I get the picture. It's just …"

"Yes. I know. People think we're a jock school. But we take our education seriously."

- - -

In the car on the way back, Andrew, for the first time in Martin's presence, bubbled with enthusiasm. "They have computer classes in seventh grade," he said. "And everyone does a sport. I can do soccer in the fall and try for basketball in the winter and baseball in the spring. And they're in a league — they play other schools. Even in the middle school. It's so cool. I can't wait."

"It's pretty amazing," agreed Martin. "I'm quite impressed. I had looked at their website, but it's much better in person. Almost looks like a college."

"Yeah. Those buildings are awesome."

"So I have a serious question for you. If you go to Cranborne, would you want to commute from our house on the bus, or stay at the school?"

"At the school," said Andrew, without a moment's hesitation. "Lavelle will be there. We're a team."

"I guess Lavelle's been a big help for you after …"

"Yeah, after," said Andrew. "He gets it. He knows about being alone."

"But he has his mother at home."

"She's hardly ever there. You saw."

"So if you stayed on campus, would you and Lavelle want to be roommates?"

"I hope so. He's my best friend."

"Well, we'll have to talk all this over. I have to tell you that going to

Cranborne is expensive."

"But the lawyer lady said there was money. Isn't there?"

"Yes, but money needs to be nurtured and spent wisely. I can see the benefit of having you go to a good school with your friend Lavelle, but we also have to consider the cost."

"How much?"

"How much what?"

"How much does it cost?"

"Thirty-two thousand dollars."

"Whoa," said Andrew. "That's a lot of money."

"As I said, it's expensive."

"And how much money does the lawyer lady say I have?"

"We won't know for sure until we make a decision about your mother's condo and your grandma's house. But I can say this much for sure. If you go to Cranborne, we would have to use some of your estate money to pay for it, and if you stay at Cranborne all the way through high school, it would use a big fraction of the lawyer lady's amount."

"What about scholarships? Didn't DeShawn say there were scholarships?"

Scholarships, thought Martin, wondering, and not for the first time, whether Lavelle's scholarship was actually being paid for by DeShawn out of his carefully saved NBA money. If so, or even regardless of whose money it was consuming, Lavelle's scholarship served multiple purposes: a star player comes to Cranborne, an under-resourced kid gets a chance at a quality education, and a life-saver is tossed to Andrew, a kid floating in a sea of loss and uncertainty.

"Yes," said Martin. "There are scholarships, but not for us. While Jenny and I aren't rich enough to pay for Cranborne without a lot of difficulty, we earn enough that you couldn't qualify for a scholarship. That means we would have to pay the full cost, and in order to do that, we would have to use at least some of your estate money."

Andrew fell silent, and remained silent for the rest of drive home, Martin wondering whether by using the estate money to send Andrew to Cranborne they would then be committed to sending both JJ and

Ellen there when their time came. Could they ever hope to afford it, with or without CC's consulting?

- - -

At the dinner table that evening, Andrew once again bubbled about Cranborne, how cool it was, the facilities, the sports, like a college.

JJ said, "So if you go to this school, where will you sleep?"

"At the school, I hope, like with Lavelle."

"So we won't see you anymore?" asked JJ, his chin wobbling a bit.

"Oh, we'll see you. Me 'n Lavelle both. Mr. Bowditch said I could come home weekends and stuff and even bring Lavelle. But this school has everything. I mean, just—"

"So you promise you'd come home?"

"Sure, li'l boss, like Lavelle says. Sure. Gotta see my little brother, right? Play soccer. Play chess."

JJ brightened. "Yeah. Gotta whomp Lavelle at chess."

- - -

While Jenny was putting Ellen and JJ to bed, Andrew asked if he could talk to Martin some more about the money.

"I wish it wasn't like this," said Martin. "Usually, children don't get involved in decisions about money. But—"

"But my Mom is dead and she left me money. And Grandma and Aunt Flora, too. So unless you spend it on Cranmore, I'm gonna have a lotta money, right?"

"Right. Since we got home, I looked at Sylvia Palmer's figures, and I'm guessing that if we don't sell any of the real estate, by the time the taxes and her lawyer fees are paid, the estate will have about two hundred and sixty thousand dollars."

"And how much more if we sell the houses?"

"She estimates about eighty thousand more."

"So that makes over three hundred?"

"Yes, about that. It's a lot of money."

"And if I go to Cranborne for six years, like you said, that would cost _st two hundred thousand, right?"

"Yes. The costs will go up each year, but the money will also be invested to earn some income. So yes, about two hundred thousand."

"And that leaves over one hundred thousand at the end?"

"Yes. Right."

"So that could be used for college?"

"Yes."

"How many kids start college with a hundred thousand in the bank?"

"Not many, I'm sure."

"Then I want to sell the houses and go to Cranborne."

"I suggest we talk about this with Dr. Schwartz on Tuesday. Okay?"

"Okay, but I know what I wanna do."

-    -   -

On Monday morning at eleven, Martin got a call from Stephen Bowditch saying that Andrew had been formally accepted at Cranborne. He would fax all the necessary forms and the first-semester tuition bill to Martin's office.

"Well, I hope you can give us until Wednesday to make a decision. I have Andrew meeting with a psychologist tomorrow, and I want to get her recommendation before committing. Is that okay?"

"Until Wednesday, we can manage," said Stephen, "especially considering what Andrew has been through. We'll hold the space."

Andrew positively bounced when Martin came home with the news, reminding him of the way JJ would bounce whenever good news arrived. And yet these two had no blood relationship. An odd similarity emerging between these step-step brothers.

-    -   -

Dr. Schwartz welcomed Andrew and Martin to her office on Tuesday afternoon, pleased to see Andrew so animated. She asked about the school, and Andrew exploded into a monologue about how cool everything was, and that Mr. Bowditch was so nice, and the Washingtons were there and Lavelle would be there, and he would sleep at the school and could come home on weekends, and he couldn't wait to start next Monday.

She then asked Martin, "Can you afford it?"

"You mean to ask me this with Andrew here?"

"Yes. He's old enough to realize that schools like Cranborne aren't free. The commitment to go there can be a big burden on a family's finances."

"But I've got money," said Andrew. "My Mom and Grandma and Aunt Flora, they left me a lot of money."

"Actually, that's true" said Martin, "and we've already had a discussion about money. There's enough in Andrew's estate to pay his tuition and still leave a nest egg for at least part of college costs. And he says that's how he wants to use it."

"Is that true?" asked Dr. Schwartz.

"Yes," said Andrew.

"So what would your mother say if she knew how you wanted to use your inheritance?"

"Mom always told me that education was the best thing you could ever get. So I think she would agree about it."

Dr. Schwartz looked to Martin, one eyebrow raised at his sudden distress.

"Yes, I think Andrew's right," said Martin, sniffing and dabbing at a watery eye. "Frances understood about education, and I think Andrew said it just right. She would approve, so I guess I do too."

On the way home, he once again asked Andrew whether it was time to tell Sylvia Palmer to sell the properties. Andrew responded, "Yes. Like I said in there, it's using Mom's money for the right thing."

- - -

At eight that evening, Sylvia called Martin at home. "I got your message. Sounds like a good decision, but I need to speak to Andrew."

Martin put Andrew on the phone.

"Yes, Miss Palmer. I understand.... Yes, that means my home and

Grandma's home get sold, but the money pays for my school and that's more important to me. You should see this school. It's awesome.... No, I talked about that already with Dr. Schwartz. She's a shrink that my dad made me go see. She's real nice, and asked if my mother would approve and I said yes and my dad agreed. Okay, here he is." He passed the phone to Martin.

Sylvia said, "It sounds like you've had all the requisite discussions."

"Well, I've tried to be careful but the key thing is that he believes that his mother would approve, and that makes it possible to come to a decision. I'm going to need to make the first-semester tuition payment within a few days, and I can manage that, but I want it recorded as an expense against Andrew's estate."

"I have a better idea," said Sylvia. "Fax the tuition bill to me and I'll pay it directly out of the insurance proceeds."

"Wow. Of course. That's very helpful," said Martin, relieved to retain the sanctity of his fund to pay off Katie. "How long do you think it will take, at this point, to get the estate fully settled?"

"I would guess two months, maybe three. We have to post notices about the property sales — things like that — and there are twenty-day requirements for each of the notification steps. I will try to wrap this up as soon as I can so we can get the audit and also get you appointed as guardian of the estate. Only after that is complete can I transfer control of the funds to you."

"I understand, and thanks so much. I appreciate your diligence, and so does Andrew. Will I have to come to Pittsburgh for another hearing?"

"I don't think so, but," and here Sylvia chuckled, "I'm going to need two notarized letters from upstanding citizens asserting to your probity, to your good character. Think you can do that?"

Martin laughed. "Will a letter from the Provost of Bottlesworth College suffice? And one from the CEO of a billion-dollar company?"

"Probably," said Sylvia, with a happy glint in her voice. "I'm going to email you a draft of typical letters so they can see what is needed."

And with that, Andrew's future seemed settled, at least for the next year or so.

* **28** *

At dinner, Jenny announced, "Lavelle's mother called this afternoon. We're picking him up at the Portland airport on Sunday at 12:43."

"Can I come too?" asked Andrew.

"And me too?" said JJ.

Jenny laughed. "Why not? Janet sounded wonderfully upbeat on the phone. I thought she would be worried about her son going so far away, but she focused on the chance for a good education and the opportunity to train with a basketball professional. She said she had never seen Lavelle so happy and excited. And also that I should thank you for everything."

Martin mused on that last remark, turning toward Andrew. "She was pretty tough on me at the beginning, remember? Wondering why I didn't simply bring you home with me that first weekend. Remember that, Andrew?"

"Yeah. But I didn't want to come at first. I didn't know anything about you except… Well, anyway, she asked me, and I said I'd rather stay with her and Lavelle. She said something about God's plan, and a cross to bear, and that was it."

"But things are working okay now, aren't they?" asked Martin.

"I still miss my Mom and Grandma, especially at night, but I feel safe here. Better than at Lavelle's house, with his Mom gone so much, and having that lawyer lady fussing over me."

"And you have a brother and a sister," said JJ.

Andrew laughed. "That too," he said.

- - -

"Hey, Drew, hey, li'l boss," called Lavelle as he exited security. "Here I am."

"Good flight?" asked Martin.

"The best part is that it got me here. Lady next to me was really fat and she kept pushing my elbow off the armrest. Anyway, I got two suitcases. Where do we get them?"

Martin herded the group toward baggage claim. "This is so cool," said Andrew. "Did they tell you we're gonna be roommates?"

"Yup. Just like back home. Roommates."

JJ interrupted. "When I'm old enough, I'm gonna go to Cranborne too."

"Really," said Lavelle, looking to Martin. "Big boss said that, too?"

Martin smiled. "When the time comes, we'll be deciding things like that. For now, I'm glad you're here."

With everything and everyone collected, Martin loaded the van and headed north. The sky was one of those mixtures of patches of blue alternated with patches of whitish clouds, some of which had ominous black bottoms. Beneath one such wraith, rain suddenly pummeled the van, dropping visibility to near zero. Martin slowed to a crawl, and he could hear Andrew catch his breath in the back seat.

"Be cool, dude," said Lavelle. "It's okay. Big boss, he drives like a pro."

- - -

As soon as the boys entered the front door, Ellen came and wrapped her arms around Lavelle's legs.

"Well, hi, li'l lady," said Lavelle. "You miss me?"

"Time for lunch," called Jenny from the kitchen. The sounds of hunger being sated competed with Jenny asking about the flight and mentioning that Andrew needed to finish packing. Martin, for his part, marveled at how much better things felt in the house with Lavelle around. It was like shattering the silence of despair. Even Ellen seemed to feel it. How would it be when both boys went off to school?

After lunch, Jenny supervised the completion of Andrew's packing while JJ challenged Lavelle to a game of chess, and Martin went to the study to call DeShawn.

"Your future superstar just ate us out of house and home," said Martin.

"He won't grow if he ain't fed," said DeShawn. "Watch for me when you drop the boys off tomorrow. Just to say hello."

"Will do," said Martin.

-    -   -

Because of the intermittent heavy rain showers, the now enlarged family was confined indoors. Andrew and Lavelle were gabbing the way boys do. JJ was attached to them like a remora, taking in everything that swam past. Ellen got tired of watching, and dragged her stuffed dachshund to her wagon and made a path through her pile of blocks where she gave the good dog a ride.

Helen and her family came for what was supposed to be a cookout, but in honor of the rain, the hamburgers got broiled in the oven. Andrew and Lavelle had retreated upstairs. Carlo managed to get JJ upset over sharing action figures, and Angela pushed Ellen down when she wouldn't release her dachshund. Lots of tears. Bill intervened with Carlo and Helen calmed the two girls down. Eventually, they gathered around the suitably protected Queen Anne, and ate dinner.

"How does it feel, the new school and everything?" asked Bill.

"It's totally cool," said Lavelle. "My Mom, she said it was the chance of a lifetime."

"And you, Andrew?"

"Yeah, it's cool. Me 'n Lavelle together."

"Well, I'm sure it will be exciting," said Helen. "That guy DeShawn really stepped in, didn't he?"

"I guess he did," said Martin. "And we have Lavelle's basketball skills to thank for that."

"You joshing, right?" said Lavelle.

"Nope," said Martin. "Not joshing."

-    -   -

The next morning, Jenny took JJ to his first day of school, starting second grade, while Martin drove Andrew and Lavelle to Cranborne, helped them unload their things, said hello and a not-so-subtle thank-you to DeShawn, and headed to his office. Kuc's new schedule for the fall involved caring for Ellen during the mornings and early afternoons, ending with picking JJ up at school. This would give Jenny the time she needed for her business and liberate Martin from weekday child-care duties, but as Martin said, he was kissing CC's ass at Autobot twice a month to pay for the freedom for both of them to work, and Jenny had to agree.

An email from Trevor contained the names and contact information for two investigators and the last known address for Martin's mother, a Greenwich Village apartment. The address was thirty-four years old. Martin decided to put this project on hold until he got the new semester started. If the flipped classroom in combination with finishing the book and his consulting at Autobot didn't eat him alive, he would hire one of them next month and see what turned up. But clearing the air with Jenny had to take priority.

- - -

That night, Martin put the children to bed, spending extra time with their baths and their books. Jenny was at her desk when Martin came downstairs. "So where are we?" asked Martin as he took his chair at the adjoining desk.

"What do you mean, where are we?" said a startled Jenny. "We're here."

"I mean us, the family."

"You sound angry. Are you angry?"

"I don't know. Maybe. We're back to just us for now, and I'm hoping…"

"Hoping what? That we can go back to the good old days?"

"What does that mean?"

"We've now got Andrew. Our family is different. There's no going back."

"Now that sounds angry. Are you angry?"

"Probably. I didn't want Andrew. He's nice. He's healthy and si and well behaved, but he's not mine, and it's hard."

"And now he's away at school. So can't we focus on just us for a little while?"

"Focus? On us?"

"Yes, us. You have been remote, to put it mildly, for months. Is Andrew so much of a disturbance that we can't be intimate anymore?"

Jenny didn't answer.

Martin pressed on. "What the hell is going on? Why can't we have sex anymore?"

Jenny burst out, "We have been in turmoil, that's why. Turmoil isn't warm and cuddly, it's nasty and upsetting."

"But I thought we had found a way through all that."

"And you think by throwing this in my face it's going to make me want to go to bed with you? That's not how it works."

"Well how does it work?"

"With tenderness, with caring. You're going back to being the same kind of overloaded self-centered person you were at CTI."

"Hey, that's not fair. I can remember you praising me after Ellen was born, how caring and everything."

"But look at you now. Instead of spending your own time with your children, you go off to an overpaid consulting job so we could hire a nanny."

"We hired the nanny so you could work, not me."

"So we could *both* work, not just me."

Martin blew out a heavy breath through fluttered lips. "This is going nowhere. I'm sorry I got you upset. I really love you, but I feel that you've gone to some dark place I can't reach. I miss you — the old you, the sexy you, my best-friend you."

Tears leaked down Jenny's cheeks. "I'm sorry. You're right. I'm upset. A lot. I love you, too, but right now, I'm a mess. Give me some time."

"Should we talk to somebody?"

"Who? Talk to who?"

"A counselor."

"You think we need a counselor?"

"I don't know. We need something. I like that Dr. Schwartz person that helped me with Andrew. Maybe…"

"No. I don't want to see her. Not now."

"Why not? What's the harm?"

"I just can't. That's all. I can't. It's getting late and I'm going to Waldoboro tomorrow to inspect some of the pieces for the Chicago job. So I'm heading for bed."

"I've still got stuff to do to get ready for Gina, so I won't be upstairs for a while."

"The babe? She comes tomorrow?"

"Where did that come from? She's a student, my TA, not 'the babe.'"

"She looks like a babe to me, but she's too tall for you."

"Dammit, Jenny. You trying to start a fight about Gina? For the record, I don't have a babe."

"I saw your eyes light up when she came and stayed over. I could smell the lust."

"So you are trying to start a fight. Well, I'm not going there. Her lease starts tomorrow, September first, she wants to get settled, and we've got a lot of work to do before classes start next week."

Jenny sniffed. "Okay, Mr. Goofus. Get the babe moved in next door."

-   -   -

As the first sunrise of September crept into their bedroom, Jenny tossed in the midst of a bad dream and elbowed Martin in the back. He woke with a start and a "what the fuck?"

"Sorry," said Jenny. "Bad dream. I must have twitched."

"Jesus, that was a tough twitch. What time is it, anyway?"

"Ten of six. I might as well get up."

"Tell me about the dream."

"I'm not sure. Something about trying to get away. From somebody."

"From me?"

"Not you. Just somebody."

"A man?"

"A man. No one in particular."

"Where did all that come from?"

"I have no idea."

-    -   -

Gina was to arrive mid-morning, so Martin had time to take JJ to school, leaving Jenny with Ellen and the residual from her bad dream. She's clearly got some kind of trouble, Martin thought. What man is she trying to get away from? *Is it me, like in disguise?*

JJ broke the reverie. "My teacher is funny looking," he said. "Miss Young."

"What do you mean, funny looking?"

JJ giggled. "She has really thick glasses and big teeth in the front of her mouth."

"Is she nice?" asked Martin.

"Yeah, she's nice an' everything, but she's funny looking."

"Listen, young man, every person, no matter how they look, is worthy of respect. We don't laugh at people because of how they look. So I don't want to hear any more about her looks. What I want to hear about is how good she is as a teacher. Okay?"

"Okay," grunted JJ. "But—"

"Not another word. Unless it's about her as a teacher."

Martin decided to go in with JJ to get a look at Miss Young, and indeed, she did have coke-bottle glasses and pronounced buck teeth, but she greeted every child with genuine warmth. He introduced himself and expressed his wishes for a successful year. JJ witnessed all this in appropriate silence.

-    -   -

Martin met Gina and the landlord at the apartment at eleven. She got a key and the instructions on the wifi and the thermostat. Martin helped carry her two suitcases, one box of books, and a computer bag up the stairs to the apartment, mulling about that crack from Jenny about "smelling the lust." Clearly, Jenny was more on target than off. Lust for attractive students could erupt anytime, anyplace, and it certainly had erupted around some fantasy image of Gina, but Martin vowed that it would never rise to a detectable level, except perhaps to Jenny's hyper-sensitive nose. He and Gina walked together to the campus, where he introduced her to Angelique and Steve Wang. There were forms to fill out for payroll, authorizations and door codes, a parking sticker, and a computer account. She would first need an employee ID number, and that required a trip to HR. By the time they got there, it was lunch time. HR wouldn't re-open until one. Martin suggested lunch at Barnaby's and a tour of the Maine Street shops.

Over lunch, Gina gushed. She talked about how successful her summer had been and how excited she was over getting a real chance to teach. When could she get to talk more with Glenda? What would she need to do before the start of class? And where was a food market so she could stock up her kitchen?

Gina's enthusiasm both warmed and relaxed Martin. He was once again devolving toward that almost parental pride he had felt when, as a sophomore, she had stood up to a grilling by a CTI faculty commit-tee, not only answering every challenge but even finding a flaw in their thinking about how to evaluate online learning experiments. There weren't going to be any problems with lust. This was going to be like it was at CTI.

After lunch, with the paperwork finally complete, Gina accom-panied Martin back to the Science Building. They went to the two side-by-side laboratories where they would be holding the flipped-classroom sessions, one of which now held the boxes of nerd kits plus two shipments of electronic components. Martin tasked Gina with unpacking everything, saving the packing slips for accounting, verify-ing that the nerd kits worked, and stuffing each kit with the requisite components. Beyond that, Gina's part of the pre-semester preparation was to build each of the lab exercises to verify that their plans for the students would actually work. She estimated it would take only a few days, surely done by the end of the week.

"So do you need me for any of this?" asked Martin.

"Nope," said a smiling Gina. "This is great. I'll get on it. One question: if I want a cup of coffee or something?"

"Third-floor lounge. At the opposite end of the hall from my office. Take what you want, no need to leave money unless you feel guilty. And don't be shy about saying hello and introducing yourself. We've got most of the School of Science in this building. Oh, I forgot. Glenda is coming tomorrow morning for a final review. We've come up with a pretty good plan for evaluating this experiment. You should join us. Ten o'clock, my office."

-   -   -

On Friday afternoon, Martin picked up Andrew and Lavelle at the Cranborne bus. The plan was for everyone, including Helen and family, to spend the Labor Day weekend at the cottage. It was crowded with four adults and six children, but there was no serious discord. Bill and Martin took the four boys to the playground in Bath for a Sunday morning basketball session, during which Martin discovered that while he was in excellent physical shape thanks to his regular treadmill and weightlifting, he couldn't shoot worth a hoot. His jump shot, once reasonably decent, had deserted him. Lavelle, for sure, and even Andrew, were better. Carlo hogged the ball too much, and JJ, with his cast removed only a week prior, had to work hard to get the ball up to the regulation-height hoops. But the outing was a happy success. Even the weather cooperated, and on the Monday holiday, as the sky reddened in anticipation of what would become a stunning sunset, the assembled multitude shared a lobster and steamer dinner, cleaned up the house, and drove back to Brimfield Junction.

Summer was now over. The book draft, while not finished, was as far along as it could be, and the flipped-classroom experiment was about to begin.

* **29** *

As Martin walked through a light rain toward campus for his pre-class meeting with Gina, he felt a familiar nervousness, squirrely wiggles in his gut — not the bad kind, the good kind — the quickened pulse of an adrenaline rush, things he hadn't felt in years. As he had often said to his research students, a bad plan is better than no plan and a good plan is better than a bad plan, and while he had a plan, he had no way to judge whether it was bad or good. Only time would tell.

He reached his office and went to the kitchenette for one more cup of coffee even though his edginess suggested it wasn't necessary. On his return, Gina appeared with a dripping umbrella. They did a joint final proofread of each of the website postings — reading assignments, instructions for getting a FIE account, online lecture assignments, instructions for getting their lab kits, the first written homework and the first set of group study problems. Finding no errors, Martin leaned back and said, "I think I'm ready. Are you ready?"

Gina sat up straight, grinned at Martin, and said, "I am so ready. I can't believe you've given me this chance. I'm totally pumped. I love... I mean this chance is so fantastic."

"Just remember, if things get out of hand at any time, you're to ask me for help. Before we go down, though, I need to hit the restroom."

"Me too," said Gina.

- - -

When they arrived at the forty-seat classroom, Martin was astonished to find almost every seat taken. He showed Gina how the podium and laptop connection system worked and got her started pulling up the course website on the projector. As Martin did a headcount, Glenda arrived and came forward with greetings.

"Quite a mob you have here," said Glenda.

"It's a puzzle," said Martin. "There are only twenty students pre-registered, so I don't know who all these people are. I trust I can introduce you?"

Glenda laughed. "As long as you don't embarrass me with embellishments."

Martin went to the front as silence descended on the gathering. "Welcome to Circuits and Electronics, affectionately known as C&E. I'm Martin Quint, and we will have a Teaching Assistant this term, Gina Farrell. Please stand up, Gina, so these folks know who you are." She stood, waved a shy hello, and sat down. "Before I begin the formal material, though, I need to ask something about this crowd. We expected twenty students and there are thirty-six of you here. I need some information."

When by a show of hands he found that all thirty-six planned to take the class for credit, he said, "Okay. It's going to be tight, but we'll figure out how to manage it. Gina will pass around sign-up cards. Be sure to give us name, email, your major, and your class schedule. Otherwise you won't get a section assignment."

After the bustle of passing cards around, Martin said, "I want to make one more introduction. Glenda, will you please stand up?" She stood, waved, and sat down as Martin continued, "This is Glenda Aldrich, a Visiting Professor of Psychology from Oxford in England. We're writing a book together about education, and this term's class is part of our research. She will be attending many of our classes and taking notes — not on you as individuals, but on the structure we're going to use this term. It's called the flipped classroom. Here's how it works. I will not be giving the lectures."

This brought an audible gasp from the assembly. "You heard correctly. If the occasion warrants, we will gather here for a lecture, but for most of the material, we'll be asking you to view online lectures at home, the ones posted by FIE, the Free Internet Education consortium. These lectures are based on this exact class, but the lecturer is

Professor Harry Huang, not me. He's quite good, actually."

A buzz started around the room. Martin spoke firmly to be heard. "And I think you'll like this." He waited for the room to fall silent. "Instead of having to listen to me in class, we're going to use our class time for collaborative problem-solving, in groups. We will, as you would expect, assign reading in the text and some basic homework problems to get you familiar with the concepts, but in class, we're going to pose some pretty challenging problems and you will need to talk to each other, work together, and use the lab kits to build actual circuits that demonstrate your solutions. Gina or I will be present throughout these sessions. I think it will be a lively and worthwhile activity. It's new. Not just for you, but also for us as instructors. You should consider yourselves as pioneers, trying something new and giving us feedback on how it's working. Does anyone have a question before we get going?"

A lean-looking male in the second row raised his hand. "Can we choose our groups? And how will you do grading if we work in groups?"

Martin nodded. "No, you cannot choose your group. We will be assigning those. Part of our educational goal is for you to learn to work cooperatively with new people. As for grading, everyone in the group gets the same grade on the group problems. For exams, of course, you each are graded individually. Now let's take a quick look at the website."

Martin blazed through a tour of the website, showing where to find everything, and then stood silent for a full minute before beginning his lecture. The room settled into the silence of an arctic midnight. "You are about to embark on the study of engineering." And with that, Martin launched into the same lecture with which he had opened C&E for years and years, stressing that engineering is the purposeful use of science, that it was up to each individual, as an educated and moral human being, to decide what was, and was not, purposeful, and that one man's purpose, or one woman's purpose, could be another person's anathema.

-    -   -

Martin asked Gina to return to his office to set up the student groups. He sighed as they worked. "Well, you wanted classroom experience. Looks like you're going to get it. Our workload has almost doubled."

"We're doing six groups, yes? Six in each?"

"It's not what I wanted. I preferred four groups of five. Some of those sixteen extras will disappear, so if we spread them around, our final group size will be end up at four or five, and that's fine. But I'm not sure how to manage this."

"Oh, I don't mind doing four groups. That's why I'm here. To learn to teach."

"I think we should both be present for all the sessions, at least until we see how things will go. So plan on lots of time in class."

As they finished the sorting process, Martin sighed, "What price success."

"What do you mean?" asked Gina.

"Last spring I taught E&M the way they do it at CTI, and it got the highest ratings of any class that had ever been taught in the Physics Department. I think the word got around."

"Just like it should," said Gina, smiling, adoring. "I'm looking forward to being overloaded by success."

"I like your attitude," said Martin.

"And you…. You're so … amazing. It's a privilege."

Were Gina's eyes misting when she said that? Martin felt a flush rise across his face. "Privilege or not," he croaked as best he could, "we've got lots to do. I hope we survive it all."

- - -

After Gina left, Martin sat at his desk, taking stock. This load of students and the new semester and the educational experiment and the thorny but positive book progress with Glenda and having Gina here and the lab kits, it was like the smell of the greasepaint to an accomplished actor. Back onto the stage, the roar of the crowd. Bottlesworth wasn't CTI, but it was real, and earnest students were coming to him to learn. Lab sessions with groups of six students were not the same as lecturing to two hundred, but they would allow real conversation between and among the students, surely a critical part of their learning process. And Gina. Lovely Gina, whose misty eyes suggested that she actually was more than a little in love with him. It wasn't the first time a student had fallen for him, and he had lots of practice easing them down. But this felt different. Not only was he committed to a semester of work with her in close quarters, he hoped he had just managed to put aside a crush of his own.

As for the crush of the semester itself, thank God she was there. Gina made it possible. He couldn't have handled twenty students by himself, much less thirty-six. And it was better than having a graduate student assistant because Gina wasn't taking any classes or trying to do her master's research. She was going to be one-hundred percent devoted to teaching for the next four months, focused exclusively on these students, and she would emerge from this semester with documented professional skills: how to listen to students, how to use Glenda's option-three conversation to build that model of how they think and revise her approach until "click," the contact is made, the light goes on, a student gets it and can proceed. The thrill of seeing that happen, up close with these small groups, one student at a time, would be locked into her bones and she'd never lose it.

-    -   -

Dinner that evening was dominated by JJ's report from his school in which he emphasized, with a sidelong glance at Martin, how nice his teacher was. But Martin also got his turn. Jenny groaned when she heard that Martin was anticipating spending up to eighteen hours a week in class, but added, "Well, at least you don't have to pick up JJ any more, thanks to Kuc."

After dinner, Jenny put the children to bed while Martin did dishes. Then he went into their study and sat at his desk, staring at a blank computer screen. After many minutes, he opened the left-hand drawer of Jenny's desk, removed the red card, and put it on her chair.

— - -

Jenny came downstairs and stopped in her tracks when she saw the card on her chair. "A red card? Really? Why?"

"Please sit down," said Martin. "I need your help."

"My help? Then why the red card?" Jenny sat at her desk.

"Because you haven't been helping, and I need your help. Badly."

"Helping with what? What's all this about?"

Martin took a deep breath before speaking. "Something is eating at you. I can't figure out what it is, but it's like a cancer growing between us, and I want to do surgery — cut it out, get rid of it. But I can't do anything if you don't tell me what's really wrong."

"This is about sex, isn't it?"

"Partly. Yes. But…"

"Then what else is it?"

"You're angry. At least I think you're angry, and you used to tell me when you were angry and we would talk about it, and make peace, and go to bed together and make love. Now all I see is angry. I feel shut out."

Jenny sat, staring at the floor, and said nothing.

"Is this about Andrew?"

Jenny shook her head without looking up. "No, I've sort of accepted Andrew. It was such a shock, though."

Martin tried to lighten things by laughing, but what came out was more like a snort. "You and me, both." Then, calmer, "But you were angry then, weren't you?"

In almost a whisper, Jenny said, "I couldn't understand how somebody as smart as you could have made a baby when you didn't want to. I still can't understand that. You said you were drunk as if it was an excuse. Being drunk is not an excuse." And a single tear fell off the tip of Jenny's nose.

"And you're not angry about that anymore?"

Jenny snarled, "I don't think so, but I can't guarantee what I'm angry about minute by minute. It doesn't work that way."

"Well I spent a lot of time today thinking about what might make you angry besides Andrew. There was money, but I took care of that. There was child care, but with the consulting money we got Kuc. And there was travel, and once we got Kuc, your travel wasn't a problem anymore."

Jenny didn't answer.

Martin tried a different tack. "Then the other night, you said all kinds of wild things, like Gina being my babe. Is that it? Having her help me teach?"

"You snuck around with her."

"I what?"

"Yes. She told me you had dinner together in Cambridge. What else did you do with her besides dinner?"

"Jenny, for God's sake. Nothing. Think, dammit. If she and I were doing anything out of order, would she have mentioned that we had dinner together? Okay, yes, I did have dinner with her. Twice. Once to catch up with a favorite student, and the second time to ask her to be my teaching assistant. That's it. Beyond that, nada. Nothing."

"But you never mentioned—"

"That's true. You were already so edgy. I was maybe worried you'd be jealous, like when you teased me about your travelling with Pierre."

And suddenly Jenny burst into tears, her face in her hands, choking sobs.

"What did I say?" said a shocked Martin. "Is this something about Pierre?"

Jenny nodded. It took more than a minute before she could choke out one word at a time through her sobs. "You...you had a drunk fuck. And we got Andrew.... And I... I couldn't...understand a drunk fuck. And then..."

Jenny's crying took over. Martin waited.

"And then what?" said Martin.

"I feel so dirty," sobbed Jenny.

"Why?"

"Because I had drunk fuck too, you idiot."

"You and Pierre?"

Jenny nodded.

"Where?"

"In Chicago."

"When?"

"The night we got the big order. We both drank too much and ended up in bed. I've wanted to tell you ever since then, but I feel so dirty, like a slut. I was so fired up by the sale. This is so embarrassing. I would have done... I mean, I needed... and I guess he did, too. I'm so ashamed. I wanted to find a way to forgive myself so I could tell you, but I haven't been able to."

Suddenly, Jenny was making sense, and this made Martin cry. He understood in a rush what it must have felt like for Camille's husband when he found out, and even how Katie had felt when she wrote "Fuck You Martin" all over their house. A stake through the heart. A stake through their marriage.

Jenny's sobbing decreased to sniffles and she looked at Martin, his face still buried in his hands. "I guess it got started by the news about Andrew, but it's not Andrew's fault. It's my fault. I'm sorry. I really am. I don't want to lose you, to lose us. It will absolutely never happen again. It was awful. What can I do?"

"Let's go to bed. To sleep, I mean. I don't know what to do. I don't want to lose you, either, but right now, it hurts too much to... We need to talk some more."

Before going up to bed, Martin went to the kitchen and got the bottle of budesonide that Dr. Sharif had prescribed. He figured he was going to need it.

* **30** *

Talk they did, mostly in the evenings while going through the motions. Yes, the motions: the good-mornings, breakfasts with the children, Martin busy with his overloaded classroom and his book, CC's consulting, the Task Force, and Jenny immersed in her business and the need to deliver for her Chicago client, the family dinners, the polite goodnights, the shared bed, the shared bathroom, and of course, throughout, the shopping, the cooking, the dishes, the laundry, the driving JJ to school, the supervising of his piano practice, the playtime and reading time for Ellen, Martin's own piano practice. Yes, all of that, but the confidence, the trust, the pleasures of intimate touch, the fire of consummation, the afterglow? In abeyance, all preempted by the need to maintain a level of calm so as not to upset the children.

On one such evening, seated side by side at their study desks, Martin suddenly asked, "I just don't get it. How can you continue to have him as part of your team? Doesn't it embarrass you? He's seen you naked. He's touched you. He fucked you, for God's sake. How can you still lead the team with him around?"

Jenny's answer was almost a plea. "He's as embarrassed as I am, for one thing, probably more embarrassed, and for a second thing, if I don't keep him on the team, my business will probably collapse. The Chicago deal depends on him. We have eighteen replica antique pieces to deliver, and his stuff is absolutely central to that contract. And if I toss him out after? Everybody will guess the reason and then no one will work with me."

There followed a stony silence, finally broken by Jenny. "And there's something else. It's been eating at me all this time."

"About Pierre?"

"Sort of. This is hard for me, so please don't blow up."

"I'll try not to. What is it?"

More silence. Eventually, Jenny spoke. "I think you have the wrong picture about what happened. It's about who fucked who. The reality is that I fucked him, not the other way around."

"You what?" shouted Martin, his voice suddenly loud enough to cause Jenny to shush him.

"Don't wake the children, for God's sake. You said you wouldn't blow up."

"Okay, okay, I won't wake the children, but what do you mean, you fucked him?"

"It's hard to describe, and I think you already know about it — sort of, anyway. When I win, I feel, like... driven... sexually, I mean. It feels like... I don't know, just intense, an urgent need."

"I've seen you get hot and bothered when you beat me at poker, but this was different, for God's sake. For starters, it wasn't with me."

"Yes, different, for sure, and not with you, which is what makes it so awful. But it was an enormous win. Huge. My business finally making it into the black. We had worked so hard and so long to win the business that when we got the actual order, I just went over the top. I wanted you, not him, but he was there and you were here. I'm not blaming him, and neither should you. You should blame me. It's my fault, period. I was drinking. Too much. More than I could handle. I've learned a horrible lesson here, and as I've already told you a thousand times, it will absolutely never happen again. He was not the aggressor. I was. If anything, he could sue me for sexual harassment and win a big settlement."

"You mean you forced him? I can't believe that."

"No. I didn't force him, but I made it hard for him to say no. He didn't protest or anything, but he knew it was wrong. So did I. And I did it anyway. We had a drunk fuck. One drunk fuck. That's it. Never again. I promise. Never again." Jenny put her head in her hands, trying to wipe tears away and control a fit of sobbing, without success.

Martin waited.

Jenny finally recovered enough to say, "I'm ashamed and wrong and terribly sorry, especially sorry I did this to you, but I can't get rid of Pierre. He's not my lover or anything, like that Camille woman was with you."

Martin's voice rasped with fury. "You're throwing Camille in my face?"

"No, I'm not throwing her in your face, I'm just saying, he's not my lover, goddamit," Jenny suddenly so loud she was now being shushed by Martin. Jenny continued in a hissing whisper. "We're not having an affair. We have no interest in each other. We were wired, and a little drunk, and we fell into bed. Beginning and end of story. Can't you see that?"

"Does his wife know?"

Jenny, calmer, said, "I'm not sure. He hasn't said."

"Does he know that I know?"

"No, I'm pretty sure he doesn't."

"Well, if we're going to go forward with Pierre in your future, he has to know that I know."

"I've thought about that, and I actually agree with you. I think you and he will need to have a talk — after I tell him, that is."

"And what would I say? How did you enjoy fucking my wife?"

And that put Jenny back into choking sobs. "Must you, goddammit?" she shrieked as she wiped her drippy nose on her sleeve. "I'm trying my best here. You put down the red card so and I'm trying. Just listen, for God's sake. He was not the instigator. If anything, he was the victim. His boss got him drunk and dragged him into bed. I'm not proud of that, but at least I'm being honest. He is absolutely not a threat to us, if we can just get past this. I think you need to hear from him that he regrets that it happened and that it won't happen again."

"But every time I think of him, in fact" — and here Martin's carapace cracked open far enough to reveal the depth of his raw inner wound — "every time I see you sitting on that Victorian settee, I imagine you spread-eagled on it, with his bare ass in the air pumping away. Getting past that image is not as easy as you think. It makes me furious."

"Please don't be crude. But, yes, I get it. It's an awful image and I agree you should be furious. But the person you should be furious at is me, not him."

"Can't I be furious at both of you?"

"Well, you clearly are, but it wasn't his fault. If you can talk to him, you'll get convinced of that, and then maybe you can focus your anger where it belongs, on me. I take full responsibility. I love you and I want to stay with you forever, but I made a mistake and I deeply regret it. I know it hurts you. And it hurts me that it hurts you. But I can't undo it, make it disappear."

Martin exhaled through fluttered lips, thinking how the sound would make baby Ellen laugh. "Well maybe you're right. Maybe I do need to talk to him. I'll think about it. In the meantime, though, it would help if you stop making wisecracks about Gina. You're not being fair to her, or to me, for that matter."

Jenny's protested. "But I can smell the lust around her. You can deny it all you want, but I know that somewhere inside of you is a wish you could get her into bed."

"For someone who just fucked one of your team members, you have a lot of nerve complaining about Gina. She's a student. She's my teaching assistant. She's young enough to be Andrew's sister. Yes, she's attractive, but she's not a flirt, she's not on the make, and neither am I."

"Are you telling me you never had any feelings for her? C'mon, Martin, I was honest about Pierre. You need to be honest with me about the babe." Jenny's tone was growing calmer.

"Stop calling her the babe. I admit that she's attractive. There are lots of attractive young women who turn up at colleges. But students are taboo. Don't you get that? Haven't you ever seen a man you found attractive but knew you would never get farther than looking?"

"Of course. There are attractive men, and I might notice them, but I don't get the hots for them the way you seem to have the hots for Gina."

"You know, she would probably be appalled, appalled and embarrassed to hear you talking this way. Maybe you and she need to have a talk, except if you did, she would probably quit and run back to Cambridge, and I would absolutely hate that. She's the only reason I can manage this semester."

"But she's in love with you."

"She's what?"

"In love with you. Or she has a super crush, whatever."

"Okay. Maybe she has a crush." Martin's tone calmed to match Jenny's. "Since you're stressing honesty, yes, I've seen some of the signs. That's not so unusual, you know. College women do sometimes fall for their professors. But she has never said or done anything inappropriate. You're being very unfair. And I'm being totally upfront with you. Let's assume for the sake of argument that she does have a crush on me. As long as I don't give her any encouragement, it will remain an unfulfilled crush, and it will eventually wither. We'll work together and the classes will get taught, she'll get the professional teaching experience she needs, I'll get the help I need, and we'll remain friends and colleagues. How is that different from you and Pierre?"

"Pierre is not in love with me."

"How do you know?"

"Ask him, for God's sake. He'll tell you. He's embarrassed even to look me in the eye. His relationship. with Anna must be under a terrific strain. It might be best for everyone if we had full disclosure. He tells her just like I told you and both Pierre and I make it clear that, yes, something bad happened — it was bad, everyone knows it was bad — but it won't happen again, and life has to go forward."

"Sounds all goody-goody, but it won't work. Anna might throw him out, then what?"

"Okay, so maybe Anna doesn't have to know, but Pierre needs to know that you know, and in fact, if he knows that you know, it sort of guarantees that things will go forward without any hint of a repeat from his side. Can't you see that?"

"I can, I guess, but by the same token, you have to acknowledge that Gina is going to stay and be my assistant and work with me and help me survive this semester."

"I'd be more comfortable if she were gone."

"And I'd be more comfortable if Pierre had never happened, but getting rid of Gina doesn't solve your guilt around Pierre. It doesn't solve anything. It makes things worse, because I will resent your lack of trust in me and in my judgment and my behavior, and I'll be overworked beyond belief by the teaching load. If you want me to be less angry, don't keep suggesting things that, in the long run, will make me more angry."

"But Gina scares me. She's so... what can I say, magnetic? Even if she's too tall for you." Jenny giggled.

"Okay. A laugh. That's better. Yes. She is too tall for me. Maybe you should just rely on that. I won't be lusting after her because she's too tall for me, and you won't have to worry that she'll steal me from you because she might have a misguided crush on me."

"Even if you have a crush on her?"

"Who said I had a crush on her?"

"I did. Don't you? Isn't that why you never told me about having dinner with her in Cambridge? You kept her secret from me."

"And is that why you went off and fucked Pierre? I thought that was about Andrew, not Gina."

"It was about Andrew, feeding into the elation over the Chicago deal. I didn't find out about Gina until I got back. By then I was already a fallen woman, in my eyes as well as yours. But when she showed up in our house, there was chemistry happening. You can't deny it."

"I can deny it. Whatever chemistry there might have been was long gone."

"You mean there was chemistry at some point?"

"Do you count a stupid fantasy level as chemistry?"

"Yes."

"Then, yes, at the stupid fantasy level. You were so angry about all sorts of things. I didn't know what was happening with us. But it didn't last long. Maybe that one dinner, the first one. Then I woke up and snapped out of it. I need to work with her, I need her help, and it's my responsibility to teach her how to teach. We're actually doing quite well together. She'll be able to handle four of the six sections on her own, and I'm finding that her judgment about the students is really quite good. I wish we could find a way for you to be more welcoming, more comfortable with her. It would make a lot of things a lot easier, especially if she sees us as a family, a unit."

"You mean if she spends more time with us as a family, her crush will dissipate?"

"I think so. I think it will."

"And your crush?"

"Long gone."

"How can I be sure?"

"Because I was just able to admit having a fantasy about her in the first place. I have to trust you about things like this. We need to trust each other."

"Yes, which means you need to trust me with Pierre."

"That's the theory. But how can we get past the fact that I can't think of Pierre without fury, without that awful image, and you can't think of Gina without worrying about my behavior. How do we get past that? I can barely even touch you in bed any more. I'm afraid of how you'll take it."

"And when you try to touch me, it reminds me of how I've failed you. I feel dirty, and I can't get turned on."

"So how do we get out of this quagmire?"

-   -   -

The following Tuesday afternoon at four, Martin and Jenny climbed the stairs to the waiting area just as Dr. Schwartz opened her office door.

"Dr. Schwartz, this is my wife, Jenny. We need to talk about our marriage."

"Do come in," she said. "Let's talk."

They emerged an hour later, an hour filled with contradictions — an expressed and reiterated wish to save the marriage amid a loud barrage of accusations, back and forth, digging-up some hurts, leaving others buried. It was exhausting, cathartic, and Dr. Schwartz's tissue box was heavily used. As they started walking together toward their car, Martin said, "Well, at least we didn't have to worry about waking the children."

Jenny smiled.

Acknowledgements

It's not easy to identify everyone who has contributed to bringing *Cross Purposes* to fruition, since my experience of the academic life has spanned many decades, with hundreds of professional colleagues and thousands of students. Further, the initial motivation to write a sequel to *One Man's Purpose* was driven by reader responses, telling me they wanted to see more of Martin Quint. But several individuals need personal thanks: Murray Smith, for his insights into language use and the structure of conversations, and Dawn Raffel, Joel Dawson, Gordon Doerfer, and Loring Conant, critical readers. My greatest thanks go to my wife Peg, who over the past few years has become almost as familiar with Martin and Jenny as I am. She not only has the patience to let me write undisturbed, she is at other times a willing and helpful critic, a sounding board. Live conversation, as a general topic, plays a big role in this book, and my live conversations with Peg played a big role in creating this book.

CPSIA information can be obtained
at www.ICGtesting.com
Printed in the USA
FFHW021841230219
50649636-56054FF